# the LADY of the SEA

# books by rosalind miles

## fiction

THE GUENEVERE TRILOGY

*Guenevere, Queen of the Summer Country*

*The Knight of the Sacred Lake*

*The Child of the Holy Grail*


THE TRISTAN AND ISOLDE TRILOGY

*Isolde, Queen of the Western Isle*

*The Maid of the White Hands*

*The Lady of the Sea*


*I, Elizabeth*

*Return to Eden*

*Bitter Legacy*

*Prodigal Sins*

*Act of Passion*

nonfiction

*The Fiction of Sex*

*The Problem of Measure for Measure*

*Danger! Men at Work*

*Modest Proposals*

*Women and Power*

*The Female Form*

*The Women's History of the World*

*The Rites of Man*

*The Children We Deserve*

*Ben Jonson: His Life and Work*

*Ben Jonson: His Craft and Art*

*Who Cooked the Last Supper?*

# the LADY of the SEA

### The Third of the
### Tristan and Isolde Novels

## ROSALIND MILES

CROWN PUBLISHERS
NEW YORK

Published by Crown Publishers, New York, New York.
Member of the Crown Publishing Group, a division of Random House, Inc.

www.crownpublishing.com

CROWN is a trademark and the Crown colophon is a registered trademark of Random House, Inc.

Originally published in Great Britain by Simon & Schuster UK, London.

Printed in the United States of America

Map copyright © 2002 by Rodica Prato

*Design by Lauren Dong*

Library of Congress Cataloging-in-Publication Data
Miles, Rosalind.
The lady of the sea : the third of the Tristan and Isolde novels / Rosalind Miles.—1st ed.
Sequel to: The maid of the white hands.
1. Isolde (Legendary character)—Fiction. 2. Tristan (Legendary character)—Fiction. 3. Mark, King of Cornwall (Legendary character)—Fiction. 4. Triangles (Interpersonal relations)—Fiction. 5. Cornwall (England : County)—Fiction. 6. Knights and knighthood—Fiction. 7. Arthurian romances—Adaptations. 8. Adultery—Fiction. 9. Ireland—Fiction. 10. Queens—Fiction. I. Title.
PR6063. I319L33 2004
813' .914—dc22
2004010503

ISBN 0-609-60962-9

10  9  8  7  6  5  4  3  2  1

First American Edition

*For the one who has gone before*

*to the Islands of Delight,*

*Unforgettable,*

*A true Irish Queen*

# the family trees of cornwall, lyonesse, and pendragon

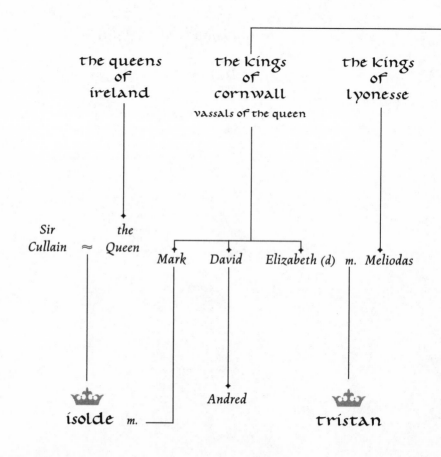

the queens
of
ireland

the kings
of
cornwall

vassals of the queen

the kings
of
lyonesse

Sir
Cullain  ≈  the
Queen

Mark    David    Elizabeth (d)  m.  Meliodas

isolde  m.

Andred

tristan

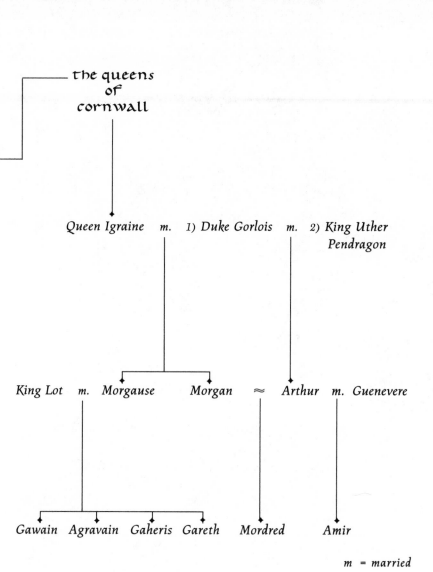

the queens
of
cornwall

Queen Igraine   m.   1) Duke Gorlois   m.   2) King Uther
                                                Pendragon

King Lot   m.   Morgause        Morgan   ≈   Arthur   m.   Guenevere

Gawain   Agravain   Gaheris   Gareth        Mordred        Amir

m = married
d = deceased
≈ = lover of

# the LADY of the SEA

At the time of King Arthur and Queen Guenevere, the King of Lyonesse wedded the sister of King Mark of Cornwall. Thereafter he was unjustly cast into prison when his wife was great with child. Then the young Queen ran mad with grief into the wood and fell into her travail betimes. There she bore a son after many grimly throes, and she called the boy's name Tristan, for her sorrows, and so she died.

Then Merlin brought the King out of his prison, and he married another queen, who ordained to poison Tristan so that her children should enjoy the land. But it happened that the Queen's own son drank the poison and fell down dead. Then the King drew his sword and said, "Tell me what drink this is, or I shall slay thee." And she fell to her knees, and told him she would have slain Tristan.

So she was damned by the assent of the barons to be burned. And as she was brought to the fire, young Tristan knelt to his father and begged the life of his stepmother as a boon.

"Take her, then," said the King, "and may God forgive her, if you can."

So Tristan went to the fire and saved her from her death, and thereafter he was known as a knight great in all chivalry for his bigness and grace.

Then the Queen of Ireland made war on King Mark of Cornwall, and Sir Tristan rode to his uncle the King and took the battle on. And the Queen of Ireland had a daughter who was known for her beauty through all the world as La Belle Isolde. She was the most noted healer of all the isles, and despite the enmity between Ireland and Cornwall, she saved Sir Tristan when he suffered a deadly hurt.

So King Mark devised to wed a maiden of such praise and swore his nephew Sir Tristan to win Isolde for him. And the Queen of Ireland ordained a drink of such virtue that the day La Belle Isolde should wed, she should drink it with King Mark and either should love the other all the days of their life. But on the sea voyage to Cornwall it chanced that Isolde drank from the flasket with Tristan, and thus happed the love which never departed them, neither for weal nor for woe.

After this the Queen of Ireland died, and La Belle Isolde was Ireland's Queen, but for a knight of Ireland who would be King. So went Isolde into Ireland to claim her own and fell into the hands of this knight, for that Tristan was away with his uncle Mark, whose great jealousy gave him no respite.

And the King of France had a daughter known as Blanche Mains for her white hands, which Princess cast great love upon Sir Tristan and would wed no man else. And by cunning she devised

to marry him, at the grief whereof Tristan ran mad and Isolde knew not where he was. Much pains ensued until that evil was undone. Yet either still loved the other through many darkly sorrows until the truth was seen.

Then Isolde sighed and said, "Well is it true, that there be in this land but four lovers, Queen Guenevere and Sir Lancelot du Lake, and Sir Tristan de Lyonesse and Queen Isolde, and so I shall send to the Queen."

Then King Mark's jealousy could not longer be contained, and word was brought to his overlord Queen Igraine that great misery was boding for Isolde in the land. . . .

—*Morte D'Arthur*

# chapter 1

orked lightning split the blackness of the sky. Swollen clouds raced screaming through the air and peal after peal of thunder came rolling in from the edge of doom. Far below, the little ship fought doggedly through the boiling sea. Soaked to the skin in spray, the figure in the prow raised a bony fist and shook it in the tortured face of the sky.

"Grief upon me!" he cried, "grief on all of us. And a curse upon you, Lady, for raising this storm!"

His words were lost amid the raging winds. All around lay nothing but a black expanse of roaring waves. Mountains of water were torn up from their depths, filling the air with the primeval smell of the seabed, where shipwrecks sleep and long-ago dead things rot.

"Aft, aft!" came a cry from one of the crew.

"See to the mizzen!" the captain shouted back.

"Spare your efforts, fools, and say your prayers!" cackled the old man in the prow. "Nothing can save us now."

The busy crew took no heed of the tall, lean figure in the prow, his crabbed hands gripping the rails, his bare head and hawk-like face defying the full fury of the storm. But crouched at the foot of the mast, the cabin boy watched the wind whip the curses from the old man's lips and shook with fear from head to foot. He saw his mother's face as she kissed him good-bye and made his own farewell to her in his heart.

Hastening past, the bosun checked his pace. "Never fear, lad," he called out more stoutly than he felt, "you'll come to no harm. The Lady of the Sea takes care of little 'uns like you."

The boy grabbed at his arm and pointed to the old man in the prow. "What's he doing, swearing and cursing like that?" he wailed. "Won't he offend the Lady and drown us all?"

Another burst of lightning shattered the sky. In the sickly light, the bosun had the color of a corpse. Shuddering, the child saw himself and all the crew drifting through the depths with glassy eyes and floating hair. He tasted the salt of his tears and the salt of the spray and felt himself dissolving into the sea, the primal ocean where all things are one. Over the side of the ship he saw great green-black masses of writhing water come to drag him down, and whimpered with dread.

"What, him?" The bosun hooked a thumb over his shoulder toward the watcher in the prow and grinned through the driving spray. "There's many would say that no ship'll ever sink as long as that crooked old carcass is aboard."

The boy's eyes widened, and he forgot his tears. "Who is he, then?"

The bosun cheerfully touched the side of his nose, and turned away. "Don't ask, lad. Don't ask."

Heartened, the boy watched the bosun race off down the deck. In front of them two mighty waves met head-on, and a towering spout of water lit the darkness of the sky. A fountain of white foam shot up into the air, and in its midst the boy saw a cascade of gold coins as bright as stars and a shining pearl the size of a seagull's egg.

The boy was ravished. It was a sign of hope.

Greatly daring, he raised his eyes and looked about. A rugged, fearful coastline lay ahead, leaping into view every time the lightning flashed. Through a break in the rocks he could see a little bay and a mighty rock within it, with a castle on the top. Cut off from the land, protected by the sea growling around its base, the great fortress stood dark and glowering, brooding over the roiling waters all about. Nothing but a narrow bridge of stone connected it to the headland opposite. It was the best defended place on earth.

Who lives there? the boy wondered. One of the Great Ones for sure.

"Into the wind!" came a distant command. "Keep her straight and true."

The little ship drove onward to the shore. Waving his arms, the old man in the prow renewed his curses, hurling defiance at the castle ahead. Assailed from right and left by the surging waves, the boat bucked and reared like a living thing, resisting the sailors' efforts to bring her to land. Undeterred, the helmsman held his course. Riding the last great wave, the little boat shot the gap between the rocks with a leap like a salmon in spring, and broke through into the safety of the bay.

In the shelter of the mighty rock, the wind dropped, and at last the old man's cries could be heard. "Grief upon you, Lady, for raising this storm! Did you think you could keep Merlin away?"

There was a stirring from the dark rock ahead. Candlelight blossomed in the topmost tower and a sound like a sigh drifted down the wind. "Keep you away, Lord Merlin? Surely you know that I sent for you?"

A PINK AND MAUVE DAWN warmed the morning sky. Muttering furiously, Merlin followed the young knight through the lofty halls and passageways of the castle on the rock. Gods above, he scolded, what a voyage that was! Never again would he come to Tintagel by sea. Last night's adventure had almost been the end of him.

But not quite. A glow of satisfaction lit his golden eyes. He and the crew had been royally received, despite arriving at the castle like drowned rats. A good night's sleep had followed in a fine feather bed, welcome even to a Great Druid like himself, a bard of the seventh seal and a lord of light. Stepping out now from a rich red-and-gold chamber hung with gorgeous tapestries, the old enchanter felt almost himself again.

But not quite, his inner voice whispered. Not quite. Oh, he looked fine enough, he knew, sleeking down his perfumed locks of hair. After last night's escape from the terror of the sea, he had gowned himself all in green for the woodland, green for the safety of earth. His long coat with its high standing collar was as dark as a midnight yew, his sleeves as they kissed the floor were a beech bud's piercing green, and the skirts of his robe sang like the wind on the mountains of home. A circle of moss agates held back his hair, and rings of jasper and beryl adorned his hands. Good enough, he decided, for any man.

But for any woman, and this one above all?

He clutched the gleaming wand he held in his hand and bared his teeth in a venomous grin. Not for her, Merlin. Not for old Queen Igraine.

Old Queen Igraine? He caught himself up. Young Igraine once, of course, and lovely enough in her youth to entrance any man. Had he forgotten that? No, he could not forget. Grief upon me, sang within his head. Grief upon all of us. Above all, on Igraine.

On . . . On . . .

Slowly they mounted to the topmost tower through wide, gracious corridors and many flights of stairs. And even here in the castle, the sea was with them still. Here in the silent corridors where no foot trod, salt-laden breezes brushed Merlin's hair and tugged at his sleeve. And always, everywhere, came the rhythmic sound of the waves, the heartbeat of life itself from the time life began.

Upward, ye Gods, upward still?

"This way, sir," called out the young knight.

On every level, the passageways narrowed down till they came to a low door in the rough stone wall. The young knight bowed to Merlin with a smile. "The Queen attends you, sir. I shall be here to escort you back when you return."

Merlin's wand was singing in his hand. Eyeing the polished shaft of golden yew, he shut his ears to its high, anxious whine, and ducked through the low opening with bated breath. The tang of the sea was even stronger now, but once inside, he might have been walking in the sky. He stood in a circular chamber at the top of the topmost tower overlooking the sea. Long windows reached from ceiling to floor all around, and the whole of the lofty chamber was flooded with light. A blazing dawn poured in from every side, and for a moment Merlin felt he could touch the rising sun as it burst from the bosom of the sea below.

In the center of the chamber stood an aged queen. Taller than most women, she had an air of remote and unquestioned majesty. Her cloak was silver, her veil the pale gold of the moon, and her robes shimmered green-gray and black like an angry sea. A deep crown of pearls encircled her head, and a gold wand of power quivered in her hand.

She bowed to him in silence, and Merlin struggled in vain to read her timeless face.

A lofty forehead, skin as pale as spindrift on the foam, and a cloud of white hair like gossamer, fine and strong. Large, liquid eyes set in a steadfast gaze, with a look that had seen a thousand years come and go. A woman of luminous beauty, with the power of a warrior queen and an undaunted soul. Ye Gods! Cursing, Merlin clutched the remnants of his composure around him like a tattered cloak. He might have been in the presence of the Great One herself.

But the woman before him bore all the signs of one bound to her mortal frame by flesh and blood. Suffering had carved deep wrinkles on her face, and a lifetime of endurance had forged the set of her chin. At some point she had known what it was to lose the will to live, and traces of that overwhelming despair hung about her still. Yet now they were no more than the shining remains of unspeakable pain transcended at last by a higher will. Here was a spirit who had risen above the fray, soared with her sorrows, and used them as the wind beneath her wings.

Alas for Igraine . . .

Merlin drew a ragged breath. Well, may the Gods forgive.

She saw his discomfort and spoke. "So, Merlin?"

Not Lord Merlin, the old enchanter noted with a sulfurous spurt of anger, nor Merlin Emrys the Bard, Great Druid, Lord of Light, nor any of the titles that honored his work as poet and prophet, dream-weaver and teller of all tales throughout his many lives. But Igraine bowed to no man, least of all him.

He forced a yellow smile. "Madam?"

Slowly he assessed the statuesque figure and immemorial face. "Lovely as ever, I see," he said with perfect truth.

In spite of himself, he felt his flesh quicken and stir as it always did in the presence of a woman like this. He spread his wrinkled hands invitingly. "Alas, madam, if only you and I . . ."

Igraine gave the ghost of a smile. "Sir, you have made many conquests in your time. I was never destined to be one of them." Her face hardened. "On the contrary . . ."

Merlin hastened to forestall her attack. "You blame me still for tak-ing Arthur away from you. But he was born to save the House of Pen-dragon, you know that. His destiny was written in the stars."

"Oh, Merlin—" Words could not convey the depth of Igraine's dis-tress. "That was not destiny. That was your desire. You wanted Arthur, so you took my son."

The tears of a long-bereft mother stood in her eyes. Merlin knew better than to defend himself.

"Yet think of him now," he wheedled. "High King of the Britons, famed throughout the land. Lord of the Round Table, and leader of the finest fellowship of knights ever seen. A King whose glory reaches as far as Rome. A byword for honor and chivalry everywhere." He held out his hands in appeal. "Did I do wrong?"

Igraine faced him with a stony disregard. "Your conscience must tell you that."

"Indeed it will," said Merlin hurriedly, "in the fullness of time. But today I am here on a voyage of goodwill."

She stared him in the eye, anger crackling around her like a storm. "When did Merlin ever have goodwill for me?"

"For your kingdom, then. For the land of Cornwall at large."

"Enough, old man," she breathed. "Say what brings you here and be on your way."

Old man, she said?

"What brings me here?" Merlin paused to conceal his rage. "Isolde!" he hissed on a slow, outgoing sigh.

Far below, the tide plucked at the shingle at the foot of the tower. Isolde, Isolde, sighed the restless sea.

At last Igraine stirred. "Queen Isolde? What of her?"

Merlin bared his yellow teeth. "Alas, she is in danger of her life. I fear if she stays in Cornwall, her days are done."

Not a flicker of emotion showed on Igraine's face. "And why is that?"

"Her husband, King Mark, is losing his grip on the land. His barons despise him and want him to name his heir. He cannot hold Cornwall much longer, and when he falls, Isolde will fall with him. His nephew

Sir Andred is poised to take the throne. And not a soul alive wants Andred as Cornwall's king."

Igraine fixed Merlin with her glimmering gaze. "Just as well then that Mark has another nephew, Sir Tristan, respected by all in Cornwall, high and low. He's been Isolde's knight for many years, and he'd guard her to the death. Why should he not succeed without harm?"

Merlin shook his head. "Blood will be shed, I know it. If you love Isolde, bid her to leave Cornwall at once. She will only be safe if she goes back to her own isle."

"So Isolde must flee to Ireland and take refuge in Dubh Lein? Indeed it is her fortress, her castle, her ancestral home. But what makes you think she will find safety there?"

Merlin started. "Why not?"

"Ah, Merlin—" The Queen glimmered at him. "I thought a Druid's ears could catch the song of a babe in its mother's womb and the turn of the tide of every faraway sea. Did you not hear of this, Lord Emrys the Bard?"

Was she playing with him? Merlin hid his rage behind an iron grin. "Hear of what, I beg you?"

"There is trouble in Cornwall, you say. But the wolves are gathering around Dubh Lein, too. Ireland's green hills and valleys are in danger now."

"From what?" Merlin cried, ready to tear his hair. "From whom?"

Isolde gave him her thousand-year-old stare. "From a race of invaders who were old when these islands were young. From the men of an ancient tribe who fell back to the northernmost mountains when the Romans came, but lived to drink from the skulls of the stragglers when the legions withdrew."

Merlin's eyes were alight with a yellow fire. "The Picts? The tribe the Romans called the Painted Ones for their hideous tattoos?"

"Yes, indeed."

"But what have they to do with Isolde?"

"They are the ancient enemies of her race. Her mother fought many hard battles to turn them from Ireland's shores."

"And they are stirring again?" Merlin let out his breath in a satisfied sigh. "All the more reason, then, for Isolde to go back to Ireland to repel their attack." He smiled broadly. "So Isolde will be fully occupied in Ireland, that's plain. And when Mark's reign ends in Cornwall, you and I are agreed that Tristan will rule?"

"Why not Isolde?"

"Isolde?" Merlin tensed. "But Mark has two heirs already, his blood kin. Against them, Isolde has no claim."

"None at all?" The Queen smiled her ancient, secret smile.

"She's Mark's wife, yes, of twenty years," Merlin snapped. "But marriage to the King is no claim to the throne."

"Nor is being nephew to the King, if the King's claim is not secure."

"What?" Merlin felt the ground slipping from beneath his feet.

"King Mark is my vassal. He only holds the throne through my goodwill. As his overlord, I can appoint another in his place."

Darkness and damnation, that it would come to this . . .

Merlin struggled to hide his dismay. "You would make Isolde the Queen of Cornwall in her husband's place?"

"Why not?" Igraine laughed, a mellow, warming sound. "She would do better than Mark. And the people would be happy if I did."

Merlin's eyes bulged. "Mark would never accept it."

"He has no power to refuse." She leveled her eyes on his. "But what do you care about Mark? Or about Isolde herself?"

Merlin puffed up his green velvet chest. "Madam, I assure you—"

"Oh, Merlin—"

Igraine broke away and strode around the room, her silks hissing like the ebbing sea. "The spirit that made you take Arthur away from me is with you still. You claimed Tristan, too, when he was a boy, and you've watched over him ever since. These are the only sons that you'll ever have, and you're determined they'll never suffer as you did, outcast and alone."

Alas the Gods . . .

Grief upon grief rose before Merlin's eyes. He saw himself again as a fatherless boy when his mother, a princess of the Pendragons, was cast out for bearing a bastard son. His own newborn son came back into his mind, in the arms of his dear young wife, who had followed her child to the grave. Once again he felt himself hunted through the forest as he was after Uther Pendragon died, and his tears for his great kinsman flowed anew. "Madam, I beg you—"

But the bell-like voice chimed on. "You care nothing for Isolde. You only want Tristan to succeed, like all your lost boys. You turned Arthur toward the Christians and promoted their faith because they invest power in men. Now you want to get rid of Isolde, because the sons of Merlin must reign alone. I see it all." She pressed her long fingers to her temples as the visions came thick and fast. "You mean to use all your ancient Welsh dragon-power to destroy the Mother-right."

"No, no," Merlin screeched. "I protest—"

Igraine held up her hand. "Fight for your fatherless men all you like, I shall defend Isolde and the Mother to the end."

"Hear me! On your own head be it—"

"Oh, sir—" Igraine turned on him, swelling like a stormy sea. "Go back to the Welshlands and your crystal cave. Learn there if you can the simple secret of life. All men are lost without a woman to love. Woman is the circle that contains all life itself, all that is human in its journey from birth to death."

"Madam, I swear—"

Words, threats, and curses were pouring from Merlin's lips. The old Queen stood for a moment surveying the tortured features and livid, twitching lips. Then she raised her hand and the young knight appeared at the door.

The old Queen bowed. "Safe journey, Merlin," she said sternly, "and be warned. Leave Isolde alone. She must find her own way through the dangers ahead. She will triumph or fail, there is no middle way, and not even the Mother can turn back the wheel."

# chapter 2

"Hear us, King Mark!"

The man at the head of the table made a final appeal. "The Gods know I've been loyal to your house." He gestured to the worn faces round the board. "We've all grown old serving you and your father, in war and peace. But we're all agreed that you must take action now."

Must, must...?

The slack figure on the throne listened with dull rage. What, a sovereign in his own stronghold to be attacked like this? A King of Cornwall to be harassed by those whose duty it was to bow and obey? He could smell them all circling now, like beasts of prey. How dare Sir Nabon and his lords tell him what to do? He had called this Council. Let them obey him—*now!*

His fist crashed to the table. "I am King here! And you, my lords, will hear me!"

Balefully, he stared down the length of the green baize. Who would challenge him? Not the white-bearded Sir Wisbeck, already a hoary ancient when Mark was a boy and now sailing serenely toward his eternal night. Nor the fat and pompous Sir Quirian, busily avoiding the King's eye. Mark laughed sardonically. Quirian might be playing manfully with the hilt of his sword, but if swords were drawn, the stout knight would not be seen.

Fools! Didn't they see that he was offering them fame beyond compare? Men would talk of the Quest for the Holy Grail for a thousand years. This nonsense about the succession must not throw him off. He hunched his shoulders and leaned forward, glowering.

"Arthur and his knights are all going on the Quest," he pronounced. "Cornwall should be there, too."

Sir Nabon watched every eye round the table turn toward the King, and stifled a sigh. Where was Isolde? No one else could deal with Mark at times like this.

Isolde...

A tall, lithe shape drifted across his mind, and he saw again the Queen's cloud, womanly red-gold hair, thoughtful eyes, and quicksilver smile. Sourly, he eyed the King's soft leather tunic and breeches of fine wool, the gold chain adorning his less than manly chest, and the undeserved torque of knighthood around his neck. Isolde had more royalty in her little finger than this man in all his ungainly body, no matter how richly he dressed.

Mark felt Nabon's honest scrutiny and thrust out his chin. "How long is it now since Arthur sent word of the Quest? He'll be leading his knights out on the road, and I should be, too."

"Oh, sire—"

Sir Nabon's voice was bleak with despair. "Your own kingdom craves your attention, not the Quest. In the north, the Picts threaten to overflow the Roman wall, and the savage Norsemen batter the eastern shore."

Old Sir Wisbeck frowned. "Hear him, sire. A ruler must do what lies nearest to hand."

Must, must...

There they were again.

Mark shifted on his throne, angrily crossing and uncrossing his long legs. "But the east coast is guarded by Arthur and Guenevere, and the Painted Ones will never come this far south. If they attack, they'll make for Ireland, for sure. And God be praised, that's in Isolde's hands. That's why she's gone to Camelot on our behalf." He straightened his narrow shoulders importantly. "Now, about the Quest—"

Nabon felt increasingly near despair. "But, sire, remember the dangers that lie nearer home."

"We need to get our young knights out guarding the roads," Sir Wisbeck agreed gravely. "Not lounging around here at the court, refusing to go to the tiltyard and drinking every night in the Knights' Hall."

"Drinking every night?" Mark's little eyes narrowed. He kneaded his belly fondly, and gave a belch. "What's wrong with that?"

"Nothing, sire," replied Nabon loyally. "But the kingdom must come first. There's no profit for Cornwall in joining the Quest for the Grail."

There was a heavy pause. Then Sir Wisbeck's frail, elderly voice dropped in once more. "And the Grail itself, sire, these objects the Christians seek—"

Mark turned on Sir Wisbeck. "The cup and plate from Our Lord's Last Supper, yes," he glowered, "and the sword and spear of His passion. What of them?"

Wisbeck's milky eyes looked deep into the past. "Many of us knew these objects by another name, long before the Christians set foot in this land. To us, they're the Hallows of the Goddess, sacred to Her for a thousand years." He held up four fingers and carefully ticked them off. "Her loving cup of forgiveness, with which She reconciles us all. Her great dish of plenty, to feed all who come. Her sword of power, and Her spear of defense."

Farther down the table, another head nodded fervently. Sir Thalassan had sailed far and wide in his youth, and the faraway gaze of the seafarer was with him still. He stared at Mark unsmiling, as powerful memories played behind his eyes.

"At sea, we had another prayer, too," he said slowly. "For us, the wide ocean was the holy grail, the mighty vessel in which the Mother holds the waters of life. And her platter of plenty is the never-failing earth."

"Yes, well," Mark huffed. "That was before the light of Christ was revealed. Father Dominian says that God has now given His true wisdom to the world, and all this Goddess-worship is a thing of the past."

A new spark of awareness burned in Nabon's eye. "And the Mother-right?" he said levelly.

Mark waved a lordly hand. "That, too, must pass."

There was a thunderous silence. Only Sir Wisbeck dared put the thought they all shared into words.

"Then what of Queen Isolde, your consort and wife? Are you saying her rule in Ireland will be no more? And what of our own sovereign lady here in Cornwall, your overlord Queen Igraine? For a thousand years, both our countries have obeyed the rule of Queens."

Nabon leaned forward urgently. "It may be true, sire," he forced out, "that the rule of women is over and done. But whatever happens, you must name your heir. As long as you remain childless, the succession lies between your nephews Andred and Tristan."

The succession, the succession . . .

God Almighty, there they were again!

Mark flung himself out of his chair and strode about the chamber, his long limbs jerking with rage. "You're a pack of chattering jackdaws, all of you. I'm sick of hearing you repeat the same nonsense day after day. Hear me, Nabon—"

But Sir Nabon was not to be silenced now. "By your leave, sire," he said trenchantly. "Sir Tristan is the choice of every man here."

Mark turned on him. "And Sir Andred?"

. . . is powerful, ruthless, and determined to succeed, ran through Nabon's mind.

"None of us will serve or follow him," he rapped out.

So! Mark gasped. They don't trust Andred. Why? What do they know about him that I don't?

Sir Quirian took a breath. "We choose Sir Tristan, sire," he said doggedly, "for his courage and courtesy that touches every soul. You saw him defeat the King of the Blacklands at the last tournament and then hand him the prize. It was to honor a close-fought battle, Sir Tristan said. But all the world knew it was pure chivalry."

Tristan, always Tristan . . .

Smoldering, Mark heard the cheers of a thousand tournaments ringing down the years. He looked at the stout knight with rising hate. All his life, it seemed, Tristan had been putting him to shame. Didn't Quirian know that every triumph of Tristan's festered in Mark's own heart? And Tristan himself surely knew that his prowess had always made Mark look poor and mean. And now every man round the table was pressing Tristan's case.

A new resolution burst in Mark's weak brain. Never would he name Tristan as his heir. Help me, God, he moaned inwardly. Lend me Your strength against Tristan, Andred, and all these meddling lords!

And Isolde.

A fresh wave of fury rose to scald his soul. Above all Isolde, with her cool, questioning stare, her fiery spirit that was always so cold to him, despite the promise of her flaming hair and her shapely body so queenly and aloof...

Inspiration seized him.

"God may yet bless our marriage and give the Queen a child," he cried. "How can I name Tristan or Andred as my heir, when they could be displaced by a son of my own loins?"

"Your son?"

Nabon stared at Mark, caught between rage and despair. He ground his teeth. And how will this miracle child come about, he snarled inwardly, when all the world knows that the Queen never comes to your bed? When for years this marriage has been a hollow sham, and you have felt free to disport yourself elsewhere? Is this an answer to our just demands? Oh, our poor country, without a leader or an heir.

He wanted to take Mark by the throat and shake him as a dog shakes a rat. Then a deep unease crept over him like a mist off the marsh. What if Mark were not lying? What would become of Isolde if Mark suddenly demanded his marriage rights? As he could, oh yes, he could. Would he take her by force? Yes, even that. Driven by greed or vanity, Mark could do anything.

Alas, poor Isolde...

Revulsion gripped Nabon's stomach. Surreptitiously, he wiped a bead of sweat from his upper lip and read the same concern in his colleagues' eyes.

"Just wait till my beloved wife returns," caroled Mark. "Then we shall see."

Around the table, the seated men tried not to meet each other's troubled gaze.

Alas, alas, Isolde...

Isolde, Isolde, mourned the restless sea.

Goddess, Mother, help her. Help us all.

Nabon buried his head in his hands and began to pray.

# chapter 3

a pearly twilight was falling on the wood. The long green shadows deepened under the trees, and the brief April sunset faded into night. One by one, all the busy creatures of the day slipped to their holes. With a thousand small murmurs and soft rustlings, the forest slowly settled itself for sleep.

The long line of knights and horses wound through the dusk. At the head of the troop, the tallest knight reined in his stallion and threw a gauntleted fist in the air. The last silver light lingered over his long, well-formed limbs, steadfast bearing, strong features, and thoughtful gray eyes.

"Halt there, every man!" he cried, "while I speak to the Queen."

Turning, he cantered back down the leafy track. In the center of the convoy were two female figures, the taller mounted on a delicate white mare, her companion at her side in the sober garb of a maid. With a sigh of content, he drew the pine-laden air deep into his lungs.

Isolde . . .

As always, the sight of her brought back the same raw catch in the depths of his heart. His horse's hooves drummed on the forest floor, and the swift rhythm ran singing through his veins: Isolde my lady, Isolde my only love.

*Ah, Tristan . . .*

Her heart in her eyes, Isolde watched him approach. The tall body she had loved for so long still sat lightly in the saddle, even after a grueling day's ride. His smile lit up the gloaming, and his hands around her waist as he swung her down from her horse made her feel alive.

He made a formal bow, "What's your wish, madam?" he asked. "Shall we press on to Castle Dore, or make camp here for the night?"

"What's my wish?"

Undecided, Isolde looked around the forest glade. Beside her, Tristan stood waiting for her to speak, and his familiar musky scent called to her irresistibly through the twilight air. She wanted to hold this moment forever, sheltering in the warmth of his great body, suspended with him in eternal time and space. Tomorrow they would be back at Castle Dore, face-to-face with King Mark and all their inescapable cares.

Back at Castle Dore?

The shadow of the future darkened around her as she stood. Then, dropping through the gentle evening mist, came a sound as soft as a sigh: *Isolde, no.*

No?

She waited, pregnant with danger, as the word came again.

*No longer.*

*Never more.*

Even after all these years, she knew her mother's voice.

*You are a Queen, Isolde, and one of long line. Your foremothers were warriors and battle ravens, the sovereignty and spirit of the land. See how they saved our people time after time, and even beat the Romans back to Rome!*

Suddenly she was a child again, watching her mother's powerful figure flashing to and fro in a flurry of hissing red silks and clattering jet.

*But Mawther—*

Isolde felt raw grief stinging her throat. How long was it since her mother had died?

*Hear me, little one. You are Queen now. What did I always teach you? No tears, no fears.*

*What are you saying, Mawther?*

*Queen as you are, you have the power of every woman, too. No woman should wait on a man to determine her fate. Your life lies before you, your future is in your hands. You must live out your destiny, and you alone must decide.*

*Must I? Must I?*

*Yes. You must choose.*

Isolde felt herself trembling from head to foot. So it had come at last, the moment she had been avoiding for all these years. The moment when her mother, her conscience, or the Great One, call it what you will, had laid bare the painful twisting and turning of her tortured life. Married to one man but in love with another from the start. Publicly a loyal consort, but in private a faithless wife.

She could still hear the faint echo quivering through the air.

*No longer, Isolde.*

*Choose.*

*You must choose.*

Ahead of them lay a parting of the ways, one road running south to Castle Dore, the other leading to Tintagel on the opposite coast. Isolde's senses swam. *Goddess, Great One, help me! What should I do?*

"Lady?" The concerned voice of Tristan reached her through the mist.

She came to herself with a shudder, and opened her eyes. "Pray you, set up my pavilion," she said clearly. "We camp here tonight."

OH, THE RAPTURE OF THE TIME they had spent at Camelot, away from King Mark's court! Yet now it was over, how short it had been. Brooding, Isolde watched her knights taking care of the horses and setting up the tents. When she had set out on the embassy to Arthur and Guenevere, the time with Tristan had stretched ahead like a dream. Now in the dark forest so near to Castle Dore, grim thoughts and fears lurked like outlaws behind every bush.

In the distance, Tristan passed among the troops. Isolde sighed. How long had she loved this man? And in all those years they had never been able to live openly together, sharing their thoughts and dreams as others did. Sadness descended on her like the evening dew. Was she doomed to live a life of stolen bliss, trapped like a fly in amber at Mark's court?

*Choose.*

*You must choose.*

"My lady?" The familiar voice of her maid sounded in her ear. "They're ready for you now."

"Thank you, Brangwain."

Turning, Isolde met the bright blackbird eyes of the woman who had come from the Welshlands to nurse her as a child and had never left her side. Those who knew Brangwain called her "Merlin's kin," and the lean, unyielding figure in her plain, dark dress clearly had something fierce and Otherworldly in her air. But now her olive-skinned face wore a broad smile as she nodded up the track. "See, lady?"

Isolde's heart lifted. "I see."

Tristan was coming toward her with that well-loved smile and reaching for her hand to lead her through the trees. Her royal pavilion stood in a clearing bathed in the last of the day's golden light, its entrance swagged back in welcome, its interior warm with bright rugs and burning braziers. One young knight was strewing the hot coals with herbs, and the sweet tang of rosemary and thyme scented the air. Another set out a tray of mead and honeycakes, while Brangwain disappeared into the inner chamber to prepare the bed. Tristan thanked the knights and dismissed them with a smile, then turned to face her, his eyes bright with joy.

Isolde could not meet his loving gaze.

*Goddess, Mother, show me what to do.*

She took off her headdress and shook out her thick mane of hair. Without the tall casque and all-enveloping veil, she looked suddenly smaller, vulnerable, and young. A familiar pang of love pierced Tristan's heart. No one would believe that this girlish creature with her tender air was a queen and warrior who had seen almost forty summers on the earth.

Tristan watched her in wonder. Oh, how he loved her, how he loved her hair! Its red-gold depths were lit with glints like fire, and her vital spirit lived in its spring and bounce. He longed to seize it by the handful and pull her into his arms. But time enough for that.

"We did well in Camelot," she said, struggling to raise her spirits with a light tone. "It's important to grasp what Arthur and Guenevere face."

"It's a twofold challenge," Tristan agreed somberly. "The Quest will be scattering their knights far and wide just as spring brings the Norsemen raiding the eastern shore."

"And none of the knights wants to stay behind in defense. Sir

Gawain and Sir Galahad could hardly wait to take to the road. But if they all go out, who will take care of the land?"

Tristan nodded. "The Grail is a wonderful prize for the knight who succeeds. But the danger of invasion is always there."

Isolde's mood deepened. "For Ireland too. You remember the dispatches that came in last night? The Picts are going to trouble us again, it seems."

"The Painted Ones?" Tristan drew in a breath of alarm. "Alas, they've always been a savage race, born to fight."

*A race of savages . . .*

Fearful images of wild and daubed barbarians rose before Isolde's eyes. "The word has reached Dubh Lein that their king is dying, and their young prince Darath is waiting to show his strength."

"And Ireland must tempt them. It's so close to their land."

Isolde laid both hands on her center. "Darath will invade, I feel it. They will need me in Ireland, I see that, too."

Tristan knew her too well to doubt a word she said. "Then we must go to Ireland, lady," he said cheerfully. "But you must not fear. The Picts are no more than pirates, by sea and land. They'll be no match for your knights and men."

*He does not understand.* Isolde shook her head and turned away.

Tristan moved forward and gently took her hand. "Lady, what is your trouble?"

*I must choose.*

She turned on him abruptly. "When we go to Ireland, we should not return."

He started at the passion in her voice. "What, not come back to Cornwall? Why on earth . . . ?"

"Mark's jealous of you. And that's making me afraid."

"Alas, lady," he groaned. "If only we knew why."

"Why? Oh, Tristan—"

She looked at him with eyes of aching love. Nearing forty, he still had the frank, open look of his boyhood, though the strong planes and angles of his face had deepened with experience and time. His fair hair sprang up from his broad forehead as thickly as it always had, and the blue of his eyes still made her catch her breath. Best of all, he never noticed how heads turned for him, male and female alike. He might have been born to put other men to shame.

And seen against Mark, who had height but not strength and royalty without a trace of dignity, who was cursed with a long, ill-made body with a muddy face and thin, graying, sandy hair—a knight who had no prowess with sword or spear and not a thought in his head of chivalry . . .

Was it any wonder that Mark felt belittled when Tristan was near?

*Mark.*

*My husband, Mark.*

Isolde struggled to collect her wayward thoughts. Tristan, too, was floundering, she could see.

"We have always tried to respect and honor him," he said in a low voice. "So why do we have to leave now? Is there anything new?"

"Yes, indeed." She could not keep the bitterness from her voice. "The Christians are increasing their power every day. They have sworn to overthrow the Goddess, and Mark does not care. That priest of his, Dominian, feeds his vanity to gain control, and Mark builds them churches to buy absolution from his sins."

Tristan shifted uneasily. "His sins—?"

"Gods above, Tristan, how long has he flaunted his mistress in my face? And what's that snake-like Elva but a sin?" Suddenly she could bear it no more. "Look at him, Tristan. He's a wretched apology for a man and for a king. He's—"

"He's my kinsman, lady," Tristan broke in, his face alive with pain. "I beg you, remember that."

*What?* Isolde stared at him. His look of reproach cut her to the quick. She opened her mouth for an angry retort, then the sound she had heard before came once again, falling through the air like the evening dew.

*Never more.*

*It is time to choose.*

She came toward Tristan and took his hand. "I must not go back to Mark or to Castle Dore," she said intently, her voice very low. "I cannot sustain this marriage any longer."

Tristan started in alarm. "What?"

Isolde held her breath. Suddenly the way ahead was clear. "I shall go back to Ireland. My country needs me. I should not be here."

Tristan felt a hollow sickness invade his heart. "But Cornwall—"

"—must do without me," she said implacably.

Never had he seen her look so cold. He struggled to understand. "But—"

"I married Mark to keep Ireland safe. The danger's been over now for twenty years. There's no reason for me to remain as Cornwall's Queen." She looked away. "Still less as Mark's wife, when I've never gone to his bed."

He flushed and looked away. "I know."

She forced him to meet her eye. "Come with me to Ireland. We'll forget Mark and Cornwall and join our lives together in my own land."

He stared at her. "But lady, he's my kinsman—my only kin. And I swore a lifelong allegiance to him."

She held his gaze and willed him to be strong. "Set Mark aside, if you can. There's something else that dearly concerns us both."

He was quite lost; she could see it.

"What else?" he said in misery, running a hand distractedly through his hair.

*Goddess, help me . . .* She drew a long, slow breath. "If I'm ever to have a child, it must be soon."

"Have a child?" he gasped. "But we've always kept our love concealed."

"So I took the way of the Mother to close up my womb." She nodded grimly. "But in my own kingdom, I can do as I like. And when I'm free to follow the Mother-right, that means I can change my consort and bear his child." She paused and clenched her fists. "Your child, Tristan, if it's not too late."

"My child?" He could not take it in. But he could see the tempest raging in her soul. *Queen or woman, what am I to be? Wife, lover, and mother, or never in this life?*

"Come with me, sir," she said suddenly.

He stood like a bear at the stake. "You know I have sworn fealty to the King," he said hoarsely.

"I need you. He does not."

She could see the sweat breaking out on his brow.

"But what of King Arthur—the Round Table—the Quest?"

Isolde's eyes flared. "What of them?"

"I am one of that sworn fellowship," he said tensely. "King Arthur may send for me to join the Quest. And I'm still Cornwall's champion. King Mark may need me to defend the land."

She stared at him, unmoving. "What about our child?"

Trembling, he caught her eye and looked away. A child? They'd never spoken of it. He had never thought of it before.

And now, go to Ireland and bring a child into the world? Reveal the secret of their love to all? He'd be forced to leave the King's service in disgrace, betraying all he had known since his life of chivalry began. And what of this new life she talked about, the little soul who would call him father and command his heart's blood for the rest of his days? Could he do it? Or was he bound to fail?

Fail the child, for sure.

Fail Isolde and fail Mark.

Fail, fail, fail . . .

Yearning in anguish, Isolde watched him pace to and fro, feeling the clash of loyalties in his soul. *Choose!* cried her silent heart. *Choose me!* But already she knew the choice that he had made.

"What will you do?" she said huskily.

"What should I do?" he cried from the depths of his pain. "I owe allegiance to Mark and King Arthur and the Round Table, too. But you are my lady and my undying love. Who should I follow now?"

"I could ask you the same thing," she said hotly. "What should I do? As Mark's wife, I should return to Castle Dore. But I choose love over duty. What will you do?"

He looked into the distance, but all he could see was the void within himself. "You are the Queen," he said awkwardly. "The sovereignty and spirit of the land."

"And you are the King of Lyonesse," she said tremulously. "But in my arms, you are a man."

What did she mean? Tristan struggled to read the mystery in her eyes.

She threw him a glance of despair. *Hold me. Love me. Do not let me go.*

He covered his face with his hand to hide his grief. "Lady, I beg you, forgive me if you can," he said huskily. "But I cannot go back on the first vow I made. I swore myself to the King before we met and pledged undying fealty on my soul. I lose my honor if I break that oath, and without my honor, I'm nothing but a recreant knight. And I could not be your knight if I broke my faith. I could not offer you a life of shame."

She was as pale as death. "So be it."

Tristan straightened up. "To Ireland with you, lady," he said bleakly, "while I return to Castle Dore to keep pledge with Mark."

"Will you come to me afterward? When can I hope to see you again?"

"Somewhere it must be written. But the stars are dark. For myself, I cannot say."

A cry of pain escaped her. "Must it be?"

"Gods above, lady," he said, his voice breaking, "I'd give my life to change it if I could. But there is no other way."

She stepped forward and lifted her hand to his cheek. "Love me one last time?"

THE NEXT DAY AT DAWN they stood in the dark wood. Ahead of them lay the fork where the two roads diverged. The whole troop stood ready to depart, and there could be no last kiss or caress under the eyes of the men. But she could hear his thoughts.

Every evening of every day, I shall pray to you, Isolde my lady, Isolde my only love.

*And every twilight when the love star glows, I shall light a candle to burn for you, sweetheart.*

Wait for me till I come to you again.

*Through the three worlds and beyond.*

Fail not.

*I shall not fail.*

Nor I, till the seas kiss the sky.

*Farewell.*

They stood for a moment, lost in their private world till the soft jingle of a horse's harness brought them to themselves again.

He fixed her with his level gray regard. "Farewell, my lady" came to her through the cold silver-gray of the dawn.

She could hardly speak for pain. "Fare you well."

Blue, green, and purple played around his head as he stood like a shadow of himself against the fading dark. He had the look of a faun in a midnight forest, wild and strange. Another moment and he would be gone.

*Oh, Tristan . . . Tristan . . .*

*When shall I see you again?*

Already she knew it was tempting the Old Ones to ask. But never did she dream what the answer would be.

# chapter 4

*I*solde, Isolde ...

Had all the evil in the land sprung from this pagan whore? Or was his own sin to blame?

"Lord, Lord, let me see Thy face!"

Groaning, the priest Dominian covered his head with his cowl and drove his misshapen body into the wind. He knew the way through the wood so well that he hardly felt the tears blinding his eyes. Was it not enough that God had sent him into the world hunchbacked and lame, so malformed that his own mother had cast him away to die? Did the Almighty have to cast him out, too?

Yet this was the way it had been all winter long. All that time, God had hidden His face. Of course the Almighty rejected those full of rage, Dominian knew that. Yet what else can I be, Lord, when You work against me? he railed inwardly, stamping along with his novice, Simeon, behind. Tell me why You have spared Isolde all these years?

Frenziedly, he beat the dripping branches away from his face.

"Isolde the pagan," he muttered, "Isolde the rampant whore, who calls herself Queen when Holy Scripture forbids women to rule. And above her is Mark's overlord, old Queen Igraine. These women are the enemies of our work. They share the friendship of their thighs with any man of their choice. Why do they flourish, Lord? We shall never win control in a land where thigh-freedom rules. We must have subject females, mute and chaste. The rule of Our Father in these islands means rooting out the Mother-right."

Dominian clutched his head. Surely God in His wisdom knew all this! Every time Isolde put to sea, He could have made the waves into her death waters, drowned the witch in a pool of her own tears. Once

He had even held her life in His hand, when she had been accused of treachery and forced to undertake the ordeal by water to clear her name. He could so easily have done away with her then. Yet each time He had spared her to triumph over His own people. Why had God betrayed him to this dark night of the soul? Neither in church nor in his private prayers had Dominian seen God's face as he used to do.

Usedtodo, usedtodo, mocked the wind in the trees. The forest path narrowed and the going was harder now. The new springtime growth of leaves on the trees impeded their way and every green shoot seemed to catch at their monkish gowns. Glaring about him, Dominian loathed all he saw. What fools people were to rejoice at the coming of spring! All it meant was melting snow and clinging mud, trees dripping down every man's neck and the lowliest brambles tearing with renewed force—

Lord, Lord, why do you hide Your face?

Walking at his elbow, the novice Simeon stole a quick look at Dominian's misery and averted his gaze. Surely his master knew the weather would be foul today? With the onset of the spring thaw, all the rest of the brethren had opted for indoor tasks, the pious in the chapel chanting Offices for the Dead and the practical scouring the dormitories for cockroaches and rats.

And with his poor hunched spine and twisted leg, Dominian might have been forgiven an effort like this. But sleet or sludge, they all knew that their leader would seek out Jerome. Even in the worst of the snow, when the drifts were over his head, Dominian had got through to his old master's cell, week after week. Sometimes he asked the brawniest of the brothers to clear the way. More often than not he struggled through alone, working his malformed body through the snow, hands and arms held high above his head, his short, stubby thighs pumping forward zealously with every step.

For Jerome was his God on earth, his all-in-all. Some of the brothers had sneered at Dominian's devotion and made it a subject for complaint. Others muttered about Dominian's failure to defeat Isolde, and the spirit of disrespect had infected them all. Overhearing their whispers, Simeon had given one a bloody nose and broken another's teeth, and had been thrashed himself for bringing violence into God's house. But how else was he to defend his master against himself?

Not far now...

Oblivious to his novice's troubled thoughts, Dominian trudged on through the heart of the wood. Ahead now lay the ancient sacred well, its moldering roof covered in damp lichen and moss. Behind it loomed the low stone hermitage, likewise dank and dripping in the bone-crunching cold.

Dominian looked at Simeon. "Wait here," he ordered.

It would do the boy good, he decided, to stand shivering in his thin habit, enduring the cold on his sandaled feet. That was nothing to his own ordeal, having to live every day without God's love. Dominian felt the jagged tears starting again. Simeon's trial would be over soon. His sufferings would last till the day he died.

My God, my God...

Jerome's narrow cell was colder inside than out. A film of ice covered the earthen floor, and the old man's drinking water was frozen in his cup. A trickle of melting snow dripped from the roof, and even the lowly bed was glistening with damp. Jerome sat cross-legged in the center of the floor, his white head nodding on its fragile neck, his frail body in its thick woolen habit no more than skin and bone. Dominian touched the cross above the threshold, stepped inside, and fell to his knees.

"Bless me, Father," he groaned, "for I have sinned."

"Sinned, my son?" Jerome swiveled his blind gaze toward the door. "How?"

"I dreamed of ousting the Great Goddess from these islands, just as God taught us in the Bible, in the holy Book of Kings. I wanted to be like King Asa when he threw down his mother's idol in the groves of Hebron, where Queen Maacha worshipped the Great Whore of all Asia and danced before her shrine."

"The Great Mother a whore?" the old man pondered. "Remember Our Lord had a mother whom He loved."

Dominian recoiled. "But Mary was chaste!" he spat out. "Not like the loose-loined women of these islands, who claim the right to share their beds with any man." He shuddered with disgust. "There was none of that for the Mother of God!"

"Son—"

But Dominian was not listening. "Was I too ambitious, Father? I only wanted to make Mark a Christian king."

Jerome's voice was as paper-thin as his frame. "Was that all?"

Dominian's cry shattered the crystal silence of the cell. "Was I wrong, Father? I meant to make all these islands a place of God."

"These islands alone?" An edge of interrogation had entered Jerome's tone. "Or did your hopes lead you farther afield?"

Dominian did not hesitate. "I wanted to lead our mission all the way to Rome. The Holy Father rewards those who serve the Mother Church well."

Rome . . .

Dominian's sight dimmed. The Eternal City on her Eternal Hill, the rock of Saint Peter, the foundation of God's church. Already he could feel the hot sun on his back, see the thousands of holy men gowned in black, white, brown, and red, keeping the flame of faith triumphantly alight among the city's merchants and tradesmen, mountebanks, thieves, and whores.

Yet he, who had dreamed of kneeling before the Pope, must now languish forever in the deserts of disgrace. And he would pay for his failure at the Last Judgment, too. There were some sins that God could not forgive.

He howled like a dog. "My God, my God, why hast thou forsaken me?"

"Take comfort, my son. Rome is not all the world." Jerome held up his hand. "Our Father alone sees what we do. And you are a faithful servant, He knows that."

The old man's fingers were as fine as twigs, his flesh translucent in the wintry light. Dominian felt a sudden lurch of fear. How many more winters could Jerome survive? And what would become of him when Jerome had gone?

From the time Jerome had found him, left to die in the wood, the old man had been the only father he had ever known. Cast out by his mother, a Goddess-worshipper, both for being a hunchback and for being a boy, he had had Jerome's love and guidance all his life. And if

Jerome left him . . . Dominian wanted to weep, to scream, to tear his flesh. Suddenly he understood how the great saints could scourge themselves hour after hour till they passed out from loss of blood. Anything was better than the pain of losing God, and Jerome was all he knew of God on earth.

"Oh, my son . . ." The old man felt his despair and tried again. "Remember, Dominian, we must keep the faith."

The faith—

Dominian thought of the ardent, intimate love Jerome shared with God. He had often overheard the old man chattering away as if to a lover, and he had no doubt that God was answering him. He searched his master's face, racked with the excruciating envy he always felt for children who enjoyed such love from their mothers in his wretched youth. Bitterness overwhelmed him. "Compared with you, Father, I have no faith!"

The old man leaned forward. "Do not deny your God."

"But He denies me."

"Never!" Jerome declared. "God loves us all, as I have loved you. And that love will never leave you. Even in death, I shall walk by your side."

"But God knows I have failed!"

"With Queen Isolde, perhaps. But you have not lost King Mark. He will never return to the Mother-faith as long as he is Queen Igraine's vassal and resents her power."

Dominian pondered. That at least was true. He felt his spirits stir.

"Take heart, son," Jerome said feelingly. "God sees your suffering and has given us the words of prayer for times like these. Come, sing with me." He struck off in a high, gnat-like tone. "De profundis, Domine—"

Dominian felt the tears rising again, but this time with a sweet healing flow. Stumbling, he began his part of the psalm. "Out of the depths, O Lord, have I called upon Thee: Lord, Lord, I beseech you, hear my voice—"

The old man reached out and felt for Dominian's hand. "Remember when you were a child and I told you of the Father who loved little ones like you?"

His heart bursting, Dominian clung to Jerome. "You said that our Lord had marked me out as one of God's chosen," he said hoarsely, "destined for a special place in Heaven."

"All true." Jerome nodded. "And truer than ever now. Hear me, Dominian." The reedy voice rose to a sonorous chant. "God is love. He loves you, as I love you, world without end."

Dominian's head was boiling. "Father—"

Jerome stared at him with his milky, blue-white eyes. "Remember, Dominian, you were not named in vain. Dominion will be yours. God will give you mastery. You and others like you will root out the Great Mother in these islands and destroy all her works. In years to come, no one will know her name."

"But how can this be?" wept Dominian. "King Mark was mine when I won him to the Christian faith. I was his confessor, his guide, his all-in-all. Yet for twenty years I have been working in vain while the pagan Isolde holds sway as Cornwall's queen."

There was a pensive pause. Then the gentle papery voice rustled again. "The King is still married. Could there yet be a child born to him?"

A child?

Born to Mark and the Queen?

Dominian burst out into a savage laugh. "Never!" he said scornfully. "I bore down on him for years to do his duty and the work of God. But the whore closed her thighs to him on their wedding day. For almost twenty years now she has shunned his bed."

"But could you not bring him to renew his vows?"

"I have tried."

"Then try again, my son. A child is all we seek."

A child of Mark and Isolde?

Dominian closed his eyes as the force of the idea took root. A child, yes! For years he had been too weak with Mark, infected by the King's own weakness and lack of faith. But this could be the new opening he sought. And if it was God's will, both King and Queen must submit.

Yes, yes . . .

Dominian's heart swelled. Step-by-step he traced his way through the task ahead. First he would have to bring Mark to the sticking point, either to master his wife or to cast her aside. And then, alas,

Isolde would have to learn that sex and childbirth tamed any woman, even her. What was marriage ordained for, after all, but as an instrument of God to keep women in their place?

And once Isolde was broken, the Mother-right would soon be gone...

A pageant of glory passed before Dominian's eyes. He saw sturdy churches rising in every town and mighty cathedrals proclaiming the faith of Rome. Crosses would crown every building in the land and mark the humblest grave. Christianity would be taught in every school and enforced on every child. Women would be stripped of thigh-freedom, and men would be given God's power and the use of the whip. Avalon would be no more, and neither man nor woman would know the Great Goddess or even remember her name.

Now God be praised! Dominian sighed with delight as fierce visions of conquest and power inflamed his mind. Then we shall once again be pleasing to Rome. The Holy Father himself will call me to his side. Our faith will take over the world when the these pagans are gone. I see it all, once Cornwall is in my grasp. And Cornwall will be mine when Isolde is no more.

"*Magnus Dominus,* great and mighty is Our God—"

Jerome launched again on his thin, high cricket's chant, his ancient countenance transfigured with bliss. Dominian gazed at him with adoration, feeling a new sense of purpose flooding his veins. He clutched the old man's hand, weeping with joy, murmuring the prayer of thanksgiving Jerome had taught him long ago. All shall be well, and all shall be well, and all manner of thing shall be well.

And this he knew to be true.

For Dominian had once again seen the face of God.

# chapter 5

So the King's loyal barons had asked Mark to name his heir? And they'd made their choice, Tristan was their man?

Trembling, Sir Andred hurried through the court. They had turned against him, then, and rejected him as the next in line? Well, they would pay the price. Of course, when he had them writhing at the end of his sword, they'd all protest that they only wanted the best for the country, the people, what you will. But he'd hang the whole pack of them when he was king.

All except Nabon. Andred paused to relish the prospect. That old fox he'd take care of himself. How would it be? Would he slowly slit Nabon's windpipe or sink a sword and twist it in his guts? As long as he could enjoy the terror in the old man's bursting eyes and catch the last rattle of breath in his dying throat, he did not care. Then he'd hang Nabon's head on the highest battlement, as a warning to others that he would not be defied.

Yes, he would have his revenge. But it would not wipe out this insult to his pride. That ever the barons would choose Tristan over him ... A murderous rage swept through Andred's soul. He bunched his fists. What in the world should he do?

He dragged an angry breath into his lungs, oblivious to the gentle, rain-laden spring air. Darkness and devils, if only Elva were here! Andred's mind turned hungrily toward his longtime love, the tall, vibrant woman who years ago had thrown her lot in with him. He'd been so sure of her love then that he'd persuaded her to make advances to the King. If Elva could capture the heart of the love-starved Mark, he had urged her, then between them they'd have the whole country in their power.

Well, the Gods loved to jest. Who would have dreamed that Elva would come to love the shallow, selfish Mark, a cowardly wretch whom all the world despised? Nothing had prepared Andred for that peculiar pain and all that had followed, the years of sharing his love with another man. But now Elva's hold over Mark was waning, and she did not know why. It had all been in vain.

A new anguish gripped Andred, and his desperation increased. Yet I can still be king and make Elva my queen. Let me get to Mark and find out . . . plan . . . decide . . .

Slowly his thoughts took shape. First he should find Elva and get her advice. Her counsel was always worth having in difficult times. Then it might be a good idea to take her with him to the King. Who knows, perhaps she could catch Mark's fancy again today, and then . . . and then . . .

His mind aflame, Andred increased his pace through the main courtyard toward the King's House on the castle mound. Ahead of him he caught sight of two knights lingering casually in the shadow of an arch. So Fer de Gambon and Taboral were lying in wait for him?

News traveled fast at court. Andred gave a mirthless grin. It would be no secret to these two royal hangers-on that Tristan was the barons' favorite to succeed. Had they come to gloat over him?

He eyed them in an evil frame of mind. A head taller than his friend, Sir Taboral cut an impressive figure in the tiltyard, where the short, bandy-legged de Gambon could never shine. But Sir Fer de Gambon regained his dignity on the ground, and his keen eye betrayed a sharp intelligence that Taboral lacked.

Why were they waiting for him, Andred wondered cynically, when surely they should be turning to Tristan to greet the rising sun? Ah, that was it. They must have realized that as soon as Tristan became king, there'd be no place for them left at court. Tristan was too honorable to entertain disreputable knights. The unscrupulous Fer de Gambon, with his ferret eyes, and the brutish Taboral would be swiftly swept away.

Still, Andred calculated, between them they had brains and brawn. And who knows how soon I shall need them? ran through his mind. They'd been useful to him before, and they could be again. But neither of them should know that till the moment came.

"Well?" he said coldly, without breaking his stride.

"There's a messenger at the gatehouse, sir," Fer de Gambon offered as he hastened alongside, jiggling his short legs to fall into step. "From the Queen."

A shock of surprise ran through Andred's frame. Isolde was due back today at Castle Dore. If she'd sent a message, she must have changed her mind. She was going somewhere else. With Tristan? And in clear defiance of her duty to Mark?

*Yesssssss!*

An upsurge of hope flashed through Andred's soul. Now how could he build on this to get his revenge on Mark... to move against Tristan... to secure the throne...?

Andred closed his eyes. An age-old, warming rage ran through his veins. Gods and Great Ones, how long had he hoped to destroy Tristan and Isolde, too? And Mark himself, now that he knew for sure that the King would not stand up to the barons to defend his right?

Well, he'd stand up for himself. From this moment on. That was the only way he would make himself king. He turned back to Fer de Gambon and Taboral with rage in his heart.

"So, sirs," he began carelessly. "This messenger from the Queen...?"

"WHAAT?"

Slowly, Mark surfaced from the depths of sleep. The warm, friendly stink of horse slobber, sweat, and wine told him he was in his chamber sprawled out in his favorite chair, after a day at the hunt and a night's drinking with his men. Later he'd have to clean himself up for the court and put on the finery and semblance of a king. But here in his Privy Chamber, he could please himself. Slack-mouthed, he settled back to sleep.

But there it was again. "Good morning, sire."

Groaning, Mark recognized the harsh burr that had disturbed more mornings than he could bear to think. "Father Dominian?" he mouthed, struggling to command his thick tongue. "What is it now?"

"Your future, sire. Your fate."

Blearily, Mark scanned the priest's burning eyes and stony face. He heaved a resentful groan. "What about it?"

"Your Queen insults you, sire," the priest began in a low, intense voice. "Moreover, she defies the law of God. It is written that a wife be subject to a husband's will. Further, that the purpose of marriage is procreation, and that is woman's task."

God Almighty, before breakfast? Before the first, much-needed drink of the day? Mark closed his eyes and prayed for the priest to die. Or to disappear without a trace, whichever would be easier for God.

But God was not listening, it seemed. In a whiff of sanctimony and incense, Dominian pressed on.

"Your barons desire that you will name one of your nephews as your chosen heir. But neither Sir Andred nor Sir Tristan is a man of faith. A Christian child of your loins is what God desires."

Mark struggled to sit up. "But you know God has not yet granted a child to my wife and me—"

"Oh, sir—" The little priest firmly brushed his protests aside. "This is your task, not God's. Every man must master his wife in marriage or cast her aside. And He ordained motherhood to tame their sex, which otherwise is rampant and sinful and born to seek command."

"Well, that's true enough of Isolde." Mark gave a furious laugh. "But God knows she's too much for me. What can I do?"

Dominian's eyes flared. "God has given to you, sire, and to every man the instrument that tames every woman, even a queen."

What on earth did he mean? Struggling, Mark closed his eyes and tried to think.

"One of His higher designs," pursued the priest. "An object of nature that fulfills the divine will. The mark of manhood, to show men they were born to rule. The weapon they may use without mercy if they choose."

Mark goggled at Dominian. His manhood? His weapon? God's instrument? Slowly, understanding dawned. God in Heaven, is that what the priest meant? But how was he to do it? Isolde followed the Mother, and believed that a woman had the right to choose who she lay down with, and also to refuse. Would she ever accept that he had a right to possess her against her will? And to force her to submit if she did not agree?

A new voice joined the jangling chorus in his head. "Good day to you, sire!"

"Jesu have mercy, not another one?" Mark shook his befuddled head. Angrily, he focused on the approaching figure, smiling as ever and spruce in black and gray, but with a distinctly meaningful glint in his eye. What was Andred doing here at this time of day? And wasn't that the Lady Elva behind?

"My lord!" A tall, lithe woman in flowing green silks greeted him with the deepest of curtsies and a flashing smile.

Mark looked at her with dislike. How long had he cared for this woman? Had she really been his mistress for all these years? He stared with a sickly fascination at the shiny green gown clinging to her long, hard, snake-like body and outlining her sharp breasts. He once thought it was wonderful and striking that she dressed herself always in green, every shade of it from lime-yellow to greeny-black. Now her scaly silks bored him, like everything else. Ignoring her completely, he turned away.

Now Andred was busy paying his respects to the priest. Time to show who was King. Mark eyed them spitefully as he heaved himself to his feet, pulling down his slubbered jerkin and straightening his hair. Why was Andred looking so pleased with himself? By the grin on his face, he was ripe for taking down.

"Andred, you know all of Arthur's knights are going on the Quest," he announced, "and Cornwall must follow suit. I've decided to send the finest knights we have, and of course that means you." He paused to enjoy the flash of panic in Andred's eye. "Unless you want to play the coward and stay at home?"

"Oh, Uncle . . ."

Andred was far too familiar with Mark's malice to rise to the bait. He put his hand on his heart and fixed Mark with a loyal stare.

"Every knight must do what he knows in his heart is right," he said soulfully. "And I have found my quest here in Castle Dore."

Mark stared at him. "Where?"

"In serving you, sire. In fulfilling your will. That is my holy grail."

"Is it indeed?" Mark grunted with hidden satisfaction. "Well, I can't argue with that."

"But the Grail, sire—"

Dominian's interest quickened. It was written that God winnowed the knights on the Quest in the winds of his wrath, and if He did, then the vainglorious, sinful Andred could hardly be spared, and Tristan, too. How wonderful if both these unsatisfactory heirs were destroyed, leaving the way clear for the rightful Christian child.

"Indeed you must send Cornwall's best knights on the Quest, sire," he said flatteringly. "And who better than the nephews of the King?"

Andred smiled to himself. "But that leaves the King unprotected," he said silkily. "Which no loyal subject would want him to be."

Dominian looked at him with eyes of burning coal. "Do you question my loyalty, sir?"

"Only your foresight," Andred returned with an easy smile. "If Tristan and I were lost, what would Cornwall do then?"

God Almighty, not the succession again? New waves of distrust awoke in Mark's fevered brain. What was Andred up to? Dominian, too? Mark gasped. He did not know. But he had to save himself from both of them.

A wondrous plan began to blossom in his mind. "Hear me!" he cried. "It's true I have only nephews to my name. But if God gave me a son . . . ?" He rolled his eyes up to the vaulted roof. "Alas, neither Our Lord Jesus Christ nor my wife's Goddess has seen fit to bless our marriage with a child. But the Queen is still within her childbearing years. With God's help and blessing, there is hope for us. You may look for a child of her body within the year."

Within the year!

There, he'd said it, Mark crowed, and now he only had to make it come true. God Almighty, but it was good to see the stunned faces around him and hear them gasp. I've fixed you now, Tristan, Andred, Nabon, and the whole pack of you.

"Ah, dear Isolde," he sighed. "How I look forward to making her mine again. And it's the right time of the year." He puffed out his chest with a wink. "The old wives say that a field well plowed in spring will yield a full harvest before the year is out."

Afloat on his visions of revenge, Mark did not pause to think how he would persuade Isolde to be his wife. He only knew that as soon as she returned from Arthur's court, he would confront her with the demand for a full married life. And this time, he would not be refused.

Well, she was on her way now. She'd be back here today and in his bed before the night was out. Suddenly, he found he was looking forward to it. She was certainly worth bedding; she'd grown better, not worse, with every year that passed. Mark gave a slow, anticipatory smirk. It would be no hardship to possess her, he was sure of that.

A child by Isolde?

Andred stood like a wolf in the forest, desperate for a scent. What in the name of the Gods did Mark mean? Did he truly intend to make Isolde bear his child? Could he force her like that? Yes, he could, if he felt himself driven to it, as he did now.

Andred raised his hand and compulsively stroked down his mustache. Only Elva knew that the well-groomed, thick black growth concealed a harelip, where Andred had been elf-shotten in the womb. No one ever saw the fine, silvery scar. But at times like this, it began to throb.

What to do? screamed his inner voice. Then he remembered the weapon he had to his hand.

"But sire—" Andred stepped forward and sadly rolled his eyes. "How, if the Queen won't be here . . . ?"

Now it was Mark's turn to goggle. "Why won't she?"

"Alas, she's gone back to Ireland."

"To Ireland?" Mark leaped as if he had been stung. "But she was due to come back."

Andred bowed apologetically and put on a sorrowful face. "She must have changed her mind."

"Changed her mind?" Mark bellowed.

"Such disrespect to you, sire," Elva put in stridently. "How can she place her wishes above yours?"

Mark's eyes bulged with rage. "She . . . she . . . ?" He could not speak. "Why?"

"She says Ireland expects an invasion of the Picts," Andred said.

Mark fought for speech. "And she thinks the Picts threaten her?"

He gave a harsh bray of contempt. "There's no danger from that pack of painted savages."

Andred gave a rueful smile. "You're right, sir, of course. But the Queen says she must stay in Ireland until she's sure it's safe. She'll be there, she says, for at least the rest of the year. She has no plans to return."

Away in Ireland for the rest of the year?

And no plans to return?

And he'd boasted of a baby within months?

Waves of humiliation crashed down on Mark's head. So he'd thought he could turn the tables on his tormentors and show them who was King? All he'd succeeded in doing was proving himself a fool.

Mark's brain reeled. It wouldn't take long for this to get about, and then every man at Castle Dore would be grinning behind his back. This was all thanks to Isolde, and Tristan, too. Between them they'd make him the laughingstock of the court.

"She ... she ... "

Gasping, Mark felt the purest hate of his life. Dominian saw his chance.

"A man should have authority over his wife," he said hotly, "and even more a king. You must order her back to court, and Sir Tristan, too."

"Oh, Sir Tristan is on his way back, did I not say?" said Andred.

What?

*Why?*

Another wave of burning suspicion flooded Mark's brain. Tristan had devotedly followed Isolde for years. What was he up to, returning alone like this? Was he after the throne, like Andred?

Gods above, were they all out to get him?

Isolde and Tristan, Andred, Dominian, and the barons, too?

With a howl of fury, Mark flung himself out of the room. Andred stroked his harelip and smiled to himself. Well, let the poison work. He caught Elva's eye. We have begun, my queen. Let us not rest till all of them are brought down.

# chapter 6

ods, it was cold! When the wind blew in from the sea as it did now, this surely was the coldest place on earth. Still, it would soon be warm enough for the King. The young man showed his teeth in a wolfish grin. When they lit the boat, his father would have the best blaze of his life.

The funeral ship perched above him on the shoreline, its graceful swan-like shape and curling prow looming darkly through the dusk. Within it lay the body of the King. The young man shook his head. After a lifetime as Prince Darath, how long would it take him to believe that his father was truly dead and that he was now King?

He turned his painted face up to the moon. Its swirls and whorls in purple, blue, and gray made him seem at one with the creatures of the night, and there was an animal grace about him as he moved toward the boat. But his curly black hair was held back by a circle of gold, and the rough plaid he wore belied his air of command. He mounted the gangplank and climbed onto the deck, grunting a greeting to the shadowy men on guard. The old King's knights were keeping their final watch, ringing the funeral vessel with plaid and steel. Even a starving tribe knew what had to be done. A king must make his last voyage in a royal craft, surrounded by all the treasures of his rank.

The ship was fine, they knew; it was the best they had. On the upper level, the King's knights had set a dozen bronze flagons, brimming with mead and enameled in green and gold. Beside them lay a set of drinking horns tipped with silver and great jeweled goblets of gold. Nearby stood jars of precious honey and boxes of salt that the tribe would hunger for in the months to come. But no one begrudged the King his final feast. With his own hands, Darath had laid out the broad platters of ash and yew, the copper knives and iron pots, and the great silver cauldron that would take a whole sheep. Now his father could feast all comers on the Blessed Isle and hold court like a king.

As he was now, arrayed in his royal glory for the final time. The women had made a deep bed of wildflowers and woodland branches, the first fragile buds of spring spread on pine and oak. The old King lay among them on a chariot of bronze, his head on a pillow of dried petals fragrant with the memory of summers gone. His body was garbed for war in a leather breastplate and kilt, with stout oxhide guards on his forearms and shins. His great gold boar collar gleamed around his neck, and a gold-plated belt encircled his waist.

Beside him rested his finest weapons of war, his sword heavy with the crust of purple quartz on its hilt and his massive bronze shield with its red-eyed, snarling boar. His battle-axe and spear lay ready at his right hand, and the deeply hacked shield protected his left arm and breast. Darath reached out and fingered the cuts and sword-slashes, remembering his father in his fighting prime. Your strength saved your life many times, old man, came the sorrowful thought. But your last enemy came upon you unseen.

He brought the double-headed battle-axe nearer to the dead man's hand and gave a last loving tug to the flowing, gray, richly forked beard.

"May your Gods go with you, old man," he muttered. "Whoever they are." He suppressed a laugh. "Perhaps you are meeting them now for the first time."

He stepped out of the boat and saw the incoming sea, a dark line of foam advancing up the shore. The straw, kindling, and pine logs all lay ready inside the hull, and when the tide turned, the funeral would begin.

The knight on guard by the gangplank turned to speak. "All has been done as you commanded. It is well."

Darath glanced back at the bier. The old King's favorite slave had been chosen to die with him, and she had reveled herself into her final sleep with hemlock and mead, enjoying thigh-freedom to the last with the knights of her choice. She lay now beside the old King, as she had done every night since he took her from her own people on some long-ago war raid, still a fine-looking woman for her years. Darath nodded to himself. His father would need her on his voyage through the Beyond. Yes, it was well done.

The voice of the knight came again. "What more is there?"

In the background, another battle-slave began to keen on a single loud, piercing note. Darath turned his head.

"Throttle that one, too," he said casually, "and lay her in the boat. She can sing for my father in the Otherworld."

He moved off down the shore, deep in thought. He did not need to look around him to remember that winter had been cruelly long and hard that year, for the stark mountains of his barren country, its stunted trees and screes of broken rock, were written on his heart. And suffering all this, Darath cursed silently, what a torment it was to live across the sea from the Western Isle, seeing her sweet, green, fertile flanks while they fought against salt winds and crumbling soil to wring a raw, rusty outcrop from the sandy hills . . .

No, it was not to be borne.

Turning his face to the sea, he swore an oath. Never again would he endure a winter like the last, trapped in the wretched homestead, waiting for his father to die. And while he paced the scrubby heath day by day, crops failed and cattle starved and cast their young. Then a wind-borne sickness blew in off the sea, and the milk failed in the women's breasts and desperate men would have eaten their plaids for food.

Never again.

He felt the approach of footsteps and turned around. Before him stood the knight who had guarded the gangplank, the leader of his father's band of knights. Once the King's closest companion, fierce and shrewd, Cunnoch had festered in inaction while the old King failed. Already Darath knew that the first great battle of his reign would be to win back the loyalty his father's weakness had lost. And whatever he did, it could not come too soon.

Cunnoch gestured dourly toward the fast-approaching tide. "It is time."

Darath nodded. Snapping his fingers, he strode swiftly across to the boat. In the distance, he could see the gathered tribe, a restless, murmuring crowd, anxious for a good farewell to the King, but held back by ancient custom: the ceremony was for the King's sword companions alone. Behind them stood the dark bulk of the mead hall, where he knew a great fire was already leaping up to the roof and the benches and tables were standing ready for the night's carouse. Drifting down the wind came the rich smell and crackle of roasting boar, and the twisting of his gut reminded him that he had not eaten for days. He stepped forward. Time to make an end.

The sea was lapping around the boat, sucking at the hull. He waited till the waves began to lift the heavy vessel from its sandy bed and draw it down the shore. Then, raising his arms, he threw his voice far out across the glassy sea to the rising moon.

"God of a thousand battles, take this king!" he cried. "Grant him safe passage through the wilderness of the Beyond. Preserve him from the Gods of blood and bone, and bring him to the Lands of the Blessed, where the harvest never fails. Give him rest there from a life of sword and spear, and let him feast with his brothers forever and a day."

There was a roar of assent from the knights around. One of them placed a torch in Darath's hand, and he hurled it deep into the boat as it slid away. The straw flared, the kindling caught light, and within seconds the whole deck was aflame. Darath stood for a moment, then turned sharply on his heel and strode away. No need to watch it sail into the night. The funeral pyre would burn for hours to come.

AT THE WAKE AFTERWARD, seated in their high wooden hall, the old King's sword companions spoke in low voices while a bard wailed in the background, singing of the King's undying honor, his prowess in battle, and his matchless life. Around them the rest of the knights reveled without restraint, men with wind-burned skins and brilliant, staring eyes, all painted like their new King in purple and blue. Laughing, they bantered to and fro in their own tongue, a high guttural sound like the call of a clan of otters, or foxes coughing in a distant den. Like their new King, they wore only a length of woven and checked plaid, kilted round the waist, with the end thrown over their shoulder or wrapped round their bodies like a poor man's cloak. Yet each tattooed face had the same high spirit and strength, and each would raise a laugh in the face of death.

But for those mourning the sword-friend of their youth, the wind blew coldly through the feasting hall. The flickering firelight streaked the older knights' faces like blood, and their stomachs shrank from the reek of tallow and the smell of roasting flesh. Cunnoch nursed his drinking horn in his hand, then took a deep gulp of the strong, honeyed mead.

"We were cursed with a failing king and an untried prince," he muttered. "Caught between an old man and a boy."

He spat on the floor. His blood brother Findra laughed and nodded toward the head of the rough wooden table, where the new King sat drinking on his father's throne. "Darath would carve you like a capon if he heard that."

Next to Findra sat his sister's son Agnomon, already a fearless fighter, but cursed with the sight. From childhood he had seen what others did not, white-faced and shaking till his visions passed, and his way of looking and speaking was not like other men.

"Our swords sicken for blood," he said now, staring out through the wooden walls. "Our children hunger while our women starve. The Dark One is coming. I can hear Her tread."

Even Cunnoch had learned to listen when Agnomon spoke. The older knight's brooding gaze turned back to Darath again. "And what will our new King do?"

There was no answer, only a bitter sigh as the three faces round the table turned toward him without hope.

> "He was a stag horned with seven points,
> He was a flood in winter,
> A river with seven lakes.
> He was a hawk gliding above the cliff,
> He was the battle glint on the enemy's shield.
> He was a shining wonder among men
> and his passing is the grave of all our hopes . . . "

Gods of Darkness, would no man strangle the bard? Darath sank his teeth into a roasted thigh, tore off a sinewy mouthful of boar's flesh, and vowed to find a new praise-singer before he died. No matter if it cost two fine horses, ten gold rings, twenty white mules, or fifty purple cloaks. The bard at his wake would do better than this maudlin lament, or he'd leave orders to slit the wailer's windpipe and end his song.

He raised his goblet to his lips, but he'd lost his taste for the thick, sweet mead and its heathery tang. Across the hall, three pairs of eyes were upon him, and he could read their hostile questions without speech. Gripping his goblet, he swung down from the throne and crossed over toward Cunnoch and his friends with a few rangy strides.

"A toast to the King!" he cried.

His father or himself? Either way, he knew they could hardly refuse. Laughing inwardly, Darath settled himself next to Findra, facing down Cunnoch's dark and impassive stare. Next to him the gaunt youth Agnomon stared and twitched as if he had seen a ghost. No time to waste, it seemed.

Far out at sea, the funeral ship sailed away in a ball of fire down the silver pathway of the moon. Darath gestured toward the sword at Cunnoch's side.

"You knew many great days with my father," he said. "Days of fire and blood. They will come again."

Was that a sneer of disbelief on Cunnoch's face? Darath pressed on. "Ireland is ours, if we want it. The Western Isle is ripe for our attack."

He was rewarded by Cunnoch's open surprise. "Ireland?"

"Their Queen's a beauty and cursed with a foolish husband, too. By force or courtship, I shall make her mine and bring all Ireland groaning beneath our heel."

Cunnoch gasped. "And how will you do that?" he demanded. "Why should the Queen yield to you?"

Darath flashed his teeth with a raw animal pride. "She's in want of a man," he said simply. "Her land is ruled by Druids and old men, and her knights have not fought a battle for years."

"But she must have a champion. As a queen, she must have her knight."

"Sir Tristan of Lyonesse," Darath confirmed. "But he was Cornwall's champion before she arrived. He's lost to her if the King needs him first."

Findra looked doubtful. "Still, all the Celtic queens know how to fight. Why, the Romans themselves lived in fear of their swords."

Darath laughed openly. "And how long since an iron sandal trod these shores?"

Cunnoch looked at him with an older man's gathering rage. "Laugh all you like, those women have often sent us running to our ships. The last Queen was called Battle Raven, and she'd roam the battlefield in a chariot of knives, swooping down on her foes like the Morrighan herself."

"Whisht!" Agnomon's strange eyes changed color, and he crossed his fingers in dread. "Don't name the Dark Mother," he muttered, "or She'll come for us tonight."

Darath leaned forward urgently. "But her daughter, Isolde, never learned to fight. The old Queen saw that war was changing and held her back. So Queen Isolde has never led men in battle with her champion and her knights fighting at her side."

Cunnoch gave him a hard stare. "How d'you know all this?"

"About Isolde?"

Darath sat without moving and felt an echo from his boyhood long ago.

What was he, fourteen or fifteen, when he first saw her at that tournament? His first outing, his first chance to show his skill, and all he knew then was the rare delight of sailing to Ireland with Cunnoch and the rest. But when they rode into the field before the combat began, there, in the high viewing gallery, had been a young lady bedecked in emerald and gold. He could still remember the look in her sea-green eyes and the fiery tangle of her red-gold hair. That was all. But the memory had been sweet, so sweet, all these years. And too precious to share with these men, who would kill a woman as soon as look at her.

"I saw her at a tournament long ago," he said casually. "You remember, Cunnoch, you were there, too." And you saved my life, hung unspoken in the air. Even now Darath sometimes sweated to recall the rogue knight who had tried to kill him from behind, and how Cunnoch threw his own body forward to take the blow.

Cunnoch glinted at him. "I remember."

"Yes, what a fight!" Findra's eyes lit up, and he turned toward Darath with the first warmth he had shown. "You were only a boy, but by the Gods, you fought like a prince. And I remember the old Queen then and Isolde, too. Ah, those women. What warriors! What Queens! Didn't they say that one of their foremothers, the mighty battle-queen Maeve, showed thigh-friendship to thirty men in one night?"

Agnomon quivered. "Beware the warrior queens of the Western Isle! Battle ravens fly in flocks that darken the sky. Beware their college of war, where Queen Aife taught a thousand queens to fight."

"Men, too," agreed Darath curtly. "The knight they call Lancelot learned all his chivalry from her. But not Isolde. Her mother sent her to Avalon to study love, not war." Smiling to himself, he flexed his body and stroked his lean, hard thigh. "And I shall love her as a queen deserves."

Cunnoch pondered. "She has no champion, you say? She can't depend on her knight?" He cracked his thin lips in a reluctant smile. "She's waiting for you, boy. Go, then, and take the Western Isle."

"I shall." Darath rose to his feet and drained off his mead. "Sharpen your swords, all of you, and summon the men. The boats are ready. We shall sail at dawn!"

# chapter 7

**W**as this Tintagel? Stiff and cold, Isolde struggled up out of a waking dream, perplexed to think of what lay ahead. Day was ending on a world that was sad and gray, a world without Tristan, without laughter, without hope. Rain hung over the headland like the smoke of distant fires, and already he was fading from her mind. His powerful body and strong-featured face would be with her till she died. But his everyday touch, the necessary feel and scent of him, these were slipping through her fingers in the vast emptiness of loss.

And what had brought her here to see Queen Igraine? Fretting, she drew a breath of the raw salt mist off the sea. What comfort could she hope to take away? She had turned to Igraine before and found strength and wise counsel in the old Queen's words. But now she would have to confess she was leaving Mark. How would Igraine treat her when she revealed that she had lost her sense of duty and announced she meant to bring the marriage to a close?

Another cold evening; another sleepless night. Isolde gritted her teeth and leaned forward to encourage her horse: Onward, my dear, there's no turning back now. Behind her the small troop of horses and men at arms plodded gamely into the wind. At her side, the loyal Brangwain threw her a loving glance: Courage, lady! You are not alone. Heartened, she returned the maid's warm smile, and together they crested the great bluff above the bay.

Below them now the land ran down to the cliff edge, and she saw the mighty outlying walls of the castle within. Who could have built this place, Isolde marveled, with its massive outer ramparts of rugged black stone? Who had raised its tall, frowning towers and laid out the series of courtyards, each leading into another, one by one? Surely some greater-than-human hand had set that great rock in the bay, crowned it with a fine castle, and fashioned the narrow bridge that was the only way across? Shivering, she waited as her captain obtained admittance, then followed the young knight leading her to the Queen.

But he did not take her as she expected across the stone bridge to the castle where the Queen lived alone. Instead, he led her through a low arch off the courtyard and down a steep flight of steps. Within a few feet, the stairway narrowed and turned, and the rocky roof became lower overhead. Step by step she found herself descending into the dark.

Now the sound of the surf became stronger, and she began to feel the nearness of the sea. As she made her way down, groping for every step, the sides of the passage were wet and gritty with salt, rough barnacles and slimy seaweed sprouting from the walls. Faraway, she could hear the plaintive cry of the gulls. But here in this dark, clammy tunnel all she knew shrank to onward and downward . . . downward . . . ever down.

Now the sea was coming to meet them; she could hear its sigh. At last her feet met sand at the bottom of the steps. The darkness lifted, and she stood in a vast cavern giving out on the open sea. The waves rolled in through a rocky arch ahead, running up the sand almost to her feet. Spindrift as fine as blossom lay on the swirling waters, and the air was full of silvery, breaking spray. Above her, great clusters of crystals hung from the roof in sparkling purple and white and rose up in glittering columns from the floor. Between them she could see the iron-bound chests and the broken masts and timbers of sunken ships, all the flotsam and jetsam of the ever-hungry sea.

She turned to her guide, bewildered. "Where are we?"

The young knight smiled. "They call it Merlin's cave."

"But I came to see Queen Igraine."

The ghost of a gentle laugh rang round the cave. "And the Queen is here."

Isolde turned. The walls of the cavern dissolved, and she thought she saw a vast shape rising like a cloud from the bed of the sea. Robed in sea-green and blue, veiled in folds of white foam, and crowned with shining stars, the great figure brooded over the waters, holding out her arms to embrace the world. Then the sight faded, and Isolde came to herself again. Before her stood Queen Igraine, clad in all the power and stillness of nature herself, but plainly an aged woman of flesh and blood.

The old Queen held up her hand. Behind her a cascade of crystal and rock formed a massive throne. "Approach, Isolde," she said in rich, level tones. "You are welcome here."

"Your Majesty."

Isolde dropped a deep curtsy, halfway between joy and fear. She felt a soaring relief to see Igraine again and drew comfort at once from her calm, lovely face. But the old Queen's erect bearing and penetrating gaze showed she lost none of her old authority. Isolde hesitated. Could she still meet that brilliant, piercing eye?

The Queen smiled. "They call this Merlin's cave, and his name serves to keep unbelievers out. But in truth I use it as my private retreat." She paused, and Isolde felt her probing, almost pitiless stare. "How can I help you? What brings you here today?"

"Three sorrows, Your Majesty—" Isolde took a breath. "My country, my love, and my life."

"Tell me the first."

"The Picts are threatening to invade my land."

"Then you must get back to Ireland as fast as you can. But do not despair. Ireland was not made to lie under a conqueror's heel. Your foremothers turned every invader back from Erin's shores." Igraine paused. "That may prove to be the least of your troubles, I think. You spoke of your life and your love."

Isolde nodded, nerving herself to speak. "When I go to Ireland, I shall not come back."

"You will say farewell to Cornwall?"

"I must!" Isolde cried. "I have labored for years to do the best I could. But my husband neglects the land for his own concerns. He cares for nothing but his wine, his hunting, and his—"

She felt a dull flush discolor her neck, and broke off.

"His mistress, you would say?" Igraine picked up, unperturbed.

"Yes, that is known to me, too. But your doubts about Mark run deeper, I suspect."

"They do," said Isolde fervently. "Long ago all the mighty kingdom of Uther Pendragon lay neglected till your son, King Arthur, won back his ancestral land. So will it be with Cornwall very soon."

A shadow passed over Igraine's face. "Tell me all you know."

With a careful attention to detail, Isolde complied. "And Mark will not resolve the succession," she finished heavily, "though his barons have been pressing him to do so for years. But Sir Andred is ready now and poised to strike. And if he seizes the throne against the will of all . . ."

She broke off. The old Queen knew well enough what would happen then.

Igraine looked at her in silence. "Thank you for your concern for my poor land," she said at last. "I am glad you have brought this to me. Mark must learn to care for his country, not for himself. I have told him so many times."

Isolde nodded unhappily. She had stood herself beside Mark in Tintagel's Great Hall and heard the old Queen issue a solemn warning: King Mark, you are my chosen vassal and will remain so, as long as my faith and trust in you endure.

And that could not be much longer. "Mark has squandered the trust that has been placed in him," she said with deep feeling.

Igraine looked at her intently. "Yours above all?"

Isolde threw back her head. "I can no longer remain with him as his wife. I have left Mark and Castle Dore, never to return."

The old Queen glimmered at her. "Never is too long a word to say."

Isolde felt a sudden onrush of tears. "When I have no respect for him and no hope of change, I cannot be his Queen."

"Then you must put the marriage aside and go your own way. That is the fate of all couples as ill-matched as you. Not all are destined to be mated, body and soul. Those who are so blessed will know what it is to walk the world between the worlds. The rest must remain bound to the face of the earth."

"Yes." Tears of anguish stood in Isolde's eyes.

*I walked there with Tristan once . . .*

*Oh, Tristan—my lost sweetheart—my only love . . .*

"Isolde?"

She felt the full force of the old Queen's subtle gaze. "This grief is not for Mark. You have another greater sorrow, I think?"

"The greatest in the world—" She was gasping with pain. "I have lost my knight."

"How so?"

"I asked him to come to Ireland. He has chosen to stay in Cornwall and follow Mark."

Igraine paused gravely. "Mark is his only kinsman and his King."

"But he owes his love to me! And now he's betrayed me, and betrayed our love—"

"Ah, Isolde . . ." Igraine took a pace away, sighing like the wind off the sea. "Beware of turning against Tristan in your heart. Do not think that he has broken faith with you."

"But madam, he—"

The old Queen held up her hand. "Could you trust a man who broke a prior oath? Who tried to please you by dishonoring a promise he had made before? The man who would do such a thing would betray you, too. Tristan has chosen the harder road and that deserves your love. He swore to serve Mark and his first duty lies there. But it will not be forever. Afterward he will know where his honor and duty lie."

Isolde felt the first faint spring of hope. "Afterward . . . ?"

"There is always an afterward," Igraine echoed, her large liquid eyes alight. "Take courage, my dear. All things must pass when the Mother turns the wheel. Your knight will ride through this dark night alone. Leave him to his journey and keep faith."

"But will he keep faith with me?"

"He will never be false to you."

*Goddess, Mother . . .*

Isolde felt her heart dancing in her breast. *So he will return. And I shall bear his child!* Then a glance at the Queen's expression cut her off sharply. "What is it?" she breathed.

"Alas, Isolde, the trials you fear today are nothing to what lies ahead. The Christians, our dearest enemies, are out in force. They hate the Mother and all that we hold dear. And now they are prowling our land as the sea howls round the shore."

"They're building their churches everywhere," Isolde agreed harshly, "and advancing their power in every village and town."

"And King Mark has been helping them."

Isolde could not hold back her bitterness. "Because they attack the Mother-right and seek to impose the rule of men."

"They have a doughty champion in Cornwall here," Igraine resumed. "An old enemy of yours."

"Father Dominian?"

"Beware of him, Isolde. He has sworn to bring you down."

Isolde nodded bleakly. "I know."

The old Queen folded her hands and brought them to her lips. "But that is not the worst. Their heaviest onslaught is on Avalon. Under them, the Sacred Island will be no more."

*Avalon . . .*

*Sacred Island . . .*

*Home . . .*

Through a mist of tears, Isolde saw again the great green island rising from the sacred lake, alive with apple blossom and the song of birds. After Dubh Lein, it had been her girlhood home, when her mother sent her to study with the Lady of the Lake. There she had learned the wisdom of the Goddess and the cornerstone of her belief. *Faith should be kindness. Religion should be love.*

"And Avalon will be no more?"

She could feel the fatal tears rising again. *I will not surrender now.* "Tell me, madam," she said thickly. "What must we do?"

"We must each become the Mother in our own lives," Igraine said intently. "Every woman her own Goddess, her own Lady whether of lake, land, or sea. But you, Isolde, are Queen of your own isle. The Mother-right is with you, and your first duty is to the spirit of the land. You will be torn many ways, but you must not lose faith. And in time, who knows? Your future may call you beyond the Western Isle."

Beyond the Western Isle? No, that was too far to look. Enough to know that the future was with her now.

"Oh, my lady ... "

Newborn dreams trembled before Isolde's eyes. Filled with fresh hope, she began to stammer out her gratitude.

The old Queen smiled her wise and ancient smile. "No more words. A ship lies waiting for you at the foot of the rock. Go to Ireland with my blessing and do what must be done. A hard road lies ahead, and the days will be long before you come safely home. But you may not leave the path you are fated to tread."

*So be it.*

Isolde squared her shoulders and raised her eyes. Through the rocky arch gleamed the far horizon, veiled by the breaking waves. Then the mists parted, and she caught a tender, fleeting flash of golden light.

She bowed to Queen Igraine. "To Ireland, then."

*Wait for me, I am coming.*

Her heart took wing, flying with the seagulls toward the faraway emerald shore.

*Ireland.*

*Erin.*

*Home.*

# chapter 8

h e had sworn to remember her every dawn and evening, and so
he did. Whenever the morning star faded or the love star lit the sky,
he gave all his thoughts and all his prayers to Isolde. When he halted
in his journey through the forest and fell to his knees, he always
meant to send love and joy winging her way. But all too often, Tristan
found himself locked in grief.

Isolde, my lady . . .

My lost lady.

Lost and gone, never to return.

Never before had he left Isolde without any idea of when he would
return. The emptiness within him was more than he could bear, and
the gnawing sense of loss grew greater every day. *Without you I am
only half myself. Less than half. You have taken the best part of me
away. That's you, my better self, my all.*

The woodland then seemed all dreary and dark, and the way ahead
full of loneliness and despair. Riding back to Mark, he had chosen the
route through the Forest Hazardous, in a fever to return to Mark as
fast as he could. If he took the broad high road, white and dusty with
the comings and goings of everyday souls, he would only fall into con-
versation about the court and the King and the Queen, and his fragile
resolution to return to Mark would be undone. Then his sacrifice
would be in vain, and all his honor would go for naught.

The forest it had to be, then. But its looming dark outline struck
him with a strange sense of dread. Roughly, he tried to shake his
courage awake. *It's a sunshiny morning in the fullness of spring. What
is there to fear?*

Set back from the path where the forest began stood a low hovel surrounded by an outlying patch of land with a few spring plantings and a byre for a pig or a cow. Built of stones and mud, thatched with branches and dried leaves, it was a poor dwelling with a hole for the window and another sealed by a rough oaken door. There were many such on the fringes of great woodlands, home to any lowly forester content to live off the soil and the bounty of the woods. The owner had carefully marked out his small terrain, and Tristan could see him now, laboring on his plot.

The smallholder straightened up as Tristan approached, leaning on his hoe. His honest face was weathered like the oaks around, and a warm, loamy smell came from him as he moved. "Greetings, lord," he called in the accent of the land.

"Good day to you, sir," Tristan courteously returned.

The old man pointed forward down the track. In the forest ahead, the branches formed a dense roof against the sky and the sun dimmed down to a dull greenish light. "There's a madman in the wood," he said simply. "Beware."

"Alas, poor soul," Tristan cried. He could not imagine what it must be like to lose his mind. "Who is he, does any man know?"

"He's a knight and a fine one, too, but no one knows his name. And no more does he remember who he is. He thinks every man wants to kill him, so he attacks all that come. You'd best avoid him, lord."

"Indeed I shall," Tristan said sorrowfully. "There's nothing but grief and dishonor in such a fight. Can you tell me where he is?"

The old man stepped up to the edge of his domain. "See there," he offered, "where the path divides? He's made himself a rough camp in a clearing down the right-hand track and hung his spear and shield on the nearest tree. That's the place to avoid."

"Thank you, good sir."

Deeply saddened, Tristan set off down the left-hand track. What had happened to overthrow the stranger knight's mind? A cruel sadness, for sure. The loss of his lady, it could only be that. There was nothing worse.

Isolde my lady...

My lady lost and gone.

Bitterly, he noted the savage repetition of his own grief. Would he lose his reason, too?

The horse pressed on step-by-step through the wood. Now the way was narrow and the trees overgrown. A thick canopy of leaves covered the path, and the undergrowth pressed in from both sides. In the warm green half-light under the shadow of the ancient oaks, gilded insects hovered with a drowsy hum. Lulled by the regular movement of the plodding gray, Tristan fell into a dreaming wakefulness. With a fleeting return of good cheer, he thought of his days on the road as a young knight, riding merrily from tournament to tournament. In those days, his loyal gray charger had known the high roads of France, Spain, and Gaul better than he had himself.

And they hadn't a care in the world. Yes, those were the days—

"Hold!" screamed a voice in his ear. The same instant, the blade of a sword flashed before his eyes.

"Have at you!" Tristan screamed back in horror, fumbling frantically for his sword. A gauntleted hand was groping for his reins as a knight in full armor lunged out from the side of the track. The terrified horse whinnied wildly and reared up, almost throwing Tristan off. Reeling, he took in the glint of the newcomer's fine armor, the edge of a vicious blade, and the metal grille of a visor, grinning like a skull. The crest of the stranger's helmet was as high as his horse. Tristan saw the size of his attacker and smelled the stranger's madness in the air. Alas, poor soul, he cried again in his heart. But save yourself, Tristan! followed swiftly, too.

Would he die here? Any second he expected to feel the point of the sword in his unprotected face. Then the knight dropped the reins and leaped back to the side of the track. Dismayed even more, Tristan saw his opponent groping for the remains of a tattered chivalry.

"Dismount, sir," the stranger shouted wildly. "This is no ambush, but a challenge, knight to knight. Arm yourself and prepare, I grant you that."

Gods above . . .

Tristan steadied the trembling gray and held his breath.

"Come on, sir!" the madman cried again. "I know you have come to kill me, but I'll fight you fair. I'm a man of honor, a knight of King Arthur's court."

King Arthur's court? Tristan wanted to weep at the pitiful delusion. Yes, and you must be one of the Round Table, too.

Alas, alas ... How could he escape from this with his honor intact?

The stranger read his face. "You don't believe me!' he trumpeted. His body shook, and he emitted a volley of strange cries. "See here, then!"

Jerking, he dropped his sword and threw up the visor covering his face. "See, see!" he cried.

Tristan took one glance and looked away. All he could see were a pair of rolling eyes, a gaping mouth with a thick, red lolling tongue, and an unkempt mass of overgrown hair and beard. A sour odor reached him, like that of a beaten dog. Clearly, the poor creature could no longer care for himself.

And there was nothing to be done for him here. With a sudden wild resolution, Tristan caught up his reins and clapped spurs to the sides of his horse. When he reached the next town, he could send back a few strong men to bring the knight the help he so desperately needed. But alone, he was powerless. And he had to avoid a battle at all costs.

"Go!" he whispered in the ear of the faithful gray. The willing horse made a great leap for its life, bounding down in the track with frantic, fearful strides. Within moments, they had left the stranger knight behind. But it would be much longer before Tristan could forget the dreadful curses that followed them, or the desolate sobs when the knight realized that he had been abandoned and left behind.

# chapter 9

*a* high tide lapped the foot of Tintagel rock. Flocks of seabirds were swooping overhead, and Isolde fancied she heard the old Queen's farewell below their plaintive cries.

"May the Great One go with you, Isolde! Return when you will, you will find me here."

Standing in the stern of the ship, she raised her hand with tears of gratitude starting in her eyes. "My thanks to you, dear lady, and farewell."

Before them the sea lay smiling, as calm as a lake. For the rest of the day, the sun shone down from a cloudless sky, the west wind filled the sails, and the little ship bowled merrily over the deep. Isolde paced the deck, dismissing Brangwain's entreaties to go below. The maid could rest in the cabin all she liked. But why should she coop herself up when she could watch the dolphins sporting around the hull or follow the play of the light on the changing sea?

"Off you go, off you go. I'll rest when we get to Dubh Lein," she promised Brangwain. But precious little respite awaited her there, she knew. The men of her Council in Ireland were old and frail. Her mother's chief councillor, Sir Gilhan, and the Great Druid known as Cormac had seemed ageless to her when she was young. But their best strength and skill had been spent over the years, and like all men, one day they must die.

She must find new councillors, then. And if the Picts were stirring, they must prepare for war. Yet were they sure that the Picts would invade? They had had no word of their old King dying or the Pictish ships putting to sea. Old men can cheat the Dark Lord many times, she consoled herself. Perhaps the old King has recovered and he's feasting his knights even now. The thought gave her some passing comfort as she gazed out over the sea.

"Good day to you, Majesty."

The captain came toward her with a smile. "We'll make Dubh Lein in good time," he declared, and her spirits rose again. Leaning over the prow, she tasted the salt of the spray and relished the beauty of the wave beneath the keel. Lulled into a wakeful dreaming, she heard the call of her land from across the sea.

*Ireland.*

*Erin.*

*Home.*

Then the wind dropped and the day began to fade. The sun sank in a sullen ball of fire, and twilight found them becalmed on a sunless sea. The rising moon looked down with an anxious light as night drained the sea of the brightness of the day. Isolde did not see the depths beginning to stir, but slowly the waves began lifting in an oily swell. Soon the boat was pitching and yawing with a sickening roll. She clung onto the prow and began to feel the onslaught of the waves. As she watched, they grew fiercer, slamming into the hull with increasing force.

"Ahoy, ahoy!" she heard the lookout cry.

Now the deck was suddenly alive with crew, some scrambling up the rigging to reef the sails, others gathering to take orders at the foot of the mast. She made her way back toward them, hearing the captain's commands already drowned out by the rising wind. Tensely, she followed the fearful gestures and cries. Far off on the horizon, twisting and turning in its own stream of light, a tornado was dancing across the face of the sea.

Within minutes it was upon them, a sudden hell of wind and black water falling with the weight of doom. Wave after mountainous wave reared up to block out the sky, then smashed down on the deck as if to crush them all. Winded and gasping, Isolde was soaked in icy water from head to foot. She clawed at the rail, secured herself with a rope, and clung on for dear life.

Now the ship was spinning in the tempest's unearthly grip, twisting and groaning like a living thing. Every plank, rope, and spar strug-

gled to withstand the strain as the vessel fought to resist the engulf-
ing wind and sea.

"Aaahh!"

Screaming, a sailor plunged from the top of the mast and was lost
in the black waters below. Moments later, a fearful crack rent the air
as the topmast followed with a dying roar. Howling, the wind rose to
toss it into the night, while the waves redoubled their furious
onslaught on the hull.

*Goddess, Mother . . .*

Isolde clung to an iron stanchion and tried to pray. But with the
next wave, the length of rail beside her splintered and was gone. As
the storm reached its height, a fateful memory returned to increase
her fears. Once, long ago, her mother, crazed with grief, had blamed
Tristan for the death of the man she loved and put a fearful curse on
him. Now the dread words returned to Isolde again.

*May the man who killed my love die a fearful death. May all those he loves
and all who love him suffer until the sea kisses the sky, and the trees bow
down their heads at his cursed feet.*

Unknowingly, the Queen had cursed Isolde, too. *May the woman
who loves him never know peace or joy. May she sorrow for him till her heart
turns black, as mine must do now for the loss of my lord.*

"Mother!" cried Isolde in terror, watching the waves grow taller
with every second. A wind from the Otherworld roared over the sea
as if in answer, and she shook with dread.

*Is it time, Mother? Have you come for me?*

She braced herself to allow the next wave to pass, then half fell,
half scrambled back toward the mast. Half-drowned, the captain huddled at its foot, roped together with some of the crew.

"Here, madam!" he cried, lunging forward to grasp her hand.
Roughly, he dashed the salt water from his eyes. "May the Gods forgive me for endangering you like this."

"Courage, sir," she shouted back through chattering teeth. "We
shall laugh about this on land."

The captain's face took on a glassy smile. "Not in this life. Sooner
or later the sea claims her own, and the Lady wants us now."

"It's nothing but a step," the bosun cried with desperate gaiety at the captain's side. "Then we sleep forever in the Mother's arms. Think of it, madam. No more work for us. Eternal rest!"

Isolde forced a jaunty grin. "Not for me, sir!" she called back. "Not yet."

Turning, she fought her way back down the side of the ship. At every step, a wave broke over her head and threatened to break her grip on the slippery rail. But a force she could not explain flooded every muscle and vein. Die now? Never. Grimly, she waded forward into the prow.

Now she felt the worst onslaught of the storm. Walls of water surrounded her, as high as she could see. Above her head, a mass of rearing, tumbling waves darkened the sky. A star blazed through the wet blackness, then it was gone. No thoughts, no words could be heard above the wind.

She stood for a moment in silence, gathering her strength. Her ears, eyes, and mouth were blocked with stinging brine. Then without a thought for her safety, she let go of the prow and threw her arms above her head. Screaming, she hurled her voice into the wind, frantic to make herself heard above the storm.

"Lady," she appealed, "great spirit and soul of the sea, spare our lives! Calm the ocean, let us die another day. A great task awaits me in Ireland, and every living creature on board has his own race to run. Bring this ship safe to land for the glory of your name!"

The wind around her seemed to increase its lament, and wave after wave of water pounded down on her head. But with every word she felt her strength increase, and a warmth surged through her she had not known before. *See, Isolde, I have lent you my power,* flashed into her mind and was gone. The thought came to her, *Am I dreaming? Are the waves abating and the waters growing calm?*

Slowly, the ship steadied, the wild motion of the sea subsiding as the wind died down. Now, on either side of the ship, the water teemed with life. Sea horses came speeding toward them, their white manes tossing on the crest of the waves, and she saw spirit shapes riding the swell all around. Silver figures swam like sea creatures around the hull, scattering white foam and glittering flakes of light. One by one they plaited their brilliant course about the ship, leaping and diving, soaring over bow and stern. Above the moaning of the dying storm, their joyful laughter resounded like tinkling bells. Isolde stood watching them in delight as the meaning of the visitation welled up in her heart. *They are the servants of the Lady of the Sea. Her messengers and maidens, come to waft us home.*

The storm was gone. Gasping, she strode back to the mast, shaking out the water from her hair. Suddenly she was cold to her bones, too cold to shiver, almost too cold to speak. The battered group of sailors awaited her, their faces etched with relief shadowed by a superstitious awe. Isolde confronted them in a silence no one could break. Then she felt a hand tug at her dress. The ship's boy stood at her side, the smallest of the crew.

"You're the Lady, aren't you?" he said trembling, his eyes like moons, "the Lady of the Sea?" He waved a small, wet paw at the dying storm. "You calmed the waters. Is it over, then? Is us safe?"

He burst into floods of tears. Isolde stooped and took him in her arms. At the feel of his small, sturdy body, a hunger for a child of her own surged up from her center and spread all through her frame.

"Hush, little one," she whispered, repeating the words of her mother when she was young. "No tears, no fears. You are safe with me."

*Am I the Lady?* she wondered afterward, when she had seen the child fed and had watched over him while he fell asleep in the hold. *Or did I become the Lady at the hour of need?* Either way, a rare force had possessed her and it was with her still.

Warm again now and well fed in her turn, she sat alone in her cabin musing as the night went on. The Lady had come to her, she was sure of that. Now she must carry that forward into the trials ahead. With the Lady's help, she would face down the dangers she feared. The Picts would most likely decide not to attack, once they knew that Ireland was defended by its Queen. Younger men would come forward to share the burdens of state, and she would know Ireland's matchless peace again.

She smiled sleepily. Brangwain was right, of course. She would rest and renew herself here, and if old Queen Igraine was right as well, she would win back Tristan's allegiance and his love. In her waking drowse, Tristan came toward her holding a brood of dream-children by the hand, all chuckling and laughing as happy children do. Her body ached to hold him in her arms, and another tender longing blossomed in her heart. *Your children, Tristan. Is that too much to hope?*

As the night waned and the daystar shone in the sky, she slept at last and dreamed sweetly of roaming Ireland's green hills and valleys with Tristan by her side. The joy of her dream bore her up through the voyage ahead and lasted until they came safely to Dubh Lein. Then a grave-faced Sir Gilhan met her at the dock with the word she had feared.

"Madam, the Picts have made landing on the northern shore, and their King demands your surrender with fire and sword."

# chapter 10

esu Maria, how he suffered for the Church! Was there anything worse than the misery of leaving Rome and traveling to a place like Castle Dore? And would any other envoy of the Pope risk his lungs, his life, even his immortal soul in this fog-infested, frozen, pagan land? These islands were indeed the end of the world. For the hundredth time, Dom Luis Carlos Felipe Arraganzo da Sevilla y Cadiz brought his scented pomander to his nose and contemplated his surroundings with truly Spanish disdain.

Yet the land of the Britons had to be won for the Church. As long as the Great Goddess was worshipped here, this false Mother was a challenge to the Mother Church.

Rome could not permit it.

"Thou shalt have none other Gods before me," Arraganzo quoted approvingly to himself. "Exactly so."

Of course, some Christians argued that the Church should not attempt to destroy the Great Whore. Christians had been chosen to receive the light of Christ, so they should have the grace to live with other faiths. What weakness, what folly was that? Why, the Jews called themselves God's Chosen, and they killed Jesus Christ! No, pagan and heathen alike were destined for the fire.

And dear God, any fire would be welcome now in this cold land! Shivering, Arraganzo knew with grim certainty that he would never be warm again till he was back in Rome. But he would never pray to God to spare him this trial or take him from this place. He had a task to fulfill, and he would not flinch.

He peered out through the curtains of his traveling litter and saw

a watery sun, with pale wisps of cloud riding in a washed-out sky.
Another dreadful morning in this place, promising another dank and
dreary day. Yet they called this summertime. He supposed he should
give thanks it was not pouring with rain. And how far had they jour-
neyed now? Every one of the tidy fields, little walls, and gray stone
dwellings in this God-forsaken country looked the same. But the oafs
he had hired at the port said they would reach Castle Dore by midday.
He sniffed the moist, clinging air with deep mistrust. The end of the
journey could not come too soon.

And then what? What would he find at the Christian settlement?
The monks' leader, for instance; could he work with him? Arraganzo
knew from twenty years' experience as a prince of the Church that a
fellow Christian was not necessarily a willing and useful brother in
Christ. And the farther from Rome, the more these communities followed their own way. Indeed, the most fervent believers could be the
most willful, especially in outlying places like this. But the brotherhood here, founded by the pious Jerome, had given no trouble before.
And its present leader, the old man's disciple, Dominian, was said in
Rome to be sound . . .

Arraganzo adjusted himself on his cushions and mused on. What
did they know of Dominian? An ambitious man, certainly. He had
long been in touch with Rome, clearly hopeful of preferment in due
course. He had made himself the King of Cornwall's confessor, that
was good, but for years now he'd been defeated by Mark's Queen.

To be sure, King Mark's pagan fancy had proved stronger than
them all. By now, even the Pope on his crimson throne knew that the
King had never brought Isolde to his bed, and the woman herself had
never abandoned the faith of Avalon or her belief in the Mother-right.
But Dominian had failed to get Mark either to consummate the marriage or to set the whore aside. Would he be ready now to try something new?

Arraganzo stroked his chin. We shall see. But either way, the will
of Rome must prevail. This monk, this Father Dominian, would coop-
erate in full, or letters of dismissal would soon be making their way
from Rome.

And at least the place would surely have a fire. However benighted they were, they must offer him warmth and shelter from this cold. After that, all things were possible, and God was good. With His aid, they would prevail. Allowing himself to dream of the triumphs to come, the Cardinal Legate shrank back into his furs and closed his eyes.

LORD, LORD, A THOUSAND BLESSINGS on Your holy name...

Trembling with joy, Dominian communed with his God, giving thanks for the miracle that deserved never-ending praise. Despite the age-old pain in his crumpled spine, the little priest knew once again the joy he had known before. Here and now, reaching out in this spare, cold chapel in mystical delight, yes, here, at any moment he would touch the face of God...

"Master! Master!" came a wild cry from behind.

The divine essence shivered and the moment was gone. In an ecstasy of loss, Dominian struggled to his feet, holding back tears of rage as his pupil Simeon ran up. In the name of Almighty God, what could justify this violent invasion, this tearing of the veil?

"Master, come!" the young monk panted. "There's a stranger on the way—come, you'll see..."

And see they did, at the settlement's main gate. Winding up the hill came a long line of horses and mules, a princely escort for the closed litter at its heart. Slowly, the procession drew up on the green with its ring of low cells where the monks spent their days. The litter came to a halt, the curtains twitched, and there he was.

"Greetings, brothers in Christ!" rang out in the accents of Rome.

With a fearful heart, Dominian saw a figure of supreme elegance in a cardinal's red robes, one whose lean, taut frame and erect bearing made him look taller than he was. The stranger had long, graceful hands and a delicately molded face with large, deep-set brown eyes and a fine aquiline nose. He smelled of pomade and all the rare scents of the south, and he made no attempt to conceal his superior air.

He stared at Dominian. "You are the leader here?"

Without waiting for an answer, he handed Dominian a scroll. It was heavy with the seals of the Curia itself, the private office of the Pope in Rome.

"My commission," purred the newcomer with all the self-satisfaction he had shown before.

Numbly, Dominian opened it, concealing the sudden rush of dismay as best he could. "You are the Cardinal Legate of Castile and Seville . . . ?"

"Luis Carlos Felipe Arraganzo da Sevilla y Cadiz y Pinca y Salamanca and so forth and so forth," replied Arraganzo with a wave of his elegant hand. "At your service and God's."

Dominian hunched his shoulders, exquisitely conscious of his coarse black habit and misshapen spine. On all sides, the brothers were gathering around in a frenzy of excitement, some gawping like half-wits, others nudging, giggling, and scratching themselves. "My lord, I do not know why we are favored with your visit—"

"I am here to urge greater efforts upon you in the name of the Mother Church."

"You have come from Rome?"

"From the ear of the Pope himself," Arraganzo sleekly confirmed. "Believe me, your labors here are of great importance to us. You did well to win King Mark to the Christian faith. But one great and enduring obstacle remains before Christianity can triumph in this land."

Dominian bunched his fists in silent fury. "I know."

"His Holiness requires King Mark's pagan Queen to be defeated," Arraganzo sailed on. "Without delay."

"My lord, this has been our aim for twenty years," Dominian protested. "And we're making some progress now. I've proved to the King that his wife is defying his rule. If he subjects her to his will, as I'm urging him, there could yet be a child born to him and the Queen."

"By what miracle will this happen, since they are known to be so bitterly estranged?" the Cardinal cruelly inquired. "Will God arrange another virgin birth?"

"Sir—" Tears of humiliation leaped to Dominian's eyes.

Arraganzo noted them dispassionately and pressed on. "Indeed, the Holy Father knows your work is sound. But it must succeed."

Dominian could have howled. "How?"

The Legate made a steeple of his hands and brought them to his lips. "You say Mark could tame the pagan Queen and bring her to his bed. But why wait for that?"

"Why wait for Isolde to return from Ireland, you mean?"

"No. Why wait for the King to act, if he ever will? Why not place before Mark a lovely young Christian or two, to inflame his desire to put his wife away?"

Inflame? Desire? Dominian pressed his fingers to the side of his head. "Oh, sir—"

Jesu Maria . . . Arraganzo watched Dominian's confusion with unbridled contempt. The poor sexless creature was more backward than he thought. Thank God they were more worldly-wise in Rome.

With a patient sigh, Arraganzo began again. "You must know all the Christians in these parts. Which of the petty kings has a fine daughter, one fitted by nature to turn King Mark's mind to lust?"

Lust? God forgive us! Dominian's spirit recoiled. "I do not know," he said brusquely.

Arraganzo fixed him with a pitiless eye. "Brother, those who do the work of God must not shrink." A faint smile pursed his lips. "Search your memory. Review every Christian maiden you know in the spirit of earthly desire." He sketched a cross in the air. "I absolve you here and now of any sin."

Dominian's stomach turned. A girl for the King to lust after? A cold sweat filmed his palms and the back of his neck. Jesu have mercy, how in God's name did he know? Trembling, he forced his reluctant mind to obey.

"Theodora," he said at last. "The eldest daughter of the King of Dun Haven, farther up the coast. God has cursed him with wives who die in childbed, leaving him many unwanted daughters and never a son. I saw him a month ago, when his last Queen died."

Arraganzo raised an elegant eyebrow. "And is the girl fit for God's work in this?"

Dominian nodded eagerly. "Oh, very devout. She knew her catechism when she was only—"

The Legate cut him off with a sharp sigh. "God will take care of her immortal soul. But her body . . . ?"

"Formed for childbearing," said Dominian uncomfortably. "You could say plump and well shaped for . . . for whatever a man desired . . ."

Fat breasts and an ample rump, translated the Legate in silence, feeling reassured. There was a pause.

"And—" Dominian burst out, then broke off.

"Yes?" probed the Legate softly.

"Sometimes she has a . . . a certain look in her eye." Dominian was squirming. "Then she drops her gaze again, like the perfect Christian virgin she is."

A perfect Christian virgin.

Yes, indeed.

The Legate smiled as a hot-eyed minx rose and danced before his eyes. He nodded. "And her father the King is nearby, you say? Where does he live?"

# chapter 11

"$\mathcal{G}$reetings, Your Majesty."

"And indeed to you."

"Good day, my lady."

"And to you. And to you."

Her heart in her eyes, Isolde watched her lords filing stiffly into the chamber and taking their seats round the Council board. How had they all so suddenly grown old?

True, Sir Gilhan had served her mother, and Sir Vaindor, sitting at his side, had once, long ago, been the Queen's chosen one. Sir Doneal had been the leader of the late Queen's knights, a position Isolde had confirmed as soon as she came to the throne. They were all her loyal supporters, trusty to the core. But looking down the table at the line of grizzled heads, Isolde knew she would need more than these old courtiers to defeat Darath the Pict.

*Oh yes, my enemy, I already know your name.* She brooded, tight-lipped. *As you must know mine. But that is all you will ever know of me.* She paused to hold down her rage. That ever the Picts had made landing on her shores!

She could still feel in her throat the sickness of disgust when Sir Gilhan had met her on the quay and broken the news. She could hardly take it in.

"The Picts?" she echoed stupidly. "Here? Now?"

"A great force of them, madam, made landing and have held their ground. Those are the first reports."

A night's sleep, torn and fitful, had done little to diminish the shock. With Brangwain's help, she had dressed carefully to meet her councillors.

"I know you, lady," Brangwain said, her olive-skinned face tight and drawn. "You'll want to be at your best, every inch a Queen."

Brangwain, too, had been at her best, as Isolde had hoped. The maid had prepared her mistress with more than her usual care. Now Isolde knew that a pale, queenly visage, enlivened with touches of pink, looked out at the world above one of the finest gowns that the royal wardrobe could afford. Her mother's crown sat with a comforting weight on her head, and she drew a melancholy joy from wearing the emeralds and green silk of Ireland once again.

But even in daylight, she was still racked by last night's dreams. Fearful images had haunted her all night long of wild invaders with blood on their swords, turning hideous blue faces toward her, jeering as they killed.

*Goddess, Mother, spare my beloved land . . .*

Weeping, she mourned the homecoming she might have had, the peaceful return she had hoped would heal Tristan's loss. Never before had it failed her, this dearly loved home of her heart. Once again her mother's voice came drifting down the winds of memory from her earliest days:

*D'you hear me, little one?*

*I hear you, Mawther.*

*Long, long ago, when the world was young, the Shining Ones made our island out of sunshine and rain. Then the Great One Herself came here to live, and called it Erin the Fair, because there was no finer land in all the world.*

*Erin, Mawther?*

*She gave it her own name. Then other lands cried for her, and she had to leave. When she left, the Shining Ones left us, too, to live forever on the astral plane. Now they shine down on us from the world between the worlds, and we mortals struggle below as best we can. But they left us the sunshine and rain, and when these two kiss, the rainbow they bear is the Mother's word to us all.*

*Word of what, Mawther?*

*Religion should be kindness. Faith is love.*

*Erin,* Isolde wept now.

*Erin, Ireland, home . . .*

And then the dark secret of the founding of Dubh Lein, an ancient settlement built for safety over a Dark Pool, where the Little Water flowed into the Greater, and both rolled on down to the sea ...

*Dubh Lein* ...

Isolde's sight shivered. And would the Pictish invaders soon be lording it here in Dubh Lein, their bare, hairy feet under her table, their tattooed bodies stretched out in her bed?

*Not while I live.*

*So then, what is to be done?*

She stared out through the window at one of those delusive days of summer, when the sun shines down from a sky as white as bone. All the world seemed fair on brilliant days like these. But those tempted out to enjoy it would meet a cutting wind and shadows as cold as the grave. And even so was life itself, every day. *Beware, Isolde, beware.*

She returned her gaze to the meeting. "So, my lords, it's clear that your fears of a Pictish invasion were not misplaced. You say our enemies are hard upon us now?"

"Camped on the northern shore, by the crannog of Black Duig," Gilhan confirmed.

"Did they make land without bloodshed?"

"Alas, no." Sir Vaindor tossed his gray head and sleeked back the remains of his handsome curls. "There were none but bog-dwellers to resist them. Peat-cutters, charcoal-makers, they slaughtered them all." He gave a boastful smile. "Now if any of your knights had been there to swing a sword ..."

Ah, Vaindor ... Isolde looked at him and fought down a bitter retort. Twenty years ago, you might have boasted of your strength. But what can you do now? *Goddess, Mother, send me some younger men. Oh, Tristan, Tristan, where are you, my love?*

"And what news since then?" she demanded.

Sir Doneal gave an angry warrior's laugh. "A challenge has come from the Pictish King."

"From Darath," Isolde spat out, perversely savoring the name. *Oh, I shall know you, sir, when we meet.* "What does he want?"

Gilhan met her eye without flinching. "Nothing but full surrender of our land," he said somberly. "You are to attend him, lady, at his settlement, with all your lords and knights, and there you will accept him as our King. Then you will bring him back to Dubh Lein to install him here."

*Install him?*

Isolde bared her teeth in a furious grin. "As my ruler, my master, I suppose, whatever he wants. Well, those who surrender can't hope to dictate the terms." She thrust out her chin. "And has he the force to back up these demands?"

Sir Vaindor played unhappily with his hair. "The sea groaned under the weight of their ships, the locals say. Now row upon row of them darken the northern shore."

"Fierce devils, the Picts, lady, and they love to fight," put in Sir Doneal with a reminiscent gleam. "Three of our men could not stop one of them when his Gods had put him into a fighting fit."

"Sir—" Isolde held up her hands. "There must be no more blood-shed."

Sir Gilhan's rheumy old eyes fastened on her in total trust. "Command us, lady, we are yours," he murmured, smiling. "Tell us what is to be done."

A pain as sharp as a fever ran through Isolde's veins. *Time was, old friend, when you would have instructed me. Must I be the master now?* She put the thought aside.

"My lady—" Sir Doneal leaned forward briskly. "We shall make a good showing, believe me, when we go north. Already your knights are clamoring to attend—"

"Go north?" Isolde interrupted furiously. "We do not go north. We send back soft words and promises and we stay here. This sea rat, this pirate, this king rat, must attend on me!"

There was a nervous silence among the men. Vaindor's mouth fell open. "But Majesty—"

"Why should a painted savage dictate to us?"

Vaindor bridled. "Because he has the men and the power to impose his will."

"And if we resist?" Isolde challenged.

Gilhan shook his head. "I fear that would only make matters worse. If we provoke him, he could carry war into the rest of our land."

"Or lay waste the north shore and kill more men," Vaindor nervously agreed. "I say we should make peace."

Isolde smiled grimly. "Oh, we shall. I tell you, sir, peace is my only aim. But it should be on our terms, not his. We must never submit to him. It can only get worse."

Gilhan's hand went to his sword. Suddenly he looked very old and drawn. "So we fight, lady?" he said as bravely as he could.

Isolde favored him with her sweetest smile. "Not yet, dear sir. No, let us play a game of delay and draw him south. While he waits, we gain time. Time to call in our men and sharpen up our swords, time to renew our defenses and make ready to fight."

"Now the Gods be praised!" Sir Gilhan chuckled. "Truly you are your mother come again. I can see her now at the helm of her war-chariot, riding down the Picts, raining spear after spear on their heads. They did not look so fearsome then, battered and bloody, scrambling for their ships."

Isolde compressed her lips. *Let it not come to this.* Aloud she said, "And we'll drive them off again. Now let us take charge of the castle at every point. And good sirs, I pray you, call up all my knights. Send out the heralds, sound the trysting horn. Let every man who loves Erin rally to us today!"

THE WOODLAND LAY BEFORE THEM, dark and deep. Drained as she was by the Council meeting and all that ensued, Isolde still felt her spirits reviving as they rode under the trees. The rich humming silence, the busy denizens with their unseen lives, the primeval smell of leaf mold, moss, and pine, the sense of a great secret slumbering at its heart, all brought Isolde a quickening in her blood. *This is what draws Tristan back to the forest and always will.* In that instant, she felt close to him again. But even this fragment of comfort was fraught with pain. *Where are you, my love?*

She gritted her teeth.

*On. Get on.*

*There's still work to be done.*

She had toiled all day with Sir Gilhan and her knights, reviewing the defenses round Dubh Lein. Among those who attended were several younger men, who all paid keen attention every time she spoke. One in particular, Sir Niall, had made himself useful with probing, intelligent questions and quiet asides. As they stood in the courtyard discussing the chances of attack, he brought up a weakness that others had overlooked.

"Remember the Dark Pool below the castle, madam," he murmured respectfully. "It breaches the walls where the river flows in from outside. This must surely have been taken care of long ago, but with your permission, I'll check that it's still safe."

"Safe?" snapped Sir Gilhan, clearly nettled, "of course it's safe." The river entrance had been barred against invaders long ago; he had overseen it himself.

In truth, it was all as Sir Gilhan had said and no more had to be done. But Isolde had drawn strength and comfort from the young man's concern. Truly, there were wise and loyal knights in Ireland now. She need have no fear of finding them when the need arose.

And now, she could turn to the real work of the day. Mounting up, she set out for the forest, with Brangwain riding behind. Slowly, she turned her thoughts to what lay ahead. Indeed, he would surely be waiting for her already, standing motionless in the shadow of his favorite tree. A Druid's ears could hear the mole tunneling in the darkness of the earth and the whisper of the spider as she spins. She leaned forward and gave her horse's mane an affectionate tug. He will certainly hear you coming, my flat-footed friend.

*Yes, Cormac will be there.*

High in the sky, the round-bodied, gleaming sun stood trembling at the high point of summer, and all the forest about her seemed alive. Rustling, the silver birches leaned down to gossip as she passed, and the wood pigeons chuckled musically from every bough. As they went deeper in, a hare stopped at the side of the path and bowed her head.

"Good day to you, little Mother," Isolde murmured.

"It's a good omen, lady," she heard Brangwain say.

And that was not the first sign of the Goddess they had had that day. When they came to the forest, its edges were foaming with May blossom, the tree of the Great One in every place where She was known. May trees lined the green tunnels as they plunged in, their branches laden with blossoms in white, pink, and red, every color of love from the pure to the passionate. *And all those shades of love I feel for Tristan.*

Then, as the greenways narrowed, they came to an oak in the center of the path. All around its broad, rugged trunk were strands of honeysuckle and ivy, closely entwined. Many years ago, in the morning of their love, she and Tristan had taken these two plants as the image of their love. "Neither one without the other," he had whispered then. "Both our hearts entwined for all our lives." Seeing them, Isolde could not hold back her tears.

At the heart of the forest stood the Druids' sacred grove, the broad grassy clearing where Cormac would be found. Only a great event like the death of the Queen would draw him away from here into the false and dangerous world of the court. Here Cormac prayed and worshipped in a world of his own, a sweet green universe of love and faith. Here the young Druids studied with him for many years to learn Cormac's wisdom and his secret lore. And here Isolde had come to learn from him, too, seeking knowledge that only he could impart.

Now the woodland fell silent as they drew near. The flighty ash trees and fluttering willows reined in their low chatter, and the white doves roosted soundlessly overhead. The clearing lay at the end of a long grassy ride, and the afternoon sun had made it a pool of gold. One tall shadow in the green gloom under the trees betrayed the presence of the man they had come to seek.

"Here, madam."

Brangwain slipped from her horse and took Isolde's reins. Slowly, Isolde dismounted and walked forward through the blinding sun in the clearing to the purple and blue shade on the other side. What would she say to Cormac now she was here?

She raised her eyes to his dark, steadfast gaze and saw with relief that he had not changed at all. In a world where the Gilhans and Vaindors grew old and gray, the Chief Druid remained eternally himself. His face, always grave and lined, looked no older, and his thick black hair showed not a trace of gray. He still wore his simple dark robes of indigo dye, though other Druids progressed to fine white wool as they reached the highest rank.

Best of all, she saw that the Druid mark pulsed with undiminished fervor between his brows. She heaved a sigh of relief. She had come to the right place. Swiftly, she prepared herself to hear what he said. Cormac always spoke without preamble, that was his way.

The Druid inclined his head, fixing her with his deep-set eyes. "You are troubled, daughter."

"More than troubled, sir. Our land is in danger. You know the Picts are here?"

Cormac closed his eyes. "I heard their oars beating on the water as I slept. Then I saw their sails in a waking dream."

"Was that all?"

"All except fire and blood and screams in the night."

Isolde shuddered. "They only know how to kill. Do we have to kill, too?"

Cormac's eyes lit with an Otherworldly fire. "The Mother teaches us to love, not hate."

"But must we fight them to protect our own?"

A warm smile of encouragement transformed Cormac's face. "You are fighting already. But with words and your own sharp wits, not with swords."

"Then you think it's right to refuse their demands? My lords are afraid that we'll anger the King of the Picts and draw down his fury on the rest of the land."

"Trust your own judgment," Cormac said quietly. "That is the reason the Old Ones made you Queen. They did not choose in vain."

Isolde bowed, deeply humbled. "Thank you, sir," she breathed.

Cormac reached out a hand and laid it on top of her head. As he blessed her forehead, she felt a tender glow. "Ah, my daughter," he sighed. "You are right to love the land. You are its spirit and its sovereignty, and you must not fail. But your heart is divided. Tell me, what is your grief?"

Isolde groaned. "I fear my marriage to King Mark is at an end. But I also fear to make the wrong move now."

"You are wise," Cormac said intently. "It is always easier to break than to repair."

Isolde clasped her hands in misery. "There's nothing for us to repair. We were married by the Christian rites, but we have never been man and wife."

"Then you have never been truly married, in the eyes of their God or ours."

"But do I have the right to leave him? I made a vow. I took him by the hand." Age-old memories stabbed at her as she recalled the long-ago service in the chapel on the rock, the sonorous Latin, the smell of incense, the chanting of the choir. Above all, the tall figure at her side in Cornwall's royal red, not the man of her heart in the blue of Lyonesse. Another hot grief, another mortal pang. *Why did I ever agree to marry Mark? If I had married Tristan, I would not be alone now.*

"Am I honor-bound to stay with Mark?" she cried. "I made a promise!"

The Druid fixed her with his burning gaze. "So did your husband. Has he kept his?"

Isolde stopped to consider. "Never," she said quietly. "He had a mistress on our wedding day. They say the affair is waning, but she still haunts the court. I have never been his, and he has never been mine."

"Then the church of King Mark joined two souls in a lie. Our Goddess teaches the truth of the heart above all."

Isolde nodded. *Religion should be kindness. Faith should be love.*

"Where there is no faith, there can be no true love," Cormac declared in his dark, resonant tones. "Your marriage to Mark was dead before it began. Give it an honest burial after all these years. That is the last office that you owe to him."

"Thank you, sir," said Isolde fervently. She felt suddenly lighter as she turned away. She would go back to Mark and dissolve the marriage in person, face-to-face. Then she could start afresh on open terms. She could live her own life. She could ...

She was suddenly aware that the Druid was waiting patiently, his eyes still locked on hers. "What is it, sir?" she cried.

"Nothing for you to fear." To her relief, she saw warmth in his gaze and the glimmer of a smile. "We spoke of what you owe to your husband King Mark. Never forget what you owe yourself."

"Myself?"

"To yourself and to the land. Long ago, our ruling Queens changed their consorts every year, for the health of the ruler and the health of the tribe. The chosen one was given to the earth, and his seed and his blood brought forth the next spring's crops. Then he was granted life for three years, then five, and then seven. These days, the former chosen ones of the Queen live out the rest of their days in her band of knights. But the Queen still has the right to change her consort at will."

Isolde listened mesmerized. She had heard as much.

"Your foremothers had the Mother-right, Isolde," Cormac's sonorous voice rolled on. "Just as you have now. The right the Mother gives every woman to choose her mate. For a queen, this right is also a duty, a duty to the land. The Queen of the Western Isle chooses for us all."

"Then I may put Mark away and take Tristan as the partner of my life?" Isolde whispered, hardly able to put her hopes into words.

"Certainly you may," Cormac responded. He was smiling openly now, a rare sight. "And remember you are still in the shadow of the great Queens of the past. Two partners in one life is a modest score."

Isolde thought of her own mother, who was never without a Companion of the Couch, and smiled wanly back.

"And when you take a new companion, you may give back to the Mother what the Great One gave to you." Cormac leaned forward urgently. "New life, Isolde. New birth. You give to the land what it gave you when you were born. A new link in the chain of being that binds us all."

*Could it be?*

Isolde held her breath. Could she break free of Mark and live openly with her love? Could they even . . . ?

A great longing blossomed within her that would not be denied. *Oh, to be with Tristan and to bear his child!* Her mind convulsed. *A boy, with his fearless bearing and truthful gaze. A girl with his fair hair and loving smile. And more little ones, too. More children like him to love . . .*

Then his loss, his absence, came back to her again and grief swept her from head to foot. She turned to Cormac with desolation in her soul.

"I thought he'd follow me," she cried. "But where is he, do you know? Is he coming? Will he soon be here?"

Now for the first time, the Druid would not meet her gaze. "Alas, lady," he groaned, "alas . . . "

Stepping back into the shadows, he looked away. The warm green gloom reclaimed him, and he faded into the forest before her eyes. Only the echo of his words lingered behind.

Alas, alas . . .

# chapter 12

O n—get on!"

Whispering, Tristan spurred his horse onward into the wood. Behind him, the mad knight's raving had faded away and the sound of his tortured sobbing was no more. As soon as he got to a town, Tristan resolved, even a village, he would send the poor soul help. But now he urged his mount to its fastest pace. "Onward, my friend. Get on!"

Willingly the gray bounded down the woodland track. The soft loam underfoot lent a spring to the galloping hooves, and the pathway opened before them into the cool green depths. Tristan did not stop till a good distance lay between him and the desperate knight.

Goddess, Mother . . .

A fearful thought overwhelmed him. If he had not seized the chance to get away, he'd have died like a dog in the wood and Isolde would never have known. When he failed to arrive at Mark's court to obey the King's command, she would have thought of him as a faithless man. If he never again contacted her after that, she would be sure he was a recreant knight who had broken his oath to them both, and simply slipped away to find an easier life. A traitor knight . . . The thought that she would despise him was more than he could bear.

Isolde, Isolde, my lady, my lost love . . .

It was a good while before he could find any comfort in his heart. But slowly the woodland took him to itself, as it always did. He heard the welcome of the forest birds, as flights of wood pigeons tumbled and sang overhead. A herd of fallow deer stopped to greet him with large-eyed stares, then bounded away, laughing and leaping for joy. A tiny shrew lifted her snout disdainfully as she passed: *Out of my way, sir, I'm busy. Why, what a ridiculous size you great humans are . . .*

"Bless you, little Mother," he breathed. He drew in the verdant richness of his surroundings, feeling his heart revive. Oak and elm flourished overhead, every tree a riot of green in the full flush of the year. He rode through white drifts of wild cherry and groves of crab apples ripening their red and yellow fruit in the sun. He came to a river and followed it to a ford, a sheet of still water lying like beaten gold. He passed through the ford and went on, pressing deeper into the forest hour by hour. After a while, he began to wonder if he had lost his way. *No*, he mused. *Hold fast to the path, and trust to the Great Ones to bring you to the light.*

And there it was, the light in the forest before it was truly dark. Glimmering through the trees stood a castle of fine white stone, with delicate arches and towers and floating traceries. A ribbon of silver water ran round its base, and its airy walkways and battlements smiled down on their own reflection shining below. It was a palace fit for a princess, for a fairy queen. Tristan urged his horse forward. On these warm summer nights when he loved to lie out in the wood, he had no intention of asking for the favor of a bed. But courtesy dictated that he should call.

He drew up to the gatehouse. "Ho there!" he called.

"Within, sir," came the reply.

Moments later, the great iron-studded double doors rolled back and two or three ancient retainers came into view. Puffing and straining, they threw wide the gates and bowed him in. In the courtyard stood another elderly man, clad in handsome but antiquated robes of rust-red velvet and carrying a staff. The breeze fluttered his white hair as he stood, and his kindly eyes smiled from a deeply wrinkled face.

"I am the Seneschal," he called, bowing deeply, "and you are welcome here, sir. May we know your name?"

Tristan vaulted from the saddle and returned the bow. "Sir, I am known as Tristan of Lyonesse."

Already the old servants were fussing round the horse and leading away the gray. The broad courtyard they stood in boasted many handsome stables on either side. But hanging their hairy heads out of their stalls were no more than three or four horses, when thirty or forty would have been expected in an establishment of this size. He turned to the Seneschal. "Whose castle is this, pray?"

"We serve the Lady Unnowne."

"You have no lord?"

The old man's face saddened. "Not since our young lady's father passed away. He built this castle as a present for his bride, a great beauty he brought all the way from France. But she never throve here away from her native land and she died when our lady was still only a child. Then last year he died, too, and our young lady fell into a sickness herself." He gave a rueful smile. "Some say that this is an ill-omened place."

Tristan felt an odd shiver, despite the heat of the sun. "Surely not," he said courteously. "But tell me, sir, what court does your lady keep here? I have only stopped in passing to pay my respects. Will she receive me, or should I be on my way?"

"She will want to see you," the Seneschal said confidently. "But do not expect a lengthy interview. Our Lady Unnowne has—" He hesitated, and seemed to be choosing his words with care. "She has not been well for some time. But you'll see for yourself."

As they spoke, the Seneschal had been leading the way out of the courtyard and up a broad flight of steps. More graceful stairs and wide corridors followed till they stood before a handsome carved oak door. As they approached, another gray-haired attendant moved forward to open it.

"My lady's chamber." The Seneschal ushered Tristan over the threshold, then stepped back. "Prepare yourself, sir, for the sight of her."

Tristan started. "What?"

The door closed behind him with a muted click of the latch. Overcoming his unease, he looked around. He was standing in a long, high-ceilinged chamber with fine furnishings and hangings on every wall. But all the windows were swathed in linen to dim the light, and a stale, fusty, choking air hung in the room. In the gloom at the end of the chamber stood a low dais, with long green curtains and a canopy of green silk edged with gold. On the dais was a deep bath of copper, with a high back and white sheets draped across it like a bed. And in the bath lay a lady, staring at the door.

Behind her were two women attendants, gowned in white, both hovering ready to minister to their charge. In the shadow by the wall stood an older man, a doctor by his bearing and dark garb. A table at his side held many liquids in colored bottles and pots, and weird-smelling pastes and potions in countless boxes and jars. The scent of lavender and chamomile rose from the bath.

"Approach, knight!" the lady called.

Her voice was light, husky, appealing, and oddly young. Tristan made his way forward, baffled. What illness was this? All he could see of the lady were her shoulders, face, and neck, and a pair of thin white arms lying forlornly along the sides of the bath. A white cloth like a nun's headdress veiled her head, and a few strands of baby-fine hair snaked out from beneath. Her face was a tight, tiny triangle, as white as her veil, with a frightened, pinched mouth. Her small hands were clenched into fists, the fingers curled over the thumbs like a child's. How old was she? He looked into eyes of flashing bronze and gold. Eighteen? Thirty-two? He had no idea.

"Forgive her appearance, sir."

It was the doctor, a quiet, older man with a face of deep concern. "My lady suffers from a tormenting skin complaint, and lying in cool water is her only relief. So she spends much of each day in the bath, shunning the sun."

Tristan thought of the sun on his back on this morning's ride and shuddered with pity for her. Now he could see that the whiteness of her arms was discolored with angry blotches of pink and red. "What a grievous affliction," he muttered beneath his breath.

But the lady had heard what he said. "Grievous, yes, it is," she said agitatedly, "but that's not all. I would not be suffering like this—trapped like this—but for an evil knight who has me in thrall."

"How, lady?" Tristan gasped.

"He wooed me—said he wanted to marry me—but all he wanted was my castle and my land," she ran on in the same breathless, broken delivery. "He deceived me cruelly—offered himself to me as a good man, then made my life a misery when I refused. All he wanted was to take my land—then force me to enter a convent against my will."

Tristan nodded sadly. There were many rogue knights and fortune hunters who preyed on heiresses left alone and undefended as this lady was.

"And now he keeps me here as a prisoner—in a trap—waging war on any knight who ventures near. He means to break me down—he tries to kill any man who might rescue me." She held out her wasted arms in a pitiful appeal. "He's a fearful fighter. No other knight has ever had him down. You must kill him for me! That's the only way I'll be safe."

Tristan gasped. "Lady, in chivalry we aim not to kill. Can't you send your Seneschal to lay your plight before the Queen? She would be ready to right such a grievous wrong."

"No one would believe me!" The young woman reared up in the bath, and her attendants leaped forward to preserve her modesty. Furiously, she dropped back. "He's a prince of deception," she shrilled. "And I have no one to fight him. We daren't leave the castle while he rules the wood."

Tristan thought of the old men around her and frowned in despair. That at least must be true.

The young woman's eyes rolled pitifully in her head, darting from side to side like a trapped fish. "He's here—he's listening—he knows what we say," she exclaimed.

"Lady, we're alone in this chamber, and your own men are guarding the door," Tristan cried. "How could that be?"

"Evil souls can take any shape they choose."

The golden-bronze eyes had turned to hard nuggets of coal. She raised one thin arm like a wand. "Will you defend me? Will you do battle to save me from my enemy?"

Gods above . . .

Tristan cast desperately about. "Have you truly no knight, lady? No man who will raise a sword in your defense?"

"I had a knight." Her small face puckered and collapsed. "The best knight in all the world. He was my love, faithful and true to me—my only friend—he loved me all my life—"

She was gasping and crying together, fighting for breath. Tristan felt like a monster. "Where is he now?"

Another burst of frantic, gulping tears. "My enemy killed him through guile and treachery."

"Lady—" Never in his life had Tristan been at such a loss.

"Sir, if you please . . . "

There was a soft footfall behind. It was the doctor again, shaking his head. "My young lady has spoken enough for one day."

"Yes, of course." Tristan turned to him with overwhelming relief. "Who has the care of her?"

The old doctor bowed. "I do."

"She has no relatives?"

"None that we know of. Her father lived in seclusion after her mother died. When he knew he was dying himself, he left her to our care."

"And the castle at large?"

"We have the Seneschal and a few menservants and maids. They all served my lady's father when she was a child."

Aged retainers then. Tristan nodded. No young knights to defend this pitiful creature, only a middle-aged doctor and a household of elderly men. He frowned, perplexed. "Have you found nothing to help her?"

"Oh, sir—" The doctor passed a hand over his brow. "We have tried all we know. White water lily, that's a known soothing agent for the skin, and lotion of cinquefoil, for a cleansing wash."

"Fern poultices, too," put in one of the women on the dais, "and drops of ragged robin to calm her down—"

"All this and more," the doctor interrupted, dismissing the woman with a brisk jerk of his head. He paused, and, like the Seneschal before him, seemed to be picking his words with care. "My lady is, shall we say, at the mercy of her fear. Of this evil knight who holds sway over her, who rampages at large in the wood and will let no one pass."

Tristan gritted his teeth. "It is true, then?"

The doctor hesitated. "It is true that she hates and fears him with all her heart."

"And on top of all this," Tristan mourned, "to suffer a dreadful, disfiguring ailment, and the loss of her mother, her father, and her knight..."

Alas, poor young thing. But still—

Tristan paused. Why was he wrestling with himself to know what to do? The lady was a woman alone, undefended and plainly sick. Could anyone have a clearer call on his strength, his truth, his knighthood oath?

You swore to assist all those weaker than yourself, he groaned inwardly, the child, the widow, the orphan, the oppressed. This lady is oppressed and an orphan, too. You undertook a life of chivalry to help such as she.

And without Isolde, that is all you have. You chose your honor above a life with her. What else can you live by now?

Tristan closed his eyes and looked into the void. Warm as it was in the chamber, he saw a future suddenly growing dark and cold. This was not his quarrel, and the Gods knew he had no stomach for this fight. But the lady's demand could not in honor be refused. He had to take on this battle with her enemy.

# chapter 13

darkness and devils, how he loved this land! Already he adored its soft contours and gentle mounds, like a woman lying down for him, ready to welcome his love. And yes, he would love the woman as well, when she came. As she must, this Queen of the Irish, this Isolde, whose fate might have made her a ruler but who'd been born a woman, too. She was coming, he knew it, like a falcon to his hand. Nothing could stop him now.

Grinning, Darath strode out of his makeshift tent to roam the smoke-filled darkness of the beach. All around him the campfires of his men bloomed through the rosy twilight, and their shadowy figures clustered hungrily around each leaping blaze. The game in the woodland was plentiful, and they were filling their bellies as they had not done for years. Darath drank in great lungfuls of the soft Irish mist and his heart leaped up. Great Gods above, here even the air was warm! He punched his fist into his palm to release his joy. The doubting Cunnoch would sing a different song now.

He came to the edge of the water where the boats lay at rest. Not drawn up too high on the shore, he had seen to that: they needed to be ready to escape if the Irish attacked. But that was looking less likely as every day passed.

In truth, how could it have gone better from the start? he exulted. A predawn landing and a lightning raid. Blue Pictish faces blazing through the dark, subduing the screaming natives with fire and sword.

And then the essential of any successful conquest: a show of blood. "Kill them!" he roared. "No mercy!"

Now the screaming was coming from his own men, too, as they

slaughtered and slashed and thrust and hacked. The bravest of the bog-dwellers had gone down to the darkness at once. Those still alive had abandoned all resistance then.

He and his men had triumphed like this from the moment they had made land. They had set up camp without danger and staked out their land. And now they must make ready to receive the Queen.

Queen Isolde, he gloated, his Queen, his by victory, by the rules of war. She'd have had his messenger, she would be on her way. How soon would she be here?

He strode about in boyish excitement, silently accusing his dead father's shade. Old man, we should have invaded this country long ago. While you were sick and dreaming and lying with your battle-slaves, we could have trampled these bog-dwellers underfoot and made their women into broodmares for our sons. We'd have had snug villages by now and fertile farms, vineyards even, as they have farther south . . .

He slammed his fists together. Well, we shall have them all now. He stroked the side of his boat and patted its great curving prow like a household pet. The hideous wooden head with its bulging eyes and sharp teeth looked back at him with a terrible grin. You'll do it, master, the carved monster leered, there's no doubt of that. As soon as Isolde comes, you'll be King.

"King Darath?" came a cry from the dark.

He hurried back up the beach, increasing his stride. A handful of knights stood at the door of his tent, with Cunnoch at their head. A larger group lurked in attendance in the darkness behind.

Darath gestured toward the interior, where a torch lit up a rough table bearing goblets and a flagon of mead. More light came from a standing brazier in the corner, where a small wood fire scented the air with pine. Once inside, he provided the older knight with a stool and scrutinized Cunnoch with care. "Be seated," he said with some ceremony.

Cunnoch stared at him impassively. "Thank you."

"You will drink mead with me?"

Darath poured a generous beaker, intent on rewarding Cunnoch for what he had done. On the day of the raid, the older knight had leaped with the first from the boat and fought madly, joyously, unflag-gingly, like a boar in rut. He had shown all the best of his animal nature—and his loyalty, too. When the killing was done and the pris-oners stowed away, they had feasted together like brothers, and Darath was content.

But it would take more than that to confirm him in Cunnoch's eyes, Darath knew. His father's old friend would judge him not on that first success, but on what followed it. So what was Cunnoch bringing him tonight?

He was aware of Cunnoch's unreadable gaze as the older man eyed him over the rim of his cup. "You have news for me?" he asked.

Cunnoch took his time draining down his mead. "Findra is back from Dubh Lein. From the Queen."

Darath felt a tightening in his chest. "He must have ridden like the devil. Well, bring him in."

Findra's eyes were blue with fatigue as he shouldered into the tent. But a smile of triumph warmed his weary face. "She will come," he declared. "She will attend you here."

Now Gods and Great Ones, thanks . . .

An answering flush raced hotly through Darath's blood. "She will yield. I shall be her King."

"Does she accept our demands?" came Cunnoch's voice from behind.

Findra grinned, his teeth white in his travel-smirched face. "Her lords say she'll make terms with the King when she comes."

"So," Cunnoch grunted.

"That's good!" More than good, Darath crowed inwardly. He pressed a beaker of mead into Findra's hand. "Drink," he said softly. "Now, is the Queen still the beauty they say?"

Findra gave a lascivious chuckle and threw the drink down his throat. "Oh, sir . . ." He groped for the words to flesh out what he had seen. "You'll enjoy her," he said at last. "She's worthy of your sword."

Cunnoch laughed. "Well, many a great queen finds a true partner in a lusty, bloodstained lad, a war-wise fighter and a man of might. Whatever her spirit, you'll master her in bed. And until then . . ." He turned to the opening of the tent and hailed the men outside. "Now! In here."

From the darkness came a volley of curses and the sound of scuffling feet. Half a dozen knights entered, struggling with a muffled captive who was resisting them all the way. Panting, the leader of the knights thrust the prisoner forward and tore off the covering. Fighting, cursing, and filling the tent with fiery rage, a woman like a creature at bay stood before them all.

And not only a woman. From the jeweled band encircling her forehead, the gold chains round her neck, and the touches of ragged finery in her dress, Darath knew she was some kind of leader, even a queen. But where had she come from? He had heard of the fabled Irish coloring and seen for himself Queen Isolde's red-gold hair, blue-green eyes, and milky skin. This woman had a tumbled mane as black as night, coal-black eyes, and a tawny skin. An older race had sired her in an older age, and the single word she spat out was in an older language still.

But they all knew her curse meant the kiss of death. Darath's eye's bulged, and he bit back a superstitious oath.

Cunnoch looked her up and down, unperturbed. She returned his stare with scorn, settling her womanly body on her heels and drawing her dark wraps around her as if ready to fight. Cunnoch laughed. "Yours, boy, and well worth bedding, too. She's the choicest of the local women, the men say."

"Spoils of war," chuckled Findra, his eyes alight. "And she's no mean prize. The people here take their lead from her. She can foretell the future and read men's minds."

Darath looked at the woman and fastened his eyes on her. "Is this true?"

She held a long pause before she began to speak. When she did, she used her darkly accented voice like a dagger, stabbing him with every word. "You want to know the future?" She spat on the floor with relish. "The Queen will not come."

Darath gasped. "What?" Fury gripped him. He would kill her. Now.

Her eyes wounded him again. "Kill me," she said contemptuously. "But she will not come."

Darath stared. She could hear his thoughts. What else could she do? "You can cast the future?" he muttered.

She raised her lip in a sneer as her only reply.

He drew the dagger from his belt, gripped her wrist, and dug the point into the flesh of her breast. "Cast, then. Unless you want to die."

A bloodstain blossomed on the darkness of her gown and the blood ran down. Ignoring it, she shrugged off Darath's grip and crossed over to the brazier, drawing a battered leather pouch from her waist. As she opened it, Darath shivered, though he could not have said why.

The woman closed her eyes and rocked back on her heels, crooning to herself in a rough guttural tongue. Soon she was lost to them and far away, but the strange chant went on. Darath felt a sudden wild loneliness grip his heart. Cunnoch and Findra were as still as stones, and he felt he was alone in all the world.

The murmuring grew louder as the song gathered pace. Moving like a sleepwalker, the woman plunged her hand into the pouch and drew out a fistful of herbs and feathers, shining pebbles, skin, and bones. As she threw it all up into the air above the brazier, Darath caught a flash of amber and pearl falling into the flames. The feathers settled last and flared up with a sudden, brilliant blaze. He did not want to think about the tiny bones.

He waited, willing his heart and mind into a dreaming calm. This was great magic, he knew, precious and rare. Only one old crone in his own land had had the skill to cast the runes, and she used to divine by pouring oil on water in a cauldron of black oak. She could call up figures in the rainbow-colored fluid and make them move in a magic far older than the Druid kind. But she saw too much, and his father had had her killed. After that, there was no one to do this work.

A rich smell from the brazier filled the air. Now it came to Darath that he would never be hungry again. Warmth ran through him, and he felt himself lying in his mother's arms. Then he saw the first girl he had loved, pink and laughing as she took him into her. Many girls and women had followed, and he knew again the same rough, rising lust he'd felt for every one. Next a tall, lissome figure swam into his ken. A cloud of red-gold hair fell round her like a cloak, and her sea-blue eyes saw into the future and beyond. Gold encircled her head, her neck, and her waist, and a band of men surrounded her with heads bowed. Darath's heart leaped and danced and sang in his breast. It was the Queen of Ireland—Isolde the Queen.

He moaned with delight. Isolde was his, she was coming, he would hold her in his arms. But then he saw that the men who had bowed before her were now all speeding away from her on all sides. Some hastened to the gatehouse, others to the battlements, and a third group into the armory, reaching for silver mail and weapons of war. Above it all rang out the two voices of war, the thin cry of the tocsin and the call of the trysting horn.

Darath opened his mouth in vain rage and could not speak. She will not come. She is making ready for war. An emptiness gripped him, cold and vast and stark. *She will not come.* Slowly the visions faded. But long after they were gone, the sound of the trysting horn echoed inside his head.

The woman's voice murmured below it, hoarse and drained. "The Queen is deceiving you. She is delaying to defend her stronghold and calling up her men. She will not come."

Darath turned away, exhausted. He knew it was true.

"Don't believe her," said Cunnoch in deep anger. "Take her to bed, use her the worst way you can. You'll get the truth out of her then."

"I won't touch her." Darath shook his head. "She's a witch, she's nothing. I have come for a queen."

Cunnoch heaved himself up and grabbed the woman by the hair. "I'll take her, then." He dragged her to the door.

Darath shuddered in superstitious fear. "And suffer her undying curse on all our heads? You must be mad." He blocked Cunnoch's path and met his hot-eyed fury head on. "Let her go. Get all the men to the boats. We're sailing to Dubh Lein."

ll done, sir." The Seneschal smiled wryly and flexed his gnarled old hands. "It's many a year since I armed a knight for battle, but I promise you, it's been done with care."

Tristan bowed. "I have no doubt of that."

Bemused, he surveyed himself in the long glass against the wall, clad in the finest armor the castle could provide. A borrowed helmet of bronze gleamed on his head, adorned with the head of an eagle and glinting with a fierce pair of ruby eyes. He had set aside his own light traveling shield for a massive antique sheet of molded bronze, emblazoned with the sign of the eagle again. A breastplate of bronze protected his upper body, and he wore thigh guards and armlets of the same design.

Yet even the familiar kiss of cold metal on his skin and the well-known bite of the straps did not seem real. He had promised to take up arms against a man he did not know, a stranger knight who had never done him wrong. But the lady swore he had wronged her and now he had to do battle on her behalf, driven by his honor and his knighthood oath. And if the lady had told the truth about his opponent, he had to prepare himself for a terrible fight.

So be it. Still struggling with his feeling of disbelief, he took his horse and rode into the wood. "Kill him!" the lady had demanded, and he was not prepared to go as far as that. But he owed her some action against her enemy.

"How will I find him?" he had asked the Seneschal.

"Take the road eastward from the castle till you come to a hollow oak," was the reply. "He has set up his pavilion in the clearing there.

You'll see his shield and spear hanging from the tree. That's the signal he's ready to give battle to all who come."

A wan morning light lit the forest path. The woodland shone invitingly ahead, welcoming him to its green, fragrant depths. A blackbird on a branch cocked its head toward him, and he read a peaceful greeting in its bright-gold eye. Then he caught the sharp, sideways glance of a killer and saw a red-gold fox slipping lithely through the grass. Even here, he sighed, death stalked in silence, and the predator was always out for its prey.

The path turned and he glimpsed the hollow oak, a gaunt ancient of the forest, huge and strange. But there was no sign of shield or spear. As he paused and cast around, somewhat at a loss, he caught a glint of armor in the distance and the clash of arms. Had the stranger knight already found an opponent today?

He pressed on down the track. Now the trees were thinning toward a clearing ahead. In the center of a wide grassy circle, three knights were struggling in a confused melee. Two of them were violently attacking a third, a much bigger man, who must surely be the lady's enemy by his strength and height. He was broad-shouldered, too, and a fierce fighter, but hard-pressed to hold two opponents off. Already the grass underfoot was trampled and bruised, and the two knights' horses had wandered a good way off to graze. Whatever the quarrel and whoever the two knights were, they had clearly been fighting the third for quite some time.

Tristan saw the attackers' swords fall and fall again, one on the big knight's helmet, one on his back.

"Hold there!" he shouted, spurring forward. "Parley, in the name of chivalry."

He bore down upon the trio, waving his sword. The two newcomers fell back unwillingly, while the third knight bowed his helmeted head and leaned heavily on his sword, gasping for breath.

Vaulting from the saddle, Tristan turned his horse loose to graze and confronted the two knights. "Explain yourselves, sirs," he said sternly. "Two knights may not battle one, as you well know. How has this breach of chivalry come about?"

The two knights exchanged a glance, and one who seemed to be the leader nodded his helmeted head. "Parley?" came his muffled voice through the metal grille.

"Parley," Tristan returned forcefully. "No more swords. You shame us all if you strike again."

The leader lowered his weapon and raised his visor, breathing heavily. At his signal, the second did the same. Tristan saw two flushed faces whose very similar dark eyebrows, strong cheekbones, and jutting jawlines proclaimed that they were brothers, even twins.

"We are knights of King Arthur," the first began, fighting to regain his breath. "We have left his court to go out on the Quest."

"Balin and Balan at your service, sir, sons of Sir Rigord of the Ravine," panted the second. A fleeting light of pride passed over his face. "We are following in the steps of those greater than ourselves. Sir Galahad and Sir Gawain have passed this way."

Balin scowled. "We were riding through the forest when we came upon this knight. We offered him single combat, but he set on us both at once."

"Without warning, not a single word," Balan added furiously. He pointed to a bleeding wound in his neck. "And he drew blood at the first attack."

Tristan listened and sighed. So the lady was right. The stranger knight was a man without honor, it seemed. He eyed the bent figure across the clearing, still breathing heavily and leaning on his sword, then turned back to the brothers and reached for a gentler tone.

"That was unchivalrous, indeed. Nevertheless, I must ask you, sirs, abandon this unfair fight."

Balin shook his head decisively. "He has injured my brother, and that injures me."

"Take it as a victory." Tristan pointed to the stranger's bowed shoulders and defeated air. "You've beaten him, any man can see that."

Balan thrust out his chin. "Oh no, sir. Blood will have blood. He broke the laws of chivalry, attacking like that. We don't owe him a moment's courtesy."

Balin laughed unpleasantly, showing his teeth. "And it's no dishonor for two to set on one when the one is big and strong enough for two. Let me advise you, sir, to be on your way. You've no call to meddle with us like this, and I swear to you, this knight will not escape."

Tristan stepped forward. "Whatever he offered you, sirs," he said with emphasis, "you may not break the oath that you have sworn. You're knights of King Arthur, you say, following Sir Galahad and Sir Gawain. What would they say to this?"

But he looked into a face of angry disdain.

"My brother is myself," said Balin slowly. "And I am he. We were born twins, and we live and die as one. Whoever is rash enough to attack either one of us can expect no courtesy or kindness at our hands."

"No parley, then!" came a bloodcurdling cry from behind. The stranger knight was coming back into the fray. With renewed vigor and answering screams of rage, the two knights leaped forward and set about him again. As Tristan watched, they had him to his knees.

"Hold there," he shouted, but his words were drowned by the clashing swords, screams, and jeers. Gods above, was he forced to intervene? Groaning furiously, Tristan slammed down his visor and reached for his sword. He would have to defend the man he had come to fight.

Already he knew it would be one of the worst engagements of his life. Many a time he had fought against two or more, and in the thick of a tournament, too, with spears and arrows falling all around. But never before had he fought two brothers, twins who seemed to share one mind, one purpose, one intent. Each knew the other's movements like his own, and together they became one terrible foe.

And Tristan's partner gave him no support. The big knight fought only for himself. Indeed, he seemed oblivious that Tristan was there. As the great figure cut and thrust, grunted, screamed, and lashed out, there was no hope of fighting together against the common enemy. The stranger's great strength and reach and his furious sweeping blows kept his opponents at bay, but did nothing to help the man fighting at his side.

So Tristan bore the brunt of the brothers' rage. Their first blows fell on him before he was aware. But he knew at once the warm sticky sensation of blood running down his side. The next second two swords were descending on his head as both brothers made him the target of their rage. Only a lightning parry and a sudden flurry of sharp jabbing blows thrust the brothers back and gained Tristan a brief respite. But moments later, they were on the attack again.

"The tide must turn," he muttered to himself behind his visor, "and the day must end." But of all his battles in recent tournaments, few or none had tried his strength like this. The stranger knight at his side was clearly suffering, too, and his armor was stained with blood. The brothers were hard and determined fighters, and their grudge against the stranger made them doubly dangerous.

At length Balan unexpectedly missed a stroke, wavered, and fell back. Balin threw his brother a swift glance of concern and lost his rhythm, too. Howling, Tristan hurled himself between them, swinging with all his strength from left to right. One sweep of his sword sent Balin sprawling to his knees, while the blow on the return stroke laid Balan flat on the ground.

Scrambling forward, Tristan set his foot on the fallen knight's chest and stuck the point of his sword into Balan's throat. Already Balin was scrambling to his feet, sword upraised, returning to the attack.

"Yield, sir," Tristan cried hoarsely, "or your brother dies."

Behind him he heard the stranger knight laughing in triumph.

"You heard the word," came a deep, exultant cry. "Yield!"

With a groan of rage, Balin threw down his sword. As he heard the weapon thudding to the ground, Balin spread his arms wide in the age-old gesture of surrender.

"I yield," he croaked.

"Take your horses, sirs, and be on your way," Tristan forced out, struggling for breath. He gestured to the red-brown crusts on the stranger knight's armor and the fresh trail of bright red seeping down his own side. "You have fought well, and your blood has been repaid with blood. You have restored the honor of your house. May all your Gods go with you on the Quest."

"Thank you, sir."

Balin gave him a reluctant bow, then helped his brother to his feet. Tensely, Tristan watched the two knights limp off, Balin supporting the stumbling Balan with a brotherly arm around his waist. At the far side of the clearing, Balin called up their horses and then helped Balan to mount. Then, taking up Balan's reins as well as his own, he led his brother slowly out of the wood.

Gods above, they've gone!

Gasping, Tristan fell to the ground and dropped his head between his knees. The reek of sweat and blood rose all around him as he gave himself up to relief. Goddess, Mother, thanks! The battle had been won without death or serious injury. Better still, he had saved the big knight's life, and by the laws of chivalry the stranger must now become his friend. He still had to challenge him about the lady in the castle, but whatever happened, they would fight no more today. Both of them were wounded and both had lost blood. Both were exhausted, and it was time for peace.

He lifted his visor and turned. The stranger knight was still standing in the clearing, sword in hand. Thankfully, Tristan heaved himself to his feet, sheathed his sword, and stepped forward to meet him, holding out his hand.

"So, sir, we meet at last," he said with a courteous bow. "I'm glad I was able to—"

A silver flicker caught the corner of his eye. He raised his head in time to avoid a rising blade. In mortal terror he leaped out of the way. But the blade flashed again. The stranger knight was aiming for his heart.

"Have at you!" came a terrible scream. The stranger fell back, then swung his sword two-handed like an axe. To his horror, Tristan saw the great body hurtling toward him to attack.

"Sir! Sir!" he shouted in wild protest, to no avail. Nothing could stop the stranger knight's forward charge.

In an instant, the knight was upon him. Madly, Tristan ducked under his sword.

"Hold your hand, sir," he howled. "I'm not your enemy. I'm Tristan of Lyonesse, a knight of—"

"Then defend yourself, Tristan of Lyonesse!"

Still screaming, the stranger knight whirled around and attacked him again. Desperation lent Tristan unwonted strength. Lashing out like a cornered stag, he swung the flat of his sword against the side of his opponent's head and knocked him off his feet. A second blow to the back of the head as the stranger went down dropped him like a stone to the ground.

Now Gods defend us...

Fresh blood was seeping from the knight's armor where his headpiece met his neck. In a panic, Tristan fumbled with the knight's helmet. Was he alive? Sweating, he struggled to turn the knight on his back, overcome with fear for his motionless foe. Blows like that could render any man unconscious, even near death.

"Air," he muttered thickly to himself, "must give him air." He pushed up the heavy visor and the knight's face came into view.

"Hear me, sir," he began hoarsely, then lost his voice.

Oh, the Gods—surely not?

A sick sensation erupted in Tristan's gut. The wild eyes were closed, and there were no hoarse threats and cries, but there was no mistaking the matted hair and beard. Here again were the beetling eyebrows, hollow cheekbones, and tortured face he already knew.

"Alas, alas!" he cried. Tears of pity rose to Tristan's eyes. Lying before him, bloodied and brought down, was the pitiful creature he had spared before. The fate he had tried to avoid had caught up with him here. He was looking at the madman in the wood.

# chapter 15

**N**othing disturbed the quiet of the moonlit bay. One by one the Pictish ships eased their way out of the rocky harbor and slid silently out to sea. Then the darkness was broken by the mournful cry of an owl. Another answered from further inland, and a third on the mountain high above echoed the trembling call.

Moments later a dark figure slipped to a hidden beacon whose blaze could not be seen from the sea. As the fierce animal-headed prows nosed onward down the coast, other owl cries and other beacon fires sent the warning south. In between, a fleet of runners and riders helped to carry the word to Dubh Lein. By the time Darath's ships made the harbor on a golden summer dawn, Isolde had been waiting for him for days. But then, she had been ready for him from the first.

"He will come," she told Sir Gilhan and her lords, "and we shall send him away with words, not with weapons. We shall give him peace, not war."

Old Sir Doneal grunted and pulled a face. "Words don't fill bellies, lady. He'll want more than that."

"He needs something to take to his clan," Sir Gilhan put in gravely. "They'll starve in the winter else."

Vaindor smiled, and Isolde did not like his smile. "And women. The Picts always want women. They used to raid us for brides in the days gone by."

Isolde froze his unwanted interruption with a stare. "That need not concern us now. He's approaching the port, you say? Be so good as to bring him to me as soon as he lands."

But not to the palace, she decided. Any invader, even a ruling king, must be kept at arm's length. Later she might admit him to Dubh Lein, if the negotiations went smoothly, step-by-step. But for now she would challenge him at the place where he came in, confronting him the moment he set foot on Dubh Lein's soil. Accordingly, she had the royal throne carried out of the palace and set up on the clifftop high above the bay. *I am Queen here. Thus far and no farther you may go* was the message she planned to convey.

What was he? she thought for the hundredth time, awaiting him now ensconced on the throne of Queens. The morning air was alive with glinting salt crystals breathed out by the restless sea, and the sun played warmly on her face and hands. Light winds lifted her hair and teased at the hem of her robe as she pondered on. Barbarian or king, knight, warrior, killer, or all of these? How should she receive him? What to wear?

These speculations had taken up many hours of discussion with Brangwain. In the end, she had dressed to receive a king, in richly fluting silks of Ireland's royal green. A green mantle of power hung from her shoulders, while an emerald-studded breastplate signaled war. More emeralds adorned her wrists, neck, and waist, and the emerald crown of Queens blazed on her head. *Well done, Isolde,* said a cold inner voice. *Fit for a king.*

*But not this King,* another voice struck back. *Where is my King, Tristan of Lyonesse? Oh, my love, my love . . .*

Grieving, she could hear her mother now. *No tears, no fears, Isolde. Remember you are Queen.*

*I hear you, Mawther.*

*No more tears.*

*No more.*

She saw Sir Gilhan move forward to greet the Picts at their ships down in the bay and usher them onto the path leading up the cliff. Knowing she was in full view of the men below, she descended from the throne and slowly, imperiously turned to face the sea, catching the wind in her cloak like great billowing wings. Only when she heard the tramp of footsteps behind did she turn back. What she saw before her made her catch her breath. *Oh, fool, Isolde! You thought you'd be dealing with a savage and you meet a king.*

Moving confidently toward her across the springy turf was a tall, lean, handsome man, cradling a bronze and gold boar-crested helmet in the crook of his arm. He wore a kilt of finely tooled leather studded with bronze and a short, sleeveless tunic of heavy oxhide, revealing broad shoulders and well-muscled arms. Round his neck was a massive jewel on a thick gold chain, carved in the likeness of a snarling boar. Four daggers of different sizes hung from his waist, and he balanced two short stabbing spears in one hand. Bangles of gold circled both his wrists, and a coronet of gold held back a thick mane of hair.

But all this paled beside the splendor of his face and arms. Indeed all his body, as far as she could see, was gorgeously decorated in shades of blue and violet, purple, indigo, and rose. She thought of the name the Romans had given his tribe, Picti, "the Painted Ones," in their own Latin tongue, but this color would never wash off. She could see the tiny raised puckers and indented scars where the dyes had been pricked deep beneath the skin.

He came to a halt, reveling in the impact he had made. Behind him stood his band of warriors, all as lean and taut as he was, all painted, too. In a tight circle at his back stood a cluster of older knights, hard-faced and hungry, already staring her down. As she readied herself to brave them in return, Darath raised his hand and signaled them to fall back. She saw anger and resistance on every patterned face, and muttered cries flew between them in their strange, strangled tongue. Then one knight, older and harder than the rest, gave a sign of reluctant assent and they withdrew.

"Queen Isolde?" he called.

She bowed and he came bounding forward, clearing the grass between them in a few rangy strides. The wind off the sea tangled his hair as he came, and he crackled with life in the glint of the morning sun. Reaching her, he scented the air like a stag, and looked hungrily around.

"So this is the fabled Island of the West?"

Isolde opened her arms to take in the rocky clifftop, the white shore below, and the wide span of the headland drifting with daisies and pink thrift. "We call it so. Greetings, King Darath. Welcome to Dubh Lein."

He grinned, a startling flash of white against the marvelous colors of his face. "We have met before."

Isolde gave a slight, superior smile. "I do not think so, sir."

"Then think again," he laughed, undeterred. "I fought before you at a tournament in Dubh Lein, when all your suitors competed for your hand."

Was he being insolent? She did not know. "Did you so? I forget."

But in truth, she could see it now. A dozen or so strangely tattooed men riding fearlessly into the field, with a tall, laughing boy at their head. Lightly armored and clad only in a breastplate and a length of worn plaid, he had seemed half-naked, a near barbarian against the rest of the visiting knights. Yet he had borne himself throughout with impressive ease, except for one moment, when his youthfulness came through. As he and his band passed the high viewing gallery where she and her mother sat, he had stared at her as if he had never seen a woman before. What was he then, twelve or fourteen? She'd been twenty herself, and that was twenty years ago . . .

She could feel his eyes on her now as they had been then, with the same boyish intensity but this time with a man's frank sexual appraisal as he looked her up and down. She returned the gaze boldly. Well, well. The boy had become a man, and a fine one, too. A fierce humor creased the corners of his eyes and drew warm, attractive lines around his mouth. He grinned at her as if he could read her thoughts, and for a moment she saw the spirit of Cernunnos, the Horned One, the God of dark secrets and ancient, midnight woods.

*Goddess, Mother, no!*

To her horror, she felt her treacherous flesh beginning to answer his hot, lustful gaze. In the next moment came a spurt of sadness and rage. *Tristan, Tristan, why are you not here? And why have I had no word, no sign from you?* Without Tristan, she was vulnerable, she knew. And she had to defeat this kingly invader by herself.

This sea rat, this pirate, this predator.

This wolf.

She drew herself up, aware all too late that this only made her more attractive in his eyes. "So, sir," she said as coldly as she could, "what brings you here?"

He flashed his lupine smile. "Life in our land is harsh. Your kingdom, lady, is a lush and fertile temptation to a red-blooded Pict."

There was a warmth of sexual suggestion in his tone. Isolde forced herself to ignore it. "And this is the reason you invade my land?"

"Invade? Did not Your Majesty invite me here?"

"Invite you—?" She caught her breath, wrong-footed by his fearless effrontery. "I must have forgotten," she struck back with biting irony.

His eyes caught fire and he heaved a meaningful sigh. "Just as you forgot the tournament where I competed in vain for your hand."

*Competed? There was no thought of it then, you were no more than fourteen, only there to try your skill.* "You were a boy among men," she said dismissively.

He gave her his most winning smile. "Oh, lady . . . "

*Boy no longer,* hung between them like a charm.

With his wolf's instincts, Darath knew when to hold his peace. She was coming, he felt it, and she had been worth the wait. Twenty years ago she was already more than he had dreamed. Then Findra had seen her, too, and had no words for what he saw.

*Now you see her again,* he told himself feverishly, proud and aloof on this windswept cliff, the loveliest, rarest creature in the world. And her spirit, her courage like the Great One Herself, so beautiful, so bold, and so alone . . .

"Sir, no more words." Isolde's voice cut sharply through his reverie. "Why are you here?"

Inspiration came to him. "I have come in search of a queen."

"A queen? But your father ruled alone, we understand."

A spasm of regret crossed his face. "My mother died in childbirth, bearing me. Neither she nor her mother left a daughter to reign. When I marry, I must take one to rule. It is my task to give the clan a queen."

Isolde laughed with disbelief. "You have come here for a wife?"

"With good reason, lady." He chuckled again. "There is a legend among us that our ancestors came from a far distant land, adventurers and hard voyagers, men without wives. When they settled, they sent for wives to the Western Isle, and some of the boldest of your women were minded to accept. They had heard of the strength and prowess of the Painted Ones and thought they would make lusty lovers and tough and trusty companions for life. But they made it a condition of their coming that the succession to the throne should pass thereafter through the female line."

There was a pause. The scent of his manhood reached her, musky and strong, and Isolde felt his bright brown eyes upon her, burning with a fire he could not suppress. She struggled to gather her wits.

"We have a tale of our own that echoes yours. Our bards say that the first arrivals in Erin came to our country from yours by a giant stone causeway linking the two lands. Then the Great Ones drowned the causeway in the sea, and they could not return. These were the days before boats, and the land bridge was gone. But when your people arrived and asked us for wives, those of our women who answered were going home."

Darath's voice assumed a caressing tone. "Have no fear, lady. Our Queens are the proudest women on the earth. Our men of power only hold sway from them. As I shall be pleased to do . . . "

*What?* Isolde passed a hot hand over her forehead, grateful for a sudden cool gust of wind. Why was she talking like this, debating ancient history with this man? Time to remind this wretched intruder who was Queen.

She stepped forward. "Sir—"

But he came to meet her and boldly seized her hand, oblivious to the watching eyes around.

"Lady, I come to claim you, King to Queen. And you will come to me, woman to man. You and I will make powerful earth magic together, and your body knows that, too."

He threw back his head and laughed, a peal of triumph that echoed round the bay. "You are mine, lady, whether you know it or not. Now, allow me to attend you back to Dubh Lein."

# chapter 16

$S$ ir—d'you hear me, sir?"

There was no response from the figure on the ground.

"Goddess, Mother, save him, save this man! That ever I should injure him like this..."

Weeping, Tristan loosened the metal guard protecting the stranger's neck and frantically chafed his wrists, trying all he could to bring the poor soul to himself. At last he saw the knight's purple-veined eyelids flicker beneath their wild mat of hair and sat back on his heels, half sobbing with relief. Gods and Great Ones, thanks! He was alive.

Eagerly, Tristan's fingers sought the leather ties on the knight's neck-guard, unlaced the helmet, and drew it off his head. Now for the first time he could see the mass of tangled hair and the unsightly growth of untended beard. How long since this man had been able to take care of himself? Impossible to say.

Suddenly, the knight beside him groaned and stirred. His eyes opened, rolled feebly in their sockets, then closed again. Gods preserve us! Tristan leaped madly to his feet. This man has attacked you twice, ran through his mind. He's raving and violent and desperately sick in the head. Hurry, hurry, or he'll attack you again! In an ecstasy of haste, he fumbled for his girdle and bound the knight's hands and feet. Then he sat down beside the great prostrate form and buried his head in his hands.

"What in the name of the Great Ones am I to do?" He groaned aloud. Wildly, his thoughts ran on. If I leave him here, even to go to fetch help, he'll be helpless against the wild creatures of the wood.

And to be torn by fang and claw when he could not defend himself . . . What a fate to overtake any man, trapped and alone.

But to move him now might stir up his madness again, and how long would the makeshift bonds hold? He's as wild as any creature of the wood and more dangerous, because of his size. Half frantic, Tristan looked up at the sky. A fat yellow sun smiled down at him through the trees, then slid behind a cloud. Well past noon, he noted, and running down toward nightfall, even on these long summer days. He had to get the knight to safety before dark.

There was another sudden movement at his side as the knight came to himself with a flurry of jerky movements and strange cries.

"Get back!" he exclaimed hoarsely. His sunken eyes darted to and fro. "I see you, all of you. Bring up your army; you don't frighten me!"

He thrashed about, straining against his bonds. Tristan took him by the shoulder and laid a hand on his head.

"There is no army, sir," he said gently. "Only you and I. And I am a knight of the King. I shall do you no harm."

The bulging eyes quieted. "I'm burning inside," the stranger said, quietly. "But when I'm not, I'm a knight of King Arthur, too." He smiled and fixed Tristan with a guileless stare. "I am one of the Round Table Fellowship of knights."

Alas, alas, poor soul . . . A knight of King Arthur? Tristan wanted to weep. He began again in a firm and gentle tone. "Oh, sir, that cannot be. I know all of them, and none of them wears a beard."

"Neither do I."

The prisoner paused and frowned. Then he brought his bound hands to his chin and felt at the mass of hair. "I don't know how this came here," he said with open surprise. "But I'm one of the Fellowship all the same."

Tristan stared at him in pity. Could it be? By the height of him, he might have been Sir Lancelot, or one of the four Orkney brothers who were King Arthur's kin. They were the tallest of the Round Table knights besides himself. But this knight was too broad for Sir Lancelot, who was as lean as a willow, and far too thin for Sir Gawain or his brothers Agravain, Gaheris, and Gareth. And the stranger was sick; who knew what was in his mind? This knight was only dreaming of being a great hero, as lesser men always did.

What was that? Tristan heard a rustling in the wood. In a panic, he leaped to his feet, reaching for his sword. Making their way stealthily through the undergrowth were half a dozen shadowy figures with others behind them, lurking beneath the trees.

"Who's there?" he cried. "Come forward, show yourself."

There was no answer. Tristan raised his sword and charged forward, repeating his cry. "Come forward, or you're dead men, all of you!"

"Hold, sir!" came the fearful response. "We come in peace. Pray you, put up your sword."

Emerging from the dense thickets of bracken and gorse was a hesitant, un-warlike figure gowned in gray. A monk, could it be? Hastily, Tristan raked him from head to foot: sandals, but no tonsure; a rough woolen habit, but no cross. A hermit, then, not a priest in holy orders or a monk. There were many such, some dwelling alone in isolated cells, others living together as brothers, renouncing the world. Some were Christians, others followed their own Gods or the God within, but all kept to the same faith of calm and goodwill. Tristan sheathed his sword. He would have nothing to fear from this man and his fellows following behind.

"Greetings, brother," he hailed the hermit, hoarse with relief.

"And to you, sir knight," the newcomer returned.

Close up, the hermit had shed his earlier fear and came to meet him with a deliberate step. Tristan saw with approval a man of middle years, upright and bright-eyed and clad in the invisible garment of inner peace. "How may we call you, sir?" the newcomer asked courteously.

Tristan hurriedly introduced himself. "And you, brother?"

The hermit shook his head. "I have no name since I forsook the world. I answer to 'Brother.' That is all I need." He gestured to the knight lying on the ground. "Truly you have done a good deed here today."

Tristan looked down uneasily at the knight, who was regarding them wonderingly with a pair of bright blue eyes. "How so?"

"To help this wretched man."

"Do you know who he is?"

"No, but we know what brought him to this pass." The hermit sorrowfully shook his head. "It is a strange, sad tale. No one knew this knight errant when he came into our lands, but the villagers say that he's one of King Arthur's knights."

There it was again. Tristan shook his head. "Alas, no. That's his delusion, I fear. What brought him here?"

"They say he was unluckily passing this way on the Quest for the Grail."

"Yes, indeed," Tristan agreed grimly. "Unlucky for the poor lady at the castle when he tried to take her estate."

A look of distress passed over the hermit's face. "Sir, he never oppressed the young Lady Unnowne."

"What?" Tristan cried. "But she told me herself—"

"She tells everyone the same tale, to hide her shame. Oh, it's true that he knew her. He called at the castle to beg a bed for the night as he passed by. Ravished by his appearance, she courted him with unbridled passion and took him to her bed. He stayed for a while, enjoying her favors, and she treated him like her husband and her lord. But one day he told her that he had to go. He was on the Quest. He could not delay."

Tristan heart dropped like a stone. "How d'you know all this? Those around her agree with what she says."

"They try to protect her out of misplaced loyalty. Most of them served her father and revere his name, and they fear she'll be dishonored if this gets out. But one of our brethren here has a sister who serves the lady, and she saw it all. The lady had set her heart upon this knight and lost her mind when he cast her off."

"So she—?" But Tristan already knew what he would hear.

The hermit sighed heavily. "Disowned and rejected, she planned a cruel revenge. She blandished him to take one last meal with her and fed him a dish that made him run mad."

Tristan gaped in horror. "What was it?"

"Who knows?" The hermit spread his hands. "It could have been many things. The red cap mushroom rots the mind and makes its victims see enemies that are not there. Then there's ergot, the blight that forms on rotting rye, which causes cramps and inner burning and hallucinations, too. She could have made him a porridge of such grains and berries as he left her castle to go on his way."

"And ever since he's been trapped here in the wood, lost to himself and in fear of everyone?" Tristan turned on the hermit in anger and distress. "Could no man help him?"

"Oh, sir, we tried."

It was another of the brothers at the leader's side, a small, timid man with shortsighted, blinking eyes. "The stranger would not be approached. There are six of us here, but we dared not go near him for fear of our lives. We could only hope and pray for a knight strong enough to overcome him, as you did."

"We have the means to heal him, now he is subdued," offered a third. He indicated the bunches of herbs hanging at his waist. "I am the apothecary of our brotherhood. Whatever poison nature ever made, she gave us the antidote."

"Are you sure?"

"I am sure we can help him. With quiet and care, most men recover in time."

The leader smiled encouragingly. "Leave him to us, sir."

Tristan turned back to the knight and knelt down at his side. "Did you hear that, my friend? These good souls will help you now. You're safe in their hands, and you'll soon be well again. Do you understand?"

A gleam of comfort flickered across the knight's face. He moved his head slowly in a sign of assent. Tristan squeezed his hand. "Farewell."

"Fare you well, sir," the hermit said.

"One thing more." Tristan searched for his purse, and pressed money into the hermit's grasp.

"No need, no need," he murmured.

But Tristan would brook no refusal. "Take it all the same."

After a few warm words of farewell, he whistled up his horse, then watched the hermit and his brothers as they lifted the knight between them and bore him away. As they went, a great coldness settled on his heart. A vast and unspeakable wrong had been done to this knight. It was time to return to the castle of Lady Unnowne.

# chapter 17

*e*ven from afar, Castle Dun Haven looked a sorry place. Weeds flourished in the battlements, and dark flocks of ravens rose cawing from their countless nest holes in the walls. Judging from its rotting timbers and limp chains, the drawbridge had not been raised for many years, and no knights emerged from the gatehouse as they approached.

A poor establishment, then. Arraganzo pursed his lips approvingly. Father Dominian had chosen better than he thought. Good, good. Here we can do God's work.

For a little desperation would be needed on the King of Dun Haven's part if they were to persuade him to part with a princess or two. As they rode through the great archway, Arraganzo noted with growing satisfaction the lack of attendance in the lower court, the solitary groom fumbling with too many horses at once, the crumbling old chamberlain who could not get hold of their names. Now they stood in a large, gracious hall that like the rest of the castle had seen better days, and Arraganzo felt the power of his purpose pulsing through his veins. They would succeed, he knew it. God was with His chosen, and He had chosen them today.

He cast a sideways eye over Dominian, who stood at his side. His pupil, Simeon, was silent and attentive in the rear. That young man would go far. The Church could use devotion such as his. And Dominian, too, seemed at his best today, his coal-black eyes burning with the light of their mission, his dark face watchful and intent. Already they had decided how they should proceed. All they needed now was the King himself.

The old chamberlain smoothed down his rusty silk gown and

began to warble tunelessly at the door. "The King...Prepare for the King—"

"Enough, enough, hold your peace."

Striding through the door was a portly man of middle height with a lined face and an irritable air. His clothes were costly but worn, and the rich red velvet straining across his gut clearly dated from earlier days. But a gold coronet gleamed upon his head, and the gold badge of kingship adorned his neck. This was the man they sought.

"Sirs—"

The newcomer came toward them, his hand outstretched, issuing all the courtly greetings of a king. But his hard, greedy eyes and pinched, suspicious mouth undermined the welcome of his words. Here was a man who gave nothing himself but was hungry for whatever he could get. Arraganzo's heart surged. Perfect. He would be ideal for God's darker purpose today.

"Greetings to Your Majesty," the Legate began smoothly, while Dominian and Simeon bowed deeply at his side. "And good wishes to you from your Heavenly Father above."

"What?" Startled, the King raised his eyes to the sky.

"You are called, sire, to do God's immortal work," Arraganzo pressed on in lofty tones. "Father Dominian tells me that you are blessed with many daughters to your name."

"Too many," the King snapped. "Far too many mouths to feed and dowries to find. Well, I can't do it, and that's that. I'll just have to put them into nunneries, every one." He glared at Arraganzo and thrust out his chin. "Is that God's purpose, sir? What's the point of it all?"

"Who can say? But God may have another aim for your fair girls," the Legate returned. He drew a breath. "Hear me, sire. Your overlord, King Mark, will shortly decide to put his wife away."

The King's small eyes widened. "He's going to divorce Queen Isolde?"

"The pagan Queen, yes," Arraganzo confirmed. "And then—"

"He'll want another wife." A gleam of calculation brightened the King's eye. He smiled. "A good Christian virgin, perhaps?"

"What else?" said Arraganzo in his silkiest tones.

"One such as your virtuous Theodora," Dominian put in.

"Yes, well . . ."

The King paused. Was "virtuous" the word for his eldest daughter's sullen, indefatigable will, her violent temper, and the greed that was already making her fat? Sly, too, he mused bitterly, doubtless already sneaking around outside and listening at the door to see what all this was about. God knows why she's so full of faults, fleeted through his brain, I've beaten her enough. Still, at least she's a virgin, I've made sure of that. And she knows her catechism. That's all they'll require.

"Theodora, yes," he said, summoning a smile. He hesitated as an almost inconceivable future took shape in his brain. That fat trollop of his, the King's wife? Could it be?

Yes!

He drove his fists into his palm and his mean eyes flared. "I'll bring her to court. I'll take all eight of them. If the King doesn't like Theodora, he can take his pick. I'll get them all new gowns—though God in Heaven, that'll cost—"

"One moment, sire," Dominian interrupted with a glance at Arraganzo. They had prepared for this.

Without hesitation, the Legate took up the tale. "At the moment, the King's forthcoming divorce is not widely known. If you bring your fair brood to court, all the other Kings will guess your intentions, and they'll do the same. Then the lovely Theodora will find other girls in her path. We need to move forward with great care if your daughter is to succeed in God's work."

"His Excellency, the Cardinal Legate and I are on our way to court," said Dominian. "Would you allow us to take her there?"

Arraganzo waved a lordly hand. "What could be more natural than that two men of God should introduce a distressed young Princess to King Mark's paternal care."

The King stared. "Distressed?"

Arraganzo nodded gravely. "We need a good reason to take Theodora into our care. Now, if the King her father is dying . . ."

"Dying, am I?" said the King doubtfully, stroking his well-fleshed cheeks.

"Wasting away," said the Legate firmly. "In pain and torment of soul."

"Unable to provide for this hapless female sprig of the family tree," added Dominian.

The King gave a cynical laugh. "Well, that's true at least." He rolled his eyes unhappily around, refusing to think about his crumbling crenellations and decaying walls. Bad enough to have to share his bedchamber with mice and rats. But if Theodora got her hands on the King...

He looked longingly at Arraganzo's gold pomander, his costly gown of velvet silk, and the massive cross of rubies around his neck. "D'you have any idea what everything costs these days? Why, the horses alone eat me out of house and home. And that eldest of mine can eat like a hog when I let her, that's why she's getting so fat—"

Arraganzo brushed his complaint aside. "So then, you throw her on the King's mercy and make ready to die."

A real alarm awoke in the King's ferret eyes. "But I don't, do I?"

"There may be a miraculous recovery," said the Legate with superb disdain. "If the girl gets King Mark to the altar and his ring on her hand."

The King hesitated. "I don't know ... "

"Come, sire," said Arraganzo with a trace of contempt, "you know she'll be safe with us."

The King surveyed the Cardinal and the priest and returned the contempt with interest. "Oh, I've no doubt of that."

"Let us see her, then," said Arraganzo briskly. If the rustlings and whispers he had caught were anything to go by, the young woman and her sisters were not far away.

"One moment, then," said the King, who then withdrew. Soon afterward he was back, escorting one, three, five, how many girls?

The Cardinal turned a laugh into a cough. Dear God, what a brood the King had been blessed with! But there was no mistaking the eldest, sailing forward like a swan at the head of the skein, her sisters trailing forlornly in her wake.

"Here they are," mumbled the King. "Theodora, Divinia, Petrina, Calvaria, Laboria ... "

"Sirs..."

Theodora was already curtsying under Arraganzo's nose, deliberately targeting the most important man in the group, the Legate noted with satisfaction as he surveyed her up and down. Ambitious, was she? That promised well. He did not like her smell, the strange warm, bready odor of all women that rose from her ample flesh, so alien to those who lived their lives among men, but he had to admit this creature was no more disgusting than the rest. Not tall, but with a bosom that would get her noticed anywhere, a plump neck and shoulders, and voluptuous hips shaped for an amorous hand. And she must be ready for a change. The faded silk she wore, long outgrown and too tight across her breasts, would make any young woman crave a new gown. As she looked around, her eye was already inquiring, anything here for me?

Good, very good! And just as Dominian had said. As she curtsied before him and knelt to kiss his ring, Arraganzo saw with unbridled delight that she gave him the eye. Himself, Dom Luis Carlos Felipe Arraganzo da Sevilla y Cadiz y Pinca y Salamanca, Cardinal Legate of the Pope and a prince of the Church! If this raw, sensual abandon did not wake King Mark's dormant desire, nothing would. "Bless you, my daughter," he murmured with deep sincerity.

Still, the wise man always made doubly sure. Arraganzo turned to survey the other daughters, who were straggling behind. The next in line was a pale, slender thing with a long white neck, folded hands, and downcast eyes. With no breasts or hips to speak of, she would appeal to any man whose secret, deep-buried longings ran to boys. And there were others, too, languishing in the rear. Divinia and Petrina, for instance; now what about them...?

"Greetings, Father."

Theodora had moved on to Dominian with another low curtsy and a slow, languorous smile. Dropping his gaze, anxious to avoid her eye, the priest was horrified to find himself staring at her breasts. Now God forgive me! Shame knocked like vomit at the back of his throat. Is this truly Your work, dear Lord? Did You die for this?

But already he could feel his protest being swept away, his

fears blown into infinity by a superior force. The Cardinal Legate was already at the door, with Theodora and another of the girls at his side.

"Come, Father," Arraganzo called in the voice of Rome. Raising a silent prayer, Dominian had no choice but to obey.

othing had changed in the Castle of Unnowne. The aged Seneschal greeted him as before, the same ancient retainers guarded the upstairs door, and the lady herself still languished in her bath with her white-clad attendants and the doctor at her side. She reared up eagerly as Tristan strode in, a look of keen anticipation on her face. The smell of the sickroom came to meet him again with its tender, healing scents of lavender and vervain. But now he noticed what he had not caught before, an indefinable hint of evil in the air.

"So, sir," the lady crowed in triumph, "you have killed my enemy?"

"Your enemy?" Tristan returned angrily. "You lied to me, lady. The knight you accused of wronging you is mad."

Her eyes grew round with hate. "He is not mad! Wicked men have the art of other-seeming—he deceives everyone."

Vividly, Tristan saw again the anguished eyes of the stranger knight searching his face like a wounded animal, the unkempt beard and dreadful matted hair. "Lady, I saw him with my own eyes," he returned. "He's out of his mind, and you made him so."

She gasped with rage. "I did not! And if I did, he deserved it."

Now it was Tristan's turn to catch his breath. "No man deserves that!"

"He treated me cruelly," she shrilled. "He took advantage of my bed—"

"You took him to your bed," Tristan cut her off. "Then you made up the story that he had done you wrong. In reality, you did a terrible thing to him. You poisoned him, lady, and robbed him of his wits."

A look of childish cunning crept over her face. "Now why would I do that?"

"Because you could not forgive him for rejecting your love."

Her head went back in a howl of pain. "Why should I forgive him?"

Without warning, she skipped from the bath as naked as a needle and ran toward him, as shameless as a child. Her long hair fell around her like a cloak, gleaming in the pearly light of the darkened room. Her skin, too, glowed with the same luster, wholesome and golden white. Tristan looked away, but not before he had seen that the whole of her body had no sign of disease.

"Lady, lady—" The women attendants swooped down and surrounded the dripping figure, solicitously enveloping her thin, childish body in soft wraps.

The doctor came forward, anxiously shaking his head. Tristan turned on him as the attendants led the lady away. "What is this? There's nothing wrong with your lady that I can see."

"Alas, sir, there is." Tears stood in the doctor's eyes. "Our lady is ill indeed, but in her mind. She was never strong, even as a child. She suffered terribly when she lost her mother, and when her father lay dying too her wits began to turn."

"But you called it a skin complaint?"

"In truth, she does suffer eruptions when her body rebels. Then she scratches her arms and picks away at her flesh if we cannot get her into the bath to calm her down and turn her mind to better things."

So that was the cause of the outbreak he'd seen on her arms . . . Tristan stared in distress. "How did this malady first show itself?"

"She stopped answering to her name and refused to accept that she came from here."

"From this castle, you mean? The place where she was born?"

"I do not come from here!" the lady cried out from the shelter of her attendants' arms, in a high, broken chime. Her shadowed, tragic eyes and sudden, odd, quicksilver smile confirmed all the doctor said.

"I was born in a silver palace with gateways of gold," she trilled on with the same strange, flashing smile. "And pillars of crystal holding up every floor. Three trees grew under my window that sang to me every day, whether birds roosted in their branches or not. There was an orchard whose fruit never failed, and a well of love from which maidens could drink their fill."

Alas, poor lady . . . Tristan bowed his head in grief.

"And the King my father loved me beyond compare. He found me in his garden, asleep in the heart of a rose. I was no bigger than his little finger, but he took me to his heart. The Fair Ones had left me there, so he reared me in a nutshell and brought me up as his own."

"And you remember that he called you after your mother, my lady," said the doctor, trying intently to engage her eye. "He named you—"

"I have no name," she interrupted, darting her eyes around like a captured fawn. "That's why I'm the Lady 'Unknown.' "

Tristan brought his hand to his head and closed his eyes. Unnowne. Unknown. Of course.

"And all this?" Tristan muttered, gesturing round the sickroom with its ointments and potions and lotions everywhere. "If they're not needed, why are they here?"

The doctor gave a smile shot through with pain. "Alas, they're all we have. We don't know how to minister to a mind that's so sick. When she scratches her arms, she often infects the skin. So we soothe her body to keep her distress at bay. The cooling waters of the bath and these lotions bring down the heat of the madness that grips her every day."

"Every day? Gods above, what a cruel affliction." Tristan shook his head. No wonder the lady had had no pity for the wandering knight.

"Every day," the doctor repeated, "she suffers some delusion or distorted thought."

"There was no lover, then?" Tristan said heavily. "No trusted knight, faithful and true to her?"

"Oh, there was." The doctor covered his eyes to hide his tears. "He waited years to marry her, he loved her so. But he went away in the end, because she could not recover her mind. He had to accept that she would always be mad."

Tristan felt grief enveloping him like a cloud. He struggled to throw it off.

"Mad, perhaps," he said forcefully, "but the rest of you here don't have that excuse."

The doctor looked alarmed. "What do you mean?"

"Why did you let her poison the stranger knight? She has made him as mad as she is and now he suffers horribly, too. Is that right?"

The doctor held out his hands helplessly. "Oh sir, we had no idea what she planned to do."

"But you still supported her afterward. You backed up her story and sent me out into the forest to fight an innocent man."

"When you came, the Seneschal and I wanted to tell you what we knew. But our lady's father had made us swear an oath that we'd be loyal to his daughter all our lives." He shook his head. "We never dreamed that our trust would be tried like this."

Pain upon pain . . . Reading the troubled face, Tristan saw layer upon layer of deep and careworn love.

"Sir, you have borne too much, you and your fellows here," he said sorrowfully. "When I leave, I'll make sure Queen Isolde knows of your plight. She'll send you some good young knights and ladies, too, to keep your mistress company and help her to better ways. You may never cure the wounds that beset her mind. But they can help you to bear the burden and cheer her life with music and dancing and other courtly delights."

The doctor's eyes were pools of wonder and hope. "Can you do that, sir?"

Tristan took the doctor's hand in both of his. "You have my word."

"Then may all your Gods give you a safe journey when you leave."

Tristan bowed. "That must be now, good sir. I fear I shall already suffer for this delay."

His meager preparations to depart were soon complete and all the castle turned out to see him on his way. The end of the long summer day was in sight, and the sunlight was fading into silver-rose, violet, and gray. The scent of the woodland rose from the mossy ground, and he drank in the wonder of life, ever springing anew.

Yet he could be lying dead now at the hands of the stranger knight. The angry brothers Balin and Balan could have killed him, too.

Tristan laughed in disdain. Killed me? I would have beaten them.

Ah, Tristan, came a somber voice from within, all men go down to darkness in the end. Who would have known if you had died in the wood? Who would have mourned your passing? When you die, what will you leave behind?

Leavebehindleavebehind, whispered the weeping willow on the bank. Tristan felt an unfamiliar agony in his soul. Who would care if he lived or died?

The greenway was opening on the high road ahead. All around him the forest bloomed in its midsummer height, lavish clusters of key-shaped seedpods crowding the sycamores as the busy oak, beech, and yew competed to unfurl their banners of green.

And he was riding back to Castle Dore? Back to King Mark?

*Fool! Fool! Triple times fool!*

He laughed in pain. A man could die in a wood—even one of King Arthur's Round Table knights, as the poor deluded stranger took himself to be—and no one would know. Was his own life, the life he so stoutly defended with his sword, no more than that, as fragile as a blade of grass?

Tristan's mind roamed on. All men, weak or strong, even knights errant like the brothers Balin and Balan, were blind to the danger that lurked in every blade. Not even King Arthur could escape such a fate. His heart grieved for all the misguided battles in which men fought each other to the death, not knowing what they did.

"Goddess, Mother!" he cried to the uncaring trees, "the love of one good woman is worth a hundred jousts."

A strange sensation seized Tristan, like a dull ache. In all his years of traveling the tournaments, men lived, men died, as the Great Ones decreed. They came out of the dark into the light, like a sparrow fluttering into the mead hall at night, and flew out into the dark again when their time was done. So it was for every man, and so it would be for Tristan himself. But what then?

With a shock he recalled that the High King himself was without an heir. When Arthur passed on, the once-mighty House of Pendragon would be no more. And the House of Lyonesse? The thought scalded his veins.

And Isolde had offered, had craved, to bear his child. He lifted his face to the rising moon and wept for his lack of faith.

"I thought of it as something you wanted, lady," he raged at himself. "I did not see ... I did not see."

Oh, fool! Blind fool. He struck his head with his hand. What else did he not see as he crept forward in his own darkness like a mole?

A point of light shimmered above the woodland and the love star was born. As he stared into its lambent, warm, opaline depths, he saw Isolde standing in an open doorway holding a lamp aloft, shining the light of her understanding upon him like the star.

Isolde, Isolde . . .

And he was riding to Mark?

Tristan turned his horse's head into the setting sun. For the rest of his life, he would always remember this moment of choice.

"Westways then, to the port," he whispered into the gray's large, furry, and receptive ear. "With your best speed, old friend. First we must find paper and ink and a messenger we can trust to send to Mark. Then westward ho! We have a boat to catch tonight, you and I."

# chapter 19

*e*vening reigned over the land, warm and still. In the bay below the Queen's House at Dubh Lein, the sea lay like a mill pond, hardly astir. On the headland above, the air was full of the drowsy, midsummer hum of insects and the call of roosting birds. The sinking sun rippled with silver and gold, touching the sleepy white clouds with tongues of fire. Brangwain sat by the open window, her neat hands flickering over a piece of stitching, her taut frame intent, as Isolde prowled the chamber, unable to rest.

Her mind picked away at the same question, like a painful scab. How had Darath imposed his will on her? Why had she allowed him to command her to his bed?

The thought of it stung like a swarm of bees. How had he turned the tables, when she'd had the upper hand? She had already succeeded in drawing him down to Dubh Lein and had met him in all her majesty on the cliff, to show him once and for all that she ruled here as Queen. And just as he should have been submitting to her, he had treated her as if he were the ruling King.

And he'd made no secret of his urge to take her to bed. *To his bed.* Her skin prickled, and an unfamiliar sensation ran through her veins. How long was it since a man had desired her like that, with hungry eyes and a rough grasp of her hand? Darath's long, painted body rose up before her eyes, and she shuddered with remorse. Why was this man invading her mind and heart, stirring up feelings she did not care to name?

*Oh Tristan, Tristan, where are you, my love?* Darath's approach had soiled her; she felt grubby and low. His words would be with her, she knew, for a long while to come, along with his hot, familiar stare deep into her eyes. *Lady, I come to claim you, king to queen. And you will come to me, woman to man. You and I will make powerful earth magic together, and your body knows that, too.*

How dare he? she raged. But deep in her heart she knew he had seen something in her that answered his animal call.

*You are mine, lady, whether you know it or not. Now, allow me to attend you back to Dubh Lein.*

She could still smell, almost taste, the coarse, wild, heathery scent of him, and feel his thumb grinding into her palm. She sweated with shame.

Yet why? When Darath spoke, she had simply ignored his advance. She had withdrawn her hand from his too-eager grasp and coolly moved on.

Coolly, but not coldly: it was vital to keep on good terms with him. So she had spoken of conditions and treaties in her smoothest tones, graciously indicating her desire for an agreement and promising to feast him like a king. By his bright-eyed glance and feral grin, he had gone back to his ship more taken with her than ever, excited by the thought of the conquest to come.

*Conquest to come, Isolde?* came a sharp inner voice.

*Yes, indeed,* she retorted just as sharply. *I shall do what has to be done. And no more. Be very sure of that. No more!*

She gave a mirthless laugh. *All very fine, and no more than a ruler should do. Then why does the thought of this Pict heat your blood? Stir up your secret parts and bring the blood to your face?*

"Lady—?"

She turned abruptly. Seated in the window, Brangwain held up her hand. "There it goes."

Isolde strained to hear. From the woodland above the castle came the strange churring call of the nightjar. Brangwain nodded to herself.

"Nightfall," she said. "They'll be waiting for us now."

Her dark-toned face alight with purpose, the maid rose and veiled herself from head to foot. Then she threw a gossamer wrap the color of twilight around Isolde, too.

"This way, lady," she said.

Lightly, she led the way down through the palace to the caves beneath. Below them lay the Dark Pool from which Dubh Lein took its name, the secret spring of sweet water at the castle's heart, the gift of the Old Ones to ensure it never ran dry.

Down they went, and down, threading their way through vast echoing caverns and rocky passages undisturbed since the primeval sleep of the earth. How did Brangwain know all these hidden places, these dark, secret ways? Isolde smiled. All the world knew that Brangwain was Merlin's kin.

Doggedly, they pressed on. As they went down, the light from Brangwain's lantern was swallowed up in a measureless cavern almost too dark to be borne. Black-winged forebodings swooped around Isolde like bats, choking her with fear. The next moment they found themselves slithering like snakes through narrow cracks scarcely wide enough to pass. In these narrow crevices in the heart of the living rock, the lantern flared over fearsome things never meant to see the light.

At last they passed into the cavern where the Dark Pool lay, and the mist off the sweet water enveloped them like dew. It came as a blessing from the Mother, and Isolde drew it deep into her lungs. Now she caught gentle rustlings and soft sighs and sometimes a brief glimpse of bright eyes in the gloom. These caves were home to many shy creatures, she knew, and she felt better for their kindly glances as she passed.

"A little farther, lady," Brangwain said again and again.

Lost in the primal night of the depths of the cave, Isolde never knew when the sweet dew of Dubh Lein's dark waters gave way to salt. But when she tasted a briny tang in the air, she knew they had found their way toward the sea. The thick velvet darkness lifted as the air lightened and stirred, and now they could almost see their way ahead. The rocky floor of the cavern gave way to sand underfoot, and the tide wept softly close at hand.

"Here, lady."

Brangwain raised the lantern, muttering to herself. They were in a wide cavern, opening onto the sea. Small, lazy waves came purling in through a rocky arch ahead and spent themselves on the sand at their feet. On the far horizon hung a pale crescent moon, tipping the black sea beneath with flecks of gold.

Isolde felt a thrill of hope and fear. *Where are we?* She looked round the cave. Inside the arch, sea terns nested in hollows in the rock while their homing males hovered protectively overhead. Farther off, a magnificent swan reposed on the top of a crag, her black eyes like jewels in her dainty head. Serene in her majesty, she ignored their approach, but Isolde gave her a courteous bow all the same: "Blessings on you, little Mother. And bless my search, I pray."

Brangwain swung the light to and fro. "Where are they?" Isolde heard the maid saying to herself. "They should be here."

There was an echoing pause. Then came a soft chuckling like the waves lapping on the shore. "We are here. See, we are all around."

Isolde gasped. "Where?"

"Here, here."

The light off the sea lit a dozen or more shapely gray forms half submerged in the water or reclining on the rocks. At first sight, Isolde took them for sea creatures with their keen bright eyes and silvery, shining flanks. She had swum with seals and dolphins as a child, and knew them as well as her human friends of those days. But these were lovely young women, at home in the sea and on land. Each shimmered in a different watery-colored silk, blue-green, shining gray, mauve, and purple-black, with ropes of shell gleaming at their waists and necks. Their long hair floated round them like seaweed, and their soft laughter ebbed and flowed with the waves. Isolde held her breath. They were the Maidens of the Lady, here to bring her on her way.

"Come."

One taller than the rest gave a commanding wave, and those in the water swam forward, drawing a boat. Isolde hesitated. *What if—?*

"Come!" The sea Maiden's command rang out again.

"This way, lady." Practical as ever, Brangwain helped her over the rocks and saw her embarked. "I'll be here when you return."

Isolde gripped the sides of the boat. With a sudden tug, the Maidens pulled the prow around and headed out of the cave. Once clear of the rocks, they took it in turns to draw the boat along, some holding the ropes while others sported among the waves. Now she saw that these easy, laughing girls were fearless swimmers and sea guardians, on the watch against those who would kill the fish. The Maiden at the prow heard her thought.

"Yes," she said in a rushing watery voice. "We protect all our kin that swim in the deep, both the little fish and the great silver shoals. But the kings and queens of the ocean"—she laughed merrily as a whale leaped far away—"they look after themselves."

Isolde looked around her in awe as the Maidens pulled steadily out into the bay. The new moon hung over the water like a prayer, casting a shining path to the world beyond. Halfway down the silver pathway to the moon stood a rocky crag, alone in the midst of the sea. Chirruping among themselves like sea otters, the Maidens surged toward it with unfailing strokes.

Now the rock loomed larger, a fortress of the sea. Beneath its ragged crest were countless caves hollowed out by the tide and great piles of broken rock around the base. The sighing sea sucked and plucked at the tumbled rocks, bedecking them with glistening beads of foam. As they drew nearer, the moon sailed behind a cloud and the world grew dark. Isolde's heart raced, and she fastened her gaze ahead.

*Goddess, Mother—*

Rising from the rock was a tall shape pulsing with power. Clustered on the rocks around her feet were a group of Maidens, all gleaming like their leader in the pale moon's watery light. Her full womanly curves were veiled in diaphanous gauze, but there was no escaping the figure's mystical force. She held a scepter of red coral across her breast, and the ring of the Goddess shone on her left hand. Pearls of all colors adorned the misty form, and a diadem of moon-white pearls crowned her head.

Joy flooded Isolde, and she wanted to weep. "Lady," she breathed, trembling with relief. "Oh, Lady—" She could not go on.

The Maidens drew up the boat at the foot of the rock. The Lady raised her arms, and her foaming robes ebbed and flowed with the rhythm of the sea. Her voice when she spoke came from the world before place or time. "Greetings, Isolde. I am glad to see you here. You have come for my help?"

Isolde thought of Tristan and her grief sprang anew. "I am suffering, Lady," she said huskily. "My true love is gone."

"The story of life is the ebb and flow of the tide. So it is with love. What do you seek?"

Isolde moistened her dry lips, holding back her tears. "When I first knew Tristan, I feared death and shame if our love became known. So I took the way of the Mother to close up my womb. But if I'm ever going to bear a child, it must be soon. Can you help me to reverse my childless state?"

"You want a child, you say? By Tristan?"

Isolde's color rose. "Who else?"

There was a thoughtful silence. "Tristan has been absent a long time. Are you sure you still think of him? Or do you dream of having a child by Darath the Pict?"

"By Darath?" she gasped.

"Why not?" Isolde caught the echo of a low, musical laugh. "He is bold and handsome and a king among men. And he is here, as Tristan is not. Tristan or Darath—which of them is it to be?"

Isolde bit her lip. *Does it matter as long as I have the child my body craves?*

But the Lady heard her thought. "Oh, it matters, Isolde," she replied in tones of clear reproof. "It matters to the child. To bring a new life into the world is not a decision a woman should take alone. A child deserves two parents and Tristan is worthy of any woman's choice."

"But Tristan is not here!" she cried in anguish.

"Do you doubt him? Always before he has returned to your side."

"But shall we ever be together?" Isolde's whole body was racked with shuddering sobs. "Sometimes I think I'll die before that comes."

"Take heart, Isolde." The Lady's voice was infinitely tender and warm. "You were not fated to live the life that others lead. But the fire of life burns green and strong in your veins."

"And in Tristan's?"

"In his, too." The great shape nodded, bathed in opalescent light. "He was born in the heart of the wood, so he will always be a creature of the land. But his heart flows with goodness as the sea teems with fish. And he will come at last to the land of his heart's desire."

"Can I trust him?"

"You must ask that question of yourself, not of him."

Isolde felt a sudden angry unease. "I don't understand."

"Examine yourself," the lady repeated in the same ringing tones. "Search your own soul. What is Darath to you?"

Isolde threw back her head defiantly. "Nothing but a threat to my kingdom. And I shall deal with that and not with him."

There was a luminous pause. "Then go your way, Isolde, as woman and queen. Reach out for the three joys of the Goddess, the three gifts She offers to every woman as maiden, mother, and crone: joy in love, the joy of a babe at your breast, and the joy of a life well lived. You have known the bliss of your body's awakening, and already you have the satisfaction of a life well lived. And now you seek motherhood, too. Will you fill the cup of life to the very brim?"

Isolde's heart burst in her breast. "Yes, I will!" she cried. "For Tristan and myself. And for the new life we shall bring into the world."

"New life, then." The Lady inclined her head.

Isolde leaned forward boldly. "Lady, teach me how to open my womb."

The Lady raised her hand. At her signal, one of the Maidens passed something hard and cold into Isolde's hand. Trembling, Isolde studied it by the light of the moon. A cunningly wrought little bottle lay on her palm, made of thick glass or translucent stone, she could not tell. Ancient runes and elaborate spirals covered its sides, and the stopper was a dewy aquamarine.

"Drink this and pray," came the Lady's voice. "It is the way of the Mother to unlock your womb."

She bowed her head to Isolde, and her veil flashed with a thousand sea drops gleaming like liquid fire. "Go now, my child, and prepare for a child of your own. And may the Mother be with you every step of the way."

# chapter 20

She was all very well as chamberwomen went, Mark thought, but God Almighty, the smell! Clean starched linen, fresh lavender and beeswax, it was too much. A big woman like her should smell of grease and fat, roast pork, old cheese, and strong beer, like a good meal in herself. In fact, all the world should smell of food and drink and horses and dogs—the more, the better, he huffed.

Still, here she was standing before him, hard-bodied and hard-faced, and she had a tale to tell that he was paying to hear. And ready and eager to hear, too. Not that she should know that. He put on a show of lordly indifference while listening intently to every word.

"Nothing?" he demanded at the end. "You've seen nothing to fear?"

The woman in the spotless apron dipped her head.

"Nothing at all, sire," she said obsequiously. "I've been watching him like a hawk as you said, but Sir Andred goes about his business all day like any other knight. At night he retires to his chamber and says his prayers." She paused. "He always prays for you, sire, and your health."

"Just as it should be, then."

Andred loyal and God-fearing? Good, good. Mark strode around the chamber, congratulating himself. A while ago he'd had enemies on all sides. Andred and Father Dominian, Sir Nabon and his lords, Isolde, his so-called wife, and even Tristan, his sworn knight, had all seemed against him then. Yet now these troubles were fading into the mist.

He frowned. True, he'd sworn to get Isolde with child, and he still had to do that. But he'd go over to Ireland if need be and make her conform. And Tristan was on his way back to Castle Dore. If his nephew had wanted to choose Isolde over Mark, he'd be in Ireland now. Mark laughed uneasily at his own distrust. Why had he ever suspected his champion knight?

And the others, too, had not proved as bad as he'd feared. His barons had been silent to a man since they'd tried to force his hand over the succession and he'd faced them down. And the good Lord in His wisdom had sent a long-nosed Spanish cardinal from Rome to occupy the interfering Dominian from dawn to dusk. With his pitiless eye and disapproving mien, Dom Arraganzo, or whatever they called him, was running the little priest off his feet. Good again! Mark rejoiced brutally. Anything to keep that carping hunchback away.

And now this woman had told him that Andred was above reproach as well. This was better than all, the best. Mark turned back to the chambermaid.

"Keep on the watch. I shall send for you again." He jerked his head dismissively. "There's a purse for you by the door."

"Thank you, sire."

The woman's dull eyes lit with a greedy gleam as she made for the door. Any day now she'd be leaving the King's service to set up for herself. A lodging house for travelers, maybe, or an alehouse in the town. Between the King and Sir Andred, she was doing well.

Of course, Sir Andred paid her better than the King, she knew he would. Well, she'd have been a fool to try to spy on Andred, he was far too sharp. But when she told him what the King wanted her to do, she'd guessed he'd reward her richly for betraying Mark's plans. And in return, she only had to carry back to Mark what Andred told her to say.

She reached for the purse, savoring the weight of the coin in her hand. An alehouse, she suddenly decided. No more making beds.

"Thank you, sir." She made a fulsome curtsy and was gone.

Mark did not notice her go. He circled the chamber again, scenting the air. How he loved these hot, lazy dog days at the end of the summer, when even the dew of the morning lay warm on the grass. When the noonday sun quivered in a sky like glass, and the evening brought brilliant sunsets of glittering gold. When a man could spend all day in the saddle swimming in the sweat off his horse's back, then sleep in the forest in his boots and begin again next day.

As he would now. Grinning with pleasure, he reached for his riding crop. Now, where to go? He was already on horseback in his mind and racing away over the sunburned heath when he heard an altercation at the door.

"The King's going hunting, he's not to be disturbed—"

"Out of my way, man! He'll want to see this!"

Mark heaved a furious sigh. Jesus and Mary, could a man have no peace?

The door opened and Andred hurried in. "A letter, sire. From Sir Tristan."

From Tristan.

Mark's heart died.

It would be the same as Isolde. She had written, too, to say she was not coming back.

Sick with betrayal, Mark took the letter and tore open the seal. The black letters ran together like a spider's crawl.

> TO MY LIEGE LORD AND KINSMAN, KING MARK OF
> CORNWALL AND THE OUTER ISLES:
>
> SIRE, YOU HAVE BEEN MY GOOD LORD THESE
> MANY LONG YEARS AND I HAVE NOT THE SKILL IN
> WORDS TO THANK YOU FOR THAT. I HAVE SERVED YOU
> AS BEST A MAN MAY WHO, ALAS, HAS MORE THAN HIS
> SHARE OF THE WEAKNESS OF MANKIND.
>
> BUT NOW I MUST CRAVE YOUR LEAVE TO GO ELSE-
> WHERE. GIVE ME YOUR BLESSING AS I DEPART YOUR
> SERVICE FOR ANOTHER LIFE. I GO TO SERVE QUEEN
> ISOLDE IN THE WESTERN ISLE. FROM THERE I SHALL
> NEVER FAIL TO REMEMBER YOUR GOODNESS AND TO
> PRAY FOR YOU.
>
> YOUR SERVANT AND LATE LIEGE MAN,
> TRISTAN OF LYONESSE

Mark stood without moving as his soul turned to stone. Tristan was leaving his service, abandoning him? He preferred to serve Isolde? So much for the wretch's allegiance. Pray for me, villain? he cried inwardly. You'd better start praying for yourself!

And the Quest? Mark wanted to scream aloud. He had boasted that Cornwall would join the Quest for the Grail, and now Tristan's desertion had put a swift end to that. As Cornwall's champion, he was leaving the country unprotected, too. Was there no end to these betrayals, blow after blow?

Slowly Mark's mind unraveled: *He'll pay for this.* Tortures and revenges flashed across his mind, jostling with tormenting images: Tristan exulting and laughing at him up his sleeve; Isolde mocking him for his absence from her bed; Isolde and Tristan sneering at him together, rejoicing in their power to destroy his peace.

Mark forced himself to breathe normally. They would both pay for this, they had to, or he would go mad. Now, what to do? He'd do it, whatever it was. He was the King.

"A letter from Sir Tristan, sire?" Andred asked, furrowing his brow in false concern. "Does that mean—?"

Snarling, Mark threw the letter in his face. "See for yourself!"

Andred scanned the letter with a soaring heart. So Tristan had left Mark to follow the Queen? Better than all, the best! Proof positive that Tristan was a traitor and the lover of the Queen. Still, he must tread carefully to bring this home. The slippery Mark would be even more unstable now.

Still pretending to read the letter, Andred watched Mark from under his eyelids as the King prowled the room, lashing out at everything in his path. One blow from his heavy riding crop sent a flagon of wine crashing to the ground, another scored the flesh on the back of one of the dogs. Howling, the poor creature limped off to lick its wound. Andred braced himself to withstand the oncoming storm.

Mark stood in the window and bayed like the dog he had hurt. "Who will deal with this traitor for me?"

Andred stood stock-still. It was the call he had waited for all his life. I will. Trust me, I will.

"Command me, sire. Tell me what is your wish," he said, holding down his raging excitement as best he could. His head was spinning. Gods above, how far would Mark go?

Mark's face contorted. "He has broken his oath. He has dishonored me."

"Such treachery deserves any punishment at your hands," Andred returned carefully, his eyes never leaving Mark.

With a furious kick, Mark drove a stool against the nearest wall. "God, if I had the right men about me, he'd pay for this!"

Andred saw the darkness gaping before him and his soul caught fire. What better chance would he have to bring Tristan down? He stepped forward with a new light in his eye. "You can trust me, sir. Only say the word, and I swear the traitor will pay."

"What?" Mark swiveled his red-veined eyes toward Andred. "How?"

Andred's mind was racing ahead. "If he's only just told you he's leaving, we can probably still catch him at the port. If you order him to be arrested and brought back here, that would give him a well-deserved shock."

A well-deserved shock, indeed. Smarting, Mark rolled the idea round his mind.

"Of course, he'd have to be waylaid and overcome. Tied and bound, too, if he won't come willingly." He paused. "A little rough handling would teach him a lesson, sire."

Mark slapped his whip against his boot. Andred was right, Tristan should be stopped. With a vengeful delight he saw Tristan, beaten and chastened, dragged back to Castle Dore. He'd make him beg for his life on his knees before all the court, then he'd throw him in a dungeon for his pains. And what if he perished down there in one of those windowless, stinking holes? That would teach him to break his allegiance to his King. Indeed, it would be a lesson to them all.

"Shall I do this, sire?" came Andred's even voice. "Do I have your command?"

Mark did not hesitate. "Yes, you do!" he cried recklessly. "Take a couple of knights, arrest the traitor Tristan, and return him to his true allegiance to me."

"And if he resists?" Andred pressed.

"Ambush him, beat him, do whatever you like," Mark shot back with murder in his heart.

Gods and Great Ones, thanks!

Andred wanted to laugh out loud. It was all the permission he needed to do his worst. And how would it be? In the heat of a fracas like that, any man could die. Perhaps through a blow to the head or by his own knife, when he drew it on others and they had to disarm him to defend themselves.

Of course, if this happened to Tristan, it would be a terrible loss. He'd be irreplaceable, there was no other word. There would never be another knight like Tristan, so handsome, courteous, and bold. Tragic indeed, a truly tragic death. Andred held back a wolfish grin. Already he could hear his own pious laments.

"Get about it, then," Mark bellowed. "No time to lose."

"No, sire. Farewell."

In a frenzy of joy, Andred hurried from the room, his mind bubbling like a poisoned well. Oh, you are mine now, Tristan, count your last hours. Our uncle the King has delivered you into my hand, and by all the Gods, I swear your day is done!

laring up through the dawn, a line of campfires lit the darkness of the shore. Soon the wind from the sea filled the air with the hot scent of fish, hare, and partridge, roasted with wild rosemary and thyme. Seated by the first of the fires, Cunnoch hunched himself over his early morning mead and looked forward to eating his fill.

And the free fish and game were all they were going to get here, he brooded, if Darath kept on behaving like a love-struck fool. He turned his back on the King's boat moored along the bay, and bitterly eyed Darath's royal pavilion farther up the shore. The young turkey cock was preening himself right now, preparing himself for his next meeting with the Queen.

Yet she'd told him already she would not see him today. Business of state, so they said, was taking up her time. Cunnoch laughed harshly. And how many times had the banquet she promised Darath been delayed?

Oh, she'd met with him, talked with him, walked with him, even ridden with him, but there was still no sign of the agreement they craved. Cunnoch closed his eyes, and the ravening hunger of his race spilled from his soul. *We want food, young Darath, not fine, flirting words. Land, not light glances from a pair of dancing eyes. There must be room here in Ireland for starving warriors to lay down their swords, or there's nothing for us but kill, kill!*

Kill and tear down, destroy, slash, and burn . . .

"How now?" came a well-known voice as Findra drew up. With him was the youth Agnomon, his sister's son, staring at sights no one else could see.

Cunnoch scowled and shook his head. He could find no easy greeting, no friendly words.

Findra nodded at Darath's pavilion, tipped now with the red-purple and gold of the rising sun. "So we wait another day on the will of the Queen?"

"What else?" Cunnoch fixed him with an eye of stone. He gestured to the army of men along the shore. "We trail after the rump of a woman, like motherless colts."

Agnomon quivered, and his strange eyes looked into a future that was plainly taking place before his troubled gaze.

"A white mare," he cried, "a white mare. And a herd led by a mare does not survive."

Findra guffawed his agreement. "He's right, you know. There's a hard winter ahead when the hay runs after the horse."

"Darath?" Cunnoch said grimly. "He can't help himself. He's in a fever to have her. And there's only one cure for that." He paused and tugged reminiscently at a lock of his hair. "You remember that woman you ran mad for when we were young? She led you a dance just like this. You had to take her by force and kill her in the end. It was the only way you could get her out of your mind."

Findra looked away. He remembered the woman all too well with her sharp eyes as black as sloes, thin body, and raven hair. But what was it that had filled his loins with fire, made him wild to possess her, then, when she refused him, had driven him out of his mind? He shook his head. Gone, all gone.

He gave a noncommittal grunt. "Well, Darath can't hope to take a ruling queen by force."

"Never." Cunnoch stared out across the bay. "But we can surely stop her from destroying him."

He got to his feet. Suddenly he had no stomach for roasted hare. Abandoning Findra and Agnomon without a word, he strode up the beach and entered Darath's tent.

"By your leave," he said rudely as he thrust his way in.

Darath sat on a camp stool at the table, oiling his hair. A stone pot of reeking bear grease stood at his elbow, and before him was a makeshift mirror of fire-blackened glass. Lifting his head, he grinned as Cunnoch scowled at him and took a seat. So the old curmudgeon had come to vent his spleen? Well, let him do his worst.

The silence deepened. Darath sucked in a breath of air, and the thick stench of the bear grease gave him strength. He cocked an eye at Cunnoch. "How goes it with you?"

"You're letting the Irish Queen make a fool of you," Cunnoch said flatly. "She's playing you like a fish on the end of a line."

"Not so." Darath gave a confident laugh and shook his oily locks to and fro. "I have hooked her, in truth."

Cunnoch's eyes bulged. "Whatever makes you think that?"

"I saw her and spoke with her. You did not."

"That's why her witchcraft hasn't worked on me," Cunnoch retorted. "But she's got you in her grip."

"By no means." Darath grinned. "Believe me, Cunnoch, I'm winning this battle of wits." His grin broadened, and he gave a lascivious wink. "She's mine, I tell you. She's falling in love with me."

Darkness and devils, what a young fool he was. Cunnoch steadied his voice. "On the contrary, you're in love with her. You've fallen like a tree in the forest, by the head. Beware of love, boy. It steals your manhood away."

Gods above, these miserable old fools . . .

Darath turned away and began deftly braiding his hair. Filling his mind with Isolde, he let Cunnoch's droning reproofs wash over his head. "You think you can court her strongly and get your own way . . . You've convinced yourself that she simply can't refuse . . . She means to flatter you till your resolution is lost and you're too soft to make war . . ."

Yes, Cunnoch, yes. Say what you like, old man. Smiling, Darath flashed his teeth at his own image in the glass and patted down his braids. In truth, he was looking well . . .

Cunnoch saw the smile and despaired. Roughly, he rallied his forces for another attack. "And she's married, of course."

"Of course." Darath gave a dismissive shrug. "But she's a follower of the Goddess, so she can change her consort whenever she likes. And since she's still childless after all these years, I'd say it's high time she did." He chuckled and stroked his thigh. "She needs a lover. A new knight."

"She has a knight." Cunnoch ground his teeth. "All the world knows that."

"What, Tristan of Lyonesse?" Darath said carelessly. "He's nothing; a queen must have her knights. And he's old. She's ripe for renewal by a younger man."

"Don't forget how old she is, too," Cunnoch said viciously. "She could almost be your mother. Another year or two and you'd be young enough to be her son."

"And none the worse for that." A look of raw lust lit Darath's handsome face. "An older woman with a younger man, that's the way of the Mother since the dawn of time."

Cunnoch was losing, he knew. But all his instincts made him fight to the end. "The Mother-right means she can change her consorts, you say. What if she casts you off in a time to come?"

Darath tossed his head with all the confidence of youth. "I'll be the one seeking fresh meat by then, not her. She'll be on her knees, begging me to stay." He looked into the future, and his face changed. "But I may not keep her that long. I can always kill her when she troubles me. And they all do in the end."

Suddenly the handsome features were ugly and cruel. But Cunnoch felt a fleeting reassurance in that. So the young whelp had not gone completely soft. And if he got Isolde into bed, he would not fail there, not when all the girls at home whispered of his prowess. If he bedded the Queen, that would strengthen their hand as they struggled with Isolde to stay. And afterward, it was true that an older woman would cling onto a young lover, that happened all the time.

If Darath let her live, that is . . .

He might bed her and wed her and kill her, and the Western Isle would be theirs . . .

Cunnoch smiled for the first time for days. And now the Queen had said she wouldn't see Darath today. So maybe he'd take the young King out on a hunt, just the two of them, so they could talk all this over in full. He could insist that Darath advance himself with the Queen, strengthen his hand, and shape up his ideas—

"Sir! Sir!" came a shout from outside the tent. A guard threw back the flap. Silhouetted against the horizon was a womanly figure mounted on a white mare. The sun glinted on a cloak of red-gold hair, a silver breastplate, and a shining spear.

"A white mare! A white mare!" came Agnomon's cry from the beach. "The herd led by a mare can never survive."

The guard bowed. "A messenger from Queen Isolde, sir. She has sent to say, will you to ride with her today?"

# chapter 22

The road fell steeply as it drew near the port. From the crest of the mountain ridge overlooking the sea, it carved its way down through thickly wooded slopes and narrowed sharply between two rocky bluffs. Dense undergrowth masked the entrance to the stony defile, and the trees wove a roof of branches overhead. It was the perfect place for an ambush, they all agreed.

An evening mist rose damply from the ground. Standing in the trees above the road, Fer de Gambon stroked his chin and looked nervously about. To his left, the powerful Sir Taboral was keeping a close watch on the highway, and farther off, two other shadowy figures waited in silence for their quarry to approach. In truth, Fer de Gambon had hoped to avoid an all-out attack, but Sir Andred's word was law. Sir Tristan was an enemy of the King. He must be arrested and brought back to court.

All very well, but...

Back at Castle Dore, Fer de Gambon had argued as strongly as he dared that treachery would be better than violence if they wanted Tristan alive. It would be easy to bribe the captain of the ship as soon as he embarked. All it would take was a fat purse of gold to see Tristan trapped in his cabin with a boatload of burly sailors to bring him ashore.

But the dark-faced Andred was adamant they must make the arrest themselves. There was gold in plenty, but it was to be used to hire a couple of local ruffians to back them up. Sir Tristan would never submit to their arrest, and he was too good a fighter for Fer de Gambon and Taboral to subdue him alone.

"And when you find these bullies, tell them not to hold back," Andred had instructed. "The King wants Tristan arrested, whatever it takes."

Fer de Gambon had followed his orders faithfully, and the two dark figures lurking with Taboral in the wood had been told they could use as much force as they liked to bring their man down. Brooding now in the damp midsummer wood, Fer de Gambon suddenly realized why Andred had been so careless of Tristan's safety at the hands of two roughnecks he did not know. Sir Tristan was not destined to survive this ambush and return to court. Sir Andred planned to use the King's orders to end his cousin's life.

Fer de Gambon covered a smile with his hand. If he was right, this could turn out very well. If Sir Tristan died in the struggle with no witnesses but himself and Taboral, then Sir Andred would be in their debt for the rest of his life. Fer de Gambon stroked down his velvet coat, and his blood raced. He could not wait to carry word of their triumph to Sir Andred at Castle Dore. He saw riches and furs and silks coming their way, and titles and land and a place at Sir Andred's elbow when he was King...

Hot dreams crowded his head. And all he had to do was to lie down in the road. That was Andred's plan.

"He won't be easy to ambush," Fer de Gambon had pointed out. "We'll never take him by surprise after all those years on the road."

Andred smiled. Tristan was still the chivalrous fool he'd always been.

"If he sees an injured man lying in the road, he'll never ride past," he said confidently. "That'll be you, de Gambon." He turned to the slow-witted Taboral, who was frowning deeply as he struggled to follow the plan. "And when he dismounts, you strike him from behind."

"Very good." The big knight's brow cleared. "I can do that."

"Get your ruffians to stand by with cords to tie him up," Andred went on. "And as soon as you've got him, send for me at once."

Then he had sent them on their way, racing to the port. And here they were, waiting for Tristan to arrive. Fer de Gambon looked down from his vantage point above the road and felt a glow in the depths of his stunted soul. The dark Gods might have created this narrow pass for this moment alone. From up here they could see Tristan approaching in good time to set up the ambush that would bring him down.

An owl hooted sadly in the distant trees. Tristan's death knell? Fer de Gambon grinned to himself. There'd be no other mourners around when Sir Tristan met his fate. He shivered with anticipation. Darkness and devils, let it be soon! He strained his ears for the sound of a horse. Was that the hollow clop of hooves ahead?

"He's coming," came Taboral's hoarse murmur at his elbow. "It's time for you to go down to the road."

A tremor of anxiety passed through Fer de Gambon. "You'll be ready for him, Taboral?" he asked. "He'll know it's a trap as soon as he sees my face."

Taboral drew his sword. "I'm ready, never fear," he boasted.

Fer de Gambon beckoned up the two dark-faced men in the rear. "And you?"

The two ruffians exchanged a glance and nodded. "Ready."

Twilight settled over the forest. The living loam breathed out the warmth of the day, and already it was dusk beneath the trees. The night-prowling creatures were beginning to venture abroad, and the earth was alive with bright eyes in the gloom. The sound of hooves drew nearer, and the unseen horseman came riding over the hill.

Tristan crested the mountain ridge with his heart aflame. He had hardly slept since leaving the Castle of Unnowne, still struggling to grasp the enormity of what he had done. Had he really ended his service with Mark? Was Isolde truly awaiting him in Ireland, ready to live openly with him as his wife?

Isolde, Isolde, at last . . .

Then the sharp shoots of bliss were almost too much to be borne. Half delirious with joy and transported with love, he had wandered the astral plain, beyond hunger and fatigue. All night he had heard the singing of the stars, and now he sang with them: Isolde, my lady. My lady and my love. As he rode to the port, he saw his past and his future becoming one seamless whole, a glittering web of hope and love fulfilled and life renewed. He saw Isolde robed in starlight and cloaked in her sun-bright hair, and he felt the trust and faith shining in her eyes. He had stood before her holding his soul in his hands and offered it up to her, perfect and whole.

He laughed to himself, but his voice cracked with strain. When she'd asked him to choose her before, why hadn't he seen then where his true allegiance lay? In all the years that he'd faithfully served Mark, the King had never once treated him with honor, either as his lord or his uncle or the last of his kin. And all that time Isolde had been strong and devoted and as true as steel.

And now, would there be a child to reward their love? In a dream, he imagined making love to Isolde as he had so often done before, but this time slowly, adoringly, like a sacrament. He pictured her lithe body swollen in pregnancy and great with child, then he saw her holding a tiny babe in her arms. Her baby and his. His mind tottered and his soul soared again: Isolde, my lady. My lady, my only love.

Slowly he became aware of a dark shape on the road. With a shock, he saw it was a body lying in the middle of the track. Sprawled facedown in the dust, the well-dressed figure showed no sign of life. "Alas, poor knight," Tristan cried.

Spurring forward, he threw himself hastily down from his horse. The knight lay in the dust, his cloak tangled over his head, much disheveled but with no sign of hurt. What had happened to bring him down like this?

He knelt by the prostrate form and reached for his pulse. "Can you hear me, sir?" he said urgently. "Are you—"

The next second, he felt the air stirring behind. Pure instinct sent him diving forward to avoid the blow. He rolled swiftly away, groping for the dagger at his belt. Even so, a sword slashed the angle of his shoulder, narrowly missing his neck. Scrambling up, he grabbed for the knight lying on the ground and sank the point of his dagger underneath his chin.

Instantly, the motionless form came to life. "Don't kill me," he screamed.

Now Tristan could see a tall, burly knight and a couple of shadowy figures lurking in the rear. Four of them? he grunted. Was that all? How many more of the murdering devils were hidden in the trees?

"Have at you!"

The big knight was charging at him with his sword upraised. But the two men in the rear did not back him up. Tristan renewed his hold on the knight in his grasp and dug the dagger into him for a second time. His own wound had opened and he could feel his blood running down, so he had little pity on the knight's frantic cries. Tightening his grip, he braved the assailant still poised to attack.

"Halt, or he dies!" he cried. "Throw down your sword and come forward, whoever you are."

The big knight threw a glance over his shoulder to the men in the rear. "Come on!" he roared.

But the two ruffians had had second thoughts. No one had told them how big and how fast and how dangerous this traveler would be. They had been promised an afternoon's brutal entertainment at his expense, shedding his blood, not risking their own skins. Their lives were worth more than money. In mutual unspoken agreement, the shadowy figures faded into the dusk.

Tristan heaved his prisoner to his feet and jabbed him violently again. "Tell him!" he hissed.

"Do what he says, Taboral!" came a frenzied scream. "Or he'll stab me to death!"

*Taboral?*

Then this wretch must be . . .

Tristan turned a wild gaze on the man in his grip. "Fer de Gambon!" he spat in disgust. "What in the name of the Gods are you doing here?"

"Don't blame him, sir." It was Taboral, his great face pale and sweating in the dusk. "It was all Sir Andred's—"

"Hold your tongue, you great fool!" howled Fer de Gambon. "Don't tell him anything."

Tristan released his hold and threw de Gambon to the ground.

"He has said enough," he ground out. "Indeed, he has told me all." He advanced on Taboral in a killing rage. "Come, sir, your sword," he said brusquely.

Without waiting for a reply, he tore the weapon from the big knight's grasp, then turned back to Fer de Gambon and did the same. In a frenzy, he hacked both the blades to bits and threw the weapons to the ground.

He could see Fer de Gambon sweating in fear. "Sir Tristan, you're a man of mercy," the knight gabbled. "Now we've told you the truth, I pray you, grant us a boon."

"A boon, a boon," echoed Taboral, though Tristan could tell he had no idea what it was.

Fer de Gambon's mean little eyes swiveled in his head, roaming from left to right in the hope of escape. "Sir, let us take service with you," he begged. "We'll follow you to the end of our days."

Tristan looked at him with shuddering contempt. "Take service with me? Not if you were the last men in the world."

Fer de Gambon's terror rose. "But we can't go back to Castle Dore."

Tristan shook his head. "Go where you will. Assassins and turncoats have no place with me."

Fer de Gambon fell to his knees and his voice rose to a wail. "Sir, we've failed the King. Our lives will be forfeit if we have to go back."

Tristan stood very still. "The King?" he demanded in a voice not his own.

"Yes, yes," de Gambon gabbled. "Sir Andred sent us here, but King Mark set him on."

Tristan stared at him. "The King." It was not a question. But he could not take it in.

"Yes, indeed." Fer de Gambon gave a shaky laugh. "Who else would have ordered this ambush? You're the King's nephew, his heir. Do you think we'd have dared to attack you on Sir Andred's word alone?"

"The King's kin?" echoed Taboral owlishly. "We'd never have dared."

The blood from Tristan's wound was spotting the ground at his feet. He stared unseeing at the bright red drops as de Gambon's words echoed round his head. Andred sent them here, but the King set them on. He knew it was true, it must be. These two cowards would never have dreamed of this by themselves.

Tristan felt his mind splitting. The dreadful knowledge worked through him, uprooting his heart, his soul. Containing the pain, he stood as still as a stone. What, Mark, his uncle, his only kin? His mother's brother and his own liege lord? Mark wanted him dead?

He fought for breath. From now on, Isolde would be all the kin he had. Praise the Gods, she was worth ten thousand of Mark. Now he knew he was right to place his life in Isolde's hands. To Ireland, then, he told himself shakily, as fast as you can. He turned away.

"Sir! Sir!" de Gambon bleated after him. "Have mercy on us, tell us what to do."

"Be thankful you've escaped death by my sword," he ground out, trembling with rage. "Make the wide world your home from this moment on, but never cross my path again as long as you live. Go now, before I punish you as you deserve. And may your Gods bring you to a better life."

"Thank you!"

"Thank you, sir!"

Catching his horse, he swung heavily into the saddle as Fer de Gambon and Taboral scrambled away. In a dream of misery, he continued his journey to the port and took ship for the Western Isle.

The captain raised a hand to feel the wind and gave a broad grin. "She's set fair, sir. We'll be there very soon."

Set fair.

Unexpectedly, Tristan found himself on the verge of tears. Goddess, Mother, he prayed, may my life's voyage with my lady be the same. In all the unfairness of life, grant us dignity and honor, truth and trust.

Weeping and rejoicing, he set his face to the west.

Wait for me, lady.

My lady and my love.

# chapter 23

*O*h, Tristan, Tristan . . .
*Where are you, my love?*

He was her first thought in the morning, and her last of the day as she lay down at night. Alone in her bed, she shivered with a dry, hard longing as her fingers remembered the touch and feel of him, and her body craved the attentions she so sorely missed.

And all the more now that she was ready to bear his child. Following the Lady's instructions with desperate care, she had prayed to the Mother the same night and begged Her help by the light of a smiling moon. Hardly able to breathe, she had taken the strange little bottle, read its ancient runes, and shivered at their raw, mysterious power.

> I AM LIFE AND THE MOTHER OF LIFE
> WHO CHOOSES ME RISKS ALL.

Dare she risk everything? She hovered in an agony of doubt. Then, in a headlong rush of courage, she brought the vial to her lips and threw the contents down. The thick, pungent liquid hit the back of her throat and made her choke. Gasping, she felt it working its way to her center, scouring every passageway and nerve. For a while she shook with a fever like a fit, then afterward she slept as sweetly as a child.

When she awoke, Tristan came into her mind in all the springtime glory of their love. She saw him tall, young, and ardent as he had been when they met, and waves of longing for him swept her, leaving her weak with desire, groaning in her bed. Then she knew that her body was urging her to make a child with Tristan, a child of their love.

These were the good days. At other times, anger shook her as a dog shakes a rat. *Where are you? Why don't you come to me? Can't you even send me word?*

Often she felt him near, and never nearer than now, when her longing seemed to bring him closer every hour. But the feeling was false. He was not near, he was not thinking of her. In all these weeks there had been no sign of him, nothing to suggest whether he lived or died. Indeed, he could have fallen by the way, tricked by harsh fate or trapped by some strange, enchanting woman, as the best knights often were.

*But you feel him approaching,* she tried to hearten herself. Sometimes she even caught his scent on the air, the rich green smell of the woodland, wholesome and sweet.

*False, all false.* Harshly, she suppressed her yearning desire. *Love deceives. And those in love always deceive themselves.*

Then a new sound came chiming into her ear.

*And never forget, my girl . . .*

Suddenly the late Queen was alive before her eyes, vibrant as ever in her flashing red and black.

*Remember, little one, all men betray.*

*Oh, Mawther, Mawther, women betray, too.*

*Women may betray, and Queens may do as they will. But never forget that you are always the Queen. You are the sovereignty and the spirit of the land. You must do what the land requires.*

*Must I court Darath, then? Humor his advances, feast him and flatter him?*

*And bed him, if need be. What else?*

This evening, a sweet silver mist rolled in from the sea as Brangwain silently robed her and groomed her and braided her hair. The queenly green silks and velvets soothed her mind, and her heart lifted as always at the kiss of her gossamer veil. When she moved, her light, drifting gown whispered like a willow in spring, and she knew the royal emeralds of Ireland in her crown put a new, commanding light in her sea-blue eyes. But every thought of Tristan was like a blow.

*What are you doing, where are you? What's keeping you away? Why aren't you here?*

*Above all, tonight.*

*Tonight I have to feast Darath. Why do I have to deal with him on my own? You'd know how to handle him for me, man to man.*

With an effort, she forced all these thoughts from her mind. This evening the needs of the country must come first. Whatever took place in her conference with Darath would shape the Western Isle for years to come.

Well, she was ready for him now. After hours of impassioned debate, she had hammered out a policy with her lords.

"We shall not fight," she had insisted. "till the last hope of settlement is gone."

"But the Picts have invaded our lands and killed our men," Sir Vaindor urged. "We should attack without mercy and kill them in return."

Isolde frowned. Vaindor would not be so eager for this fray if he had to fight himself. But it was easy enough to throw younger men's lives away.

"We must find out what they want," she responded firmly, "and what we can offer them without danger to ourselves."

Sir Gilhan seconded her gravely. "There's danger here, yes. Already they've gained a foothold on our northern shore, and they're here in Dubh Lein as our invited guests. We must be careful not to give too much away."

"Or too little," came the voice of old Doneal. "If we throw them off as a dog shakes off fleas, they'll only be back next spring to bite us again."

Hour after hour the discussion raged to and fro. At last she had won their agreement, but would Darath accept what she had to say? She gritted her teeth. *Only if I woo him and win his consent. Flirt and flatter, remember, advance and retreat. I must play him like a fish on a line. But never forget that this fish has teeth like a pike's. And all this I must do for Ireland, not for myself.*

*All for Ireland?* A mocking voice sounded inside her head. *Is that true, my dear? Aren't you enjoying the admiration of a fine young man?*

Was she? Was that what Darath had started to mean to her?

Thoughts and fears swirled round her head like wasps. But welling inside her she could feel a raw sensual curiosity, an excitement not felt for years. *Will he? Won't he?* danced unbidden through her mind.

*Will he? Won't he?*

*What?*

She did not know.

Well, she'd find out tonight as soon as he arrived. "We must take the lead from the first," she instructed Brangwain. "I am Queen here. He must see that I'm in command."

Coolly, she waited for the tread of booted feet, the cry of the guard, and the opening of the door. But one glance at Darath made her think again. He had dressed for battle, and it was clear that the struggle between them would not easily be won.

His leather kilt was the same chestnut brown as his eyes, adorned with a thousand studs of yellow gold. His shadowy gaze was lit with the same pinpoints of light, and she tried in vain to read the expression on his face. Strangely wrought swirls and scrolls in bronze and gold embellished his cloak, designed like his fabulous tattoos to bring him the power of the dragon and the magic of the boar. With an odd, unpleasant sensation she saw that despite all his finery, he still wore his four favorite daggers at his waist. *What, man? Even here, in a lady's chamber?*

He followed her gaze and laughed. "Lady, would you have me leave my friends behind? They are dearer to me than anything could be to you, for they've saved my life many times. Let me introduce you."

Fondly, he fingered the richly jeweled hilts, moving from the shortest to the longest as he spoke. "The youngest brother, that's Flesh-Biter here. Then there's Blood-Drinker, and Sun-Darkener comes next. But those who taste the oldest of my little clan know the truth of his name. I call him Go No More."

Crooning, he fingered the deadly, shining blades. *He loves them!* Isolde stood gripped with shock. Mesmerized, she watched the play of his hard brown hands and the glinting gold bangles snaking up his naked arms. His kingly bronze collar depicted a savage boar, and his belt bore a pair of stags fighting to the death. Already she felt his unbridled animal power. Smiling a wide, white smile, Darath struck home.

"Lady, I've offered you my bed and sword. What's your reply?"

Isolde gathered her strength and struck back. "What would your countrymen say to a ruling queen?"

"Only what they've said for a thousand years," he laughed. "We Picts trace our descent through our mothers, as you do here. The women rule, the men go to war."

Isolde raised her eyebrows. "Is it so?"

"From the dawn of our race. You and I spoke of the time of the mingling of our blood, when our forefathers courted your foremothers and won them as wives, on condition they could always be queens."

"I remember," Isolde cut in. "And the bravest of our women returned to strengthen your land." She paused to get his attention. "As some may do again."

Darath cocked his head, suddenly alert. "The women of Ireland return with us to our land? How?"

*Good!* She had taken him off balance. She could see he had no idea what she meant.

"We have women here in Ireland who still long for lusty lovers and men they can trust. Your people are weakened by famine and sickness and the loss of your crops. Let your men woo and win the boldest of our girls, and we'll send them to Pictland with grain for their sowing and cattle for their byres. There's not a female in Ireland who can't raise a crop and milk a cow. You and your men can take back our living treasure to restock your land anew."

"Take back?" he demanded, unsmiling. "You have decided, then, that we must leave?"

"Oh, I think you know you must," she replied in her gentlest tones. "Or we'll hack you to pieces and sweep you into the sea. This is your choice. You may leave your bones to rot on Ireland's shore or depart with honor and with the best of our women as wives."

His eyes widened, then darkened again. "Why should I believe you?"

She laughed in her throat. "Believe me, this is the best of what we have. I'm offering you honest plain dealing between a woman and a man, the way of the Mother as it has always been."

"The way of the Mother?" Catching her mood, he drew nearer, a dark light in his face.

She stepped forward to meet him and gave him her hand. "The way of a man with a woman since time began." She looked into his eyes and pushed on. "What do you say to my proposal, sir?" she asked huskily, lowering her gaze.

He took her hand and drew her toward him with an uncertain grin. Isolde suppressed another gleam of delight. *So I've surprised you again. Good, good!*

"Your proposal, lady?" he said urgently. "What about mine?"

The tattoo on his shoulder was gorgeous, rich, and strange. Her fingers itched to follow its lavish scrolls and trace the curves right up to the base of his throat. The strong scent of him reached her now, the moorland tang of his skin and the oil in his hair, the leather of his kilt and the sharp smell of danger he conveyed. Breathing deeply, she laid her hand on his chest with teasing slowness and prepared to disengage. "Oh, sir—"

She was rewarded with another sideways glance and for the first time felt ahead in this battle of wits. *Only keep him guessing,* she schooled herself, *play him to and fro, and you'll win the day. Then there'll be peace for Ireland and throughout all the isles. No killing at all, but the chance of love for our women and the hope of new life.*

*New life, yes!*

She scented the smell of victory in the air. An unfamiliar sense of her own power bloomed in her heart and ran triumphing through her veins. It lasted till she caught a commotion in the corridor, the jangle of spurs and a sudden shout from the guards.

"Out of my way!" she heard. "I must see the Queen."

Then the door opened and Tristan came striding through.

# chapter 24

$a$t first, all he saw was Isolde. The long, slow evening was fading into dusk, and her fiery hair burned dark in the silver light. Her sea-washed eyes called to him as they always did, her fine green gown shimmered with her every breath, and already he could feel her body in his arms.

Then he saw that she was not alone. Two figures were standing at the end of the chamber, Isolde and a man he did not know. A Pict, that was clear from his painted face and body, but whoever he was, he was standing too close to Isolde, far too close. They were not heart to heart or lip to lip, but the man's keen brown eyes did not hide the secret of his desire. Already the painted stranger could picture Isolde's long slender body lying next to his, Tristan could tell.

And Isolde? His head reeled. When he came in, she had been smiling, almost glowing with delight. Isolde *smiling* at this . . . this barbarian the way she always used to smile at him? And then leaping away from the stranger, dropping his hand? Tristan saw all this and could not believe what he saw.

He stared at Isolde as if he were seeing a ghost. A pale flush of horror had silenced her now, but she had been deep into her dealings with the Pict, that was plain. He had not slept on the voyage, daydreaming of this moment, and see what he had found. He laughed in disbelief and could not breathe for pain.

*Goddess! Mother!* Isolde berated herself in a torment of grief. *If only he'd come at another time! Then I'd have been beside myself with delight, rushing forward to throw myself into his arms. And now he's caught me with another man, a candlelight banquet ready by the wall and the sense of love in the air.*

*Darath's love.*

*His rival.*

*Another man.*

There was no sound but Tristan's labored breath. The three stood like standing stones, trapped in a moment as long as eternity. But every nerve and vein in Isolde was on fire. *Tristan—oh, Tristan—why did you come like this?*

She knew at once how it must look to him. It came to her in a second of bleak awakening that he'd never been present at her meetings with fellow rulers before, had never watched her mix statecraft and seduction as all women leaders did. It must look to him as if she desired Darath. *Goddess, Mother, show me what to do!*

And she could not even greet him as her body craved. One glance at the hawk-eyed Darath told her she had to keep up the pretense that Tristan was only one of her knights. *Oh, my love . . . I can't even hold you or kiss you or touch your hand.* Aching in every nerve, she stepped forward to meet him with a hollow smile.

"How are you, sir?" she said in her brightest tones. "I am glad to see you here."

False, brittle words. The smell of betrayal hung heavily in the air. Tristan looked at Darath and hot loathing filled his mind. The Pict was shorter than he was but almost as big-built, with shoulders like a stallion's and well-muscled thighs and flanks. He wore the deep bronze belt of a warrior, carved with running stags, and the boar collar of a king with the same hammered design.

Yet there was something womanly and repulsive about his braided hair, each knot knitted tightly at the scalp, then woven into its neighbor across his broad head. The florid blues and purples of his tattooed skin darkened his face like a creature of the night, and his eye upon Tristan had all the kindness of a wolf. Was it for this barbarian that Isolde had decked herself out in her favorite silks and emeralds with a hundred adornments besides?

Gods above, was she courting him? A lightning bolt of panic split Tristan's brain. Isolde had married before to keep Ireland safe. She only took Mark as her husband when she feared he would invade the Western Isle. Now, with Darath on her doorstep, would she try it again?

The Gods alone knew.

For a moment Tristan tasted the madness of jealousy, then he struggled with himself to set it aside. The Pict was a King, a fellow knight and a guest. The laws of chivalry and hospitality demanded that he be treated well.

"So, sire," he forced out. "Tristan of Lyonesse at your service. May I know your name?"

"My name?"

Darath felt Tristan's hatred and grinned. He loved to provoke these old men. "I am Darath the Pict," he threw out, "and I yield to no man."

Isolde treated him to a flashing stare. "Come, sir, you both meet as Kings. We'll have no fighting talk."

"As you wish," Darath shrugged. He would not concern himself with this blundering fool. Whoever had said he was the Queen's chosen one? If he'd been anything to Isolde, he'd have been here at her side.

A cruel laugh twisted his face. And look at him now, pale and sweating and speechless as a ghost. Get to your bed, old man, he conveyed in a soundless sneer. What, has the sea voyage been too much for you?

Isolde followed Darath's gaze. With a shock, she picked up Tristan's pallor and the sickly gray sheen on his skin. His left arm was hanging awkwardly at his side, and he was swaying on his feet.

*Goddess, Mother, are you sick, Tristan? What's happened to you?*

She turned to Darath. "Sire, I have had your proposal and you have had mine. Let us take time to consider, then meet again." She switched her attention to Tristan. "And Sir Tristan, you have traveled hard today. You must be ready to take to your quarters and rest."

"Till tomorrow, then." Darath sauntered forward and lingered over kissing Isolde's hand.

"Tomorrow, my lady," Tristan echoed in a deadly tone.

"Good night."

Stiffly, Isolde bowed them both out of the room. Even then she dared not give vent to her distress. The walls of a palace had ears, and her enemies and invaders were at the gates. When the stronghold of Dubh Lein was her own again, then she could weep her fill.

*Tristan, Tristan, my love, forgive me?*

*Goddess, Mother, spare him. Spare us both.*

# chapter 25

**n**ight had settled over Dubh Lein hours ago. The guards at the gates were drowsing over their pikes, and the prying eyes of the court had long closed in sleep. But Brangwain hurried through the shadowed corridors with her heart in her mouth. She did not trust that painted devil, the King of the Picts. And if he knew she'd been scouting the corridors so that the Queen could slip into Sir Tristan's quarters unobserved...

Brangwain heaved an angry sigh. Oh my lady, my lady, she mourned, what ill luck you had. What spiteful demons brought Sir Tristan here just as you had the Pictish King by the hand? And why was Sir Tristan already wounded and sick?

That at least they had dealt with, Brangwain reflected with a faint return of hope. Whoever attacked him had given him an ugly cut, but he was easier now. Brangwain sighed with the sense of one job at least well done. On Isolde's express orders, she had gone herself hotfoot with herbs and salves to minister to him.

When she got back to the Queen's chamber, Isolde was waiting by the door.

"All clear, my lady," Brangwain breathed.

Isolde nodded her thanks and slipped out as light as a ghost.

"Wish me well, Brangwain." Her words floated over her shoulder as she hurried away.

"I do, I do." The maid crossed all her fingers and plaited them into a knot. "Goddess, Mother, go with her all the way."

WILLOW BARK FOR REDUCING HIS FEVER, she'd ordered that. It would work against bone pain, too, if his wound was deep. Honey-salve for the sword-cut and all-heal to knit his flesh, he'd had all that. But she needed to see him to know how badly injured he was. And she could not do that till all the world was asleep.

*Oh, Tristan, Tristan . . .*

Feverishly Isolde hastened through the dark corridors to Tristan's side. She could hardly contain her tension. *Almost there . . .*

He was leaning out of the window as she came in, staring into the dark. He turned toward her, heavy with the smell of the night and the wildness of the midnight in his eyes. He had thrown off his jerkin and sword-belt, and his shirt hung loose above his dark breeches and boots. Now she saw the dressing on his shoulder where it met his neck, and could tell at once it was a considerable wound. But that was nothing to the hurt in his eyes.

They stood staring at one another in silence, then both spoke at once.

"How are you? What happened?"

"Lady, that stranger knight—?"

They broke off again, as tongue-tied and awkward as lovers half their age, and the pain between them as deep and wide as the sea.

Tristan was the first to recover. "I beg you, lady, tell me why the Pict is here?"

She felt angry and guilty at once. "The Picts have made landing on our northern shore," she said levelly. "Darath invaded with a mighty force of men."

He let out a sharp breath of surprise. "What did they want?"

"Ireland's total surrender to their will."

Tristan gasped. "Is that all?" he said sardonically.

Isolde hesitated. She dared not tell him of Darath's advances to her. "Yes," she said stiffly. "That's all."

He gave an angry laugh. "Isn't that enough? And when I arrived, I suppose you had summoned him to dismiss his demands with scorn?"

*Oh, Tristan . . .*

Isolde groaned inwardly. "No, I had not." She drew a careful breath. "I've been negotiating with him since he arrived."

"I don't understand," he said. He was very pale. "Why don't you take up his challenge?"

"And go to war?"

He nodded, his eyes on hers. After so long apart, the sight of her was a radiance to him, like sunlight on water or starshine dancing at night. For her sake, he could do anything.

"Sound the trysting horn, lady," he urged, "and raise all your knights. We can beat these invaders away from Ireland's shores."

"That has been done. All the knights of the island are here at my command."

Tristan's face cleared. "Then I'll lead your army and drive their King out myself."

She could hear the edge of rivalry in his voice. "Alas, no," she said in a low voice. "It may not be."

"Gods above, why not!" he cried in a sudden passion. "The knights of the Western Isle aren't afraid of the Picts. I'll direct the battle. You shall command it from the nearest hill."

*Goddess, Mother . . .*

"Enough men have died already. Many poor crannog-dwellers perished when the Picts came in."

Tristan tossed back his hair. "Then I'll challenge him to single combat," he said furiously. "I'll beat him like a dog and force him to withdraw."

"I want to avoid any fighting," she said slowly. "For now, I want to see what talk of peace will do."

"Peace?" Tristan's eyes flared. "Madam, war is the only language he'll understand. Kill or be killed, that's the law of the Picts."

Would he ever share her passion to keep the peace? "We may not kill," she said stubbornly. "It is against our faith. You know the Mother teaches love, not death."

He paused. A new coldness had entered his tone. "Even when they've killed your people?"

She heard her own voice growing colder as she replied. "Even then. Wrong added to grievous wrong does not make a right."

He looked at her with a strange and hostile regard. "This Darath . . . their King—"

Could he possibly say the name with more contempt? "Yes, sir," she answered through gritted teeth.

"You know he would kill you if he wanted to?"

"Kill me?"

Whatever she had been expecting, it was not this. Kill her? Darath? The man who had flattered and caressed her, blandished her to his bed?

"That's ridiculous." Isolde set her chin. "You don't know him. You can't say that."

Tristan turned away, defeated. Believe me, I know, hovered on his lips. There's no mistaking a killer when he looks you in the eye. Why would Isolde defend a man who had murdered her people and invaded her land? *Because she cares for him!* fell on his mind like a blow.

He could hardly bear to think it, let alone put it into words. Does she love him?

Surely she can't?

No, Isolde, no!

The gulf between them widened as they stood. She put out her hand to touch him and, with a dull horror, saw him flinch away. A thin film of sweat broke out on his brow, and she saw him sway.

"What happened to you?" she said in deep distress.

"I was ambushed on the road." He laughed bitterly. "By the knights of King Mark, no less. One struck me, but it's nothing. It's a clean wound; it will heal."

"Mark ordered your death?" She could not believe it. "Whatever for?"

"Because I sent word I was leaving him to follow you."

Isolde closed her eyes. So Tristan had made the choice she was praying for him to make, then he'd arrived to find her with another man...

*Oh, Tristan, no...*

"And Mark tried to kill you? No, no," she said helplessly. "It could not be."

Tristan stared at her implacably. "He sent Fer de Gambon and Taboral under Andred's command. They waylaid me. They were out to take my life."

"There you are, then," she cried, grasping at straws. "It's Andred, not Mark, behind this. Mark's a coward, but he's not a murderer."

"Trust me, lady . . ."

Tristan clenched his fists and cursed himself for a fool. Why hadn't he brought the rogue knights along with him? She'd have had to believe him if she'd heard it from their own mouths.

"Lady, lady," he groaned from the depths of his heart. "Mark tried to kill me. Your husband wants me dead!"

Isolde stared at him in anger. It could not be true. His mind was inflamed from his wound. He was not well. "Oh, sir . . ."

But why were they arguing like this? She hadn't seen him for weeks, and still he hadn't even tried to touch her hand. Why didn't he reach out for her, take her in his arms? If only he would hold her, kiss her, lie with her skin to skin. Whenever they'd been at odds with each other before, making love had always set them right . . .

*Tristan, Tristan, my love . . .*

She moved forward and took him by the hand. "Can we talk of something else?"

He did not respond, she saw with a sinking heart. But she pressed on as lightly as she could. "You know we spoke before about having a child."

"A child?" He looked as if he had never heard the word.

"Our child, Tristan." She gave him a tremulous smile. "And now it may come about, just as we talked of it in Castle Dore."

"We—?" Tristan turned away. "How may this be?"

His coldness was infectious. "I have seen the Lady," she said stiffly. He made no reply.

Gods above, did he have to make it so hard? "To have a child," Isolde repeated in rising distress. "I have taken the way of the Mother to unlock my womb."

"So." Tristan set his shoulders, a sign she recognized. And still he would not answer her or warm to her touch.

Did he believe her? She could not read his face. What was he thinking? His gaze was as opaque as milk. But suddenly she knew he did not trust her anymore. Above the wholesome scent of herbs and salve, she caught the sharp smell of doubt and rank distrust. And already he was drawing away from her, like a hurt creature of the forest seeking its lair.

She reached out in panic. "At least lie down with me for comfort. Let me hold you in my arms."

The gaze he turned on her was wild and aloof. "You must excuse me, lady."

"Excuse you...?"

*Goddess, Mother...*

Her heart plunging, Isolde pulled away. In all these years, he had never refused her before.

"I—" He broke off and turned his face away.

Isolde nodded, humbled and aghast. "Oh, your wound, of course... I'm sorry, I should have thought..."

He bowed his head. Neither of them could speak. Sadness fell between them like a weeping cloud. She gathered her forces and moved toward the door.

Never before had they parted without a kiss. She stood, hoping but hopeless, waiting for his farewell. But he did not stir.

"Good night," she said, in a voice not her own.

She had to strain to catch a low murmur in reply. She left him standing like marble, an image of nobility and pain. She was not to know that the fever from his wound had flared up again and his body was aflame. But above that, one thought was poisoning his mind and coursing through his veins like boiling oil.

*She does not love me.*

*She's chosen Darath the Pict.*

*And if she's taken the way of the Mother to unlock her womb, it's because she wants his child!*

# chapter 26

adam, you haven't had a wink of sleep all night."

Isolde smiled sadly at Brangwain. And neither have you, she did not need to say. They both knew that the maid, like a faithful shadow, slept when Isolde slept, ate when she ate, and laughed and wept with her, too. Now, in the gray light of dawn, Brangwain's dark-complexioned face looked drawn with fatigue, and there was a deeper question in her sloe-black eyes: what's to be done?

With another strained smile, Isolde acknowledged her concern and turned away: *I know, Brangwain, I know.*

The very thought of Tristan was a pain as sharp as toothache, as bad as the gnawing of the inward cankers that ate people alive. Isolde caught her breath. *Goddess, Mother, whatever shall we do?*

"I was so longing to see him," she said hollowly.

Brangwain nodded. "I know."

But not like this, hung between them like a sigh.

"I must not lose sight of Ireland," Isolde murmured. "I can still save our country from war."

"Ireland, always Ireland." Brangwain pursed her narrow lips. "You must think of Sir Tristan, too."

"Oh, I do, Brangwain, I do." Isolde held back a sad smile. Brangwain always championed Tristan with all the passion of her steadfast heart. "But I can't behave as I want while the Picts are here. I can't have him at my side during the day, I can't eat with him and dance with him at night, I can't even send to greet him in the morning in case someone spies the messenger going to and fro."

"You're right not to trust the Picts," Brangwain agreed grimly.

"That Cunnoch of theirs is a dangerous man. And any of them could have bribed the servants to snoop around."

Isolde felt a wild impulse to laugh. *My own servants spying on me? On us, on our love?*

She had come to Ireland to be free, and here she was trapped again in the toils of secrecy and deceit. Her soul convulsed. *Oh, Tristan, surely we must breathe the open air before we die! I beg you, help me to deal with the Picts and put an end to the threat we face. Don't destroy the fragile truce I'm building with Darath. Trust me to do right by the country and by you.*

She closed her eyes and put her whole heart into a prayer.

*Have faith, my love.*

*Hold on.*

A sad-faced sun was climbing up the sky and its pale, chilly rays were finding their way into the room.

"I must send to Darath," Isolde said slowly. "But I shan't even mention what we talked about last night. It's vital to keep him guessing about what happens next."

"Well, Sir Tristan's arrival will have helped us there," Brangwain put in with a sardonic smile. "The King of the Picts can hardly have been ready for that."

"No, indeed." Isolde felt her spirits rally. Brangwain was right; Tristan's sudden appearance could be turned to good account. It had certainly taken Darath by surprise. And Tristan loved her. He would not fail her now.

She threw back her head. "Send to Darath," she ordered crisply. "Tell him the Queen bids him welcome to the day. Say that I may ride today or I may not. Ask him to hold himself in readiness to meet later on. But only if affairs of state permit."

HE WOULD GO TO THE TILTYARD, that was the thing to do. Never mind the wound in his shoulder, anything was better than pacing like a caged beast in here. Tristan glanced around his quarters, feeling the walls closing in. He had always before loved the loam-washed apartment, with its fragrant, honey-waxed floors of golden oak. Its spacious rooms and rich furnishings seemed to him a mark of Isolde's love, and here they had known many passing moments of joy.

But with every thought of Isolde, the memory of Darath came treading heavily on its heels. Shaking, Tristan realized that he had never felt jealousy before. Now it stalked his mind like a lover's bane, and he knew he would neither sleep nor eat till it went away.

What was she doing now? he tormented himself. Was she with that painted creature, with *him*? He could not name the Pict, even in his own mind. The sun was up; the Pict could be with her already, smiling at her side. Or perhaps she had only pretended to send him away last night, and he'd shared her bed...?

And what about his men, that whole pack of tattooed barbarians camped out on the shore? Peace and kindness, she had insisted, faith and love. But didn't she see that the Picts must be strengthening their hold every day? Sooner or later it would come to a battle, he dared swear to that. If ever he'd seen an animal born to fight, it was Darath the Pict.

And born to...?

No!

He would not think of Isolde that way.

The madness of jealousy jabbed at Tristan again. With a flash of horror, he saw that he would gladly kill Darath, strike him down *now!* Then, in the coldness that followed the hot rush of blood, he'd abandon him like a dead dog and leave his body for the crows and wolves. The thought sickened him. Tristan, Tristan, what have you become?

Hurry, hurry, leave this place, get out...

With fingers as dead as sticks, he fumbled on his armor and reached for his sword and lance. Outside the chamber, the air was chill and sweet as late summer took on its early autumn tones, the wholesome world of nature a welcome respite from his overheated thoughts.

"Sir Tristan!"

"Why, there you are, sir."

As he strode through the palace and down through the outer courts, knight after knight hastened forward to shake his hand.

"Sir Tristan, by all that's wonderful," one cried. "God's above, you are welcome here."

Laughing, another appealed to his fellows standing around. "Who better to lead us against the Picts?"

"Welcome back to Dubh Lein, sir."

"Thank you. Thank you."

Every warm greeting revived Tristan's flagging heart. He had a part to play here, he knew it. Isolde loved him, and he had the knights' respect. They would follow wherever he led, and she would not fail him now. And she always had the interests of the country at heart. She knew what a queen had to do.

He pressed on to the stables with a lighter step. Once mounted and in the saddle, he turned the gray toward the tiltyard, stroking his neck. He could hardly feel the wound in his shoulder now. Yes, this had been the right thing to do.

"Just a pass or two for exercise, old friend," he murmured. "To blow the cobwebs away."

As they rode out of the castle, Tristan saw with relief that he had the tiltyard to himself. The long grassy enclosure held no other jousters thundering up and down, trying their skills on the targets all around. The straw knights sat on their wooden horses with their battered shields, waiting forlornly for a real knight to approach, and the rings dangling along the length of the track swayed idly in the breeze. Tristan could do what he liked. He chuckled with delight. Already he was starting to feel like himself again.

"Have at you, then!" he roared to the empty air.

He eased the gray forward, aiming for the target at the end of the green. Picking up the pace, he forgot the pain in his shoulder and blessed his luck that his sword arm was unhurt.

"Take that!" he cried. He slammed two of the straw opponents with a satisfying thud, sending each of them spinning as he galloped by. Returning down the other side of the green, he caught ring after ring on the point of his spear, dropping each one just as deftly in time for the next.

The flying hooves of the gray cut into the turf, and he drew the smell of the newly bruised grass deep into his lungs. He felt the jolt in his injured shoulder with every stride, but he did not care. As he roared at the dummy knights and raced to and fro, every stab of the fiery pain made him feel more alive.

"Go, friend. Go!"

Leaning forward, he breathed his excitement into the horse's ear. The willing gray hurtled eagerly up and down, turning tightly in its own circle at the end of every charge. At last its pale flanks were dark and foaming with sweat, and the pain in Tristan's shoulder was too much to be borne.

"Enough, boy," he murmured, easing up on the reins. The horse slowed and came to a halt, snorting heavily. Only then did Tristan become aware of a figure on the shadows by the gate, leaning against the wall. When had this stranger wandered into the tiltyard unseen and stayed to watch his ferocious mock battles and war-like display?

But it was not a stranger. It was the man he hated most in all the world.

As their eyes met, Darath straightened up and slowly brought his palms together in mock applause. "Well ridden, Sir Tristan." He waved sardonically toward the reeling straw dummies and wildly swinging rings. "You killed all your deadly enemies."

*And I could kill you!* In an instant, all Tristan's good humor vanished like summer snow. What a fool he must have looked, what a fool! All the time he'd been galloping up and down and cavorting like a boy, the Pict had been laughing at him, enjoying the show.

He could hardly speak for rage. The pain in his shoulder was much fiercer now, and he knew he was sweating from the strain. Darath sauntered toward him, smiling a slow smile. His white teeth gleamed in the sunlight, and Tristan wanted to knock them out of his head.

"So, sir," Darath went on, "I must leave you to your exercise. The Queen has sent for me."

Tristan tensed. Isolde had sent for this creature and not for him . . . and she'd be waiting for him now, in delight, in hope? He reached for the calmest tones he could find. "Farewell then, sir."

"Farewell."

Darath turned away, then swung back on his heel.

"Unless—?" he murmured speculatively, eyeing Tristan up and

down. He had nothing to lose. Isolde was not awaiting him; he had only made that up to annoy this old man. Maybe there was more sport to be had out of Tristan, after all? Old or not, he still looked like a fair fighter, and the chance of a pass in the tiltyard was not to be denied. Darath grinned. It was a while now since he had lifted a lance or swung a sword. And he'd vastly enjoy putting this great booby down.

Darath flexed his shoulders and bunched his hands, then favored Tristan with a smirking glance. "Is your sport done for the day?"

"It is."

"Is it indeed?" Darath persisted. "Must you leave?"

Don't listen to a word of this, urged Tristan's inner voice. Ride away. But a sudden hot thought made him look at Darath anew. Here, right here in the tiltyard, he could deal with his enemy now. He could beat the filthy wretch hollow and force him to leave Ireland as the price of his miserable life.

He ignored the pain shooting down his arm. "Must I leave?" he echoed Darath in mocking tones. "Not if Your Majesty will accept a challenge at my hands."

Darath stared at him. Then, with great deliberation, he drew the largest of his daggers from his belt and threw it to the ground. Tristan's horse shied violently as it quivered between his hooves.

"A challenge?" Darath laughed offensively. "I accept."

There was no thought in Tristan's mind now but *kill!* He cleared his throat and tried to find his voice. "They'll find you a mount at the stables and assist you to arm. I'll wait for you here."

Darath swept him an insolent bow. "Not for long, I hope."

The lean figure strode away in the sun. Watching him, Tristan felt himself growing cold. Shivering, he tried to reclaim his former heat: he'd need all the fire he had to do battle with the Pict. But the fine flame of hatred was gone. With growing dread he sat on the sweating gray, feeling his stomach for the fight draining away. One grim thought haunted him like a ghost. I wanted to kill you, Darath. Will you now kill me?

# chapter 27

b ow are you, my dear girl?"

Lovingly, Isolde reached up and stroked the satin-smooth nose of her sweet-natured mare. These pure white native ponies with their cornflower blue eyes had been bred for the Queens of Ireland since time began. Though shy, they were fleet and fearless and never held back. And this one, she knew, had no fear of the Painted Ones.

"You want to go out, my dear?" Isolde whispered in the mare's long, silky ear. "Well, you shall. Would you like to ride over the marshes today to see the birds?"

She swung cheerfully into the saddle and looked about. The first breath of autumn had brought a welcome bite to the air after the long endless days of summer heat. Soon the bright red and yellow leaves would be dancing about the yard, and the breeze already bore the tang of the turn of the year. Isolde stroked the mare's neck. "Ready for a gallop, then?"

All around her the stable yard was abuzz. Familiar with the hubbub of the morning ride, Isolde did not notice the excitement in one corner, where a group of the stable lads were still recovering from the appearance of the stranger in their midst.

"Remember the colors on him?" sighed one, lost in hero worship. "On his face, I mean, and the patterns on his shoulders and arms?"

"Yes, but when he gets into the tiltyard, it'll be his strength that counts," put in a small, skinny youth. "He looked as if he could take on an ox."

"And he's going to battle Sir Tristan?" giggled a third. "They'll kill each other. Neither of them will give in."

"Hush your mouth, lad."

Suddenly the stable master was among them, clipping ears left and right. "The Queen's riding today," he went on, "so get about your work, all of you."

Heads ringing, the lads scattered, bobbing and bowing to Isolde as they ran. She watched them with amusement and a deeper impulse, too. *May the Mother bless you, boys.* These were her people, and she loved them as her life. Every little thing like this made her glad to be home. *You will have many Queens and rulers in the Western Isle,* she thought, *but never one who loved you as I do.*

The morning sun was glancing over the grass. Raising her head, she saw the messenger she had sent to Darath hastening back toward her through the outer gate. "So, sir," she hailed him. "What news from the King of the Picts?"

The messenger shook his head. "The King was not with his people down by their ships. They said he'd come up here to the castle to attend on you. But as I came past the tiltyard, I saw him there."

Isolde did not move. "In the tiltyard?"

"In combat with Sir Tristan." The messenger shook his head. "I don't know how that came about."

*Oh, I do. It started the moment they met.* "Thank you, sir."

The messenger bowed and disappeared. Isolde sat on her horse like a woman of stone. *Darath and Tristan fighting? Goddess, Mother, the madness, the sadness of men! Who started this? Did it matter, when they both wanted to do it, no matter what the cost?*

She paused in sudden fear. *Oh Tristan . . . fighting with a wounded shoulder, too?*

*Even so, you could still kill Darath.*

*Or maybe he'll kill you.*

She leaned forward over the horse's neck. "Hurry, hurry! Go for me, girl," she breathed.

The mare sprang into a canter, clattering over the cobbles as fast as safety allowed. Isolde clapped her spurs to the mare's heaving sides. *Goddess, Mother, let me not come too late!*

"AGAIN, SIR!"

Panting, Tristan hardly recognized the sound of his own voice.

Gods above, what a fool he had been! Whatever had possessed him to throw down a challenge when he was exhausted and Darath was fresh in the field? When he had an injury and the Pict was fighting fit? And more, when his opponent was a much younger man?

Tristan gritted his teeth. That had been the worst folly of all. Endowed with the raw animal strength of youth, Darath was beating him. In this fiercely fought contest, the King of the Picts had the edge.

Which only made Tristan want to kill him more hotly and hopelessly with every stroke.

"Again!" he cried hoarsely. "Again."

But his enemy needed no encouragement. Darath was already hacking and swinging with the best.

Indeed, he had shocked Tristan from the very first. All his life, he saw now, he had been better than those he fought. Even at the court of Arthur and Guenevere, where the best knights in the land were to be found and the knights of the Round Table practiced their skill, only Lancelot or Gawain could occasionally bring him down. Lancelot had an unequaled suppleness and athleticism, and Gawain an almost unbeatable height and bulk. But he, Tristan, had both.

Or used to have, he cursed himself with a hard-breathing oath. When Darath returned, he had reentered the tiltyard at a gallop, bearing down on Tristan like avenging doom. Taken by surprise, Tristan had felt the wind of Darath's spear as the deadly blade caught him and sliced his side. With a swift sideways feint he'd missed the worst of the blow, but the sharp point had laid open the flesh and given him a painful wound.

First blood to Darath, then. Tristan spat with rage. Gods, how he hated him! In the second charge, fury lent strength to his spear, and, to his delight, the blow landed fair and square. But Darath took the impact, stayed in the saddle, then rode on. Tristan gasped in disbelief. Never had he seen that before.

"Again!" he called. "Again!" But nothing he could do succeeded in bringing his opponent down.

Still, I'll wear him down in the end, ran through Tristan's fevered brain. Get him off the horse, fight him on the ground. That's where his own height and weight would surely tell. But while Tristan was still contemplating that, Darath flung himself out of the saddle, all too eager to continue with dagger and sword. Tristan reached for his own sword, Glaeve, with little of his customary verve.

"Come, friend," he whispered bleakly, "let us do what we can."

*Morethanthat*, sir, *morethanthat*, the great blade hissed in response. Heartened, Tristan hefted his weapon and stepped into the fray, but his enemy was already hacking about him with a flurry of swinging blows. Recoiling, Tristan planted his feet on the ground and communed with his Gods. Let me beat this vile wretch, he prayed. Strengthen my arm, for the sake of my lady and love.

"Have at you!" Darath growled.

"And you!"

Tristan's stomach clenched as he ducked another swing. Leaping forward, he brought Glaeve down with all his force, and had the satisfaction of seeing Darath's head running with blood. The next moment he caught sight of Isolde in the morning sunlight, spurring madly toward the tiltyard across the plain. She was racing down from the castle, and even at this distance he could see the anger in her every move.

"Hold, sir!" he cried hoarsely to Darath, dropping his sword.

"D'you yield?" Darath shouted eagerly.

"Never!" Tristan snarled. He gestured toward the horizon. "But see there—the Queen."

The flying figure drew nearer with every stride. Together they waited, catching their breath and leaning heavily on their swords. Isolde watched the heaving, panting figures as she galloped up and could hardly contain her rage.

"So, sirs," she ground out, dragging the mare to a halt. Then her eye fell on Darath, his face a mask of blood. Her gaze switched to Tristan, and she raked him from head to foot.

"How did this begin?" she said in a deadly voice.

Darath saw Tristan's discomfort and gave a wolfish grin. "With a challenge, Your Majesty."

"Whose?" demanded Isolde in the same frozen tone.

Tristan stepped forward. "Mine."

There was an endless silence. Then Isolde fixed her eyes on the men on the ground and addressed them both. "You're injured, King Darath. You must retire to your ship, and I'll send my own healer to dress your wound. Sir Tristan, you will attend me back to Dubh Lein. And I shall feast you both in the Great Hall tonight."

She turned away without waiting for a reply.

*Goddess, Mother . . .*

She could hardly wait till she had Tristan alone. Riding back up the castle mound, acknowledging the bows and greetings of the people along the way, had never been such an ordeal before. She struggled to contain her temper as they made their way up through the courtyards to the Queen's House and into the safety of her chamber. Being forced to keep pace with Tristan's slow, painful movements enraged her still more. Gods above, he'd already been wounded once. Was he determined to injure himself again? Or had he only wanted to hurt Darath, whatever the cost to her hopes of making peace?

Brangwain took one look at her mistress as they came in and slipped away. "If you need me, lady, I shan't be far away . . ."

The door closed behind the maid's anxious back. Isolde turned on Tristan. His clothes were splattered with mud, and he reeked of sweat and the iron stink of blood. His eyes were black, and his face was wreathed in pain. Still, she must speak.

"You had a reason for this challenge, sir?"

Tristan felt his heart failing. This icy coldness was more than he could bear. With an effort he brought himself to meet her eye. "I thought I'd defeat the Pict and drive him from these shores."

"When you knew I favored negotiation?" Isolde flared. "When I wanted to avoid bloodshed above all else?"

"This was man-to-man," he returned stiffly. "He came upon me in the tiltyard and braved me out."

*So you had to fight him, of course.* With an effort, Isolde bit back the sharp retort. "For Ireland's sake, all I wanted was to keep the peace."

"If you say so, lady."

Isolde tensed. Was that a flicker of scorn in Tristan's eye? "What would you say, sir?"

"The King of the Picts is a personable man," he said harshly. "Any Queen might take pleasure in dealing with him. And many men would count themselves lucky to be in his place."

"You think there is something between us?"

"I can see it with my own eyes."

"Be careful, sir." Isolde held herself very still. "This is statecraft, not seduction, whatever you may think."

"Isn't it both?" he flashed back. "You married King Mark to save Ireland from war. Who could blame you if you tried the same again?"

She fought for control. "The same again—?"

Tristan did not flinch. "Buying off the King of the Picts by offering yourself."

She gasped with rage. "You think I—?"

"You are the Queen. You will do what you will do."

"Do you doubt me?" she cried.

"Lady, I don't. But a man like the Pict plays a woman like a fish on a hook."

"And you think I'm a woman like that?" She was almost beside herself.

All women are clay in the hands of unscrupulous men, leaped into his mind, but he managed to leave it unsaid.

"You may be playing him, too," he said slowly. "But should I stand by in silence when I see him fooling you?"

"Fooling me? How?"

"Flattering you. Courting you with fine words. Treating you like a woman and not like a queen."

Was it true? Isolde felt a tide of blistering ire. "And you would have done better?"

"Yes, indeed," Tristan fought back. "I would have beaten the Pict and forced him to yield. If I had, he'd be gone by now."

"Oh, so?" She could hardly contain her rage. "From what I saw in the tiltyard, he was beating you!"

The look of hurt on his face was his only reply. Angrier than ever, she tried to console herself. How dare he mistrust her so? How could she ever have called this man her true love, when he knew her so little and doubted her so much? And how could he be a suitable consort to her now or the father of her child?

She felt him moving toward her and looked up. His face was dark with a passion he could not express. "Send him away," he said on one low, intense note. "Send him away, or I must leave you now."

She looked at him with the blind black anger of love and for a terrible moment wished that he were dead. "Go, then, if you must."

"Lady—"

The look in her eyes made Tristan catch his breath. He had never wanted her more in all his life. Blindly, he moved to fold her to his chest. If only he could take her in his arms. But to his shock, she recoiled from his touch like the plague.

"I can't love you like this," she said with a fierce intensity. "If I lie with you, we could have a child. I'll never bring a child of anger into the world. If we do this at all, it must be with love."

"You wanted my child before." A new horror struck Tristan. "It's the Pict, isn't it?" he said wildly. "You want a child by him!"

"It was your child I wanted!" she burst out. She knew the pain between them was growing every moment, but she could not stop.

"But not now?" She could see he was white with shock. "You don't want a child of mine—?"

"How can I?" she raced on. "First you insist on choosing Mark over me. Then you come back without warning and make trouble like this." She turned away from him, ready to tear her hair. "How can I even think of bearing your child?"

He could hardly speak. "You mean to discard me. Then you'll take the Pict."

"No, I won't!"

"Will you make him your knight? Will you take him to your couch?"

"Tristan—"

"Will you marry him?"

"This is nonsense! Believe me, Tristan—"

"How can I?"

Isolde clutched her head. "D'you think I'm lying?"

Did he think that...? A thousand devils were dancing in Tristan's head.

Yes, he did, this very minute...

No, never in the world...

Clutching his head, he cried out like a stag in a trap. *Betrayed,* began to hammer at his mind. Betrayed by Isolde, ambushed and betrayed by Mark. There was no one left to trust in all the world.

He went through the sketchy motion of a bow. "I must leave you, lady," he said hoarsely. His eyes were as black as pits.

Terrified, Isolde reached out a hand. "Don't—"

But already he was halfway out of the room. And beaten in body and mind, she let him go.

# chapter 28

$a$ cloud-laden wind was sweeping in from the sea. In the woodlands behind Dubh Lein, the fiery berries of the rowan were setting the margins of the forest aflame, but everything else in the world was drowned in gray. Isolde stood in her window watching the falling rain. *Oh Tristan, Tristan . . . Where are you, my love?*

Meanwhile, she had to deal with Darath, and that was hard. Harder than ever, now that Tristan was gone.

Gone? Yes, without a farewell. Yet still she could hardly believe it. *Where are you, my love?*

At first she thought she would see him again that night, when all the court assembled in the Great Hall. They'd quarreled bitterly, that was true, but by nightfall all her anger had drained away. Remorse and fresh hope tripped over one another in her mind. *We can do better, love, we'll recover from this . . . I should have been more patient and loving, more, more, more . . .*

Then her heart leaped with the fresh and joyful thought, *At least he's still here. Tristan's here in Dubh Lein and he loves me still.* Thinking like this made Darath fade from view. *When I feast them together tonight, Tristan will outshine Darath as the sun outshines a star.*

*Tristan, oh, my love . .*

*How long till evening comes?*

"Come, Brangwain, make me fine," she ordered the maid, her skin crackling with excitement at the thought of seeing Tristan again. The long, slow, silvery hour when twilight descended and the fires were lit had always been her favorite time of the day. Old friends and new gathered by ones and twos, communing by candlelight as the wine went round. For Isolde, the scent of apple wood on the hearth and the candles' soft glow, the ruby gleam of the wine and the warmth of the flames, all blended together into one seamless joy. Tristan was here. He would be waiting for her now.

But he was not there when she entered the Great Hall. As she moved among the crowd, her eye never left the door. *Where are you, my love? Hurry, come to me, I am here.*

But he did not come. Sir Gilhan and her lords, her courtiers and her knights, all claimed her attention and wanted her company. Darath appeared in the doorway surrounded by his knights, and they made a magnificent entrance clad in leather, bronze, and gold, drawing breathless sighs from every woman in the room. The salt of the sea and their own wild animal tang came in with them, and the air in the chamber quickened with their approach. And still Tristan did not come.

"He must be keeping to his chamber, lady," Brangwain said, her face tight with concern. "To rest and recover himself."

Numbly, she agreed But his last words loomed dark in her mind. I must leave you, lady, he had said. Leave her? Did he mean leave and go away? Or had he simply intended to bid her good night? She could not get fears like this out of her head.

When did she know for sure that he would not come? Was it when her eyes were squinting from looking at the door, and she could no longer order the servants to delay the feast? When Darath seized her hand to lead her to her seat, and she knew he would not have dared if Tristan had been there? When she saw Darath's men exchange a flurry of bright-eyed nods and grins, and she knew they were sharing their master's triumph in their strange, yelping tongue?

She could not think of eating. Tristan was alone in his quarters. Was he injured, was he ill? But enthroned on the dais in full sight and sound of all, she could not even send a servant to find out for fear of drawing attention to herself. And Brangwain was probably right after all. Perhaps he only wanted to be left to rest. If he needed help, he could always send for her.

The night was long. She forced herself to entertain Darath royally, talking and laughing with his companions, too. But every moment dragged by like impending death, and she could not fight off a sense of dread. Now the feast was waning as the night wore on, and her hopes were fading, too. Dully, she watched the candles' winding shrouds making their way down each white, waxen stem.

At last all the farewells were made, and she could withdraw. In the chamber, Brangwain helped her to disrobe and hastened away.

"Till tomorrow, lady," she whispered. "And may the Great One Herself watch over you tonight."

Dry-eyed, Isolde nodded and retired to bed. She would not weep. Tomorrow she'd send for Tristan and repair this rift. She'd make him see that she loved him after all. She would make things better. Everything would come right. Tossing and turning, she dozed in and out of newly minted hopes and bright dreams.

A fitful night gave way to a troubled dawn. Dense, clay-colored clouds boiled up from the face of the sea and lumbered over the horizon, darkening the sky. Crosswinds rose to meet them and it started to rain. Rivulets of water ran down the greeny glass as Isolde stood in her window watching time tick away. Time passed unnoticed but for slow loss of hope. And still the clouds wept till all the world dissolved in tears.

*Where are you, Tristan? Where are you, my love?*

"News from the harbor, lady." Brangwain came through the door grimly shaking the rain from her cloak. "My lord has taken ship."

"Taken ship? Without saying good-bye?"

"They said at the quay that he sailed away last night."

"On the evening tide?"

"No, at noon."

That meant he had gone straight from her chamber down to the dock. Isolde's mouth was dry. "Where did he go?"

Brangwain pursed her lips. "No one knows. He boarded the ship, paid the captain, and away they went."

*Gone, then, without a word.* All her rage returned and filled her to the brim. *Is this the way to treat a woman who has loved you faithfully for all these years? Is this how you leave me—without a word of good-bye?*

Isolde's head lifted and her shoulders snapped back. *You may leave me, sir, but I will not leave you. As soon as I can, I'll come seeking you.*

She fixed her eyes on Brangwain. "Any word from the King of the Picts?"

Brangwain snorted in disgust. "He's here, madam, in attendance outside. He says he'll wait all day if he has to, but he'll see you in the end."

"Very well." Isolde drew a breath. "I did not send for him, and I can't deal with him now. Let him wait."

THE KING OF THE PICTS MADE TO WAIT like a servant—like a dog? Brooding, Cunnoch watched Darath from beneath his lids as the younger man paced the antechamber to and fro. Darath had lost his mind to this Irish queen, that was plain. All that Cunnoch and the others had warned him against had come true.

And still the young fool would not hear him. Furiously, the older knight eyed the faint rays of sun through the window and resolved to try again. They had walked up to Dubh Lein in the first chilly fingers of dawn and waited out the downpour that ensued. Now the sky was clear, and there was no reason why the Queen and Darath could not walk or ride out. Except that she wanted to keep him dangling here.

Cunnoch crossed to the window and pretended to study the sky. "The rain's stopped," he announced unnecessarily. "If the Queen won't see you, we should get back to the ships."

Darath stretched his lips in the semblance of a grin. "Oh, she will."

"What makes you think that? I swear she has no intention of seeing you today."

"I have a better opinion of her than you do."

Cunnoch shook his head. "Why d'you trust her?" he growled. "Can't you see what she's doing to you?"

Darath looked at him with an expressionless stare. "What's that?"

Cunnoch gestured toward the window, which framed a skein of wild geese forging its way through the sky. "Autumn's here now and winter's on its way. Once the storms set in, we're caught like rats in a trap. The Queen won't even have to call up her knights. When our supplies are exhausted, we'll die of hunger as we'd have done if we'd stayed at home."

Again he received the same bland, empty look. "I know," Darath said.

Cunnoch gritted his teeth. "Why are we here?" he ground out.

Darath fixed his gaze on the ceiling. "To win the Queen."

"In marriage?" Cunnoch fumed in disbelief. "She's playing with you, boy. She won't marry you. Sir Tristan's her knight, and there's many here who'll swear he's her only love."

"And he's gone."

"Forever?"

Darath bared his teeth. "I'm ready to deal with him if he comes back."

"And of course Isolde would be pleased if you did that," Cunnoch scoffed. "D'you think she'd ever forgive you for killing her knight?"

Darath sighed. Why was Cunnoch trying to provoke him? Sooner or later he'd have to admit he was right. "Hear me, Cunnoch—"

"Sire—" came a voice from outside. The door opened and a servant entered with a bow. "This way, if you please, King Darath. The Queen begs your attendance now."

# chapter 29

How beautiful are Thy ways, O Lord our God!

Sighing with satisfaction, Dom Arraganzo pressed forward into the Audience Chamber of Castle Dore. If he had ever doubted God's wisdom in making women the lower creatures of His world, he saw the divine purpose now. It was absolutely right that the female of the species should be kept out of the world, restricted to nunneries and confined to women's quarters when they were at home. Dealing with the two daughters of the King of Dun Haven had made him more thankful than ever that he lived his life among men.

For the two Princesses walking behind him now were a living advertisement for the sins of Eve. Oh, he was sure they were following him demurely enough, as they all made their way into the presence of King Mark. With his liberal chastisement, their father had certainly taught them how to behave. But what a pair they were!

The fat one—lean as he was, Arraganzo could not think of her any other way—Theodora as they called her, embodied all Eve's greed, cupidity, and lust. The thin one, Divinia, was consumed with the same beady-eyed curiosity that had caused the Fall of Man, a deadly hunger to know things women should not know. Neither of them had a shred of respect for men, not even a Papal Legate or their father the King. Arraganzo sighed. It was clear to him now why their father had beaten them so much. If he'd been the King of Dun Haven, he'd have laid on the rod himself.

Still, they would undoubtedly interest King Mark. Either of them would make a stir on her own, and together they formed a challenge to any man. One round and plump as a pudding, one slender and fragile like a hazel twig in spring. One dark, one fair; one inviting, one cool and remote. The fat one trussed up in a rich mulberry velvet with a heavy gold train, the thin one floating in a cloud of pale blue voile. Arraganzo reviewed his own handiwork with pride. Whatever could be done for these two girls had been done to the hilt.

And now they were about to be put to the test. Ahead of them Mark gazed openmouthed from his throne, already transfixed by the sight of them. Around him, the busy courtiers whispered and stared, assessing the procession as it came along. In the front, Arraganzo was a vision in scarlet from his cardinal's cap to his hand-stitched kid-skin boots. Behind him came the two sisters, striking in their contrasted shades of earth and sky, attended by their maids in virginal white. Bringing up the rear like two dark clouds were the black-clad Dominian and his pupil, Simeon. Arraganzo purred with delight. No wonder Mark was goggling like a fool. Castle Dore had never seen anything like it before.

They came to a halt at the foot of the throne. Dominian moved forward with a clumsy bow.

"Your Majesty," he proclaimed, "may I present a visitor from the Holy See, the Pope's emissary from Rome, the Cardinal Legate of Spain?"

Mark gazed at Arraganzo, overawed. "We are honored, my lord."

"Oh, sire, the honor is mine." Arraganzo made a courtly Spanish flourish and stepped aside. "And may I commend two young Christian princesses to your care." He waved a hand at the fat one. "Princess Theodora," he declaimed.

Simeon gave Theodora a violent jab in the back. Prompted, Theodora fell to her knees and clasped her hands. "Sire, give us your blessing."

"And the Princess Divinia," Arraganzo intoned.

Hearing her name, Divinia knelt, too. "Bless us, sire," she breathed in a high, lisping voice.

Arraganzo leaned forward. "Their father the King is dying," he said quietly. "He begs Your Majesty will take them as your wards."

"My wards, eh?" Mark murmured, stroking his chin as he eyed the two girls up and down. The well-covered one was a fine-looking wench, to be sure, but the half-starved waif in blue was appealing, too.

And both were staring at him with huge sad eyes as if he were the most important man on earth. Well, nothing wrong with that. Nice to see two young women showing such mature judgment and good sense.

He turned to Arraganzo. "Soon to be orphans, you say?"

Arraganzo inclined his head. "Unless they find a new father in yourself. A king should be a father to his people, as Our Lord decreed. And sometimes he may be more."

Mark's shriveled spirit soared. Oh yes, oh yes. It would be an excellent thing to have these two beauties at court, hanging on his every word and following him devotedly to and fro. He could certainly be a good father to them, and maybe more. Well, to one of them, at least. Now, which one?

Then an inner prompting made him shake his head. He turned to Arraganzo with regret. "Alas, I have another commitment I can't escape."

Arraganzo raised a magnificent eyebrow. "And what is that?"

"The Quest for the Holy Grail," said Mark importantly. "Half the knights of the Round Table have already set out, and my knights and I must play our part in that. We'd have been on the road by now but for Tristan's treachery and desertion, the villainous wretch."

Dominian folded his hands. "Sire, the Quest is not your concern. You may leave that to King Arthur and his knights."

Arraganzo nodded. "There is more than one way to do God's work, my son."

"But I swore to join them," Mark protested. "The names of the Grail knights will never die. I want to be remembered along with Lancelot, Gawain, and Galahad. We'll still be honored in a thousand years."

Arraganzo stepped forward, drawing himself up. "Do not desire to join the fellowship of the Grail," he said commandingly. "The Quest they follow is only one of many of God's works. As you see, He has another task for you here. The lives of these two virgins lie at your feet."

Virgins, eh? Mark felt his interest quickening at the thought. Virgins, yes, of course, they wouldn't have known any men. Neither of them would scorn him and spurn him as Isolde did. And fresh meat would be more than welcome after the stale, resentful mistress he had cast off.

"And think of this, sire," Arraganzo resumed. "The Holy Grail is the pure vessel of Christ's passion and the symbol of His love. It can only be found by the most peerless knight in the world, free from sin, without weakness, taint, or shame."

He paused, closely watching Mark's face. Not me, then, was clearly written in every twitch of the King's muddy countenance and shifting, flickering eyes. Certainly not me.

Arraganzo seized his moment and pressed on. "For the rest of mankind, there is another grail. That is the holy innocence of a maiden, whose pure body they desire to penetrate. Mortal men may possess that holy grail through carnal knowledge of a virgin's inviolate vessel when they plunge themselves in her maiden form."

"Is it so?" Mark was overwhelmed.

"It is God's word and will," the Cardinal Legate averred in his most thrilling tones, "His sacred mystery revealed to His lesser creation here on earth. A man loses himself in a woman to gain what all men seek. That is the terror, that is the miracle."

Mark looked at the two Princesses with new eyes. Terror and miracle, eh? he chuckled to himself. Which was which? The fat one could well be a terror, but the shy one might prove to be a miracle. The quiet ones were often the best in bed.

"So, sire?"

Arraganzo, Dominian, the two Princesses, and Simeon the young monk were watching Mark in a silence that gripped all the court. He struggled to find a masterful, kingly tone.

"If God wills me to take these two lost maidens under my wing," he declared in ringing tones, "it shall be done. Bring them to my privy apartments, where I may consider their needs."

He rose to his feet. Barely containing themselves, the courtiers bowed as the King, the Princesses, and the men of God left the chamber, then fell to gossiping with a vengeance as they all followed out. At last the chamber was empty but for a lone figure lurking in the shadow of the dais. Breathing heavily and gripping the hilt of his sword, Andred tried in vain to still his raging discontent.

What else, he fumed, did the jealous Gods have in store for him? First the failed ambush as Tristan rode to the port, leaving his deadly rival alive and at large after all the money he had spent to achieve the opposite result. Then those cretins Fer de Gambon and Taboral limping back to court, ready to blackmail him as soon as they dared. Already he could hear their weaselly demands: We need money, sir, and a place at court, then help us to a piece of land or a small estate. He sucked in his breath and gave a mirthless grin. He'd probably have to kill them now, of course. The only question was when.

And now the accursed Christians were on the move. Andred groaned aloud. If they got Mark interested in a Christian girl, that scarlet-clad eminence from Rome would have the marriage to Isolde annulled before you could say "pagan whore." That very night one of those princesses would be in Mark's bed. Nine months later there'd be a bouncing Christian bairn and Andred would be as Isolde and Tristan were, no longer wanted or needed, a part of Mark's past.

And with no hope of coming to the throne.

So, then . . .

Motionless, Andred thought long and hard. What to do? Wait till he saw which princess caught Mark's eye, then have her killed before the wedding day? Lay false information that they were unchaste and get them both sent back to Dun Haven in disgrace? Poison them with a draught that mimicked the wasting sickness that was so often the death of young maids? Or better still—he laughed soundlessly—poison Mark?

He laughed with bitter delight. Already he could see Mark falling prey to the cleverer of the two Princesses who were even now trotting happily into the King's House. A savage, baleful grin took over his face. Do what you will, uncle dear, I shall have you in the end. And princesses both, enjoy your time in Castle Dore. It will all be over before you've even begun to understand what you're doing here.

# chapter 30

The mountain range lay black against the sky. Below it, the land ran gently down to the sea, where the line of the forest broke around a sheltered bay. From a distance, the whole landscape seemed asleep. But the early morning foxes, weasels, and stoats, like the ravens, crows, and blackbirds wheeling overhead, were intrigued to see that they had company.

Winding down the valley came a procession of horses and men, bright with lances and banners and gleaming with silver and gold. The new dawn, still red and raw in the sky, lit their path through the trees and down to the sandy shore. Isolde rode with Darath at the head of the glittering line, while all his companions and knights rode behind. Apart from the few who had stayed to guard the ships, all the Picts were there in force.

As they had to be, Isolde knew, if her plan was to succeed.

*If . . .*

No one trusted her judgment, she knew. She could hear the Picts now muttering behind her back, sharing their doubts and dissatisfaction in dark tones. Even though she did not understand what was said, there was no mistaking Cunnoch's sharply expressed suspicion and its echo in Findra's low, guarded replies. Findra's young kinsman, Agnomon, was staring and muttering to himself as he rode along. All Darath's men were against her, that was plain. Even their familiar strong, heathery smell had changed to something more feral and furtive as they hid their fears.

And in Dubh Lein, too, her lords had dismissed her scheme. In her own home and heartland, even the loyal Sir Gilhan had turned against her as he never had before.

"It'll never succeed," he said flatly. "Not with the Picts." He leaned forward across the Council table, folding his battle-scarred hands. "At least take a troop of our soldiers to keep you from harm."

Isolde shook her head. "That would only convince the Picts they have something to fear."

Gilhan frowned in despair. "Madam, this may well cost you your life."

"My life?" She had laughed then, an unconvincing trill. "As long as our men do their part, the Picts won't kill me. Why should they?"

"Oh, madam—" Sir Doneal burst in with savage scorn. "A Pict never needs a reason to kill. If they spurn your offer, kiss the world good-bye."

*The world and Tristan.*

*Oh, Tristan, Tristan, where are you, my love?*

Her heart wept. Then her mother's voice came dropping into her ear. *No tears, no fears. Remember you are Queen.*

She stiffened her spine. *And a queen does what is best for the land.*

She felt a hot hand on hers and came back to herself. "You are silent, lady. What are your thoughts?"

It was Darath, of course, riding too close to her side. She flashed him an enigmatic smile. "Why, nothing I care to reveal."

"No?" His bright eyes were alive with malice. "Let me guess. You're pining for Sir Tristan, your long-serving knight."

Had she realized before how cruel he could be? With a great effort, she shrugged the comment off. "A queen will always have her knights."

He looked around and laughed with open disdain. "Even here?"

She speared him with a glance. "A thousand knights leap to my bidding here. Why do you worry about one?"

Darath returned her shrug. "He was a gallant opponent when we fought. I hope his wounds have not taken a turn for the worse."

*What wounds? Oh, Tristan, did you suffer more than I knew?* She struggled to recapture a light, bantering tone. "Enough of Sir Tristan. The King of the Picts has all my interest now."

*As does delaying you here till the storms of the season set in,* she did not say. *Keeping you and your Picts in Ireland as winter descends. Do you see that, sir? Do you understand the game?*

Her thoughts were thudding so loudly she felt he must hear. *If not, you play into my hands. You invaded our land in midsummer, when the sea was calm. But now*—she looked at the wintry sea and wanted to laugh—*trapped by storms, cut off from hearth and home, my enemy becomes my prisoner.*

*And I alone hold the key to this island of ours.*

"See, sir."

She pointed ahead through the trees. As the forest thinned out, they saw a wide natural harbor with a row of neat houses behind, all clustered together around the edge of the bay. Between the forest and the houses lay a ring of tidy homesteads and well-kept farms, sheltered by the trees from the worst of the winter storms.

On the beach, a row of fishing boats lay drawn up above the waterline, each with its ropes and nets coiled neatly inside. Passing between the houses and pausing to laugh and gossip on the sand were the women of the village, old and young, many of them with babies on their backs and children round their knees, but all healthy and strong. Most had the red-gold hair and pale skin of Ireland, but here and there were some with a fall of hair as black and glossy as a beetle and eyes as blue as a speedwell in spring. Even in the dull light of a December day, the village teemed with life.

Isolde watched the young mothers and their babies with a peculiar pain. *This is how I would be, if I had Tristan's child.* She forced her mind away.

She turned to Darath and gestured to the scene below. "What do you notice here?"

He was dazzled by the women, she could see, especially the tallest, a queenly young thing with a basket of fish at her feet. He shook his head, unable to tear his eyes away. "Nothing."

"Nothing?" Isolde questioned. "Look again. Some time ago a huge shoal of fish was seen far out at sea, greater than any have ever seen here before. All the men, young and old, took to the boats to harvest this rare tide. None of them came back. Ever since we call the village Womenswold, 'the place of women,' in our tongue."

She had caught his interest, she could see. "What happened?" Darath demanded, openmouthed.

"No one knows. A great wave, perhaps, to overwhelm the fleet, or some monster of the deep. Afterward the sea threw up the masts and timbers of the sunken ships. But the men were gone as if they had never been."

Darath's gaze swiveled back to the beach. "So all these women live here as widows or virgins in a world without men?"

"And not by choice," Isolde agreed somberly. "Their life is very hard."

She pulled her horse around and looked Darath in the eye. Behind him she could see Cunnoch and his knights, tense and alert, drinking in every word she said.

"Sir, when we met," she began, "you spoke of the past, when the men of your land wooed the women of ours. Here in this village it could happen again. If you and your men court these women and win their consent, I promise a bride-gift for each marriage made. Do this, and you and your men will return to Pictland far richer than you came, with grain for your barns and cattle for your byres. Above all you'll have strong healthy women to renew your race. And there will be kith and kin bonds between us from now on."

He gave an arrogant laugh. "I came here for a queen, not for a fisherwife. And I will not leave without taking you to my bed." He turned to look at his knights, grinned widely, and raised his voice. "We refuse."

Isolde smiled. "Think again, sir." She drew her sword and flourished it over her head. At her signal, the dark forest came to life. A thousand lances glinted among the trees, and a thousand rays of dancing, broken light flashed on the arrowheads pointed at the Picts.

"It's an ambush!" screamed Cunnoch, diving for his sword. "She's going to kill us all!"

"Agnomon, here!" Already Findra had gathered the staring young man to his side and was prepared to sell his life for his sister's son.

"You have nothing to fear," Isolde called back to them in ringing tones. "Your lives are safe. My word is still is my bond. And you see I'm alone and undefended among you here. But I give you a choice. Take the offer I have made to your King, woo our women, and marry those who will consent. If they are unwilling to leave their native place, wed them and make your homes here. You'll be dearly welcome if you stay in Ireland with us."

They were staring at her like rabbits at a snake. Determinedly, she pressed on. "For every woman who goes back to your land, we'll send cattle and grain. She and her man and her children will always be able to come back to the Western Isle at any time. And any man of the Picts who marries one of our women becomes one of us, too. That is our offer."

She paused, and drew a deep breath. "Take it, and peace and plenty lie ahead. Refuse it"—she gestured toward the forest with its hidden force of men—"and we give you war, blood, and defeat." She lifted her sword and swung it through the air. "Like my mother and all my fore-mothers they call the battle ravens of the Western Isle, I shall sweep you into the sea."

"But lady—" Darath's face was glistening like a man in the throes of death. "I wanted your love," he said in a faint, ghastly voice.

Isolde shook her head sadly. "Sir, I am not for you. Somewhere the woman awaits you who will be your Queen. And all women are queens where the Goddess rules."

Darath mustered a sickly grin. "Perhaps," he murmured.

Isolde nodded. "Take time to consider your choice. We sent orders ahead that you and your men are to be welcomed here. But you have your own welcome, as you can see."

Smiling, she indicated a group of the villagers drawing toward them up the path from the beach. At their head was the tall young woman Darath had noticed before, with a cloak of black hair and piercing forget-me-not eyes. She wore a handsome cloak of silver gray fur, and her step had the leap of a salmon in spring.

"Welcome, strangers," she called boldly, eyeing the Picts up and down. "I am Medhebar, the head of this village here. Do you come as enemies or friends?"

Isolde looked at Darath. "What will your answer be?"

"Friends, lady," he cried hoarsely.

Medhebar opened her arms and gestured to her basket of fish. "Then come and feast with us. You're just in time for the catch."

Already the younger Picts were jumping down from their mounts. Cunnoch still sat on his horse, snarling fiercely at all around, but Findra and Agnomon were yielding, Isolde could see. She smiled at Medhebar. "Thank you for your gracious hospitality. We are pleased to accept."

As she dismounted, she saw that more and more of the Picts were doing the same. She turned to speak to Medhebar, who was still keenly assessing the newcomers with open interest and delight.

There was a voice in her ear. "Lady, what of me?"

Darath stood before her like a man bereft. Suddenly he looked young and forlorn, a lost boy. But there was only one answer she could make to Darath now.

"Sir, your fate lies before you. Another woman is waiting to take you to her arms."

"Not you, then." He gritted his teeth, and she felt his pain. Then he flashed the familiar grin and tossed back his hair. "At least give me something to remember you by."

She laughed, startled. "What?"

He held an endless pause. "A kiss."

Isolde paused. But why not? He was a gallant loser, and the peace she had won for Ireland was worth the price.

"Come here," she said. As he stepped toward her, she took his face between her hands and kissed him on the lips.

"Lady!" he gasped. She felt him trembling. Then he threw his arms round her and crushed her to his chest.

"Again!"

*Oh, Tristan . . .*

Once, long ago, Tristan had kissed another woman, and the fear that he'd been unfaithful had killed her heart. But then she learned that the woman had helped him escape from prison and that he had bought his freedom with that kiss. *I am not betraying Tristan,* she told herself. *Or if I am, I am buying Ireland's future with this kiss of mine. I am making allies of the Picts, not enemies.*

His kiss was fleshy yet hard, a boy's kiss, not a man's. Again her deep hunger for Tristan began to stir. *Where are you? Will I find you again? If I do, can you forgive this? Can I ever forgive you?*

She hardly felt Darath disengage from her, but she could tell he was reluctant to let go his hold. As she opened her eyes, his were shining with desire.

"Darkness and devils!" he cried passionately. "If only you would take me to your bed! Think what ancient dragon magic we two would unleash, the warrior daughters we would make and the blood-drinking sons. It's a sin against nature to deny me that."

"You will have warrior girls and fearless boys," she promised him with a smile. "Believe me, that is written in your stars."

"As you are in mine," he murmured, kissing her hand. "Call on me again if ever you need a sword. I'll be your champion till the day I die."

"And before that, sir, you will bring your Queen and your warrior brood to visit us here." She paused for emphasis. "In peace. You must swear an oath of peace."

"That may be hard." Darath glanced broodingly at his lords. "Still, we have had the blood adventure we wanted when we left. Our hungry swords have had their meat and drink."

"And lady, you have given us a promise of hope," Findra put in. "If we go back with all the goods you have promised us, we are not leaving here as beaten men."

"And remember, we leave with our lives." Agnomon's strange yelping voice had lost none of its power to disturb. "With all our blood still beating in our veins, not spilled in a foreign land to fatten the earth."

"That too, boy," Cunnoch agreed with a dangerous grin. "If that's all we care about."

"Think, Cunnoch—" Darath leaned forward intensely to engage the older knight.

Cunnoch made a fiery response, and the talk went to and fro. Isolde stepped quietly away, holding her peace. There would be more arguments yet among the Picts, she was sure of that. Cunnoch would not readily abandon his lust for war, and at least some of the knights would follow him. And the women of the village would take some hard wooing by the Pictish men: they thought too well of themselves in Womenswold to yield at the first blush.

But as was the way of the world since time began, the young men would try. She saw with interest that the younger Picts were already shaping up to the challenge. While Darath and his knights remained huddled in a tight conclave, some were shyly approaching the unmarried girls, others boldly approaching the young mothers, tousling the heads of their babies and teasing the boys.

*This will succeed,* came to her with deep thankfulness. *It will come about.* It would take time—*how long, Mother, how long?*—and her work would not be complete till the last of the Picts had sailed with the last of the brides.

That meant weeks, even months, of patient discussions, easing the fears and concerns of both sides. These were big decisions, and they could not be rushed. But then she would be free to leave Ireland and follow Tristan, wherever he had gone. She would have done her duty to the land, and she'd be free to seek her love.

And then—*Goddess, Mother, speed my sails and direct my flight!*

Then, and only then, could she take ship to look for Tristan. But she would search high and low. She would never give up.

And one day . . .

One day . . .

*I shall find you again, my love, though you've gone to the ends of the earth.*

# chapter 31

*a* low gray light was glimmering through the trees. All the world was asleep underneath the forest's green eternal roof, and the woodland creatures still huddled in their holes. It would be noon before the brooding red morning sun lent any warmth to the dank, chilly earth. But the woodman moving quietly along the narrow path knew when his quarry would be out that day, as he knew many things town people never guessed.

Yet he would be a townsman before he died. Let it be soon, Great Ones, soon! he implored his Gods. The life of the forest had kept his father contented for three-score years. His brothers and sisters likewise all serenely carried on the ancient ways. But ever since boyhood, he had craved the world of the town.

His sharp eyes glistened. The men there wore cloaks and tunics of fine wool, not rough hempen shirts, homespun breeches in dull woodland green, and pelts for a coat. They had daggers and swords swinging at their sides, while he had only his short, pointed killing stick in one hand, a bow in the other, and half a dozen arrows on his back.

Well, not for much longer. He knew how to better himself. No other forester for miles around could equal his catch, and he had trapped and sold his furs and scrimped and saved, working like a dog. Even now, in the dead of the year, when all the earth slumbered and winter struggled to give way to spring, the game was there if you knew where to look. And if you had what it took to stay on the hunt while others gave up. He set his chin. He would not—could not—give up.

Not if he wanted to leave the forest behind. Yet he knew that for some, the world of tree and leaf that he longed to quit was a sweet refuge and a second home. While he dreamed of a brick-built house with shutters at the windows and a solid roof of tile, others came here to live under the shelter of bracken, wicker, and furze. Take the newcomer now, the stranger who had slipped in almost unnoticed a while ago. Whoever he was, he lived as lightly as an animal, moving from place to place. Despite the cold and damp, he made no fires and curled up like a fox in a hollow at the end of the day.

And here he was again. The woodman paused as he saw signs of a careful passage through the wood, traces so slight that they could hardly be seen. Could a wild dog, a badger, or a wolf have broken the tips of that fern and trodden those new shoots of grass? Yes, indeed. But was he sure that this animal was a man? Without a shadow of a doubt.

And what kind of man hid here and did not want to be seen? An outlaw, of course. But for every rogue or villain who tried to hide, there'd be half a dozen or more who wanted him caught. They'd often pay good money to know where he was. Money a poor man could use and needed now.

The morning sun was lifting above the trees. A squirrel stood poised on a branch overhead, illuminated by the sudden shaft of light. Moving with care, the woodman reached for his bow and arrow and shot it down. As he crossed the clearing to retrieve it, he thought of the price the glossy red skin would bring when he sold his pelts. Good enough, but not as much as the bounty he'd get for a human hide.

He scratched his thin beard and grinned. Next time he went to market in the town, he'd ask around. No harm in seeing if there was a hue and cry out for any wanted men. He flexed his shoulders, feeling the sun on his back. Spring was coming, it was getting warmer every day. And before winter, he'd have no need to care about rain, frost, or snow. The bad weather would be for those in the forest to bear, as they always had. But he'd be snug and warm. He'd be living in town.

I'M COMING, TRISTAN.

*Wait for me, my love.*

Was he still her love? She did not know.

Some days she yearned for him with a hunger so cruel she thought she was losing her mind. At other times, she felt like cutting him out of her life. After twenty years, that he could misjudge her so . . . mistrust her so . . .

Isolde lost her breath whenever she thought about this.

And to fail her so badly just when she needed him most, needed him both for herself and for Ireland, invaded by the Picts. But he only wanted to treat her as a woman, not as a queen. And he'd stupidly tried to deal with Darath man-to-man, not King to King nor even knight to knight.

Darath . . .

She drew the soft morning air deep into her lungs and felt comfort return. That at least had turned out as she had hoped. Weeks had gone by as Darath's men courted the women of the Wold, who wanted to prove that they wouldn't be easily won. Their leader had come to Isolde, laughing at the men's pride. Medhebar's fine eyes were dancing as she came through the door, pushing back her dark hair. She smelled of fresh winds and the wide open sea, and she would be a prize for any man. Isolde's heart lifted to see such beauty. *My people. My land.*

"Lady, the Picts think they are offering us the world," Medhebar said. "But we see a hard struggle ahead in a barren, stony land."

Isolde paused. "I'm sure you're right about that. But you struggle here, and your lives are often hard. Over there every woman would have a man at her side. Picts are loyal and strong and ready to play the man's part. Here you have to be both women and men."

Medhebar looked at her thoughtfully. "We hear other things, too. Some say that they kill their women from time to time."

Isolde sighed.

*Ah, Medhebar . . .*

*All men kill women from time to time. That is life.*

*In spirit, if not in body. That is love.*

Aloud she said, "Men can only kill women if the women themselves are not strong. Your fate has taught you how to take care of yourselves. Those who go with the Picts will have the strength of the other women around them, too. Along with your faith in yourselves, that's all you'll need."

"And the Picts will be leaving hostages in Womenswold," Medhebar added with a dancing gleam in her eye. "Some of their men want to stay back and marry here."

Isolde laughed. "Then you have good surety that they will behave."

She paused, her head on one side. Some of the leading Picts had courted Medhebar, flocking around her like moths to a flame. Darath himself had come to Ireland in search of a queen. Now that Isolde had refused him, would he think of Medhebar?

She smiled at the lovely young woman. "And you? What will you do?"

Medhebar gave her mischievous smile in return. "I shall go with the new brides to Pictland and see them settled there. Then I can see what that life might hold for me. After that I shall decide."

Isolde nodded. Young as she was, Medhebar was wise. *Grant me wisdom now, Great One,* she prayed. *Or at least the common sense that I should have at my years!*

At last they all sailed away, and Isolde was free to leave. Now she could start the search for her lost love. All winter long she had thought and dreamed of Tristan. Now, with her duty done, she was in a fever to be gone.

But still the country came first. On her quest, she would find it hard without Brangwain. But she knew she had to search for Tristan alone. And who better to take care of Dubh Lein while she was away?

"Do this for me, Brangwain? And for my lord?"

"If you say so, my lady," came the subdued reply.

It was not in Brangwain's nature to defy Isolde's command. But the maid could not suppress her concern as she said good-bye.

"Where are you going, lady?" she said, her lilting accent sharpened by distress. "At least tell me that."

A soft, sad smile spread over Isolde's face. "Why, I think you know already. Where else would Tristan be?"

Brangwain's tensely coiled body relaxed in some relief. "Yes, of course, my lady. Now I understand."

Isolde nodded. Where else would Tristan go but back to Cornwall and back to the wildwood? All the world knew that his mother had run mad with grief when her child was due and had given birth to Tristan in a hollow tree. Born in the depths of the forest, he had always been half woodland creature, half man, and he had carried the greenwood within him ever since. *Oh my love, you may be a knight of the Round Table and King of Lyonesse,* Isolde thought, *but you are at one with the hawk and the stag in your heart.*

"Cornwall, ho!" cried the captain as at last they embarked. The sea had been calm, even smiling, and the winds were kind. The weather smiled, and the voyage from Ireland passed by in a dream. The worst of the winter storms were behind them now, and the Lady had leveled the waters and made the way straight. *Thank you, Lady. And Great One, my thanks to you.*

Yet all the way over from Ireland she had asked herself, *Will he really be there?* The world was wide, and no one knew better than Tristan where a man could disappear. In his tournament days, he had ridden the high roads of France, Spain, and Gaul, and other kingdoms besides. He had seen lands of ice where the sun never rose, and others where for months it never set. They had talked, as lovers do, of traveling together to the very ends of the earth. Would he now try to lose himself there alone?

No, she knew the place, for sure. He would go back to Cornwall, but surely not back to King Mark. Now that he believed that Mark had tried to kill him on the road, would he risk his life by returning to the court? Would any man choose to reenter the lair of a wolf? Not unless he had completely lost his mind.

Yet it must be Cornwall, she was sure of that. A wounded beast always drags itself back home. Tristan had been a wanderer all his life, but there was one place on earth that he called his own. Long ago he had won an ancient castle by the fortunes of war, and the Gods themselves might have fashioned it for him. Locked away in the depths of the forest, it lay deep in a cleft in the mountain, overgrown by trees. Whoever had built it, back in the mists of time, had set it into the face of the hillside to keep it secret from passing eyes. The knight who owned it had killed many men for his sport and had chosen this retreat to hide from the world.

The dead knight had called his fortress Castle Pleure, because under him it had been a place of tears. When he claimed it for Isolde and she gave it to him, Tristan at once renamed it Castle Bel Content, for the great joy that they had discovered there. But the crumbling old grange was not really a castle at all. It had no towers, no moat, no battlements, no means of defense. All it offered was a sanctuary away from the court, and for many years they had found it a safe place to hide.

*And that is why I know I'll find you there, my love.*

So she had set her course for Cornwall and the forest there. She had slipped into the land by a quiet, faraway port, to keep any word of her arrival from reaching Mark. She could not think of going to Castle Dore till she'd found Tristan. Then together they would decide what to do.

*Together . . .*

*Soon, my love, very soon.*

Now, where was she going? Distracted, Isolde drew her horse to a halt and looked around. Days and nights of traveling by sea and land were behind her now, and every hour she had felt herself drawing nearer to him. Sometimes she thought his spirit was just within reach, around the next corner or over the next hill.

*On, go on.*

*Only a little farther.*

*Oh Tristan, Tristan . . .*

The morning sun was sailing up the sky. The earth groaned and stirred, awaking from its winter sleep. The living fragrance of the forest was all around her now. She sighed, and filled her lungs with the sweet breath of hope. Soon, very soon, she would have him in her arms.

Step-by-step she pressed on through the wood. *Not far now.* Already her mind was leaping ahead with joy. Only Brangwain and a trusted few knew of the peaceful, secluded old grange, which they had kept secret for just such a time as this. No one would find them or trouble them while they rested here.

Indeed, without help, no one could find it at all. In the depths of the forest, travelers passed the wooded cleft in the hillside unawares. Even the door was mantled with thick ivy, hiding the way in. A sudden fear overtook her: *Will I remember where it is?* She urged her horse forward, holding her misgivings down. *Look out for the hidden hollow in the side of the hill. Where the undergrowth is densest, the way in is there.*

Even then, she nearly passed it. But a voice from long ago murmured, *It is here.* Dismounting, she secured her horse's bridle and turned the beast loose to graze. Slipping into the narrow cleft, she plunged through bramble and fern and found her way to the door. She was troubled to see that the low door looked unopened since the last time they left. But Tristan of all men knew how to cover his tracks. Of course, he would make the entrance look undisturbed.

*Oh Tristan, Tristan, my love . . .*

Trembling, she opened the door. Passing over the threshold and into the wide hall, she had to hold back her tears. *Goddess, Mother, how I love this place!* Ivy mantled all the windows, and every room was bathed in greenish light. But all the rooms inside were clean and dry, and a sweet loamy fragrance hung in the air. After the chill of the forest, the old grange was warm, and she felt a kindly welcome in the soft green gloom.

Her heart soared. "Tristan?" she called. "Are you there?"

She moved eagerly forward through the well-furnished apartments, bright with rugs and tapestries, all glimmering with the same woodland light. One room gave onto another, low, spacious chambers floored in mellow oak, looking out through green curtains of ivy to the forest beyond. Still calling, she threw open a pair of doors.

"Tristan? Are you there?"

A slight movement on the floor caught her eye. A brown wood mouse sat up on her haunches, holding Isolde in a long, steady gaze. Her huge dark eyes were liquid with unshed tears, and her fragile pink hands were clasped in deep concern.

Isolde stood stock-still. "What is it, little Mother?" she whispered fearfully.

The small plump creature bowed her shining head. *You know, Isolde, what has brought me here.*

And suddenly she knew. Tristan was not there. And the Gods alone knew where in the world he might be.

# chapter 32

The tiny messenger bowed again and was gone. Isolde moistened her dry lips and tried to form a word of blessing as she went. *Thank you, Little Mother. The truth must always be welcomed, however it hurts.* Yet still her inner voice said, *He must be here.*

"Tristan? Are you there?"

Nothing but echoing silence throughout the house.

*Tristan, where are you?*

*Answer me, answer me, love!*

*You're here, aren't you?*

*I'm coming, I'll find you, never fear.*

Blindly, she crashed through room after empty room. But she would not give up hope. At the top of the house was the attic, and there, if anywhere, Tristan must come to rest. She had nursed him there for weeks as he recovered from his near-fatal battle with the knight who had owned the castle before. After that they had briefly stayed on, living for the first time almost as man and wife, and her sore heart revived to remember the joy of that time. Tucked away under the eaves, the long rambling attic chamber looked out over the trees, and all day long the sun filled it with light. It had little round windows that smiled like kindly eyes, and the birds in the branches used to sing them to sleep.

And now it stood empty and gaping, bare of everything except a film of dust. Disturbed by her entrance, the tiny motes leaped and danced, lit by the slanting rays of the afternoon sun. Unmoved, the solid old four-poster bed, the oak chairs and tables, and the dusty armor-stand all stared back as if to say, Greetings, lady, what are you doing here? Half dazed, she watched them as her last hope died.

Tristan was not here. He was not in the house. He had not returned like a wounded beast to his cave.

*Wrong, Isolde!* She stood nursing her failure, aching with emptiness. How could she have been so wrong?

In a dream, she turned and left the empty house. Her horse came at once to her call, and she mounted without thinking and set off into the wood. *Where am I going?* she wondered, and back the answer came. *Search the wood. The truth lies in the wood.*

Closing her eyes, she placed herself in the Goddess's hands. *Take me to Tristan,* she prayed, *help me find my love.* A dove called mournfully from a distant pine, and the trees overhead sighed and nodded their heads.

*In . . .*

*Deeper in . . .*

As the afternoon lengthened, she scoured the depths of the wood, checking this way and that for any signs of life. At last she saw a thin plume of smoke rising above the trees, and the forest thinned out toward a clearing ahead. A little farther and a low hovel came into view, its door standing open to catch the last of the sun. She caught a glimpse of someone inside and shivered with the violence of sudden hope. Had Tristan taken shelter in this woodman's hut?

*Tristan, Tristan . . .*

Now she was near enough to see through the door. In the fading light, the rough, windowless croft was already dark inside, but she could make out the shape of a man moving around. Tall and broadshouldered, dressed in woodland green . . . *Oh, Tristan . . . Tristan . . .*

In a passion of haste, she threw herself down from the horse and stumbled frantically to the door.

*Tristan, Tristan, are you there, my love?*

But the tall man who blocked her entrance was not Tristan but a hard-faced, bearded stranger with a brace of dead partridges dangling from his hand. Behind him more game hung swinging from the roof, and the air was full of the stink of curing pelts. He had recently killed, she could see; he had blood on his hands.

"I heard you coming, lady," the woodman said unpleasantly. "What d'you want with me?"

He had another smear of blood on his right cheek. On the floor of his hovel lay heaps of the day's kill. A mouthful of broken teeth flashed as he spoke, and there was something hostile in his level stare. Isolde drew herself up. Did he think she was going to try to steal his precious catch?

"Forgive me if I intruded into your domain," she said stiffly. "I am seeking another man, and I thought he might have sheltered here."

She's looking for the stranger.

A shoot of triumph ran through the woodman's brain. It has to be him, there's no one else hiding round here. And just look at the woman who's asking after him now. To judge from her, whoever he may be, there'll be money in this for sure.

Greedily, he eyed Isolde up and down, taking in the rich velvet riding habit, the soft leather cloak, and the matching gloves and boots. Jewels in abundance, too, at her neck and waist. Her headdress was far finer than any he'd seen in town, and the Shining Ones themselves might have woven her veil.

Who was she? Never mind. He could smell money, money in his hand.

"No offense," he said carelessly. "Who are you looking for, then? I might have seen him, I'm out in the forest all day."

"Oh, sir—"

Isolde hovered in an agony of doubt. If Tristan was here, this wretch was likely to know. But she could not trust him, she was sure of that.

Yet what harm could he do, living in the forest like this? If he talked about her, who on earth could he tell? And there was no one else to ask.

"Have you seen anyone?" she questioned, reaching for her purse. "Or anything?"

He pretended to think. "Yes, I have."

"Who?" she burst out, her eyes wild with hope.

"Well, there's the other woodlanders," he said cunningly. "Them as live hereabouts."

"No, not a woodlander," she cried. "This is a knight I seek. A man of distinction. He comes from the court."

A knight of the court. The woodman held his breath. Now he knew that the stranger was a court renegade, a knight on the run. The King himself might pay to know where he was.

"Sorry, lady." He tugged at his scrubby beard and shook his head. "No one like that round here, we're too far from court." He nodded at the purse in her hand and gave a meaningful glance. "We're all poor folk in the forest, every one."

"Thank you, sir."

Drooping, she pressed a coin into his hand and turned to go. He watched her ride away sadly through the trees. A silver-green twilight was falling over the earth, and the sweet mists of evening were rising from the ground. The forester cocked a practiced eye at the clouds. Rain was on its way. There was no more hunting that he could do tonight.

But tomorrow . . .

Tomorrow he would make his way to court.

Yes, it would be a long way, but no farther than a determined man could walk. Someone there, maybe even King Mark himself, would surely pay for what he had learned just now. A runaway from the court was hiding in his wood, and a fine lady was scattering gold to find where he was.

The woodman clutched Isolde's gold coin in awe, feeling his future unfolding as he stood. Then he took himself in hand. Just finish with the kill, my lad, and get yourself to bed. Tomorrow morning, you'll want to be off at dawn. But as you go through the town, take a look at the houses there. One of them could be yours before the winter comes.

Get to court, tell the King, and see what happens then.

Off before dawn, that's the way.

Just get to the King.

START BEFORE DAWN, that's the thing to do.

Numbly, Isolde took up the reins and rejoined the forest path. Make a fresh start tomorrow, look farther afield. Night was falling, and there was no shelter here. Back in Castle Bel Content, at least she'd be warm and dry, and the food in her saddlebag would see her through the night.

Then tomorrow...

She put the thought from her mind. Tomorrow would have to take care of itself.

The twilight forest was settling for the night. All around her the woodland creatures were snuggling down in their beds with small contented snufflings and soft sighs. Loneliness fell on her like a weeping cloud. *Every bird, every bat has a mate; even the weasel and the tiny shrew have someone to comfort them. All except me.*

As she made her way onward, a light rain began to fall. *All the world is in mourning for my love.*

The bracken and fern grew tall at the side of the path. Brooding, she cut and slashed at it with her whip. Where was he? She had come all this way looking for him, when he should be seeking her to make his peace. He'd done all he could in Ireland to make things hard for her, then he'd disappeared. Was that the act of a loving partner or a loyal knight?

A watery winter moon shone fitfully through the trees. Farther down the path, she saw a hollow oak and knew at once she had not passed it before. In the gathering dusk, she had lost her way.

With a sinking heart, she retraced her steps. The drizzle was steadier now, and dark thoughts seemed to lie in ambush behind every tree.

If only Tristan had not challenged Darath and forced him to fight...

If only she had not been so ready to let Tristan go...

But she must not give way to dark thoughts. *Enough, Isolde,* she berated herself. *Keep to the path. That will bring you home.*

*If I can call it home when my true love is away.*

*Enough!*

The cold and damp had pierced her to the bone. She huddled deeper into her mantle and tried to warm her fingers on the horse's furry back.

"A little farther, my dear," she whispered, stroking its neck, "and then we'll go no more today."

She knew she had to watch out for the entrance to the grange. The narrow crack in the hillside was so easy to miss. With a half sob of gratitude, she spied the way in. *Goddess, Mother, thanks!* Food, warmth, and shelter lay behind the clustering oaks.

She turned off the path and plunged into the undergrowth. A dark, hooded shape was standing beneath the trees. Fear choked her throat, but she stifled the urge to scream. *It's him!* she howled inside. *It's the woodman with blood on his hands. He's followed me. He's going to attack me now!*

But he did not move. Muffled from head to foot in woodland green, he was waiting as patiently as a hunter for his prey. Her heart in her mouth, she tore the horse's head around.

"Go!" she whispered urgently in its ear, clapping her spurs to its side.

*Goddess, Mother, save me . . .*

But the watcher in the dark was ahead of her. A powerful hand reached out, seizing her reins. The muffled shape was so near that she could smell the scent of the woodland on him, wild and strong. Whinnying in terror, the horse reared, but her attacker made a grab for the bridle and dragged the horse down. Madly, she raised her whip to lash at him, but she had no room to strike, he was much too close.

"Get off!" she howled, beating him with her fists. Vainly, she tried to spur the horse away. The poor beast screamed with pain and reared again.

*Goddess, Mother, save us! Spare us both.*

At last he wrestled the panicking horse to a halt. Then he threw back his heavy hood and tried to speak. The words choked his throat, but she heard them just the same.

"Lady, oh, lady—do you not know me, my love?"

She looked and did not know the man who spoke. Then she looked again and saw him clad in his own radiant soul-light, unmistakable. He was dressed in a tunic and cloak of woodland green, and the silver shield on his back caught the green of the trees overhead. Her soul soared in a starburst of delight. It came to her that she loved every star in the sky and every grain of sand on the earth below. She loved the leaves that framed his head in green and gold, and she would weave them into a bower where she could lie with him forever and a day.

*Tristan* . . .

All this ran through her mind as she heard the words, "Come to me, lady—my lady and my love."

# chapter 33

*ristan* . . .

She slipped from the horse and fell into his arms. Inside the cloak he was warm and dry, and she felt the riotous thudding of his heart. She groped for his hand and pressed it to her lips. "Oh, Tristan . . . "

Like a westering bird, she flew into his embrace. His kiss was all she had been dreaming of, and more. They clung to each other like children lost in a wood. There was no need for words.

A rain of kisses fell on top of her head. She shivered with shock and could not hold back her tears. He stroked her face and pulled back in concern. "Oh—you're so cold."

She laughed, half delirious with joy. "Not anymore." She clutched onto him, suddenly afraid. "Hold me."

He folded her into his cloak. "Lady, I shall never let you go."

How long they stood together she could not tell. At last an owl cried out and Tristan stirred.

"It's late," he said urgently. "I must get you to shelter, or you'll catch your death of cold."

Swiftly, he unsaddled her horse and tethered it loosely to graze. Then he took her hand and drew her toward the grange. "This way, lady. We'll be safe in here."

A welcoming candle bloomed in the wide, low hall. He led her straight to the little chamber at the rear of the house where they used to sit when the household was asleep. With a pleasure too deep for words, she saw the room had been made ready to receive her, and there was a merry fire blazing on the hearth.

She looked at him, marveling. "How did you know I was here in the wood?"

"I heard you near the forester's, and I guessed you'd be coming back here." As he spoke, he swiftly relieved her of her sodden cloak and wrapped her in a rug that had been warmed before the fire. "So I hurried back to make ready, so that you'd have somewhere warm and safe to sleep."

"Oh Tristan . . ."

She feasted her eyes on his face. His gaze was full of anxious concern for her, but he had a good color and his eyes were clear. He had lost the tormented air he had had in Dubh Lein, and the weeks in the forest had given him a new calm and strength.

He read her thought. "So will it be for you, away from the court," he said gently. "Here in the woodland—"

"Darath has gone," she interrupted fiercely. "I sent him away."

He did not reply. She was startled to see tears standing in his eyes. "I always meant to," she stammered, "surely you knew that."

"You sent him away? Without bloodshed?"

"Yes."

"How?"

"We offered them cattle for their byres and the chance to win brides for their beds. That was what they had come for after all."

She could see Tristan struggling with himself. "Then you were right," he said at last, "and I was wrong. I was sure you'd have to fight them to drive them out."

"I was wrong, too," she said slowly. "I should have tried harder to explain what I was trying to do. I got angry with you instead. I thought you were trying to spoil my negotiations with Darath because you wanted to do battle with him yourself."

"I did," he said awkwardly. "I thought he was taking you away from me."

"Oh, my love . . ."

"I thought you were only drawing out the discussions so you could be with him. I was afraid you planned to take him as your knight instead of me."

An ugly flush of unhappiness crept up her neck. "I should never have made you think that. I was only trying to capture his interest and make it harder for him to attack Dubh Lein."

She hesitated, conscious of Tristan's eyes closely searching her face. Should she tell him that Darath had wanted to take her to his bed? That she had been attracted to him in return? That she had kissed him on the mouth when he demanded a price for agreeing to go away?

She drew a deep breath. "Tristan," she began.

"Ah, lady—" He put a finger to her lips. "Let's talk about this another time."

*But not now.* Isolde nodded, and a great tear of weariness rolled down her cheek. The next moment she was weeping in his arms. "Oh, Tristan . . ."

"No tears, my love," he said tenderly. The kiss he gave her healed her very soul. He stroked the length of her body, and she felt herself reviving at his touch. After a while she was no longer tired and cold but floating on the tender wings of bliss.

"Come to me—"

She reached up and pulled him down to her side. Suddenly, she was starving for his love, longing to possess him, blind to all thoughts but one.

It came to her with a gasp of delight that they were closer to freedom than they had ever been. Both Igraine and Cormac had confirmed that her marriage with Mark was dead. Give it an honest burial, Cormac had said. That is the last duty that you owe to him. Now she could go back to Mark without fear and dissolve the marriage in person, face-to-face. Afterward she could live life on her own terms.

They should go back to Castle Dore soon.

But not tonight.

Tonight she would sleep like a child in Tristan's arms. Together they would climb softly upstairs by candlelight to the moonlit attic at the top of the house. There they would heal all the sorrows that had kept them apart, and with tears and kisses they would be reconciled. Afterward, she would lie and watch his sleeping face for hours until, overflowing with love and joy beyond words, she fell into a deep and dreamless sleep.

*And will tonight be the beginning of new life? Not Tristan's and mine, but the child of our love?*

She smiled dreamily. *Who knows? But we shall find out.*

From Tristan's face, she could tell he was thinking the same. She gave him a glimmering smile. An answering smile crinkled the corners of his eyes, and a look of infinite sweetness swept over his face. Never had he looked so dear to her, so fine.

His spirits soaring, he took her by the hand. As long as the world was asleep, they were safe. Then a thought of pure joy burst in his thankful brain. There was no need for secrecy any more. He threw back his head and laughed aloud with delight. By breaking his oath to Mark, he had earned the right to take his beloved in his arms. Their love was open, he could shout it from the hills.

"Lady, lady," he whispered. He caught his breath. How long had he waited to say these words to her?

"Come, my love. Let me take you to bed."

THAT WAS THE FIRST NIGHT they spent in the chamber above the trees. The next morning she woke to the first sweet breath of spring. Looking out of the window, she saw fresh green shoots sprouting merrily on all the tops of the trees. Had winter been slipping away unnoticed while they'd been apart? Or had the dark days fled as soon as Tristan appeared?

In the days to come, she had time to puzzle it out.

That, and so much else.

"Why did you leave me like that?" she asked him one day in a low, unhappy voice. "Sailing away without a word of farewell."

He flinched. "It was time for me to go."

"Why?"

He lifted his head, and his eyes were full of pain. "I was jealous of Darath, which a knight should never be. I was breaking my oath of chivalry and wronging him, but above all, I was making things worse for you."

"Yes, you were." She could not hold back a flash of bitterness. "It was hard to deal with Darath when you came back."

"I know. He could see how much I hated him, and he was able to use that against you. I knew if I stayed, you'd never get the better of him."

"But to go without a word—"

"I didn't trust myself to say good-bye," he said with painful honesty.

"But why didn't you leave me word where you meant to go?"

"Because I didn't know. But I knew if you wanted me, you'd find me in the end."

"And you were right." Breathless with joy, she ran her fingers over his forehead, smoothing away the troubled lines on his brow. "Now kiss me, my love?"

But still she had to know what he'd been doing in the time they were apart.

"How have you been living?" she asked the next day as they walked in the forest in the morning sun.

"Like any other forester," he replied.

She looked round, bewildered. "But there's nothing here."

He gave a crooked smile. "There's all you need in the forest if you know where to look. Don't forget, Merlin lived wild in the woods for years after Uther died." His grin grew broader. "And he's no woodman, lady, as you know."

The smile that she gave him then lit his soul. "And you are the best in the world." She laid her hand on his. "Will you teach me?"

SO BEGAN THE HAPPIEST TIME they had known, living together in the depths of the wood. Earth had slipped the chains of winter, and spring was under way. Day after day, the sun knocked on their window to wake them, and the great forest opened its hidden ways and took them to its heart. Hand in hand, they roamed far and wide, greeting their woodland neighbors like their kin. The lively hares were their children, the roe deer their sisters and brothers, and the many-antlered stags their great cousins in all their pride.

As they went, Tristan taught her all his forest lore: never to eat where they had gathered their food, never to sleep where they had eaten, and never to lay their heads in the same place twice. At night, they made their beds in warm, safe hollows guarded by thickets of quickthorn and knotty furze.

Afterward, Isolde thought she never slept better than in those woodland retreats, roofed by mighty evergreens and guarded by thick walls of bramble and fern. Night after night, she lay with Tristan at her side and the Goddess moon riding the sky overhead. As sleep descended, she lay snug inside her cloak, counting each shining star and hearing them sing.

In those long, dewy nights, she saw the world with new eyes. Sometimes she thought that the Fair Ones shadowed all in green came out of the hills and hollows to bring them sweet dreams, and every tree leaned down its tender, new-budding head to kiss them good night. And with such thoughts, sleep was not far behind.

When morning came, they fed on sweet roots and springwater and strong-flavored, chewy leaves. Then they set off for the day's adventures, slipping as light-footed as deer between the greeny-black holly and bloodred-berried yew. Tristan's face and body grew browner, and each lengthening day seemed to lend him new strength. She saw him newborn in springtime beauty, as if the sun itself were coursing through his limbs. Here in the forest he was utterly at home, moving with ease through its dark, fertile depths. Here he taught her how to lose herself in the life of the wood, till her spirit left her body for the astral plain. And here they trod the world between the worlds, searching, ever searching, with each new foray. Within days, they had transcended their mortal clay and wandered the realms where the Great Ones lived.

"Oh, my love, let us embrace this time of peace," Tristan said somberly, "and then, my Queen, we'll decide what to do."

She looked at his dear face, aching with love. Once again she saw the wonder of his broad, high forehead and frank open gaze, his strong cheekbones and well-shaped mouth. Beltain was coming, the feast of fires and flowers, the mystic time when spring ripened into summer and the doors of the Otherworld opened wide for love. What better time to renew the ties that bound them, heart and soul? And where better than the heart of the greenwood?

In the heart of the wood and many leagues deep in love, they did not see the lone figure on the high road, doggedly making his way to Castle Dore. They did not hear the woodman's description of them as he whiled away his journey rehearsing what he would say. "There's a knight, my lord, in the forest and a fine lady, too, with a head of red-gold hair and the sound of the Western Isle in the way she speaks . . . "

But there was more, much more, that the woodman himself did not know. So they could not have guessed that his was not the only treachery afoot, and that evil was already brewing at the court of King Mark. They rose every morning in the pearly dew and looked into each other's eyes and rejoiced to be alive, like the little gilded flies of midsummer that sing and dance and live for only a day.

*onfitebur tibi, Domine . . .*

Is that how the psalm began, Theodora asked herself? "I will give thanks to Thee, O Lord with all my heart: I will sing of Thy marvelous works . . ."

Yes, I will give thanks, the Princess promised herself smugly, I'll sing out to God with all my heart. She looked around the sunlit guest room of Castle Dore. Could anything in the world be more marvelous than this?

Across the chamber, her sister Divinia was coiled up in a window seat overlooking the castle grounds, basking in the warmth of the sun. Pale as ever but less waif-like now, Divinia returned Theodora's glance with a languid yawn.

"Are you tired, sister?" she said.

Theodora had to laugh. Back in Dun Haven, they'd have been working like slaves from the moment day broke till they dropped into their beds. With their stepmothers dying in childbirth one by one, there were always babies to be cared for and a troubled household to run. Then, by candlelight, when night came at last, there were clothes to be made and blankets and sheets to be patched. Here they were ladies of leisure, guests of the King, spoiled from dawn till dusk.

There was a knock on the door. Theodora opened it, and dismissed the servant outside with a curt word. Then she turned back in triumph into the sunny room. "Look at this."

Her eyes glistened as she held aloft a plate of sticky sweetmeats and slices of almond bread dripping with lard. Greedily, she began to stuff them in her mouth.

"I thought they'd never come," she complained. "I must have sent for them an hour ago."

Divinia's stomach turned, and she had to look away. "Father would beat you if he saw you being such a pig."

Theodora plumped herself down on a cushion and grinned through a mouthful of grease. "Father isn't here."

"You're getting fatter every day," Divinia pouted at her sister spitefully. "He's bound to know as soon as we get back."

There was a pause while Theodora emptied her mouth. "You can do what you like," she said clearly. "But I'm not going back."

There. She'd said it, the thing they had both been afraid even to think.

Divinia's eyes bulged. "Not ever?" she whispered fearfully.

"Never. I don't care who I have to marry to stay here."

"Not even the King?"

Theodora set her plump chin. "Especially him." She gave a disbelieving stare. "Whatever you think of him, he's still the King. You know what that means."

Divinia felt sick. "But he's stupid. And he's so smelly and horrible and *old.*"

Theodora's eyes lit up. "The older, the better," she grinned malevolently. "The sooner he'll die. And then I'll be Queen, and no one in the world can tell me what to do."

"What if he won't marry you?"

Theodora set the empty plate aside and stretched her ample body like a cat. "Someone else will. There's plenty of men here at court."

"You mean one of those filthy old lords that stare at us all the time?" Divinia shuddered. "I'd rather die."

"You don't mean that." She looked at Divinia and fixed her with a frown. Surely even her dim-witted sister could see that this was their only chance of escape?

"Listen to me," she said with all the force of a nature long suppressed. "If I marry the King, I'll keep you here as my lady in waiting, and you must promise to do the same for me. Unless you want to go back to Dun Haven and live as we did before, with Father and the girls."

Divinia lost some of her fragile color and shook her head. "No, I don't."

"Father's wives keep getting younger, don't forget," Theodora prodded. "The next one'll be the same age as you and me, and we'll have to take orders from her and do what she says. Is that what you want?"

"No." Divinia's porcelain skin flushed. "I can't do that."

"Well, then." Theodora surged up to Divinia and pulled her to her feet. "We've got to marry the King or someone else. Father Dominian will soon be here to take us into court. Let's see how good we can make ourselves look by then."

She set to work on Divinia with a will, pinching her cheeks and fluffing out her hair.

"Bite your lips to make them red," she commanded, ignoring the flurry of protests and cries. "And here, wear these earrings, they'll give you more of an air."

By the time Father Dominian was expected, the younger sister had been subtly transformed. Still pale and ethereal, she now glowed a silvery pink down to her fingers' ends, wherever Theodora's vigorous pinching had produced the desired effect.

"Between us, we'll catch one of these lords" was the brutal calculation of the older girl, "even if it's not the King himself. And all we need is one to stay in Castle Dore."

"Are you ready, my daughters?"

Hovering in the doorway, reluctant to come in, Dominian averted his eyes from his two charges and their flowing robes, which clung too closely and revealed too much.

"I have come to take you into court," he curtly announced. "The King is holding an audience today and is graciously pleased to invite you to attend."

Theodora paused to arranged her veil to show more of her plump, white shoulders and well-rounded neck. Then she pulled down the front of her dress and brazenly tweaked up her breasts to make a better display.

"We're ready," she said to Dominian with a lusty smirk.

"Follow me, then," Dominian said, shrinking in his soul. And may God in His wisdom have mercy on us all.

The little priest bowed his head in painful prayer as he led the two Princesses away. *Salvum me fac, Domine.* Help me, help me, Lord.

He had rarely been so unhappy in his life. Is this truly your work that I do now, O Lord? Strengthen and guide me, for I am losing my way.

# chapter 35

The days were slipping away like pearls on a chain. To see Tristan's face was a daily delight. When the wood pigeons crooned their hearts out in the topmost tree, Isolde thought they were singing for him alone. And when the great seven-pointed stag called to his mate through the echoing groves, it seemed to Isolde that she heard Tristan's voice.

Now summer ripened to its peak in the fullness of the earth. From early morning, the air was golden and warm beneath the trees, heavy with the scent of the season and teeming with life. Together they ranged far and wide throughout the wood, learning its hills and hollows, its dark rocks and sunlit ravines.

Each day brought new enchantments, new delights. A triple rainbow one day when it rained. Another day, two proud swans sailing down a stream, one fore, one aft, guarding the dusty brown skein of their offspring paddling in between. And best of all, in the secret heart of the wood, a cloven oak covered with ivy and honeysuckle intertwined.

Isolde reached for Tristan's hand. "You remember, love?" She could not go on for tears.

"Remember?" Tristan's laugh caught in his throat. "How could I forget?"

They stood silent then, marveling at this memorial to their love, the sign that the fates had given them so many years ago. In the heart of the darkest forest, so their pledge had run, the ivy and the honeysuckle flourish as one. And so it will be with us, our lives so intertwined that every curve and line of one will follow the outline of the other in deepest love.

They had made another promise at that time and held fast to that, too: *This love may never leave us now, neither for weal nor for woe.*

And as they held that moment in their minds again, she found the strength to ask him what they should do.

He gripped her hand. "You think we should leave the wood?"

Isolde nodded unhappily. "We can't live like this forever."

He took her by the shoulders. "Are you unhappy, lady, here with me?"

She could see the pain in his face. Tears sprang to her eyes.

"I'm happier here with you than I have ever been," she told him, her voice breaking. "But sooner or later we have to return to the world. We're like midsummer flowers, Tristan, growing tall in the sun. But winter must come."

As she spoke, he felt a winter chill invade his heart. Thin fingers as cold as death wound themselves around his hopes, and he knew the fear of summer's end that haunts all who live in the wood. Already he could feel the wind blowing stronger and see the bracken turning from green to red. Soon at night they would hear the king stag belling from the far hilltop, and wake at dawn to the wild goose's parting cry.

But still he wanted to stave off the moment if he could.

"If it's winter you fear, let me take you back to the grange," he offered. "I can keep you like a queen in Castle Bel Content."

She could hear her heart crying, *Yes, let's do that. I want to stay here!*

"And I could love you like a king," she said wanly, stroking his hand. "But we're only safe as long as we keep on the move. We'd be trapped like rats in Bel Content if Mark and Andred tracked us there."

"As they will," he added, almost to himself. "They must." She had never seen him look so grim.

An endless moment passed.

"Oh, my lady," he breathed. He tipped up her chin to look her in the eyes. "I'm a hunter, at home in the heart of the wood. But you're a child of the sea. You want to go back to Ireland so you can have the ocean, the tides, the waves, and the shore."

Tremulously, she shook her head. "Neither is more to me than the other. It takes the sea and the land together to make a world."

He folded her into his cloak and softly quoted a fragment of an ancient runic verse, cherished between them whenever they were apart.

> *Bel ami,*
> *si eczt de nouz*
> *Ne vouz sanz mei,*
> *ne mei sanz vouz.*

" 'My dearest love,' " she translated back to him, " 'this is our fate, neither you without me, nor me without you.' "

They stood together in a silence too deep for tears. Together they had walked the world between the worlds, and now it was slipping away. Isolde could hardly speak for pain.

"We should go back to court," she said through cold, stiff lips. "Then I can end this hollow marriage with Mark, and you can leave his service with honor, not as a fugitive."

Tristan stared at her in horror. "Go back to court?" He laughed in disbelief. "Mark tried to kill me, lady!"

Isolde dropped her gaze and looked away. "You don't know that."

"I know that Andred and his two villains made an attempt on my life," he spat out, "and they said that the King himself had ordered my death."

"But that's just what Andred would have told them, don't you see?"

"Lady, lady," he groaned. "Blame it all on Andred if you like. But surely you understand that Mark himself—"

"No, I don't," she interrupted. "Mark is many things, but he wouldn't do that."

Tristan nodded bleakly. Isolde refused to believe her husband could be a murderer. What could he say? His tongue lay like lead in his mouth.

Dimly, he heard Isolde speaking again.

"I want to separate from Mark with dignity. Then we'll go home to Ireland and live in peace."

He could not contain himself. "And you think Mark will simply let us go?" Dark visions of the future crowded his mind. "It's true that we'll have to leave, if we want to be safe. Sooner or later one of the woodland folk will give us away. But let's be very careful about what we do next."

A new excitement was written on Isolde's face. "You think we should make straight for the coast and sail to Ireland?"

He caught her rising spirits. "Anywhere in the world!"

She gave a tremulous laugh. Should they do this? Could such a thing be right? She could hardly breathe. "And I'll write to Mark from there."

Goddess, Mother, thanks! Tristan bowed his head. "To Ireland, then," he cried.

Isolde looked at him through a veil of tears. How she loved this man!

*Ireland.*

*Erin.*

*Home.*

# chapter 36

*S*o then, who do we have today?"

Resplendent in all his finery, Mark lolled back on his throne and looked out over the Audience Chamber with a sense of satisfaction filling his soul. See, he could dress up grandly when he chose. No well-worn riding habit this morning, as familiar and wrinkled as a second skin, but the very best that the royal wardrobe could afford. Silently, he preened himself on his tunic of bright scarlet, the weight of the gold chains around his neck, and his cape of cloth-of-gold. From the crown on his head to the tip of his red leather boots, he fancied he looked every inch the King.

And what other king took care of his people like this? If he was choosing for himself, he'd be out in the sun right now, racing through the forest with his band of knights or plunging his overheated body in the sweet sharp shock of a freezing mountain stream. Instead, he was pent up indoors, enthroned on this dais, giving himself freely to any wretched peasant or muddy oaf who turned up at court. He could see them all now, huddled around the door, lining up to press their stinking petitions into his hand and beg him to right some ridiculous wrong.

And all this under the eye of his lords and courtiers, too, every one clustered around him, beady-eyed, waiting for him to do something wrong. His eye fell on Andred, poised and ready at the foot of the throne. Thank God he had someone to handle all this for him.

"So, then, Andred," he huffed, "what's on today?"

Andred cast a cold eye round the chamber, taking in the gaudy courtiers chattering round the throne and the dull motley of townsfolk and villagers clustered by the door. Gods above, how these hovel-dwellers stank!

"Today will be like every other audience, sire. We'll be through in a trice. There's nothing here to keep you from your sport."

"Good, very good," Mark yawned. "Begin, then."

"Before we do, my lord, I have a private communication for your ears." Andred broke off and allowed a delicate pause. "The Lady Elva craves permission to return to court."

"Who does?" said Mark obtusely.

"Your admirer, sire. Your former mistress—"

"Yes, yes," Mark interrupted nastily. "No need to remind me, I haven't forgotten that. What does she want?"

"A while ago, you suggested she retire from the court. A spell in the country, you said, would be good for her health. She sends to say she feels much recovered now. Will Your Majesty allow her to come back to Castle Dore?"

The crowd ebbed and swirled in the doorway, then parted to reveal the black habit of Father Dominian, who was entering with the two Princesses in his wake. Both fixed their eyes on the throne, dropped their eyes, and curtsied fulsomely as they came in. Mark eyed them in deep appreciation and played thoughtfully with his lower lip. Perhaps it might be a good idea to have Elva back.

He turned to Andred with a careless laugh. "Would she make them jealous?"

Andred started, taken by surprise. "Who?"

"Those two."

Mark gestured toward the two sisters, now standing with Father Dominian below the dais. Nearest to him, Theodora was decked out in a bloodred gown with floating panels of mulberry, nightshade, and gold. Beside her, Divinia wore a simple silk shift of blushing pink with a train of ivory velvet, looking for all the world like a plate of strawberries and cream. Mark's appetite rose. He wanted to strip her and eat her, nibbling her ears, her nose, and the tips of her childish breasts.

Then his eyes turned back to the toothsome, well-bosomed creature at her side. Either one of Theodora's luscious, trunk-like thighs was worth the whole of Divinia's skinny carcass to a red-blooded man.

Who would trifle with a girl like a bowl of fruit when he could sink his teeth into a thick slab of sirloin well marbled with fat?

Mark wagged his head owlishly and gave a braying laugh. "She loves me, you know, that girl Theodora. They both do, of course, but the younger one would never say it to my face."

Andred fought down a seething bile. Well, could that be because she doesn't love you at all, he wanted to say? That she laughs at your thinning hair and expanding paunch, and dreams of a lover who doesn't stink of horses and dogs?

Mark peered at Andred. "You've gone a peculiar color," he observed. "Are you all right?"

I will be when I kill you, erupted in a silent scream from Andred's dark soul. And both those dim little Christian whores as well, and Tristan and Isolde too, don't forget them...

He stroked down his mustache. "This is good news, sire," he said unctuously. "But the Lady Elva—is it your wish she should come back to court?"

"Why does she want to come?" Mark demanded.

"To please you. She only has your interests at heart."

"Does she, though?"

Mark paused to think. Already Elva had dwindled in his mind. For the life of him, he could not remember why he had sent her away. Oh yes, she had kept trying to order him about, that was it, nattering night and day. Always insisting that a king should do this, a king should do that, behaving as if he was the subject and she the one in command. A warm glow of resentment lit his feeble brain. She was as bad as Isolde—or worse. Neither of them ever treated him like a king.

Not like the two little Princesses from Dun Haven, who knew both their God and their King. He looked down from the dais at Theodora, who was fluttering her fleshy bosom most attractively.

"No," he said firmly to Andred. "Elva must not return. You can tell her that from me. Now see to the petitioners, will you? They don't all need to approach the throne; you can deal with them."

Mark dismissed Andred with a nod of the head and the sense of a job well done. Already his mind was turning to the time after the audience when he'd have the Princesses alone. His blood thickened.

He was itching to get his hands on both of them, the dainty morsel in pink and white and the older, heavier, gamier bird. Yes, of course it was a sin to lust after a woman while he still had a wife, let alone lust after two. But he wouldn't be the first man to take a brace of fine sisters to bed, one after another like two courses at a meal.

And there was that Spanish cardinal, the fine cleric from Rome, coming in through the door, Mark noted. Well, he was the man for the task, he could sort this out.

"Good day, Dom Arraganzo," he caroled. With one stroke of his pen, the Papal Legate could annul the marriage to Isolde, and pouf! The whole wretched union would be gone, would be no more. Then he'd be free to marry one sister and hold the other in reserve to be his mistress later on. Now, which one to marry? Better to begin with the lesser and keep the stronger for another day. He pointed to Divinia and patted his thigh.

"Come here, my dear," he called.

"A moment, sire."

It was Andred, pressing up to the foot of the dais with a woodman in tow. The man wore a rough coat of scarred and ill-matched pelts, cobbled up from the damaged skins he could not sell. A pair of shifty eyes looked out of a hard-bitten face, and he grunted a greeting through a mouthful of broken teeth.

Andred pushed him forward urgently. "This man has news, sire, that you'll want to hear."

The man grinned and showed his teeth. "There's a knight in the forest, a huntsman as skilled as any I've known. He's been slipping around, hiding out there for a few weeks now. Then a fine lady came looking for him and gave me gold. She was ... "

Mark sat like a man made of stone. A fine lady with the sound of the Western Isle in her voice and a head of red-gold hair.

Isolde.

Looking for Tristan, who else in the world could it be?

He let out his breath in a hiss.

Issssolde.

And Tristan.

*So my traitorous nephew has come secretly back to Cornwall to do* me wrong, and my wife has been trailing him through the wood, like some gypsy whore cast off by her traveling man.

Isolde chasing Tristan.

And both of them utterly careless of any harm they might do to him.

Rage filled his brain. Dimly, he heard Andred's voice above the angry roaring of his mind.

"Did she find him, fellow?"

"He's a man of the woods, sir. He found her."

"How do you know?"

"Because they're living together like woodlanders, moving from place to place. They think they've gone unnoticed, but I know where they are."

"Wait outside, then," Andred said dismissively. "We'll call on you in a while."

"You owe me a reward," said the forester triumphantly. "I'm a poor man, and I've come all this way to court."

"You'll be paid, forester," Andred retorted with an ominous glint. "But for now, get out and wait to be told what to do."

The woodman hurried out. As he did so, a furious muttering broke the silence he left behind. Both the Dun Haven Princesses had rounded on Father Dominian and were confronting the little priest.

"*Isolde?* That's the name of the Queen. So she's come back here?" Theodora stuttered, her eyes as round as moons. "You told us she'd gone to Ireland and that she wouldn't come back. We thought the King had finished with his wife—annulled her, or whatever it's called. And all along—" Her eyes bulged as if they would burst.

"It's adultery," piped Divinia, her watery features blazing like sea fire. "And fornication, too, setting us on to court him like a single man."

Father Dominian held up his hands. "Daughters, daughters, please—"

"And in the meantime"—Theodora was gathering fury as she spoke—"the missing Queen lies in the woodland with a runaway knight. More sin and wickedness to taint us both. And the King— what's he doing about that?"

"Now God preserve us!" gulped Divinia. "And our immortal souls." Clasping her hands together, she began to pray.

It's adultery...

Sick to his soul, Mark contemplated the wretchedness of being once again a married man. It came to him that he had enjoyed flirting with the Princesses more than anything since his bachelor days. For a while he had felt like a single man again, and he wanted that back.

But not with these two, oh no! Listen to them now. The younger one wailing about her immortal soul and the older revealed as an angry virago all too ready for a fight. Isolde, Elva, and now this fat bitch to boot—they were all the same. All they wanted was to dominate and domineer.

And who was King here, after all? He leaned forward from the throne.

"Step forward, Princesses, and make your farewells," he called dangerously. "I must attend to affairs of state, and you must return to Dun Haven while your father lives. When he dies, I shall vest your wardship in the hands of the Church. And in the meantime, I wish you Godspeed from Castle Dore."

He did not heed the stunned silence that followed his words. Andred was the next to feel the weight of his angry eye.

"Get a band of men together and send for the dogs," Mark hissed. "Tristan and Isolde have taken shelter in the forest, and we're going to hunt them down."

# chapter 37

ods above, how he hated this midsummer sun! Even more than he hated every flake of winter's snow. Hated the seasons in the forest, even when the woodland wore its fairest face. You lived out too long when Uther Pendragon died, Merlin reflected savagely as he went along. The sun, the wind, the rain, the ice, and the frost—every one of them was a little death to those who spent their lives out of doors. Even to a bard, a Druid of the seventh seal, a Lord of Light. Even to Merlin himself.

Plodding onward at his own pace, the white mule Merlin was riding rolled one blue eye and one brown, and reflected, too. What painful creatures these two-leggers were! Born without hair or fur, how poorly they withstood the weather all year round. Yet still they held themselves equal with the Gods, whereas in fact—

"Hold your tongue, fool," said Merlin rancorously, "and let's get on."

The mule nodded, and both travelers gave their attention to the road ahead. At least in the greenways they were sheltered from the heat of the sun. Carved out by wanderers and drovers and millions of unknown feet, the ancient tracks were so deep and overgrown with trees that a traveler could cross the whole of the island in these green tunnels without being seen.

On! Merlin berated himself, on! Or you will come too late.

Too late to save Tristan.

Ye Gods, Merlin mourned. When would these human creatures be able to rule their own fate? Even a Lord of Light could not be everywhere. Yet who would work for these islands, if not himself? Who but Merlin, from the dawn of time?

"Who brings in the winds from the mountains?" he began in his high, bard-like chant.

> "Who teaches the sun when to rise?
> Who cares for the cattle on the hillside
> And the child in the wood?
> Who feeds a man's hunger and heals his thatch of wounds?
> Merlin! Merlin!
> Merlin through all time."

Good, yes, very good, and every word true. And how these hidden greenways soothed his soul. Merlin cast an appreciative eye up the steep banks running away toward the horizon on either side. Whoever was out and about could not see him here. No one should know how Merlin came and went.

Especially when he had failed.

Failed first of all with Igraine, when the old Queen would not choose Tristan over Mark and see that Isolde was sent out of the way. And failed again now, losing Tristan in the forest, just as he'd lost Tristan's mother all those years ago.

Gods above, how had it come about?

Weeping with fury, Merlin cracked each of his knuckles till his fingertips shot out blue flame. How could he have missed Tristan in the wood? The young knight was there, he knew; all the woodland creatures told him so. They had seen him slipping through the trees with all the skill of a wild thing, covering his tracks, lying low, and finally going to earth.

Yes, of course, Tristan was there! Merlin moaned. He had felt him, smelled him himself. Yet even the woodman, a creature of the forest, could only detect his presence. He could not track him down.

And failing Tristan, the old enchanter groaned, he'd failed Isolde, too. He could have spared that vital spirit from all the dread events that lay ahead. But Tristan was the focus of his love. Tristan, like Arthur, was the child of his dearest soul.

And Tristan's road ahead was dark indeed. Alas for the unmothered child and the fatherless boy. Tears sprang to Merlin's eyes.

"Grief upon me!" he gasped. "Grief upon all of us." He raised his eyes to the brilliant sky. "Spare Tristan!" he implored. "Spare both of them."

"Merlin, Merlin, news—!"

There was an angry clacking from above. Hopping about on a branch overhead were four magpies, flashing their blue-black wings and chattering to themselves.

"Oh, so? What news?"

Merlin cocked a cold and weary eye. How little enthusiasm he had for these vain and noisy gossips of the wood! But even a fool said a wise thing sometimes. "Speak," he said.

"Isolde was seen leaving Dubh Lein—" began one.

"—for Cornwall," the second burst in self-importantly, like a child. "For Castle Dore—"

"No, no!" screeched the third. "She went to seek Tristan in the wood! In the wood! In the wood!"

They squabbled on. Merlin looked at his fingertips and toyed with the idea of blasting them all with blue fire. But as the tale unfolded, his ears began to twitch. The woodman had betrayed the lovers to Mark. The King was calling up his knights and dogs to hunt them down.

"Is it so?"

Well, then, so much for Tristan.

Isolde, too.

He lifted his eyes to the black mountains ahead and the tears flowed again. "And may the Mother take care of them now, for I cannot!"

"ARE THE DOGS READY?"

One look at King Mark's livid face made Andred speak as calmly as he could. "Very nearly, sire."

Mark looked around the stable yard with undisguised rage. All around him his knights were fighting to hold down their horses, and he could hear the dogs baying madly from their kennels behind the stable wall. The scent of a manhunt was in the air, and every creature had picked up the bloodlust of the mounted men. He glowered at Andred.

"Then tell me why the dogs aren't here."

Andred paused for thought. Because the kennel master had no idea that you would burst from the Audience Chamber and demand the hounds right *now,* he wanted to say. Because it's noon, the hour when the creatures get fed. And because everything seems too slow to a man out for revenge.

"I'll go and find out, my lord," he said.

Mark watched the retreating figure with a sudden hot spurt of mistrust. Was Andred betraying him, just as Tristan had? Were they both working together against him? No, that was ridiculous. But why else was Andred delaying the dogs like this?

His horse tossed its head, impatient to be off, and he jabbed it savagely in the mouth. "Stand still, stand!" he snarled.

"Sire, a word?"

Pulling his horse's head around, Mark saw Sir Nabon approaching with a heavy frown. Jesus and Mary, what did the old fool want? It was bad enough to endure him speaking his fill in the council chamber. No reason to put up with his sermonizing now.

"Later," he called, and turned his horse away.

But Sir Nabon moved deliberately to block the horse's path.

"Now, sire, if you please, before you do this thing," he said trenchantly. "Your Queen and Sir Tristan are not animals to be hunted down. I beg you, my lord, give up this unworthy chase."

"Unworthy?" Mark gasped in sarcastic disbelief. "And they're not animals, you say? What d'you call it, then, rutting like beasts in the wood?"

Nabon's face tightened, and he fought down the impulse to reach for his sword. He would have killed another man who spoke so grossly of the Queen. But this was the King.

"For the sake of the country, I must ask you to think again," he said as forcefully as he dared. "The word of the forester does not mean that the Queen and Sir Tristan are guilty of adultery."

Mark's eyes bulged. "What else does it mean?"

"There is no proof."

"For God's sake, man, they've been alone together for weeks in the wood. What more proof d'you want?"

"They could still be chaste. They could have lain apart."

What was old Nabon saying? Approaching from behind, Andred caught the tail end of the councillor's speech and increased his pace. Isolde and Tristan chaste? What nonsense was this?

And worse, was Mark wavering in his revenge?

Composing his face into an air of concern, Andred hurried up.

"Indeed, sire, they could have been chaste," he intervened. "The wise man never leaps to conclusions, as Lord Nabon says. But if they were loyal to you, why did they stay away from court for so long? What have they been doing all this time in the wood?"

He was relieved to see the thunder and lightning return to Mark's clouded face. He bowed politely to Sir Nabon and pressed on. "They could be plotting together against the King. Even if they're not lovers, as you say, they could be traitors to the King and the country, too."

Mark's stubby finger jabbed accusingly at Sir Nabon. "Well, Nabon. What d'you say to that?"

Andred slipped in again smoothly before Nabon could reply. "If they were innocent, what do they have to hide? Why not simply return straightaway to King Mark, the Queen's loving husband and Sir Tristan's generous lord?"

Nabon could have answered that twenty times over, but he dared not speak. He was no match for Andred's snake-like intelligence and silver tongue.

A new edge had crept into Andred's voice. "And besides," he insinuated, frowning thoughtfully at Mark. "You'll remember, sire, that they've ignored you before. This isn't the first time that Sir Tristan has chosen to follow the Queen instead of you, or that the Queen has followed her own desires."

"Desires?" Mark spat out.

Good, good! Andred thrilled at his own cleverness. Every word he said was feeding Mark's fury and his hunger for revenge. And now see what was coming from behind . . .

Andred fervently thanked his Gods. If this did not inflame his uncle's rage, nothing would. With luck, Tristan would not get out of the forest alive.

"Hear us, sire!"

*Eripe me, Domine . . .*

Deliver me, O Lord, from the evil man, Dom Arraganzo prayed vigorously as he strode along. What, Mark thought he could send the Princesses back to Dun Haven after all the work that Arraganzo and Dominian had done? He thrust his elegant nose high in the air. He would not flinch from the damage to his kidskin boots plowing over these cobbles and dodging the reeking droppings as the horses pranced about. If this royal sinner was thwarting God's holy plan, then it was surely time to intervene.

Oh, so? The Cardinal Prelate bearing down on him, and Father Dominian hobbling along, too? Struggling, Mark held down a yelp of rage. He thought he'd got rid of these two when he sent the Christian Princesses back home. Where would it end?

"Sire, I have just left two young women deep in grief," Arraganzo fumed. "They say you plan to cancel their wardship and return them to Dun Haven at once. I have come in all haste to put an end to this."

Mark reached for an iron-hard smile. "Sadly, it's true."

Arraganzo stared him in the eye. "Then I must ask you to reconsider, my lord. This must not be."

Must, must not . . .

Mark was in no mood for this. "I am King here, sir, remember?"

Arraganzo reached for a flattering smile. "And a king has obligations. He leads his people by gracious and kingly behavior, as you do, sire. It is for this that the Princesses love and admire you so much."

Mark's vanity was tweaked. "They love me, eh?"

"Both of them," said the Cardinal firmly. "Especially Theodora, who told me of her love for you in tears."

"Theodora?" Mark was instantly suspicious again. "She's the one who started dictating what I could and couldn't do."

Dominian stepped forward. "This is why God has given husbands the right to control their wives. When you marry her, she is yours to rule and to chastise till she learns your will."

"You hear your Father confessor?" Arraganzo declaimed. "You only need to learn how to tame your wife." Without warning, he dropped the flattering smile and fixed Mark with an eye of stone. "And you may not decide for yourself that the maidens go back. It is utterly against the will of God."

Dominian supported Arraganzo with his coal-black eyes on fire. "The Almighty Father in his loving kindness wants you to have a pure and gentle Christian wife."

"And now you may make a marriage with a girl you desire," Arraganzo sailed on.

"And one who desires you, Uncle," Andred followed with a slight but suggestive leer.

Jesus, Mary, and Joseph, was there no respite? When would Andred, Arraganzo, and Dominian hold their peace? Mark heard their voices buzzing like hornets and gadflies in his fevered head and felt that one or other of them would sting him to death. His father's voice reached him from a lifetime away.

"You'll never hold onto the throne, boy, you're weak through and through. Any fool will always be able to tell you what to do."

Mark's lips parted in a ghastly grin. And did you still think that, Father, when I let you die? When you were wounded in the forest and I refused to go for help, no matter how much you shouted and threatened me? You were very intent then on telling me what to do. But I proved to you then that I had a will of my own. How surprised you were!

He laughed for pure joy at the thought of his father's death. And then I became King. His chest swelled. So I've earned the right to do what a king has to do. He lifted his head, reveling in the access of power.

"All in good time, Lord Arraganzo. Today I have a quarry to hunt down." He raised his arm. "Mount up, men!" he snarled.

There was a commotion in the yard as the dogs came flooding in, a tide of barking, yelping, heaving brown and white. Andred turned to the nearest groom and signaled for his horse.

"Sire?"

There was a faint cry from the castle walls. A moment later, a man-at-arms came clattering down from the battlements.

"Word from the lookout, sire," he panted. "The Queen and Sir Tristan have been sighted. They're riding in."

# chapter 38

*C*astle Dore.

Isolde sat heavily on her horse with Tristan at her side and shivered at the sight of the white walls and graceful towers, bright with the banners of Cornwall fluttering in the sun. What had brought them here?

Grimly, she searched her soul, wondering if this could be right. In truth, all she wanted was to be back with Tristan, roaming in the wood. Yet here he was, too, white-faced and watchful as they rode up to the castle and in through the massive gates. The sun smiled down from a sky as clear as glass on a day that would normally have set the blood coursing through their veins. But all she could feel was the shadow over their lives.

It had all seemed so simple before. Of course they should go back to Ireland, not to Castle Dore. Mark was not to be trusted, they knew that by now. And what did they owe him more than they had already done?

But that was the question that continued to haunt Tristan.

"If I want to quit Mark's service with honor," he brooded, "I should kneel before him, beg his permission to leave, and kiss his hands in farewell."

Isolde laughed harshly. "You know what Mark thinks about honor. Will he let you go?"

"I don't know," Tristan admitted. "But the laws of chivalry say that no knight can be forced to serve against his will. If Mark refuses, I can take my sword, my shield, and my horse and ride away to find another lord." He gave a lopsided grin that pierced her soul. "Or a lady, like the one I found so long ago. One word from Mark, and I can follow the love of my life."

"Oh Tristan . . . "

They kissed as if it was the first time their lips had met. At last, she hesitatingly resumed. "But can we risk it? Your life may be at stake."

"I have to try. Only then can I call myself free."

*Erin is free.*

She could hear Ireland calling with a passion that tore her in two. *In Ireland, we would be free.* But unless things were settled with Mark, would they ever be safe?

"If we go back to Ireland together, Mark will be publicly shamed. And if his pride has been hurt, he'll have to seek revenge," Isolde said slowly.

Tristan sighed. "Lady, I think we have to go back to Castle Dore. Let's make a clean and honorable break with the past, then afterward we can live as we want."

Isolde fought down her misgivings. "Well, then, let's do it. We'll ride in together, and then we shall be free."

*Free of Mark . . .*

She hardly dared think it. After almost twenty years, could it ever come true?

The courtyard ahead of them was seething with life. Forty or fifty men were mounting up while a pack of hounds raced round the cobbled square. At the center of the whirlwind were Mark and Andred, both mounted on the strongest chargers Castle Dore could provide.

Tristan drew in his breath. "They're going out on the hunt."

"To hunt us?" Isolde turned pale.

"Who else?"

*Then he's already decided to kill us.*

She pulled her horse's head around. "Run for it, Tristan!"

"Isolde!" Mark hailed her loudly from the center of the throng, carving his way toward them with Andred at his side. "Welcome, Isolde. And Tristan, greetings to you."

"Greetings, my lord." Isolde tried to smile.

Mark gave a glittering smile. God Almighty, Isolde was a fine woman, even though she was looking so pale and breathless now. But how dare she ride back in like this, as if nothing had happened?

"We had heard you were lodging in the wood," he said. He waved a gauntleted hand at the baying hounds. "We were on our way to look for you."

Out of the corner of his eye, Mark caught the Cardinal Legate and Father Dominian staring in stark disbelief, and his shriveled heart soared. How wonderful to make those pompous religious asses goggle and glare!

He pointed to the two clerics. "They thought you had fled the country," he caroled. "While all the time—"

Isolde bit her lip. "Sire, let me explain—"

"Later, later." Mark brushed her aside. She'd speak when he was ready and not before. "Tonight I shall feast you as the Queen deserves. The Pope's emissary has been longing to make your acquaintance, haven't you, sir?'

Arraganzo bowed toward Isolde with a tortured smile. "As you say, sire."

I'll feast her and find out what she's up to, ran through Mark's fevered brain. Tristan, too. What are they doing here? Does Isolde expect to come back to me as my wife? If she does, I should force her to follow it through. A wild thought struck him. Why, I could still get her with child before the year is out. That would show all the world who ruled here as King!

"A feast, a feast!" he brayed. He threw up an arm, and called the chamberlain to his side. "Make the Great Hall ready for the finest feast tonight. The King will honor his returning Queen!"

The courtyard erupted in a mighty roar of whistles and cheers as the knights showed their approval of the revelry to come. Mark's mean heart swelled. He looked at the downcast Isolde, and malice filled his soul. By heaven, I've got the whip hand over her now. And she's still my wife. She's made me look a fool, and she'll pay for that. If I ply her with drink, I can take her tonight. Dominian is right, I've waited far too long.

In the hubbub, he found Arraganzo by his side. He was pleased to see the Cardinal looking yellow and jaundiced with rage.

"And what of your wards, sire, the Princesses of Dun Haven?" the Legate forced out. "The girls who so tenderly hoped to marry you?"

"Oh, they can stay here at Castle Dore, never fear. Leave them to me, and you'll find they'll be in good hands," Mark said truculently.

His soul soared. Now that Isolde had returned, he could do anything. If she was ready to obey him now as his wife, he'd have her as his Queen and the mother of his heir, and keep the two girls as well. They could enliven the times when there was no hunting and life at court grew dull. His grin broadened. It was the best of both worlds, and just what he deserved.

"See, nephew, see?" he hissed into Andred's ear. "You thought Isolde and Tristan were traitors. But here they are, both of them, just as I ordered. The Queen has come back to fulfill her marriage vows to me."

"As you say, sir." Andred bowed his head.

Mark's mood swung upward like a weather vane. Already he could see himself presiding at the feast, a goblet in his hand, the thick red wine running into his veins like blood and the pleasure of forcing himself on Isolde to come. It was time for her to be a wife to him, whether she wanted it or not. Tonight he would make the baby his barons desired.

He snorted with mirth. He'd get his revenge on Isolde, and at the same time Nabon and the others would be silenced, too. Better and better, the best! For one long, lovely moment Mark had the world at his feet, a new world of power, fulfillment, and control.

But the voice at his elbow put an end to all his dreams. "No feast for us, sire, I beg."

He turned to look at Isolde. Never had she looked so pale and cold. "I must talk to you now, indoors," she said through icy lips.

"What, now?"

"Alas, yes."

Why alas? Brooding, Mark dismounted and led the way indoors. Surely Isolde wouldn't try to thwart him as soon as she was back? He strode into the nearest chamber and turned to face her, with Dominian and Andred at his side.

Across the room a solitary fly was beating against the window, trapped inside the panes of greenish glass. Mark tugged at his collar. God, it was stuffy in here. He stood shaking his head and pulling at his ear, hardly able to believe what he was hearing. What was Isolde saying? And could she possibly mean what she said?

'Sir, I've come to give you your freedom and to claim my own. Then I mean to return to Ireland and resume my throne."

"What nonsense is this?" Mark gave a blustering guffaw. "You're not free, Isolde, you're my wife, and the time has come for you to be a wife indeed."

Gaping, she saw the lascivious light in his eye. "Wife . . . to you?" she stammered.

"Who else?" Mark shot back. He took a step toward her. "My wife in truth, Isolde, as well as in name."

"Sir, we have been ceremonial partners, you and I," she forced out. "Our marriage has been a sham for all these years, and we must put an end to this pretense."

"You're right about that," Mark agreed with a coarse laugh. He seized her by the wrist. "We're going to make this a marriage in the eyes of the world. A full married union, Isolde, what do you think of that?"

Triumphantly, he looked at Dominian for approval, and saw that Tristan was standing aghast, as pale as death. As well he might, Mark rejoiced. A child would put an end to any hopes Tristan had of Cornwall's throne. And that would show them all who ruled here as King.

*Goddess, Mother, help me . . .*

"Sir, I cannot contemplate what you suggest." Resolutely, Isolde struggled to set Mark straight. "If you're thinking that way, then you're deceiving yourself. I've taken spiritual counsel in Ireland, and my Druid has pronounced that our marriage is ended, if it ever began. From this moment on, I can no longer be your wife."

"You've consulted your Druid, lady?"

It was Dominian, violently thrusting his squat body to the fore. "What has a pagan priest to do with this?"

"Our Druids have the same spiritual authority that your Christian priests claim. And mine confirms my judgment that this marriage is no more."

"And this gives you the right to end a marriage by your own will?" the priest mocked savagely. "How can that be? You married the King by the rites of our Holy Church, and our God allows women no say at all in that."

Isolde's temper flared. "Under the Goddess, priest—"

"Your Goddess is no more!" Dominian shrilled. "We have taken your temples and overthrown your shrines. Your so-called Hallows are now lost to the world, and in times to come, no one will remember that a woman God once ruled. All men will know the story of our Holy Grail, and not a soul will know that we took it from the loving cup of the Mother when she supplied all who came to her feasts."

"Oh, priest—" Isolde could not contain herself. "D'you think people are fools?" She gave a bitter laugh. "Yes, your followers are ruthless, determined, and strong. Violent men always win in the short term. But in times to come, all women, and men, too, will understand that you usurped all the powers of our Goddess, our Mother the earth, to feed all her children and provide for all who come."

"Blasphemy!" put in Dominian with a face of fire.

Isolde thrust her face into his. "Do you know, priest, or do you care that our very word 'lady' means 'She who feeds us with bread'? That your men priests have only wine to pass off as blood, while every mother gives her blood to make the human race?"

Dominian's face was glistening with bile. "In the name of God, hear me—"

"No more." She waved a hand. "Faith should be kindness. Religion should be love. You will never convert me to a religion of sin and death, least of all one that gives your sect the right to destroy all other beliefs. It may take a thousand years, but a day will come when all men and women will know that you and your kind overthrew the Great Mother and installed a God of hate."

She turned toward Mark and felt herself swelling with power. "I am Isolde, Queen of the Western Isle, and I divorce you now, King Mark of Cornwall and the isles. All bonds are dissolved between us from this time forth. You are no longer my husband, and I am not your wife. Let us think and speak kindly of one another in times to come. You will find me in Ireland, and you will always be welcome there."

There was an echoing silence. Tristan stepped forward and fell to one knee, offering the hilt of his sword to Mark.

"I, too, must take my leave of you, King Mark. My duty to the Queen demands that I follow her as her knight. I beg Your Majesty to grant me my discharge from your service with honor on both sides."

Mark groped for words. "Go then," he said thickly. "A true lord releases his knight at a request like this. And the same must be true of a husband." He turned to Isolde. "Take up your new life in Ireland. You are free to go where you like. I wish you both well."

*Free?*

*Free to go?*

Isolde could not believe it. Her head was reeling. *Am I dreaming this?*

Suddenly, she felt Tristan's hand gripping her elbow, urging her toward the door.

"Out, lady. We must get out," came a fierce, almost soundless whisper in her ear.

She fumbled a bow toward Mark.

"Thank you, my lord," she said hollowly. "We shall send from Ireland to hear news of you, and we shall always be glad to have your news in return."

Trembling in every limb, she let Tristan lead her away. Her legs would hardly carry her to the door, but beyond it lay the world she had longed for all her life.

*We shall be safe and free now, Tristan and I.*

*Goddess, Mother, thanks!*

"May God bring you both everything you deserve," Mark called after them. But they did not stop to ponder what he meant.

# chapter 39

*S*o, Andred?"

Andred paused. He must not openly show his delight, he knew that. He must not even glance toward Dominian, who must surely be rejoicing at this turn of events as much as he was. But could there be anything more thrilling than Isolde's declaration of divorce and his uncle's rage? The King's dull, pebbly eyes were glittering like polished stones, and he was slashing around him savagely with his hunting whip.

And Tristan, too. Oh, you have done for yourself now, dear cousin of mine, Andred exulted darkly. Did you think for a moment that Mark would let you go? He bit back a sudden wild laugh. What knight has ever left Mark's service before, let alone one who thought he could ride off with the King's wife?

"And I talked of a great welcome feast, Andred?" Mark raged on. "I promised to honor the pair of them in open court? God in heaven, and I boasted that Isolde had come back to me to renew her vows?" He writhed with shame, almost beside himself.

Andred sighed. "Sire, you were not to know what they planned. They must have been deceiving you for years."

"And I believed them," Mark yelped. He rounded on Dominian, who was standing hunched to one side, his hands in his sleeves. "What a fool I look now, eh, Father? What a driveling fool."

Fool indeed and worse, Andred rejoiced to himself. A flabby-mouthed boaster, a deceived husband, and a king with no understanding of people or events. Silently, he set himself to stoke the flames of revenge.

"Alas, sire," he said mournfully, "if only you had not sworn to give Cornwall an heir."

Mark's eyes bulged. "God Almighty, yes, I did that, too!"

"Before the year was out, I think you said. And now the whole country is waiting for the Queen to be with child . . . " Andred spread his hands and allowed his voice to trail off.

Mark's color deepened. "And now the two of them must think they're home and free."

Dominian nodded. "They'll be sailing away to Ireland as fast as they can." He paused. "Probably today."

Mark could not bear it. "God in Heaven, I'll never live this down." Unless . . .

Dominian set himself to add fuel to the fire. "Remember, sire, that God is on your side. If the Queen will not accept her wifely destiny, you may set her aside. Then the way is clear for a Christian marriage."

"Set her aside? You mean confine her to a nunnery and let her end her days there?" Mark paused. "That's far too good for her." He paused for thought. Both Isolde and Tristan should suffer as he was suffering now. They should both die.

Dominian tensed. Lord, Lord, he prayed, do I have the pagan whore in my hand at last?

"Sire, let me urge you to act," he said with all the burning force he could command. "You must—"

Must, must!

The throbbing in Mark's head intensified. When would these weevils stop telling him what to do?

"Oh, I'll do it, never fear." Mark gave a horrible laugh. "Don't forget, Father, you told me that God had given every man the instrument to control his wife. It's the mark of manhood, to show that men were born to rule. The weapon they may use without mercy if they choose."

Dominian brought his hands together. "All true, my son."

"I'll do it, then." Mark's eyes were very dark. "I'll find her in her chamber and do it now."

GODS ABOVE, IT WAS STIFLING IN HERE! Isolde paced her chamber, struggling to breathe. Was the stale air of the court choking her after the freedom of the forest and the life she had lived with Tristan? Or was it a looming fear she could not escape?

She tried to gather her thoughts. Tristan had gone down to the harbor to command a ship. When he returned, they could simply slip away. *Get ready, then, and go. You need nothing from here. Everything you want is in Ireland.*

But still the walls and ceiling seemed to be closing in. *Too hot, too hot . . .*

She tore off her headdress and tossed it onto the bed. Crossing to the window, she threw open the casement, surprising a sad-eyed dove roosting on the ledge. Fluttering away, the graceful creature flew in a circle, then returned to its perch. Just as I did, Isolde thought, her mind darkened with fear. Flying free as a bird in Ireland, I came circling back here.

Restlessly, she paced up and down the chamber. *Goddess, Mother, tell me what to do.* Mark gave us soft words, but there was something dark and dreadful in his eye. Did we make the wrong decision when we returned?

Dimly, she heard an echo from the window where the white dove perched.

Wrong, came a sorrowful cooing. Wrong, wrong.

"Is that you, Little Mother?" Isolde gasped for breath and hurried across the room.

True, true. Solemnly, the lovely creature awaited her approach.

"Have you come to tell me that we shouldn't have come back?" Isolde forced out. "But we thought in all honor to Mark that we should return."

Wrong, wrong, cooed the dove. All the sadness of the world shone in her large dark eyes.

Isolde's heart tightened. "Mark is my husband now of twenty years. He's Tristan's kinsman, too. I thought we would be safe."

Wrong, wrong.

Isolde willed herself to stay calm. "So now we must get away from Mark as fast as we can."

The bird dipped her sleek white head. True, true.

"And there's Andred." Now Isolde's inner voice joined the anxious debate. "He's against us, too."

Two large round teardrops stood in the dove's dark eyes. True, true, she lamented, too true.

"Goddess, Mother, why did I ever think we'd find safety here?" Isolde cried in despair. Closing her eyes, she tried to piece out a plan.

"I'll send for Tristan and we'll fly at once. But will Mark pursue us? The world is wide, Little Mother. Where should we go?"

She opened her eyes. But the bird had flown. The next moment a harsh voice sounded in her ear.

"Talking to yourself, Isolde? Losing your wits?"

A sick terror seized her. *How did he get in?*

She turned, holding down her fear. Mark stood before her, breathing heavily, so close that she could feel the pulse of his throbbing rage. A livid flush discolored his face, and a strange odor hung about him that she had not known before.

"What is your will, sir?" she said evenly.

"My will? Oh, that's good." He gave a frightening laugh. "When did you ever care about that?"

Isolde drew a breath. "What is this?"

"Why, nothing but your husband, come to claim his rights. You've fobbed me off for over twenty years. But every bird comes home to roost at last."

A tremor seized her. *His rights?* She stared at Mark in horror. His eyes were black with anger, and he was tugging open his tunic at the neck. Now she recognized the unpleasant smell that hung about him like a dead man's shroud. *It's the smell of sex, and sex with him would be death.*

She shuddered with revulsion. *Goddess, Mother, no!*

Mark saw it and lost all control.

"You're too good for me, is that it?" he shouted, beside himself. Now he knew what to do. He'd drag her down from her pedestal and squeeze her windpipe till those green eyes popped. He gripped her by the throat.

"Come here!"

"Mark—" She struggled to break his hold.

A vicious blow caught her across the head. "You're mine now, don't you see?" he panted. "You came back of your own free will, and I'll have my marriage rights, by God I will!"

He tightened his grip on her neck till she could not breathe, but still the stink of him filled her nose and mouth. He hit her again in the face, and she tasted blood.

*Don't go down, don't go down . . .* Her senses reeled as she fought to stay upright.

"You're mine, Isolde," the hot hissing voice came in her ear again. Knocking her down, he fell on top of her with all his weight and drove the breath from her body.

"Don't fight me," he rasped.

Steadily, he increased his pressure on her neck. Isolde felt her lungs bursting, and her senses swam. The flagstones beneath her were as cold as the grave. One thought alone filled her tormented mind. *I have taken the way of the Mother to unlock my womb. If he rapes me now, I could bear his child.*

Now his mouth was slobbering into hers and sucking at her face. His hand was clawing at her breasts, tearing her bodice, heaving up her skirt. Never had she felt so doomed, so helpless, so weak. Great tears of hopelessness gathered in her eyes.

Then a voice from the cradle came dropping through the air. *No tears, no fears, Isolde. Remember you are Queen.*

*Remember, Mother? May I never forget!*

Screaming inside, she heaved up her body, throwing Mark off to the side, and furiously brought up her knee between his legs. With all her force, she did the same again, then jabbed her fingers into his eyes, clawing at his face.

"Get off me!" Howling, she tore at his eyes, his nose, his mouth, and kneed him again and again without remorse. "Leave me alone!"

With a cry of agony, Mark rolled away, hunching himself into a protective ball. Instantly, she was on her feet and running for her life.

*Tristan, Tristan . . .*

She burst out of the chamber and into the corridor.

"Lady!"

Tristan stood frozen in surprise outside the door. As he looked at her in horror, she could see herself through his eyes, beaten, bruised, and torn, blood trickling from her lip. Gasping, he caught her body in his arms, breathless at the livid marks on her neck.

"Mark?" he demanded in a choking voice.

She nodded. "He—"

"Ohhh . . ."

He could not speak. Beside himself, he cradled her in his arms, showering kisses on her face and her poor mottled neck. Then their lips came together in the deepest need and despair. They kissed as if the kiss were their last on earth.

Then a sound from behind made them spring apart. Andred stood in the corridor with a troop of men, smiling the worst smile they were likely to see. "At last," he said softly. "Now we know."

Tristan ground his teeth. "Andred—"

"No more words, traitor." Andred held up his hand. "You must speak to the King."

He nodded behind them as Mark came limping up. Long red scratches marked his face from forehead to chin, and Isolde took a forlorn pleasure from the sight of his battered eyes and mouth.

Andred bowed to Mark, unable to contain his delight. "We've caught them, sire, in each other's arms."

Tristan bowed to Mark. "My lord," he said thickly, "I beg you, let me speak." But Mark ignored him.

"Arrest them both, Andred," he ordered through swollen lips. "But imprison them apart to await separate fates."

Tristan stepped forward with his hand on his sword, "Sire, I must be with the Queen."

Mark swiveled his gaze toward Tristan with a black-eyed stare. "Oh no, my dear nephew, the Queen must be with me. And as for you, Andred knows what to do with a traitor, don't you, Andred?"

"Yes, sire," Andred put in, grinning like a pike.

"Go to it then," Mark ordered. He snapped his fingers at the captain of the guard. "Take the Queen away and hold her under lock and key till I come to the cells. Don't look so aghast, Isolde. Surely you knew I'd reserve your punishment for myself?"

*h*e should have killed Andred, Tristan saw that now. He'd had his hand on his sword; he could have finished him off then. But he'd hesitated to strike, and now they were lost.

He could have . . .

He should have . . .

*Fool! Useless fool!*

"So, Tristan?"

Andred was at his side, bursting with joy. Behind him stood half a dozen men-at-arms.

"I have you now, Tristan!" he exulted. "You heard the King's orders. You are in my hands."

Dazed with shock, Tristan felt his sword torn from his grasp and his hands roughly bound behind his back. Helplessly, he watched Mark and his men make a wall around Isolde and lead her away. He saw her head turn toward him as they approached and caught her last aching glance as the tall, burly forms hid her from his view. Then she was gone, and only the lingering trace of her scent remained.

My lady.

Oh, my love.

And he had allowed her to fall into Mark's filthy hands?

*Fool! Triple times fool.*

"So, Tristan?" Andred's joyful voice came again at his side. He turned and felt his own sword prick his throat. As he stood there, bound and defenseless, Andred waved Glaeve in his face and deliberately jabbed him again, delightedly watching the blood running down his neck.

Was Andred deaf? Tristan wondered dully. Didn't he hear the

furious screaming of Glaeve, snarling and resisting in Andred's usurp-
ing grasp? Kill, kill! howled the great sword in outrage. Kill him,
master, kill!

Andred lowered the sword.

"That's enough for now," he chuckled, his eyes alight. "We don't
want you to die too soon."

Behind Andred stood the captain of the guard. As Tristan looked
at him, the good man looked away, shock and resistance written on
his face.

"Have no fear, soldier," Tristan said hoarsely. "The Gods will never
blame you for this."

"The Gods?" Andred burst out laughing. "What do they care? But
I'm forgetting, cousin, that you'll soon be with them yourself. When
you get to the Otherworld, you can tell them what you think. Forward, then!"

He waved Tristan's sword and pointed down the corridor. Uneasily,
the men-at-arms formed up.

"This way," Andred ordered. "To the cliff."

Why to the cliff? Tristan wondered with unnatural calm. Because
it would be easier to make his death look like an accident? Or simply
because the tide would bear his body out to sea?

Out to sea . . .

Goddess, Mother, yes!

He closed his eyes in prayer. Out to sea and drifting with the tide.
Far, far away from the world with its terrible hurts and its hatreds, its
fever and fret. Floating into the arms of the Lady, the Mother of us all.
Goddess, Mother, Lady of the Sea, he prayed, may my fate be no worse
than this.

And my lady's.

Oh, Isolde, my sweetheart, my lady, my only love. His heart
clenched like a fist. Oh, my love, my love, what are you suffering now?

A heavy hand fell on shoulder.

"Come on, sir," the captain muttered under his breath.

Prodded forward, Tristan stumbled where he was led. Leaving the
castle, they climbed to the top of the cliff. A high wind moaned around
the headland, lashing the sea, and the air was heavy with great weep-

ing tears. Gods and Great Ones, Tristan prayed from the depths of his heart, if you're weeping for my lady, take pity on her now.

"Come on, sir. On you go. Up the hill."

Up and up.

Where were they taking him?

With every step, his misery increased.

The road curved around a bluff and crested the top of the cliff. Below them, the sea beat on the rocky shore. Where was he destined to breathe his last, Tristan wondered with sardonic detachment, or would any of these rocky outcrops do?

The road rounded the last craggy bluff. Clinging perilously to the edge of the cliff, a little stone building lay ahead on the side of the road, and suddenly he saw where they were taking him. Gods above, it was the chapel on the rock, the church where Mark and Isolde had been married and he himself had given the bride away!

Suddenly, he felt again its wintry cold, the desperation of a place imbued with the chill of death. They called it a chapel, but it was no more than a simple cell, built in ancient days by one of the earliest holy men in these parts. The holy man had chosen its location, too, a stark structure of cold stone on the edge of a cliff, hovering over a dizzying drop to the sea below. The old hermit had been so strict and pure of heart that he could not bear to live near lesser mortals loaded with sin. Tristan shivered. Who would choose to shun his fellow men and live such a drear, lonely life? Why did the Christians make everything so hard?

The captain's gruff voice sounded again in his ear. "This way, sir. In you go."

Rough hands thrust him over the threshold, and he found himself inside a bare, whitewashed cell. Thin slits in the side admitted a dim light, and an unglazed window at the end overlooked the sea. Below it stood a simple black square of stone. This was the altar where the old hermit had prayed long ago, and where Father Dominian had married Isolde and Mark.

Tristan gasped. Gods and Great Ones, was this Andred's idea of a joke? His sight faded, and he saw himself standing in the little chapel by Isolde, as he had done on that ill-fated day. Through the mists of time, he saw again the white-robed choristers, the stone altar blazing with candles, and the priest in his glittering vestments intoning the prayers. His head swimming, he thought he could still hear the ancient stone walls echoing with the sound of the long-dead choir caroling hymns and psalms to welcome the bride. *Jubilate Deo*, swam across his mind, Rejoice, rejoice in the Lord . . .

The priest's voice rose over the choir. Beloved in Christ, we are gathered here—

Now Isolde stood beside him as she had that day, veiled from head to foot in white silk like a shroud of snow, a winter queen: cold hands, cold heart, all cold. Mark stood beside her in red fox fur and red velvet, with Cornwall's ancestral gold crown on his head and a rich show of jewels adorning his hands, neck, and breast.

Outside the unglazed window, a winter sun shone as white as a sea-washed bone. A biting wind blew in through the slit in the wall, bringing with it a flurry of snow. In a dream, he watched the white flakes drifting to the ground.

*Who gives this woman to be married to this man?*

*I do.*

*I now pronounce you man and wife* . . .

"Sir Tristan, ho?"

It was Dominian, the priest.

And here they all were now, in the present, just as they had been then, the little priest and a crowd of knights, all thrusting into the chapel, packing the cold space behind him and crowding the clifftop outside. Tristan laughed. He was going to die before an audience, it seemed.

Andred read his face. "Yes, we're all here to help you make a good end," he gloated. "Rest assured, Tristan, we shall pray for you."

Dominian, too, could scarcely contain himself. "And I urge you to make your own prayers, Sir Tristan. You have grievously sinned."

"Only by your laws, priest," Tristan returned hoarsely. "Not by mine."

The croaking of a raven sounded overhead.

"That's your death warrant, Tristan!" Andred cried, reveling in his power. "We're going to throw you from this chapel onto the rocks below. Then the sea will take your body, and when it's found, no one will know how you died."

Tristan flexed his wrists. "Andred—"

But Andred was not to be stopped. "Think of it, Tristan," he crowed. "While Mark is punishing your lady, the fish will be feeding on your flesh and gnawing your bones."

Tristan's mind split. "Yours, Andred, not mine!" he howled.

The blood rushed to his head, and the world turned black. One thought alone was thundering through his veins. Dimly, he heard Glaeve's fierce cry: Kill, master, kill! Swelling with rage, he clenched his fists and, with all the force at his command, broke free of his bonds.

"So, Andred!" he gasped.

Leaping forward, he wrenched Glaeve from Andred's hand and drove the blade straight into Andred's heart.

"Wha—?"

Andred's eyes widened, and he slumped to the floor. His mouth fell open, and his soul fled from his body with its last ragged breath. Howling with rage, Tristan leaped across the lifeless form and flourished the point of his sword at the nearest knights.

"Bear witness, all of you," he panted, "that I never wronged this man. Yet he has hated and pursued me for twenty years. Still, the Gods are just. In seeking my death, he has met his own." He waved Glaeve round his head. "Tell this to all the world, if you call yourself knights. Now get out of here, if you wish to live!"

But they were already falling over one another in their haste to get through the door. With a final volley of curses, Tristan slammed the stout oak behind them and thrust home the bolt.

On the roof above his head, the raven gave one last ominous croak and flew away. Andred's death knell then, not his. Tristan's spirits soared with the bird into the airy void.

"Thank you, brother," he cried.

He could hear the knights muttering and arguing outside.

"—what now?" he caught.

"Send for the King," came another voice. "He'll decide what to do."

There was an unpleasant laugh. "Well, he's safe enough here while the King makes up his mind . . . "

Tristan smiled and shook his head. Not for much longer.

He ran down the cell and lightly leaped up on the altar, then climbed through the window giving onto the sea below. Standing on the ledge, he looked down at the drop, light-headed with excitement and relief.

Below him, the sea lashed the rocks, and mountainous waves drove in to break themselves on the foot of the cliff. One after one, the white-crested, stormy billows raced madly into the shore and ran out again on a high, fretful tide. Tons of water shattered into shining pieces like shards of glass and then formed again with a sullen, menacing roar. He was almost too high to hear the voice of the sea, but he felt its sucking and sighing all the same.

Now he thought he saw maidens below him in flowing gray robes, splashing and sporting like seals among the waves. Fearlessly, they swam to and fro, floating between the sharp rocks, laughing and calling out to him. Come, Tristan, come! One swifter than all the rest leaped out of the water and dived back again in a tangle of bright hair, red-gold like Isolde's in the morning light.

My lady . . . Oh, my love—

Come, come . . .

Every shell on the seashore was singing to him now. Tristan listened, and his soul was at peace. To jump from the cliff was no more than falling in love, a mighty leap of faith, springing off into fathomless nothingness to make safe landing on some far distant shore.

Wait for me, lady, in the World between the Worlds.

With one last prayer, he gathered all his strength and leaped into the void.

# chapter 41

They buried Andred where he fell, in the chapel on the rock. On Mark's orders, he was laid beneath the bloodstained flagstones in the crypt, beside the mortal remains of the hermit who built the cell. The Cardinal Legate performed the funeral rites with all the magnificence of the Mother Church, and Father Dominian gave a solemn sermon heaping praise on Andred as a fallen hero, one worthy to share the last resting place of a saint. The chapel, too, was as fine as it could be that day. Banks of candles, clouds of incense, and a white-gowned choir pouring hymns of loss and grief into the air all combined to send Andred's soul winging on its way, wherever it was destined to go.

But there was to be no ceremony for Tristan, by the King's decree. Let the sea take him, and the fish gnaw his bones. Death by water was too good for the deed he had done, the blood-murder of his own kith and kin. He had cheated justice by taking his own life, and now his sin and his punishment both lay with God. But had he lived, Mark threatened in a rage terrible to behold, he would have found out what it was to rob both his King and his country of Cornwall's rightful heir.

"Rightful heir?" scoffed Sir Nabon angrily when the word went around. "When we could never persuade the King to name an heir at all?"

"And when Andred's own actions have robbed us of Tristan, too," put in Sir Quirian heavily.

His fellow councillors nodded. Old Sir Wisbeck could hardly speak for tears. "Goddess, Mother, have mercy on us all."

"But how can She spare us from the wickedness of our fellow men?" demanded Nabon savagely. He buried his head in his hands. "Oh, my poor country! What else do the Gods have in store?"

THERE WERE PLENTY OF WOMEN he could have, Mark was sure of that. Once he was done with Isolde, his choice was not limited to the fatherless pair of Princesses from Dun Haven, the fat one and the thin. Indeed, he could hardly be bothered to think about them now. Tightening his girdle and thrusting his sword into its sheath, Mark pursed his slack lips and set his face like stone. First he would deal with Isolde, he promised himself. Then he would take time to consider Cornwall's next Queen.

He sent for the captain of Castle Dore. "You're sure she's held fast?" he demanded.

The captain nodded. "Deep underground, my lord, bolted and barred. But every day she demands to be released. She wants a trial, she says, to clear her name."

"Clear her name?" Mark turned a poisonous hue. "And how does she think she'll do that?"

Like most of Castle Dore, the captain had heard the wild rumors flying around and did not know what to believe. But he knew that he had never seen the King like this before.

"I couldn't say, my lord," he said, backing off. "All I know is, she's asking to see you."

"Is she, indeed?" Mark's eyes widened with a violent gleam. "Then we should do what the lady wants, don't you agree?"

The captain paused uncertainly. But he had no power to prevent Mark from visiting the cells. Carved out of the heart of the rock, the underground passageways had no natural light, and as they went down, Mark's eyes shone in the dark with inhuman glee. Indeed, he was rubbing his hands with delight as he climbed down the steep, slimy steps from the outer world with the last of the daylight fading around his head.

At the foot of the steps, the captain's lantern lit up a dank and dismal tunnel with a row of barred doors on either side. The captain gestured to the nearest cell, keeping a careful watch on Mark's face.

"We've done as you ordered, sir, kept her in the dark," he offered. "And on short rations too, just enough to keep her alive."

Mark smiled like a snake. "Is she yielding, then? That should break her spirit pretty soon."

"Not so's you'd notice, sire," the captain said stolidly, avoiding Mark's eye. "We hear her talking and singing to herself. Sometimes she chuckles and laughs, as if she had a friend in there. Whatever she's doing, it keeps her spirits up."

Mark smiled again, baring his teeth. "We'll see about that." He pointed toward the door. "Open up."

With a rattle of keys, the slab of oak swung back. The stale air of the dungeon came to meet them, and with it the dank breath of the heart of the living rock. The captain held up his lamp, and a white face at the back of the cell swam into view. As the two men watched, there was a flurry of soiled green silk, wild eyes, and disheveled hair as Isolde rose to her feet and surged forward into the light.

"So, madam?"

Mark thought he had prepared himself for anything Isolde could say. But her first words still took him by surprise.

"Why am I locked up?"

"What question is that?" he sneered to cover his surprise. "You're awaiting charges, madam, like any criminal."

Isolde squinted at him. Her eyes were paining her in the lamplight, and she was struggling to stand upright, but the sight of Mark's raw hostility restored her strength. "Pray you, release me at once. I am no criminal, and the least of your subjects is entitled to fair treatment at your hands."

"Fair treatment?" Mark's cry of outrage echoed around the cell. "Let me remind you that adultery is treason to the King. But you'll soon know all about treason and adultery, my dear. And the penalty."

Was he smiling? Half blinded by the lantern, Isolde could not see. But she knew that Mark was deeply enjoying himself.

"Yes, treason," he gloated on. "And now my faithless nephew is counting the cost of that, too."

"Prove it!" Isolde cried. "Prove that Tristan was ever a traitor to you or to Cornwall."

"He was your lover, madam!" Mark raged. "What more proof d'you need? When you gave yourself to him, you cheated me of what was rightfully mine."

Isolde thrust out her chin. "I was never yours, and you were never mine. We never pledged ourselves to each other, you and I. Tristan is my chosen one, by the laws of the Mother-right."

" 'Is,' lady?" Mark widened his eyes and began to enjoy himself. "Oh, of course, you don't know."

*Know what?* She could not help herself. "What is there to know?"

Mark laughed for joy. With a sharp shaft of pleasure, he thought of Tristan's broken body, mangled by its fall onto the rocks and rolling helplessly with the uncaring tide. "Tristan is dead."

*Dead?* Her heart set like a stone. "You've killed him."

"No, not I," chortled Mark.

"Andred, then."

Mark's face convulsed. "Nor Andred, neither. Andred's a dead man, too. Your paramour killed him."

"What?"

"Tristan killed Andred, then killed himself."

"Never!" A wild laugh of derision burst from her.

"Oh, it's true. Your noble knight killed his own cousin, then dashed himself to death." Mark was rubbing his hands with a kind of glee, she saw with disbelief. "He jumped onto the rocks from the chapel on the cliff."

*It's a trick. He's trying to break my spirit.* "I don't believe you. It's all a lie."

"You'll have the proof soon enough. The sea always gives up its dead."

"Spare me your empty threats," Isolde spat out. "And spare yourself. I'm not afraid of anything you can do."

"Oh, you will be, Isolde, you will. By the time I've finished with you, you'll be begging my forgiveness on your knees and groveling to me for the chance to live. You'll beg for the chance to submit to my rightful desires and bear my child."

Isolde heard herself laughing, a harsh, hateful sound. "And then you'll kill me. You only want me to see me brought down and destroyed. You don't want me as a wife."

"But you're still a desirable woman, as Tristan well knew."

Mark came toward her till she could smell his sweat. He thrust her into a corner and laughed in her face. Now his hand was moving over her body, groping for her breast.

"You say I don't want you," he breathed into her neck. "My dear wife, how would you know?"

THE SUN WAS SETTING on a sea as smooth as glass. But no matter what face the Lady wore, he loved her just the same. Sighing from his heart, the young sailor gave thanks that he had found his path. Not a dull highway on the land such as dusty, earthbound folk trod, but the whale-way, the waterway where the great beasts swam.

And he had seen them himself, with his own dazzled eyes. What a voyage, eh? Dreaming, the boy recalled distant islands where the hot, spice-laden air greeted seamen as they sailed in, and the skin of the people had a tawny-amber bloom. Where they sold pearls in the market as big as pigeons' eggs, and moonstones lay by the wayside on mountain paths.

But there was danger in this glory, too. He shuddered to remember other young lives like his suddenly lost: one shipmate stabbed in a brawl before he could draw his knife, and three dead of a strange shaking fever in the same day. Still, he was alive, he'd lived to tell the tale. And soon, very soon, they'd be landing at Castle Dore, and he'd be sitting by his mother's fire, doing just that.

"All well, sailor? Keeping a good lookout there?"

He had not heard the captain's easy tread.

"Oh, sir," he blurted out eagerly. "How far to land?"

The captain gave an understanding grin. Even the hardiest sailor longed for home.

"Not far at all now, lad." He eyed the boy keenly. "Just you keep your wits about you. The nearer to port, the sharper the watch has to be."

"Aye, sir."

Heartened, the boy fixed his gaze on the horizon, determined not to miss the first sight of land. But lost in thought again and aching for home, he did not see the darker black shadow on the gray-black face of the sea. Like a cloud in springtime, it came and went, rising and falling with the swell of the waves. But then it rolled over, and he saw a human face. Bloated and disfigured, gray-black like the water and with blind, sightless eyes, but a face just the same.

"Man at sea!" he croaked, almost speechless with dread. Gods and Great Ones, what an evil omen to welcome them home like this!

Within seconds, every deckhand was swarming to his side.

"Who is it, lad?" one of them cried.

"Not one of ours," he stuttered in reply.

"No matter for that," bellowed the captain, arriving to take charge. He jerked a thumb at the nearest mariners. "Get a boat down there, quickly, over the side. Two more of you follow with grappling hooks. Let's save the poor devil if we can." But already he could hear the sea calling, *too late.*

From the deck, the young sailor could hear the cries below.

"Get a rope around him."

"Gods, he's heavy!"

"Is he still alive?" called the captain.

"Dead as a doornail, sir."

"All the same, steady now, haul him aboard."

Alas, poor soul, the young sailor mourned in his heart. He knew that the heaving billows hid many secrets of the deep. Beneath the face of the ocean that mere mortals saw, lost sailors and voyagers went down to a better place. A world of glittering palaces lay below the waves, with vast hills and valleys and forests and shady groves. There the drowned sailors lived like Great Ones and took their ease, feasting on emerald tables out of sapphire bowls.

But the great battered body now lying on the deck was not one of them. He would never see his mother's face again, or sit by the fireside listening to old tales. Some woman who loved him would be mourning his absence, too, waiting to welcome him home to her arms. But the dripping hulk would have only one last resting place. Six feet of earth would be his housing now.

"Land ahoy!"

The lights of Castle Dore appeared at the head of the bay. Already they could hear the crash of the waves on the beach and the raw rattle of shingle in the dying tide. Out at sea, the silvery bar of the horizon darkened slowly toward night.

The captain folded his hands and lifted his gaze to the sky.

"Lady, take this soul," he prayed. "He's just one of the lost family of the sea."

# chapter 42

$\mathcal{A}$ savage sea howled round Tintagel rock. Overhead, the birds ran screaming before the storm and found what shelter they could from the furious wind. The creatures of the sea slunk down to the depths, and night-riding demons terrorized the sky. Inside the ancient fortress, the earthly occupants slipped fearfully to their beds. But a light burned steadily in the topmost tower, and within the spacious chamber, all was calm.

A tall figure stood at the open window, impervious to the wind and the driving spray. The sea dew settled on a fine white head and added new brilliance to the crystals in the ancient crown. The stately form held a shuttered lantern in her hand whose beam fell on a storm-battered seagull on the window ledge. Trembling, the bird poured out her troubled heart. And alone in her aerie, old Queen Igraine listened with a heart that echoed the brave messenger's distress.

"So then?" she questioned the seagull from time to time, stopping her to make sure she had the story right. At last she gently touched the bird's snowy head. "You have done well, my dear. Rest now till daybreak. You will be safe here."

She watched from beneath hooded eyelids as the bird's head dropped wearily upon her ruffled breast. Then she turned back into the room, pacing the floor.

"In the name of the Mother," she muttered, "we may not forgive."

The candles burned on. Then an angry clacking brought her to the window again. Perched on the ledge high above the ocean's roar was an old sea eagle, his windblown feathers tipped with gray and white. As Igraine approached, he fixed her with a glaring yellow eye and opened his beak.

Igraine listened to the furious cawing with a stony face, then held up her hand. "No more, Merlin!" she commanded. "I know all this and more."

Enraged, the bird resumed his high-pitched rant, his raw screeching notes blending with the howling of the wind.

"Yes, I know, I know," Igraine repeated. "But all this was written a thousand years ago. If you'd been there, could you have saved Tristan?"

She paused, ignoring the eagle's protests. "But think of Isolde, half-raped, then cast alive into a house of death. Punished by the one who promised to protect her when she gave him her hand. A woman alone, overpowered by men. What of her fate, Merlin, tell me that?"

THEY THOUGHT SHE WAS ALONE, but what did they know? When they left her in the darkness of the cell with nothing but water and a lump of stale black bread, they thought she'd run mad from loneliness and despair. And once the light of the lantern had faded into blackness again, it was hard, yes, hard to keep her spirits up. But those who had condemned her to this place had no sense of the world that lay beyond their ken.

*Good day, Isolde.*

Isolde smiled. She put out her hand and felt the greeting from a sleek-as-satin nose.

"Good day to you, Little Mother," she said warmly to the small, unseen presence that drew up to her side.

*How are you?* A wave of loving concern lapped over her like a midsummer tide.

She gave a rusty laugh. "Not as well as I should be, but better than I could be, and that's the truth."

*Hold fast to that, Isolde,* came the heartfelt response. *Do not let Mark break your spirit. Let all that you endure strengthen your resolve.*

She burst out laughing. "Mark break my spirit? He'll have to kill me first."

*Beware of that, Isolde.* She heard a deep sigh. *I fear he plans to do that, to take your life.*

"What, murder me? No, never." She hesitated, sucking in her breath. "Oh, I know he wants to bring me to my knees. He couldn't wait to tell me Tristan was dead. It's a lie, of course. I know that Tristan would never take his own life."

*But Mark also came to renew his attack on you.*

Frowning, Isolde shifted her back to find a more comfortable place against the unyielding rock. "He pinned me against the wall and tried to touch me, that's true. He pushed me into a corner and turned my stomach with the way he smelled. But as soon as he began, I struck back. And he remembered what had happened last time he made that mistake."

There was a soft whisper of amusement in the dark. *Oh, Isolde, it's good to see that Mark has not destroyed your spirit.*

She felt a sudden surge of sardonic mirth. "Nor will he, Little Mother, as long as I walk this earth."

There was a sudden silence. Then her unseen visitor spoke in a voice full of tears. *Oh, Isolde . . .*

Isolde craned forward anxiously. "What is it?"

*Listen!*

"I can't hear anything."

*Alas, alas . . .*

The voice was fading away. A sick dread swept through Isolde. "Don't leave me, Little Mother, don't go—"

*Farewell.*

The air stirred, and the creature was gone. A few moments later she heard what the sharp, shell-like ears had already caught. Slow, careful footsteps on the stone stairway meant that one of her tormentors was coming down. And more than one, to judge from the voices reaching her now.

"Careful, man. Keep your end up. I can't get him down by myself."

"This is madness. Gods above, what a weight!"

"King's orders, remember? And watch your tongue. The King's not far behind."

The second speaker groaned and gave a laugh. "But will he give us a hand to get this back up again?"

Now the shuffling and grunting was drawing up to her door.

"Stand aside," she heard the captain of Castle Dore say.

Then came the jangle of great keys and the solid oak swung back. All she could see was the captain's lantern, like a sudden starburst in a moonless sky. Then slowly her eyes took in the scene behind.

Framed by the doorway, a pair of shadowy figures began struggling with a heavy burden into the cell. Staring in disbelief, she watched two men-at-arms manhandle a makeshift stretcher through the door. On it lay a tall, well-built body covered by a cloth.

*Not Tristan.* She could not breathe. *Goddess, Mother, say it isn't so . . .*

Panting, the men set the litter down on the floor. Behind them Mark entered, treading on their heels. A grin of sadistic delight disfigured his face.

"Remember, Isolde, I told you Tristan was dead?"

She forced herself to speak. "Yes, and I throw that lie back in your teeth."

Mark's eyes lit up. He pointed to the body on the bier. "Then who do you think this is?"

Isolde held her breath. *Don't say anything. Don't play his game.*

But Mark needed no other audience but himself. Reaching down, he twitched the cloth off the motionless form.

"Let me show you, dear wife!" he crowed.

*Goddess, Mother . . .*

On the bier lay a man with Tristan's broad shoulders and narrow, horseman's hips. He had Tristan's long legs, too, clad in his fine woolen breeches and boots, though sea-stained now like the tunic he wore. Still, she knew the blue tunic and the tattered cloak.

But not even the dead man's mother would have known his face. Battered beyond all recognition, it was a featureless mass of dead flesh and bone. Her eyes shied away, and she could not look at it. But one thought pierced her mind. *This could have been Tristan when he was alive.*

*Oh, my love, my love . . .*

"It's not true," she said hoarsely. "It's a trick."

"You think so?" Mark hissed. His eyes were very bright. Reaching down, he picked up one of the dead man's hands. On the ring finger gleamed a band of antique gold.

"Ohh—" She thrust her fist in her mouth. *Goddess, Mother,* she howled in the madness of her soul, *help me, help me now!*

It was the ring she had given Tristan when they first pledged their love. It was all she had had from her father, her mother's first chosen one, a knight and hero of Ireland she had never known. He had died in battle before she was born, but he had left her this ring, and all her life she had waited to give it to her true love. It had fitted him perfectly, a deep band of red gold on the fourth finger of his broad brown hand. She had seen it there, held it, and kissed it for twenty years.

*Ohhh . . .*

Isolde closed her eyes. *Have you left me then, love? I never thought you'd go ahead of me to the world between the worlds. But I knew in the end that this world would break our hearts.*

Opening her soul, she soared into a lament.

*You were the best and truest knight that ever lived. You were the gentlest in war and the most fearless in peace.*

*Not a horse but knew the kindness of your hand, not a widow or a child but felt the strength of your arm. No companion knight relied on you in vain, no lady but was honored by your courtesy.*

*You were handsome in body and soul, generous beyond measure, and brave beyond all reproach. You were my first love, and you will be my last. There is no love, no life, for me without you.*

*Go then, my love and my delight. Wait for me in the world between the worlds and I shall follow, I shall be with you soon.*

She turned to Mark, quite composed. Never would she let him see her grief.

"So, sir, you have your triumph. Do what you will with me, I am done with you. If you will not release me, I will live out my life in prison now that Tristan has gone. It can't be long now you've almost starved me to death. And I pray you, trouble me no more. I'd die a thousand times rather than see you again."

Mark's face turned livid. "I can make you think again," he said thickly. "You know the penalty for a treacherous, adulterous queen."

Isolde shrugged. "Take my life; it holds nothing for me. I shall keep faith with Tristan till the seas rise to swallow me or the earth lies heavy on my bones."

Mark could not believe it. How could she cheat him of his rightful revenge?

His mouth worked with a passion he could not contain. "I'll burn you alive!"

She gave a ghostly smile. "Then I shall be with Tristan."

He moved toward her with slow, deadly steps, his face glistening with menace.

"You say that now," he spat out. "But death at the stake is a terrible way to die."

Isolde shook her head. "You offer me the very thing I seek."

"Think about it, my dear. It will help you mend your ways."

"Oh, sir." She was infinitely weary now. "None of us dies a death of our choosing or by our own desire." She paused. "But while you threaten me with death, spare a thought for your own. We all come from the cauldron of rebirth. If you hound me so cruelly to my grave, how will you answer the Old Ones in times to come?"

"Words, empty words," Mark scoffed. His eyes were alight with new venom. "I must bring down your pride and your beauty, too, since that's been the basis of your pride. Your beauty has been the ruin of you, so I must arrange the ruin of it in turn."

"Do what you will," she said quietly.

He rounded on, his face wild and alight. A mad vein was jumping at the side of his eye.

"Oh, I shall, never fear. And I have the very thing in mind for you. If I burn you to death, you'll only suffer for a while. Then the winds will scatter your ashes and, as you believe, the Mother will take you home. But what do you say to a slow death, my dear wife? Not so very painful to the body, alas, more of a creeping numbness in every limb. But an endless, exquisite agony to the soul."

Isolde looked at him, struggling to hide her fear. What did he mean?

Mark cocked his head to one side and held up his hand. "D'you hear that?"

Click, clack...

Click, clack...

The noise in the corridor made her blood run cold. With it came a heavy, shuffling tread and the regular thud of a stick on the ground. A limping figure was advancing toward the door, dragging its feet and sounding a wooden bell. Already she knew what the next sound would be.

"Unclean! Unclean! All good folk fly this place..."

It was the cry of the leper from the earliest times. Frozen, she saw a tall, muffled figure in the doorway, hooded and stooped in a covering of filthy rags. His hands and feet were bound up in bandages yellow with pus and stained with blackened blood. He clutched a wooden clapper in the remains of his fist.

Isolde's hand flew to her mouth. *Tristan?* Once, long ago, Tristan had rescued her from Mark's anger clad in a leper's disguise. The wrappings all lepers wore had concealed his face, and the fear of leprosy had kept suspicious souls at bay. But the first words from the newcomer's mouth dispelled all hope. It was a voice every bit as cruel as Mark's, the raw, unknown guttural of a desperate man.

"I'll need some help to get her to the leper house. You promised me a couple of your strongest guards."

"And you'll have them, never fear," Mark snapped at him. "A whole troop if you like. Just keep her confined and do what I've told you to do."

The man gave a terrible laugh. "No fear of that, sir."

Mark turned on Isolde. "Madam, you've ruled in two countries, with princes and kings at your feet. Now you'll live in a hovel without the strength to move. You'll be hobbling on sticks like this creature, scarcely able to walk. And soon you'll be crawling, begging on your hands and knees."

Isolde bared her teeth. "The Gods themselves will never see that day."

"You'll sing another tune in the leper house." Trembling, Mark turned away.

The leper shuffled forward. "Oh, we've plenty of singers there," he guffawed. "And she'll make a fine addition to our choir. And don't forget you said I could—"

"You can do what you like." Mark hooked his thumb violently toward the door. "Take her away, man. She's yours."

# chapter 43

*W*ait *for me, love.*
*Wait for me, wherever you are.*

They carried her from Castle Dore under cover of falling night, huddled inside a litter, for she was too weak to walk. Not a soul in the castle or the town saw her go. The townsfolk would surely have seen the great traveling bed, swinging between four horses plodding along, and the strong guard of armed men guiding it on its way. But they would only think that some high and mighty dignitary was abroad, not their onetime Queen, bound and gagged to make sure she did not utter a sound.

Lying on the litter hidden from all eyes, Isolde swore a great oath. One day her own people, the knights of Ireland and her trusty councillors, would raise heaven and earth to find her and avenge her wrongs. Then she would have satisfaction for these cruelties. But until then, she could only suffer and endure.

As they cleared the town, the trees were black against the sunset and hunched like desperate men. Curled up on the lumpy mattress with the stale smell of the musty hangings in her face, Isolde watched through a crack in the curtains and saw her future running away from her like sand. But she did not care. Tristan was dead. There was no life for her now.

She could not weep. She was lost in a pit of grief, but she had no tears. It was strange to be so unfeeling, so numb. Working the gag from her mouth, she struggled to sit up.

"Soldier?" she called. "Soldier? Is anyone there?"

There was a long pause, then the curtains twitched apart. She saw a mailed figure stooping down, and the honest face of a young captain came into view.

"Where are you taking me, soldier?"

With a shaft of pain, she saw he could not meet her eye. Doubtless all the men around him felt the same.

"To the leper house, lady," he mumbled with an aching heart. Gods above, when he'd signed on as a guard at Castle Dore, he never reckoned on anything like this. How would he tell his wife that they'd taken the Queen to a leper house today? He'd never be able to speak of it for the rest of his life.

"And where is that?" the low voice persisted.

"Outside the town," he replied. "Lepers are forbidden to live with other folk, so they've got a place of their own in the forest."

*Where they mean to lock me up with the man who came to collect me and take me away?*

"Very well," she said. In truth, why should she care?

The path wound onward through the dripping trees. At length she felt the horses slowing to a halt. As they set her litter to the earth and pushed back the drapes, she saw the leper she had met in the prison dismounting from his mule. Two of the men-at-arms pulled her from her couch and untied her bonds, then fell back in alarm as the leper approached. He swung himself forward on his crutch, smelling of rotting flesh and pus and blood, and waving a bandaged arm at the hovel ahead.

"Your new home, lady," he leered.

Ahead of her a long, low building crouched in a clearing, surrounded by a circle of ancient pines. Though they called it a house, it was no more than a rough shelter of wattle and daub, with two dark windows staring at her like blind eyes. But there was no mistaking the huddle of crutches and sticks round the door.

Around her the men-at-arms were muttering and shuffling their feet, eyeing the building with fear, impatient to get away. The young captain came toward her, white-faced.

"In you go, lady," he said.

She stood for a moment quite numb, unable to move. The nearest of the guards drew back, leveling their weapons as if to thrust her forward at the end of their pikes.

The leper laughed. "Just see us inside, lads, and leave her to me. I guarantee she'll be safe once I get her through the door. That's what I promised the King."

He nudged Isolde's back, and she forced herself not to flinch. *Whoever he is, he has his dignity. Whatever he was, he was better than he is now.*

The smell came to meet them as they neared the door, the same blend of sickness, pus, and blood that the leper himself gave off. Behind it rose a low jumble of moans and cries, a wailful chorus of misery and pain. *We've plenty of singers*, the leper had said to Mark, *and she'll make a fine addition to our choir.* Her stomach clenched to feel the force of his words.

The rickety door swung inward at his touch. Inside, she saw a wide hall lit only by the logs of a central fire. The leaping flames cast a flickering, bloodred light on a host of wild faces leering at her like demons of the night. As her eyes adjusted to the gloom, she saw a hundred and more sad outcasts, most of them pitifully deformed. Some had dreadfully swollen trunk-like arms and legs, others had no extremities at all.

*Alas, poor souls.*

*And this is what it means to be a leper, thrown on the dung heap of the world, no more than human refuse to be swept away?*

She gazed round in despair. Some huddled against the wall, moaning softly or talking to themselves. Others hunched round the fire in the center of the room, sharing a moment of wild gaiety around the flames. But most of them lay sprawled on rough piles of stinking rags, lying together in a hopeless, tangled heap, arms, legs, and stinking bodies intertwined. As the muffled figures lay mumbling and railing and crying out in their sleep, she could not tell if they were men or women, rich or poor, old or young. Even nature's dearest gift, the sense of self, had been lost to these desperate souls.

And they were not all adults, fully grown. Among the ravaged faces and wasted limbs, some of them would still be children in the world outside. And Goddess, Mother! Was that a woman with a baby at her breast? They lay on a floor of packed earth, without flagstones, rugs, or bracken between them and the worms. *Well, I shall be down there soon,* Isolde thought without a shred of self-pity, bowing before the others' pain. *Lay me in that world beneath this world and I'll be with Tristan.*

The lepers round the fire raised their heads to look at the new arrival as she came in. The light from the flames and the smoke inside the room lent a dreadful air of the underworld to their hooded faces, overbright eyes, and roughly bandaged forms.

"Welcome to the house of the outlaws!" cried her escort with a flourish that chilled her blood.

One of the men round the fire turned around in anger to answer the leper's hoarse cry. "Outlaws we are," he cried back. "But not of our own free will. We broke no law. We never chose to murder, rape, or steal."

"Yet we linger here, souls that the world hates and shuns," another sorrowful voice seconded. "Our punishment is worse than that of those condemned to suffer by law for what they have done. They know that sooner or later their agonies must end. But innocent as we are, we must suffer till death."

*Alas, poor souls, maimed and sick by nature and then punished for it so harshly, too . . .*

Isolde stepped forward, her heart in her mouth. "Oh, sirs—"

But the leper leader was before her, bearing down on the speaker with an unmistakable threat.

"Shut your mouth, will you?" he said menacingly. "No more of that." He gestured toward Isolde with a terrible leer. "We have a new inmate, my friends, and she's gently born. So let's have no more complaints. Madam here expects the very best. Which is why I'm taking her to lie with me."

He pushed Isolde onward down the room. At the end of the communal chamber, a wicker partition fenced off a private space, and a crude length of sacking served it for a door. The leper hooked it aside with the remains of his arm and drove her through. The light of the fire hardly penetrated the space within. All she could see was a huddle of bed rags on the floor, with the same sickly sweet smell of disease that the leper himself gave off.

Her sinister guardian threw back his hood, and she saw that he had no hair. No eyebrows or eyelashes, and not a hair on his head. Great suppurating sores covered his scalp and marched on down his neck, and she flinched to see the raw red craters oozing with yellow pus. He read her shocked face and laughed.

"Oh, it takes all your hair, this disease. Good thing I'm such a beauty without it, eh, my love?"

He came lurching toward her. Her legs, her body, her heart turned to stone. Close up, he smelled even worse.

*So, Isolde, is this your punishment?*

*Tell me then, Great Mother, what was my sin?*

"Well, Lazaran?"

A woman was standing in the corner of the room. Dusk as it was, she glimmered in the shadows with her own light. Her long black hair was shot through with gray, and her shapely face had a luminous sense of wisdom, peace, and calm. Tall and unmoving, she had the air of a queen of the forest, a mother deer of many summers who has seen many great stags come and go.

"Well, Lazaran?" the mellow voice resumed.

The leper twitched away from Isolde as if he had been stung. "Madrona!" he cried in a fury. "What are you doing here?"

"I have come to greet our newcomer."

Who was this woman? Isolde fastened hungry eyes on her. She had been a fine lady once, that was plain, and a grave beauty hung about her still. Her manner and bearing had a unmistakable nobility, and she carried herself with an undefeated pride. Isolde caught sight of a thick girdle of amber beneath her cloak, and at her waist she wore a bronze workbox on a handsome chain, containing all the implements of the lady of the house. Isolde looked at her in pity and wonder. Living here, the woman must know that she would never use her scissors, pins, needle, or comb again. Yet there was still the remains of a tattered dignity in her air.

The woman searched Isolde's face, then surveyed her hands. "You are not a leper."

"No."

"Do you have reason to think you have caught the disease?"

"None."

"Have you been confined here by family or friends, who fear you may have been in contact with leprosy and may pass it on to them?"

"Not at all."

She fixed Isolde with a gaze as still as water in a woodland pool. "Then why are you here?"

"On the orders of the King."

The woman nodded as understanding dawned. "You are the Queen."

"Of course she's the Queen," hissed the leper. "But keep it to yourself. I don't want all these reprobates knowing who she is."

Isolde felt her cracked lips smiling with bitter irony. "I was the Queen. But I have fallen foul of the King. All this has been contrived by my husband, Mark."

The woman did not look surprised. "You defied him. That was something he could not forgive. So he chose the leper house as his revenge."

Isolde gave a cracked laugh. "Can you believe it?"

The woman gravely inclined her head. "It's a punishment that jealous husbands like to inflict. And if you catch the infection here, that will suit the King, too. If you die in the wood, forgotten and unseen, no one can accuse him of your death."

Isolde nodded grimly. "And you? What brought you here?"

The proud head went back. "I came here to be with my son."

Isolde's eyes widened. "By choice?"

"It would be any mother's choice. I was a widow with an only son. We were well-to-do, we had our own estate. But my son traveled overseas and came back with the disease. I wanted to be with him and nurse him till he died. At least I could do that."

The woman glimmered at her with a grief too deep for tears.

Isolde dared not speak. After a while, the level tones resumed. "And afterward, I had nowhere else to go. My son is buried here, and I wanted to stay. The Gods had decreed that I would not catch the disease, so I go on taking care of those who have." A tender smile appeared on her careworn face. "They are my family now. And when I die, they will bury me with love. Not everyone can say that."

"Madrona? Madrona?"

A childish voice broke in on their debate. The rough sacking parted, and a slight, clumsy form came shouldering through. In a dream of misery, Isolde saw a young boy of eight or ten swing himself into the room on a rough forked crutch and reach out to Madrona with a hopeful smile.

Madrona's face lit up. "Come here, my prince!" She swept him into her arms.

Isolde felt her tears rising for the first time. "What a dreadful affliction this is."

Madrona paused. "There is not much pain. Lepers soon lose all feeling in their limbs. The worst is the numbness and slow loss of strength. In time, the disease burns itself out, and some suffer little at all."

"Is that enough, madam? Or will you talk all night?"

Isolde turned. The leper was looking at her with a savage, brooding desire, as if he was already fingering her flesh.

"Come, lady." He bared his teeth and reached out a bandaged hand.

Isolde took a breath and readied herself to fight. *But Goddess, Mother . . . to think of inflicting pain on a creature in pain . . .*

Madrona stepped forward, the child in her arms. "Think again, Lazaran," she said.

He turned on her heavily. "Think what?"

"Do not do this. Be wise and leave her alone."

"And if I don't?" he jeered.

Madrona turned away, as if bored. "Do what you like, the woman's nothing to me. I'm taking this child to bed, so I'll leave you alone. But if she's the Queen as you say, you'd better take care. The King's thrown her to you in a fit of rage. What if he changes his mind?"

"He wouldn't do that," Lazaran growled, his eyes darting to and fro. "He said I could do what I liked."

"And you believed him?"

"He's the King!" the leper blustered. "He gave me his word."

"Just as he gave his word to this very Queen," Madrona returned, "when he stood beside her in church and promised to care for her all her life. And look at her now. If he'll destroy the ruling Queen, my friend, what will he do to you?"

"Why should he do anything to me?" But the swollen face was dark with suspicion now.

"He could change his mind tomorrow and want her back. And in the meantime, you'll have raped her and beaten her, too, because you'll have to do that to force her to submit. If you've despoiled his darling, he'll flay you alive, no matter what he says."

The leper's tongue flickered out round his lipless mouth, and he seemed to shrink inside his rags before their eyes.

"Curse you, you're right," he snuffled with a savage oath. "Kings, like the Gods, love to play with us. He probably wanted to torment me with her. Or else he wants her here in torment, waiting for the blow to fall."

Madrona nodded gravely. "That's very likely."

Lazaran's bloodshot eyes flared. "Well, he won't make a fool out of me. I can bide my time. He's given orders that she's to be kept short of food, so the sickness will seize her all the quicker as she grows weak. When it does, he won't want her anymore. Then she'll be mine, and I can do what I want."

He turned on Isolde with the swiftness of a snake. "And it won't be long, my darling. Give us a kiss till then?"

# chapter 44

T he big knight rode out of the forest in the hour before dawn, when the last of the night stars still trembled in the sky. As he crested the hill and began the long, slow descent to Castle Dore, some of the townsfolk saw his great frame, dark in the mist against the rising sun, and were stung into a moment of wild hope.

"It's Sir Tristan!" shouted one of the watchers at the ford, leaping and splashing about in the shallows for glee. But he was a poor natural, simple since the day he was born, and in times gone by he had seen Queen Guenevere attended by a fairy host, a watery giant who lived under the ford, and the massed armies of Uther Pendragon at their last stand. So no one was inclined to believe what the shouting lad said. And the wiser sort knew the leap that Tristan had made. No man on earth could have survived that fall.

"It's not Sir Tristan, no," one of the women said gruffly. "He's gone from us now, my lad. He'll come no more."

The staring boy cocked his head to one side and grinned. "Who is it, then?"

This was the question in all the townspeople's minds as the stranger rode down the valley and up through the town. Men noted his fine weapons and splendid armor and put him down as a prince from Outre Mer. Women saw his worn face and haggard air and knew that even if he had come from that unknown kingdom beyond the sea, he had suffered cruelly, and very likely for love.

Who was he? followed him like a whisper wherever he went. And the same question was put again by the chamberlain when the stranger rode up to the great gate of Castle Dore and asked for King Mark.

"Who are you, sir? And what is your business here?"

The stranger shook his head. "My name is nothing, and my business will be brief. But tell your King that he may admit me without disgrace. I am a knight of the Round Table, and King Arthur is my lord."

"A knight of King Arthur, eh?" Mark demanded when the word was brought. "Gods above, fool, show him in at once! You can't keep a man like that dancing attendance in the gatehouse without food or drink."

Which is exactly what the King would have done in another mood, the chamberlain reflected rancorously as he bowed himself out. But between Mark's royal rages and his frightening black sulks, there was no serving him at all these days. Still, the stranger must be treated with chivalry.

"This way, sir," he offered politely, leading the newcomer up through the courtyards and cloisters to the King's privy chamber. He knocked and threw open the door.

"Sire, the stranger knight is here to pay his respects."

"Come in, come in," Mark cried.

At his invitation, a lofty, broad-shouldered figure moved into the room, carrying his helmet in the crook of his arm. The newcomer was clean-shaven and well-groomed, with long fair hair neatly trimmed and curled; but his broad face was never meant to be so thin, and his features bore signs of sickness and suffering. His large frame, too, was painfully lean for his height, and he walked like a man far older than his years.

Mark leaned forward on his throne, a sharp impulse of alarm springing inside his skull. Who was the gaunt stranger, and what did he want? Forcing a smile, he waved a welcoming hand.

"Greetings to you, sir," he caroled cheerfully. "What brings you to our court?"

The stranger bowed. "I am seeking Sir Tristan."

Mark tensed imperceptibly. "Are you, now? Why so?"

"I've come to thank him for his goodness to me." The knight laid his great hand on his sword. "I want to pledge him my oath of undying brotherhood."

"Gods above, man," Mark cried in a nasty tone, "what did he do?" The knight looked away with an awkward shrug.

"I can hardly answer that," he said uncomfortably, "except to my shame. But I am more than the battered knight errant you see now. I was once a man of honor, a knight of King Arthur and one of his Fellowship."

"A knight of the Round Table?" Mark's eyes narrowed. "Who are you, then?"

"They call me Gawain. I was Arthur's first companion, and I've sworn to be his last."

Mark's ungainly body twitched with shock. Was this worn, haunted creature the great hero Gawain, famous alike for his roistering ways with women and his tireless strength? The eldest of the four great brothers from the Orkney Isles? In truth, Gawain was King Arthur's cousin and closest kin, and they shared the same fair coloring and outstanding build. But just look at him now, Mark snarled inwardly. Darkness and devils, was everything these days turning out for the worse?

"Sir Gawain!" he said furiously. "I would not have recognized you."

A shaft of black humor crossed the wasted face. "After the time I spent in the forest, my own brothers would not have recognized me."

Mark stared at him. "What happened there? You've been sick? Imprisoned?"

"Both, to my great misfortune. I dallied with a lady in the forest, and she mistook my aim in courting her. She thought I was wooing her to be my wife, when all I wanted was the comfort of her bed."

Mark nodded viciously. "Well, what else are women for? That's all the comfort they can give a man." He felt his uncertain temper pricking him again. "And some of them won't even do that."

Gawain gave a painful grin. "Well, if I offended, I had my punishment."

Mark gave a venomous chuckle. "She locked you up, eh? Threw you into her dungeons and refused to let you go?"

"Worse. She trapped me in the prison of my own mind. She fed me poison till I lost my wits. Then she set me free to run mad in the forest, challenging all comers to fight me to the death."

"God Almighty, it's a wonder you survived," Mark marveled.

Gawain nodded. "Some knight on the road could easily have finished me off, or else I'd have died of starvation in the wood, living on acorns and roots like the wild swine." His burst of dark laughter sounded more like the Gawain of old. "It's a high price to pay for a few nights in bed."

"Women are strange beasts," Mark said feelingly. "They're monsters, in fact. A man can never trust them. They're not like us."

Gawain frowned. If women were monsters, he pondered, why did men desire them so much? And why did the King seem to hate the entire sex? But at least he could second Mark's conclusion with all his heart.

"That's the truth, sire," he agreed solemnly. "Women are not like us."

Mark leaned forward and jabbed him in the chest. "You agree with me, then? A man has to keep them down. The Romans knew that, they had the right idea. And now the Christians are saying the same thing. Women should be subject to men. It's the will of God."

The will of God that men should keep women down? Gawain thought how much he loved a wild and willing girl and felt his doubts about King Mark rising again. What man could want a woman who didn't desire him, too? Who didn't lust after him as much as he lusted for her, hungering for him till her back teeth ached? Why should men want to keep women down, when it was often hard enough to arouse them at all?

Gawain stroked his chin and made a diplomatic bow.

"As you say, sire, women are a trial to men. And I would still be subject to the lady of the castle if Sir Tristan had not saved my wretched life. He came across me when I was running mad in the wood and refused to fight me, though I challenged him to the death. Then he took me to a hermitage to be healed. He did not recognize me because I'd changed so much, and I didn't know him because I was out of my mind. But the hermit and his fellows helped me to recover my wits, and my first task now is to thank him on my knees."

Mark quivered and drew back. "Who, Tristan?"

"Yes indeed," Gawain said wonderingly. "Will you send for him, sire?"

Mark crossed his legs and shifted uneasily on his throne. "Didn't the chamberlain tell you when you arrived?"

"Tell me what?"

Mark rolled his eyes. "Alas, I have a great sadness to report. My beloved nephew is dead."

Gawain turned pale. "Dead? How?"

"He ran mad and threw himself off the cliff."

Gawain clutched his head. "In the name of the great Gods, why?"

Mark heaved a heavy sigh. "It's been a time of loss. Tristan's wits turned when the Queen caught leprosy, lost her beauty, and retired to a leper house to die."

Gawain shook his head, stunned. He could hardly believe it. "A double blow for you, sire," he forced out at last.

Mark brought a bunched fist to his eye and knuckled out a tear. "A tragedy beyond all. But fear not, Sir Gawain, we shan't neglect a guest. We'll feast you tonight, and you shall eat like a king. After your ordeal in the forest, you deserve no less." He gave a sudden chuckle, startling Gawain. "I have a pair of sisters here at court, one so fat that she's falling out of her gown, and the other so slender she hardly fills her shift. You can take your pick."

Gawain bowed his head. Was the King serious? All this when Tristan was dead?

"Sire, I thank you for your courtesy, but I fear I must decline," he returned in a low voice. "After what you've just told me, I'd be poor company at a feast. If you'll forgive me, I will take my leave."

Gawain was going? Good, very good. Mark congratulated himself on his luck. The sooner the big knight was gone, the better it would be. Gawain must not know what really happened here. And as soon as Gawain was gone, he'd have a chance to work out the story he was going to tell the world, including the treason of the two lovers and Andred's death. God only knew how he was going to explain the loss of both his nephews to his overlord, Queen Igraine. But he would worry about that when the time came. Uneasily, he put the thought aside.

"Come, then, Sir Gawain," he said in ringing tones, "let me speed you on your way. And when you next pass a church or a holy place, say a prayer for me in my terrible loss."

# chapter 45

Was she still in the leper house in the wood?

And was it still summer or the deep, dead heart of the year?

Isolde lay huddled on her pile of rags on the floor and found no answer to hard questions like these. But always she dreamed of better times to come. Alone in her cell, except when Madrona was near, she had all the time in the world to think and dream.

Yet even in this strange misty time and place, some things were real. The noise and the sickness were real, as were the cries and groans and the lepers' eternal stench, and her own body's weakness, increasing every day. She was ill, she knew, and there was no escaping that.

How was she ill? She had no idea. Sometimes she thought it was hunger that had brought her so low. Mark had kept her half starved in the cell at Castle Dore, and now that she lived with the lepers, she ate even less. At dawn every day, all those who could walk or crawl set off to the town to beg for food. They haunted the back kitchens of great houses to pick up the waste, then scavenged the refuse dumps of Castle Dore till they had filled their greasy satchels with all they could find. As dark descended, they would carry the booty home, back to the hut in the forest where the rest lay in hope.

When the food-bearers arrived, the excitement was intense. The housebound lepers all came crowding around as the satchels were turned out, jostling and cursing and fighting among themselves. But Isolde had no stomach for these foul and broken scraps. She could not even stand the smell of the sweet and savory leavings all jumbled together. The whole mess was hardly fit for pigs. Madrona tried many times to coax her to eat, then turned to stronger tactics when gentleness failed.

"Come, lady," she said forcefully, kneeling beside Isolde with a bowl of slops. "I've begged off your body from Lazaran's lust because you're the Queen. It'll be a poor recompense for me if you let yourself die."

"Yes, indeed," Isolde said, or tried to say.

In truth, she did not know if the hoarse whisper echoing around her mind ever reached her lips. But the older woman had cared for her from the moment she arrived, and Isolde wanted so much to do what she said. Madrona had even taken her into her own cell, the only private corner apart from Lazaran's in the whole house.

But when Madrona urged her, "Eat, lady! Eat!" she found herself dreaming of the midwinter feasts of the past. The foul hovel around her melted into the mist, along with the endless low moans of the lepers and the stink of their fleshly decay. Then the reedy lament of the flutes came into her head, and she saw figures dancing in an ivy-clad hall. Great bundles of pearly mistletoe gleamed on high amid spiky branches of holly bright with berries as red as blood.

And then Tristan was in her mind, too, his harp sweeter and his leap higher than that of any of the revelers in the hall. His eyes were brighter than any berries, and when he smiled, his lips and teeth put the red of the holly and the pearls of the mistletoe to shame. When she saw him like this, dancing and singing with his harp, it came to her that he was surely dead.

"Oh, oh," she wept. "Oh, oh . . . "

*I did not believe you, Mark, when you told me so. You hated me and Tristan, so I thought it was a trick. You wanted to break my spirit, and I could not let that be. But now it must be true.*

Tristan could not have come to her to dance and sing if his spirit was still chained to this mortal earth. It meant he was already walking in the Beyond, and not a soul could call him back again.

*Oh, oh, my love.*

*My only love lost and gone.*

"Wait for me, sweetheart," she whispered. "I will soon be there."

Now she blessed her sickness, for it would bring her to Tristan sooner than she might think. And now she knew that whatever afflicted her, it was not hunger as she once had thought. Every day she forced herself to eat something to please Madrona, but her pains did not ease.

Soon she could no longer hold down any food. At night she shivered, and all day long she burned. When she felt the fever running through nerve and vein, she called to Tristan in her heart: *Soon I'll be with you, love. Wait. I'll be there.*

"Do I have the disease, Madrona?" she asked hopefully, through pale, dry lips. "Am I a leper now?"

The older woman looked at her with a heavy heart.

"Not as I know it," she said carefully. "But you have a sore fever, and that's bad enough. And if you don't take some liquid, you'll burn up." She reached for the beaker of springwater on the floor. "Let me moisten your mouth a little. Just a little . . . Good, that's the way."

But no one could live on water and hope to survive.

"She must have milk," Madrona told Lazaran.

"And where will that come from?" the leader of the lepers sneered.

"From a cow," she retorted, "as it always did. Will you beg some for her in the town?"

The leper shook his muffled head. Sourly, he gestured to the band of tense and hungry beggars, all clustered behind him ready to depart. "With these wretches to manage? Not I."

"But the Queen—"

"I'm off." He cut across her with a heartless wave. "If you want milk for our fine lady, beg yourself."

Which is how Madrona came to leave Isolde alone, having first tenderly covered up the feverish figure on the floor.

"I don't like leaving you, but won't be long," she assured Isolde, tucking her up firmly inside the pile of rags but leaving her arms free to throw off the covers if she got too warm. She set the wooden beaker near Isolde's hand. "Try to drink some water while I'm gone."

What was Madrona saying? Whatever it was, it could only be kindly meant. Isolde nodded dreamily.

"Thank you," she tried to say.

Through drowsy lids, she watched the older woman move toward the door, pausing to blow out the candle on the way. Now it was almost dark in the windowless cell.

"I hate to leave you without any light," Madrona murmured. "But if one of the others blundered in ..."

Isolde nodded again. If the candle went over, the rags on the floor would catch fire. Then, within minutes, the whole flimsy dwelling would burn down. Death by fire would be a cruel way to the Beyond. But it would open the gates to the Otherworld and bring her to her love.

She raised her hand and struggled to sit up. "Farewell."

But as soon as Madrona had gone, she slid down again, curled up the way a child would against a beating that must come. Meanwhile, Madrona set off down the track that led to the town, and Lazaran followed after her with his motley crew. So none of them saw the dark figure in the wood, watching and waiting till the last of them had gone. And still he waited, as motionless as a stone and as patient as a fox at a rabbit's den.

Time wore on. At last the stranger was satisfied no one would return. Moving as lightly as a shadow, he left the shelter of the trees and crossed the clearing to the leper house. He paused on the threshold for a swift look back, then shouldered through the door to the place within.

Once inside the house, he froze against the wall, blending into the dark roughcast and loam. Before him lay all the lepers too crippled to go to town or too sick to stir, some moaning softly and twitching in their sleep, others snoring like cows bellowing to be milked.

*Not there ... nor there ...*

*Over there, then?*

*No.*

The newcomer surveyed the sad heaps of lost humanity one by one, but he did not find the face that he sought.

Huddled by the walls and clustered round the fire, the inmates slept on unaware. The few who stirred and opened one eye saw nothing but a heavily muffled creature like themselves, his hands and feet bound up in pus-stained rags. Like them, he had bandaged his head to hide his face, and a ragged cloak concealed his stooping form. But he limped along nimbly on his makeshift crutch as he passed down the hall to the curtained cells at the end, snatching a candle from the wall as he went.

In there?

No.

A swift glance round Lazaran's private place showed an empty bed and not a soul within. He turned to the next sheet of sacking and swept it back with one stiffly bandaged arm.

In here, then?

And there she was. All alone, curled up on the floor.

No one else by.

His alone.

*Yesss!*

$\mathscr{G}$od speed you, Sir Gawain."

The whole castle had turned out to see Gawain on his way. All except Tristan and Isolde, he thought heavily. His heart bursting, he acknowledged the cheers and waves on all sides. Every one of the servants hanging out of the windows, crowding the courtyard and filling every door, bore him the same goodwill, he knew. And the little priest who had just addressed him spoke for them all.

"Thank you, Father," he replied.

The priest squinted at him. "Where lies your way?"

"I am going to seek my three brothers and take up the Quest with them."

Dominian's coal-black eyes burst into fire. "God will bless you, my son," he said fervently. "You and your fellow knights. And one of you will bring home the Holy Grail."

Gawain rubbed a rough hand across his chin. "Not I, alas," he said ruefully. "It's said that the Knight of the Grail must be peerless in battle, the finest fighter of our fellowship. Most of us think that that's Sir Lancelot."

Dominian's face darkened. "God has also decreed that the knight who succeeds in this most holy quest must be free from sin. And Sir Lancelot is—"

"Is what, sir priest?" Gawain broke in with a truculent air.

Father Dominian gave an angry cough. "He is known to be the knight who serves Queen Guenevere. Too closely, some men say."

Gawain stared him down. "Come, Father," he said heartily, after a pause. "Even in a Christian kingdom, a queen must have her knights."

Mark twitched his shoulders and stepped forward. Jesus and Mary, what an oaf Gawain was, to speak of knights and queens after what Isolde had done! But the big knight had no idea of her treachery with Tristan, that was plain.

"Enough of this," Mark cried. "It's all superstition; we don't know the truth." He turned to the priest. "Tell me, Father, how can the Grail prophecy come about? Where will you find a man without stain or sin?"

"In a pure virgin, on the pattern of Jesus Christ himself," Dominian replied with a baleful glare. "Our Lord was not known to women, as you know."

"Well, we have one like that in Camelot now," said Gawain thoughtfully. "The boy Galahad might work your miracle. He's a knight of the Round Table, too, young as he is. He's only just come to court, and he has no interest in women, as far as I can see."

Dominian switched his gaze from Gawain and stared balefully at Mark. "And all men know how women lead men to sin."

"True, alas," Gawain said grimly. "As I know to my cost. Well, let me be on my way. The rest of us may never find the Holy Grail, but we can honor King Arthur by taking up the Quest. We can all glorify the Round Table Fellowship and do deeds of worship as we go along."

"Indeed you can," cried Mark. God Almighty, he raged inwardly, would Gawain never go? With a clumsy gesture, he clapped Gawain on the back. "Remember me to your dear brothers, Sir Agravain, Sir Gaheris, and Sir Gareth. King Arthur must be grateful for such fine kin. You four Orkney princes will be an adornment to any quest."

"God bless you, Sir Gawain," Father Dominian said intensely. "May He watch over your every step and speed your way."

Gawain moved forward and took the reins of his horse. "Thank you both."

Mark stepped back and raised his hand. The heralds on the battlements raised their trumpets and flourished a fine fanfare of farewell. The silver notes slid down through the chilly dawn air as Gawain mounted up and made his last farewells. Then he turned his horse out through the gateway with a leaden heart.

Not another word of Tristan or Isolde on Mark's lips, he pondered in some distress. Why wouldn't Mark talk of them? It was as if they had never lived.

"Goddess, Mother," he muttered, "save me from the Christians and their prayers, and watch over my steps as I go. And if you can—" he paused to scratch his head—"I beg you, give me some understanding of what has happened here."

TAP, SCRATCH . . .

Tap, tap, scratch . . .

Isolde never knew if the sound of the crutch dragged her from sleep, or if some other sense warned her of the dark figure approaching through the door. But suddenly she was coming to the surface from the depths of a heavy dream. She was lying on the floor and someone—a man—was standing over her.

"Who's there?" she whispered.

There was no reply. All she could see was a candle clutched in a none-too-steady hand and a muffled figure looming behind the flame. She strengthened her voice. "Who is it? Answer me."

There was a long, slow pause. "A friend," she heard at last.

A friend? She did not know the hoarse, breathy voice. The newcomer held up his candle.

"See, lady?" he said.

She could see nothing. Who was it? Isolde tried to sit up, determined to confront the intruder on his own terms. But as she did so, her head swam and she fell back. *Goddess, Mother, this fever* . . . She broke out in a cold, clammy sweat.

The newcomer moved a step forward, and the candle trembled in his hand. Her eyes failing, Isolde could not hold him in her view. Then her sight shimmered, and she guessed what he was. The tall, shrouded figure was a fetch, a spirit of Otherwhere, one of the three worlds, perhaps, or the astral plane. A ghost warrior even, come from the world below, or a messenger from the Dark Lord Penn Annwyn, sent to bring her home. A dew lay on his rusty rags that was neither rain nor seawater nor mist, but like the tears of the Mother for the sorrows of the world. Was he her death?

"Who are you?" she said wonderingly, without pain or fear.

His voice when he spoke was bitter, strange, and remote. "A homeless wretch who has to hide his head. A poor castaway like all the inmates here. Except you. You're the Queen."

"The Queen?" Isolde's face cracked in a mirthless smile. "Yes, that's true."

"And still married to the King?"

"True again, sir."

What did it matter to him? she wondered. Why was he questioning her relationship to Mark?

*Unless . . .*

Her heart lurched with fear. Unless he planned to take her to his bed. She was the only woman not deformed and disfigured in all this house of disease. If his thoughts were turning that way, he could take her now.

*Goddess, Mother . . .*

Her mind labored to save herself. *But he'll leave me alone if he fears to offend the King.*

*Yess!*

Madrona had saved her from Lazaran by using this ploy. It was the only weapon she had, alone as she was.

"Yes, fellow," she said strongly, "I'm the wife of the King. I'm here under his protection, and his men are watching us now."

She heard him catch his breath. After a heavy pause, he began again. "If the King is protecting you, why has he put you here?"

"I am here of my own volition," she heard herself say. "Having crossed the path of some lepers, I feared I had caught the disease. So I persuaded the King to let me retreat to this house, to find out if I was infected or not. But the King is anxiously awaiting my return."

"Is he, now?" Again she caught the heavy, indrawn breath. "But around town they're saying that you're to be burned. For treason and adultery, they say."

She tried for a careless laugh. "You know better than to believe what people say."

"So you're not in danger?"

*Gods and Great Ones . . .*

Isolde's senses swam. She was dreaming, she knew. She must be, if she thought she knew the voice, a voice she'd never hear again this side of the grave. She raised a hand to her head and felt the fever raging to her bones.

*But the voice . . . ?*

*He sounds like—*

*No! No, no.*

Her heart convulsed. It was a trap, it must be. If he sounded like Tristan, it was another man.

Who was he, then?

*Gods above, who knew what he was?*

She summoned the last of her strength. "Get out!" she shrilled. "I am still Queen. Leave this place at once."

But instead he came closer, lowering his voice. The wavering candle danced round his hooded face. "Answer me this, lady. I hear you have lost your love."

*Lost my love?*

*Lost Tristan?*

She could take no more. Let him do what he wanted with her, she would never deny her true love for any man's threat. Whatever he did, it would only hasten her end and bring on the time she would be in Tristan's arms.

"Lost my love? Not so." Isolde gave an Otherworldly smile. "He comes to me between daybreak and evening tide, between dawn and dusk. He waits for me on the margins of the day, and his hand helps me forward into dark or light. At the water's edge, he is always waiting for me. And when I come to the last crossing, he will be there."

"You have not lost faith, then."

She laughed through her pitiful cracked lips. "I'll sooner lose my life."

"But they say that Tristan is dead."

"Not to me." Again the ethereal smile. "Never in all three worlds to me."

"And the King is giving it out that you'll die, too."

"Very likely."

"And you're not yourself, lady. How long have you been sick?"

Now the voice was familiar in its every urgent throb, and the mists were gathering inside her head. "No matter. I have a fever. Go away now. Save yourself."

"Save myself? When you lie here so ill? Goddess, Mother—"

She heard a stifled oath. Then the stranger was on his knees beside her bed, seizing her hand and bringing it to his lips. "Oh, lady, lady—"

*I have died,* she thought, *and gone to the Island of Bliss. I know this voice . . . this hand . . . this kiss . . .*

The stranger was weeping quietly at her side. It was a long time before he found his voice. When he spoke, she knew what he would say.

"Ah, lady, lady . . . Do you not know me, my love?"

# chapter 47

Tristan alive?

*Oh, oh . . .*

Tristan here and folding her in his arms?

*Oh . . . oh . . . oh . . .*

Her senses spun. Or Tristan dead and with her in the Otherworld? Was it all her sickness and the madness it brought? She could not tell.

It came to her then. *I have lost my mind. Or else I have died, he has died, and we're walking the world between the worlds.* How could Tristan be alive when she had seen his great body, his clothes, and his ring?

"Who are you?" she said hollowly.

By way of answer, he crushed her to his chest, raining kisses on her lips, her head, her neck. Tears as soft as dew fell on her upturned face as he muttered his broken thoughts into her ear. *Wherever we are,* she thought in a dream, *this is Tristan, this is the man I have loved.* His kiss on her throat revived a thousand joys, and his scent embraced her, musky and hot and strong.

"Tristan?" she said timidly, like a child.

His heart surged. Gods above, how she had suffered while he'd been away! He could hardly bear to hold her thin body and look into her eyes, shadowed with horrors too great to be borne. As he cradled her in his arms, he felt her burning skin and saw her cracked, parched lips. A thought came to him like the call of a distant bell: I shall kill Mark. The man who will do this has no right to live.

Slowly, her darkened eyes fastened on his face, then wandered away round the cramped, fusty cell. She raised a hand, but it fell back into her lap. *I have no strength,* she thought, but she was too weak to tell him even that. A soft breath of laughter escaped her, and she saw a sudden flare of panic in Tristan's eyes.

Why was she laughing at such a difficult time? *Goddess, Mother, have I lost my mind?*

"Lady, I know you're not well, but tell me if you can. These men Mark has set to watch you—are they here in the leper house or in hiding outside?"

"Nowhere." She laughed again. "There's no one there."

"You made it up?" He laughed in disbelief. "What for?"

She shook her head, too weak to reply. But he understood.

"You thought I'd come to rape you," he said savagely. "So you wanted me to think the King's men were on guard."

*When you'd come to save me,* she wanted to say. *And I only succeeded in dragging the whole thing out. Because then you had to find out if it was true. And I kept up the whole story to protect myself.*

But she could not get any of the words out of her mouth. It was all too hard.

"Lady—"

She became aware that Tristan was bringing the beaker to her lips. Obediently, she tried to force some of the water down. Tristan watched her in evident pain. "Tell me," he said quietly, "when did you last eat?"

"Are we dead?" she replied inconsequentially.

"I don't think so, lady," he said smiling, his eyes on her face. "I'd like to convince you that I'm still alive."

"I don't know," she said slowly. She raised a hand to his face. "Mark brought me your dead body."

"Oh no, lady," Tristan laughed harshly. "Not mine."

"But he wore your clothes."

"Easily obtained from my quarters by Mark's men."

"And he had the ring I gave you on his hand."

"Your father's ring?" Tristan held out his left hand. "But see, I have it still. And you know I'd lose my hand rather than this ring."

She reached for his hand and stroked the band of gold. With its strong lines and simple design, it would have been easy to copy or substitute. And Mark would have had no problem in deceiving her in the darkness of the cell, when his only motive had been to torment her.

"But I did see a body," she said sorrowfully. "Whose do you think it was?"

"Alas, who knows?" Tristan groaned. "Some poor drowned soul washed up at Castle Dore. Travelers, fishermen, those who don't wish to live, there are many who die like that, the lost children of the sea." He paused with a grim sigh.

Isolde felt her tears beginning anew. "But my love, my love... Andred took you off to kill you. How did you survive?"

"I jumped from the window of the chapel on the cliff."

"With a sheer drop onto the rocks below?"

Tristan nodded. "I didn't care if I lived or died. But I made the mightiest leap of my whole life. I thought I was jumping into the arms of death, and I meant to embrace the Dark Lord with all my strength."

Isolde looked at him enthralled. Born in the wild, Tristan could leap like a stag, and his powerful frame would have taken him far from the shore.

"So you cleared the rocks?" she asked, marveling.

"With the help of the Goddess, I did. And the tide that day was unusually high. As I jumped, the sea rose to meet me and broke my fall."

Isolde gave a beatific smile. "The Lady takes care of her own. But what happened then? Oh my love, my love, wherever have you been?"

He reached out to stroke her face to comfort her. "I was swept out to sea on the turn of the tide," he returned. "And then I exhausted myself, struggling to get back. When I was finally picked up by a ship, I was close to death."

"And they brought you back," Isolde said joyfully.

Tristan laughed. "Alas, no. The ship was bound for France. I found myself set down on their coast without a penny to my name and hardly a stitch to cover my nakedness. But the captain took pity on me and trusted me. He lent me some money and helped me to an inn. I rested there till I'd recovered my strength, then made my way back by the fastest ship."

"And found me gone," Isolde said grimly.

"Indeed I did." Tristan's voice darkened at the memory. "Mark is giving it out that you are dying and may be dead."

"Of leprosy?"

"Or some other dread disease."

Isolde tried not to sound bitter. "That would suit him very well."

Tristan lightly shook her shoulder. "Except that you aren't going to die." Briskly, he crossed to the sacking over the door and squinted down the long hall to read the sky outside. "The day is waning. It's time we were on our way."

Isolde passed a hand across her face. "But where are we going? How are we going to live?"

There was a muttering from the inner room.

"Lady, we have to go," Tristan replied urgently. "We mustn't be caught here when the others return."

"Goddess, Mother, yes!" Isolde gasped. How could she have forgotten the danger they were in? She tried to get to her feet.

"Let me help you."

Tristan could not bear to watch her struggling. His heart burned to see her wan and wasted frame and the charcoal smudges round her suffering eyes. Swiftly, he leaned down and took her in his arms.

"I'll carry you to my horse," he said. "It's not far. That'll be the quickest. We have to get away as fast as we can."

"I can walk," she protested hoarsely.

He brushed this aside. "Lady, we have to get you out of this leper house. Then I'm taking you to a place where we'll both be safe."

*Will we?* The unspoken words hung trembling between them.

*Will I be free of leprosy?* ran through Isolde's fevered veins.

*Can I keep my lady safe?* beat in Tristan's mind.

But one thought chimed between them in perfect accord.

*Whatever happens, we shall never be divided again.*

# chapter 48

W here are we going?"

"To safety, my love. Have no fear."

*To the wildwood, then. That's the safest place Tristan knows.*

"Where are we now?"

"Getting there, lady."

"Is it much farther?"

"Not too far. Hold fast to me and I'll bring you there."

*Yes, bring me to the wood. Then we shall be safe.*

"It's so dark, Tristan."

"Courage, sweetheart. Not much farther now."

"But it must be midnight or more. When shall we be there?"

"Soon, soon."

*Soon, soon, soon . . .*

"Are we there yet?"

"Almost, my lady. Can you see a light?"

"Where?"

"Straight ahead."

"No, I can't."

"Look again, lady. Look through that clump of trees."

"Over there?"

"Yes. I set the lamp in the window to light us in."

"Oh, Tristan—it's the castle in the wood . . ."

"Don't weep, my love. I swear we'll be safe here. No one knows the secret of the hidden grange. Hush now . . ."

There was a lengthy pause. Then he said, "Oh, lady, oh my love . . . Do you hear the owls calling and the roe deer's cry? The whole of the wildwood is welcoming you home."

"THIS WAY, SIR."

The Audience Chamber gaped ahead, stark, cold, and bare. But all too soon it would be filled with warm, jostling bodies, when the crowd of people at the gate would be admitted to the presence of the King. Mark himself would not make his entrance till all the petitioners had been admitted to the hall. But when he came, he would take his seat on the dais, and Sir Nabon made for it with a deliberate tread.

"Follow me, sir," he encouraged the knight close behind. "If you stand here by the throne, you'll be first to speak to the King. And I know he'll be anxious to hear what you have to say."

"Thank you, sir," said the knight with a courteous bow.

Nabon waved his hand. "No thanks are due. A message from your mistress is of the highest importance to her vassals here. How is Queen Igraine?"

The knight's handsome young face suffused with respect and love. "As ever, Sir Nabon, a wonder to us all. Ageless and beautiful, merciful and wise."

Nabon grunted in misery, eyeing the sealed parchment the knight carried in his hand. Mark would need more than the old Queen's mercy to right the cruel wrongs he'd committed of late. And Queen Igraine was only mortal, after all. What could she do?

He wanted to weep as if his heart would break. If it had not broken already, with Tristan dead. And Isolde as good as dead too, locked up with the dead and dying by the will of the King . . .

Stop it, old fool! he chided himself fiercely to banish the tears gathering in his eyes. The Mother herself will not let Isolde die. And who knows but that this knight has brought help from Queen Igraine?

He turned his gaze to the knight. The newcomer was regarding him with a sympathetic but puzzled scrutiny.

"Are you well, sir?" he asked.

"Of course I'm well, yes, yes." Tetchily, Nabon brushed the question aside. "Let's just make sure you're the first to speak to the King. He won't be long now."

From the corridor came a distant, slow-growing roar. Nabon nodded. "The guards have admitted the people. Any minute they'll come pouring in. Just make sure you hold your ground."

Moments later the doors of the chamber went back and a tide of humanity washed into the room. Old and young, thin and fat, well-dressed and poor, all thrust their way in and flocked toward the dais. Behind them came the weaker vessels: women with children and babes in swaddling clothes, the aged, the lame, and the infirm. The sour smell of their bodies came in with them: soiled clothing, stale food, and greasy hair. But rising above it, breathing from every form, was the fragile scent of expectancy and hope.

Hope? thought Nabon bitterly. There was nothing to hope for from Mark. But Igraine, now . . .

He looked again at the knight holding the old Queen's message in his hand. Perhaps there was something here?

"Make way for the King!"

The heralds were busy clearing a way through the crowd. Behind them came Mark decked out in full array, gowned and cloaked in ermine and silk and velvet of royal red. He wore his father's crown upon his head and seemingly half the gold of Castle Dore round his neck. He looks almost dignified, thought Nabon bitterly. Let's hope he receives Igraine's knight with dignity, too.

But following Mark were half a dozen young men who made Nabon's heart sink to his boots. Gods above, he snarled, that ever I should regret Andred's death. But since Andred had gone, there was no one to restrain the King. Mark wanted what he wanted, like a child, without thought of the consequence. And without Andred to check Mark's violence and greed, the King had become increasingly dependent on rogue knights like these, unscrupulous men of little chivalry.

And now the entire court had fallen silent, all staring at the dais and waiting for the audience to begin. Nabon's flesh crawled. Happily, Igraine's knight seemed not to notice Mark's entourage as he stepped forward and gave his deepest bow.

"I bring you a message, sire, from Queen Igraine. My lady, your overlord, salutes you through me and desires you will read these words from her own hand."

With another flourish he knelt and delivered the scroll to Mark at the foot of the throne. "I am also ordered to wait for your reply," he went on. "I'll be ready to leave as soon as you've decided what you wish to say."

"Very well."

Mark stared at the letter with dread swelling around his heart. What did it mean? What would Queen Igraine say?

Forcing himself to act, he broke the seal. The black letters within leaped out at him like spiders and seared his eyes. Every word frayed his self-control and heated his blood.

QUEEN IGRAINE TO HER VASSAL AND SUBJECT KING MARK, GREETINGS FROM THE ROYAL STRONGHOLD OF THE ANCIENTS, TINTAGEL ON THE ROCK.

SIR, WE HAVE HEARD SAD NEWS OF THE DEATH OF YOUR NEPHEWS AND THE SORE FATE OF YOUR QUEEN. AS WELL YOU KNOW, YOU HOLD YOUR THRONE ENTIRELY AS OUR VASSAL AND ONLY BY OUR GOODWILL.

WE REQUIRE YOU THEREFORE TO COME TO TINTAGEL FORTHWITH AND PRESENT YOURSELF IN PERSON BEFORE OUR THRONE. YOU MAY ACCOUNT FOR YOUR ACTIONS WHEN YOU COME AND MAKE ALL EXCUSES THEN THAT ARE FITTING TO BE MADE. BUT YOU MUST KNOW THAT SUCH TREATMENT AS YOU SEEM TO HAVE GIVEN TO YOUR QUEEN WILL NOT BE ENDURED IN THE LAND WHERE THE MOTHER RULES. DEEDS OF EVIL CANCEL OUT YOUR VASSAL BOND TO ME. PREPARE YOURSELF THEREFORE TO LAY DOWN YOUR THRONE.

Lay down the throne?

Mark choked back a laugh of murderous, seething rage. So he'd lost his lands and his throne because he'd got rid of his treacherous nephew and put his whore of a wife into the leper house? God Almighty, he should have strangled her long before this with his bare hands!

Steadily, the mist rose behind Mark's flaming eyes. Strangled Isolde? He should have had her burned. Stoned. Flayed. Torn limb from limb.

And now...

He felt himself slipping. He could see the dark abyss ahead.

And now he must go to Tintagel and face the old Queen? An odd smile split his face. Well, he'd go there indeed, but with an army of men. They'd storm the fortress and take the castle on the rock, then he'd hang the old Queen by her fingernails from the very top.

Or else he'd have her burned, like Isolde.

Stoned.

Flayed.

Torn limb from limb.

"Sire? Sire?"

It was the chamberlain, shaking in every limb. "Sire, there's an army of lepers at the gate. Their leader says he's brought news that you'll want to hear. But already the guards have barricaded all the doors. They won't let him in except by your special command."

Mark's brain twitched and sang like the string of an overstrung bow. "Then give it them!" he shouted wildly. "Let him in, you fool!"

"Admit a leper?"

"God save us, they're unclean!"

Crying out in fear, the waiting petitioners began to make for the door. Swiftly, a crush developed as they trampled each other in the rush to get out.

"Back! Back!" howled the oncoming guards, forcing a way through with their pikes. Behind them walked a lean, muffled figure, his bandages round his face, slowly and sardonically swinging his wooden bell.

"Unclean!" he cried with a terrible laugh. "Unclean." He reached the foot of the throne and made a clownish bow. "News of your Queen, my lord."

Mark's soul leaped up with a wild, dreadful hope. "Is she dead?"

His burning brain reeled. Now that Tristan and Andred had gone, if she were dead, too, there'd be no one alive left to tell the tale. Then he could say that all three had died of a terrible fever that had driven them mad. Possessed by evil spirits, Tristan had killed Andred, then hurled himself madly to his death, and Isolde had run away to the leper house. Dead, yes! How marvelous. *Yess, dead!*

"Not dead, sir, no," said the leper with a leer. "In fact, the opposite. Lively enough to have made her escape."

Mark's eyes bulged. "She's escaped?" he yelped. "Got away?"

The leper nodded. "I left a houseful to watch her while I went to town, knowing she was too ill to move." He shrugged. "When I got back, she was gone."

Gone...

Mark felt himself slipping again. "She was sick, you say?" he asked hoarsely.

"She had a fever. She was too weak to sit up or walk by herself."

A dark shaft of horror opened at Mark's feet. If Isolde had left the leper house in that state, who had taken her away? Who would have wanted to do it? Who would have cared for her enough to risk his life?

There was only one answer.

God Almighty, could Tristan be *alive?*

Mark could not bear it. Yes, it was true that Tristan's body had never been found. And, of course, when another body had been washed ashore, he had used it to convince Isolde that Tristan was dead. Indeed, those who saw it thought it might have been Tristan himself. It was about his height and weight, and the dead man was impossible to recognize because his features were gone.

But Tristan never had hammertoes, as the dead man had. Still, dressed in Tristan's clothes and Tristan's boots, with an old ring on his finger from the royal treasury, he looked convincing enough. And every day Mark expected to hear that Tristan's real corpse had been found.

So far, it had not.

God have mercy, *was he still alive?*

Nabon hurried forward. "The Queen's gone, did he say? And in a state of fever, too? We must find her, sire. I'll send for the healers, and we'll get out a search party. I'll get the torches and dogs here at once—"

"Silence, Nabon," Mark hissed. Inside his head, the world was breaking apart. But one thing was becoming increasingly clear. Tristan himself could be alive or dead. But someone had spirited Isolde from the leper house. She could not be allowed to get away. He had to find her and this unknown accomplice at once.

"Hot pursuit!" he cried. "Raise a hue and cry."

"Hear me, sire."

"I want the country scoured from end to end."

Nabon clutched his head. "Sire, I beg you—" he cried.

"Raise all the knights and barons under your command," Mark ordered, his eyes aflame. "We ride at once to hunt Isolde down."

# chapter 49

*a*ll round the ancient grange, the forest slept. Tucked deep in its narrow valley, the house slumbered, too, enjoying the sweet calm of ages beneath its thick roof of trees. Overhead, a slender new moon silvered the green of the leaves, and the night-roosting birds sighed and held their peace. But in the midnight woodland, one soul was awake. The man slipping silently through the trees came to rest beneath a towering oak and paused for thought. This was the place. The fugitives had to be here.

He chuckled to himself and rubbed his hands. He had to admit it was a good place to hide. A narrow track leading into an almost invisible cleft in the hillside veiled by long fronds of trailing ivy and honeysuckle. Yes, they were in there, he was sure of that. Moving forward again with great stealth, the dark figure staked out the narrow approach to the hidden grange.

It was true there were no signs of human presence and little to be seen. If they'd come on horseback, the horse had been turned loose a long way back, and hardly a blade of grass had been disturbed. Yet still he'd wager his life they were inside the house buried deep in the side of the hill, with a dark lantern and a banked-down fire. And if they were in there, he'd found what he sought.

But careful now, he schooled his impatient heart. Move slowly, watch and wait. No mistakes now, not so near the goal. He must pause and think and plan. And when he was ready, that would be time to act.

The mournful moon retreated behind a cloud. A deeper darkness fell upon the earth, and the night grew darker still beneath the thick roof of leaves. Better and better, he prided himself, the best. Oh,

this had been very well done, and the triumphant ending would justify it all!

"TRISTAN?"

Isolde came to herself with a groan. When would she stop waking in
a panic, dreading to find herself back in the cell? But before the fear had
had time to take shape in her mind, he was at her side. "Yes, my love?"

At the sight of him, she could not hold back a smile. "Nothing—I
only wanted to know you were here."

A muffled candle lit the little room, and he knelt beside her in
silence in the shining gloom.

"I'll never leave you now," he said at last. "I'll always be here."

She looked round the comfortable den with an uneasy laugh. "Not
here, don't say that, it's bad luck. Not anywhere in Cornwall. We must
get away."

He took her hand. "Lady, I swear we'll set out for Ireland as soon
as you're well enough to move."

"And that won't be long. Oh, Tristan, how can I thank you for nursing me back to health?" She lifted his hand and placed in on her forehead. "See, the fever's all gone, thanks to you."

He laid the back of his hand against her cheek. "It's true," he said
tenderly. "You are better today."

"And I'll be able to ride again in a day or two. It's only a question
of building up my strength." Tears sprang to her eyes. "And thank the
Gods, I didn't catch leprosy. We're so lucky I was spared."

"Well, the fever was bad enough," Tristan replied. "You could have
died from that."

"And I'm sure a lot of those poor lepers will," Isolde sighed. "There
will always be sudden infections like that when a lot of sick people are
huddled together in one filthy place."

A shadow passed over his face. "If only I'd come for you sooner
than I did. But it took me so long to get back from France."

"Oh, my love, I won't hear another word," she said firmly. "You
came as fast as you—"

"Ssshhh!"

Without warning, he froze and laid a finger on her lips.

Isolde started. "What—?"

He shook his head at her: *Don't speak!*

"There's someone outside," he mouthed.

*Goddess, Mother, save us . . .*

She could not move. They sat in silence, as she frantically strained her ears. There was nothing to hear but the night sounds of the wood. Then . . .

Was that a stealthy footstep right outside the door . . . ?

She could smell the living essence of her fear.

"Courage, lady," Tristan hissed. He pulled her close to his chest. "Listen to me," he whispered in her ear. "This is what we'll do . . ."

THE VALLEY HE STOOD IN was as dark as the grave. So no one saw the intruder as he left the shelter of his tree and glided forward through the starless night. Mantled with thick curtains of ivy and huddled into the hillside like part of the rock, the hidden old grange kept its secrets well. But the newcomer had had long enough now to understand how it lay.

This way, then . . .

Quietly, easily, man . . .

Some distance from the door, he paused to think again. Careful, now. All could still be lost. But they were inside for sure, and this was the only way out. He could not miss them now.

Around him, he knew, the whole valley waited and watched. The night-roaming creatures cowered in their holes, and even the soft loamy earth forgot to breathe. Trembling, the moon hid its head. It is time, thought the watcher to himself. It is time.

Silently, he lowered his visor to cover his face and unsheathed his sword. There should be only two of them inside, but it always paid to be careful at times like this. Hefting the weapon in his hand, he moved forward, intent on the ivy-curtained door directly ahead. To his surprise, it swung back on its hinges and a shaft of candlelight streamed out into the dark. Behind the candle, a female figure craned forward, shaking with fear.

"Who's there?" she called. "Who's there?"

Isolde! The intruder laughed. Gods above, there she was...

Still laughing, he strode forward through the door. The next second he felt a kick like a horse in his back and found himself sprawling face downward on the floor.

Tristan slammed the door and jumped on the prostrate form.

"Quickly!" he gasped, planting his full weight on the intruder's back. "Quickly now, tie his hands."

In an ecstasy of haste, Isolde fumbled to tie up the stranger's wrists with all her force. Then she drew her dagger and dug the tip of the blade into the soft flesh behind the intruder's ear.

Tristan scrambled to his feet and leaned down to roll the helmeted figure onto his back.

"Who is it?" Isolde cried. "Surely Mark can't have found out already that I've escaped? And he must still think you're dead."

"I don't know," he panted. "But I'll get the truth out of this fellow now." He wrenched off the heavy helmet. "So, sir," he cried savagely, his knife at the stranger's throat. "Who are you, and what d'you want?"

Isolde leaned over him. "And don't expect any mercy from us, if you've come from Mark," she said furiously.

The stranger threw back his head. "Come from Mark, lady?" A burst of laughter shook his long, thin frame. He fastened his gaze on Tristan. "Why, Tristan, what kind of welcome is this? Do you not know me, old friend?"

"Know you?" Tristan leaped to his feet in a towering rage. "I've never seen you before in all my—"

But Isolde was staring at the newcomer with her eyes out on stalks. Gods above, how often had she seen this face?

And to think they had treated a knight of Camelot like this...

A fellow of the Round Table... King Arthur's nephew, the closest kin of the King...

*Goddess, Mother, forgive us!*

"Look at him, Tristan!" she shrilled. "It's Gawain!"

# chapter 50

awain indeed!" the big knight chuckled in delight.

"Oh, my friend—" Tristan gasped. He reached for Gawain's wrists and slashed madly at his bonds.

"Thank you, sir."

The big knight lay on the flagstones rubbing his wrists and gently feeling the broken skin behind his ear. Tears sprang to Isolde's eyes.

"And we attacked you—we feared you came from Mark. Oh, can you ever forgive us?"

Gawain heaved his great body off the floor and turned to face them with a somber air.

"Dearest lady, believe me, I would have done the same. King Mark is your enemy, there's no doubt about that."

Briefly, he recounted what had passed between him and Mark. Tristan listened impassively, but his eyes were alive with pain.

*Oh, my love . . .*

Isolde felt his sorrow resounding in her own heart. *Alas, it still hurts you to know how Mark has changed. It is true he loved you once as his dearest kin, his knight, his champion, and his chosen heir. But he has long since nourished a deadly jealousy of you.*

She turned to the newcomer. "You are welcome, Sir Gawain. I promise you we shall make up for this discourtesy."

Tristan shook his head. "Gods above, old friend, how did you get here?"

"It's a long story." Gawain grinned. "Do you remember the madman in the wood?"

"The knight who had lost his mind?" Tristan gasped. A burst of understanding lit his face. "Was that you? And I didn't recognize you then, either. Gods, what a blindworm I've been!"

"But you saved my life. And when I recovered, I went to Castle Dore to thank you in person for everything you'd done."

Isolde heaved an angry sigh. "And doubtless Mark told you a string of terrible lies."

"Of course," Tristan said bitterly. "So how did you find out the truth?"

Gawain shook his head in puzzlement. "I hardly know. Mark told me you'd run mad and thrown yourself off a cliff because the Queen had caught leprosy and gone to a leper house to die. I believed him at first. After all, why should the King of Cornwall make up a story like that?"

Tristan nodded grimly. Gawain was known to be a better fighter than a thinker, rarely one to question what he was told. Mark must have hoped that Gawain would carry this lying tale back to King Arthur and that the whole of Camelot and his fellow knights of the Round Table would swallow it, too.

He could tell that Isolde was thinking the same thing.

"What made you change your mind?" she asked Gawain.

"When I rode away, I had time to puzzle it out," Gawain explained. "You were the King's oldest nephew, his knight, his heir, and his closest kin. Andred had had a full ceremonial burial, yet he was holding no funeral for you at all. So you were obviously in some kind of disgrace."

Tristan threw a glance at Isolde. "That's right."

Isolde caught her breath. "The King had discovered our love," she said with difficulty.

"Ah," said Gawain gently and without surprise. "Indeed, something of the sort occurred to me. So I left Castle Dore by the high road, as if I was heading off to join my brothers on the Quest. Then I slipped back under cover of darkness and made a few inquiries around the town. It didn't take long to find out that Sir Tristan had been taken to the chapel under heavy guard and had never come out." He bowed to Isolde. "And that Your Majesty had been first imprisoned and then carried off to the leper house under duress."

Isolde closed her eyes. "What did you do then?"

"I went to the leper house to find you, madam. I thought that you'd tell me the truth about Tristan, whatever it was. And when I found you gone, I followed your tracks back here."

"Well done, good sir," Isolde said fervently.

Gawain leaned forward, beaming with pride. "And now I can thank you, Tristan, for saving my life. Gods above, what a friend you were to me that day! Count on my sword for the rest of our days."

But Tristan was not listening. "You said you tracked us here?"

Gawain grinned. "Yes, in the end. It took me a good while. You're a fine woodsman, Tristan, you know that."

Tristan turned pale. "How did you track us?" he forced out. "I went backward and forward to confuse the trail. We rode through rivers and over stony paths to throw off pursuit—"

"Oh, you didn't make it easy, I'll grant you that." Gawain chuckled with glee. "But as I soon as I saw one print of your old gray's great hoof, I knew you must have come to rescue the Queen. And now we can all—"

"Devils and darkness, man!" Tristan cried. His eyes were staring, and he grabbed madly for his sword.

"What?" In an instant, Gawain was on his feet, looking wildly about him, too, and picking up his sword. "What is it?" he cried.

Isolde groaned. "Don't you understand? Gods above, Sir Gawain, if you found us, then others can, too! All they have to do is to follow your tracks."

Gawain's great face fell. "But you don't know that anyone is after you."

*Oh, we do.*

In truth, her heart had been dropping with every word Gawain said. One thought possessed her like a darkening cloud. *Mark is on his way. Any moment he'll be here.*

Tristan read her mind. "Any moment," he agreed, his voice thick with dread. "We must leave at once." He gave a terrible laugh. "If we still can."

In one swift movement he blew out the candle and made his way to the window, peering out into the night. Beyond the curtain of ivy, there was nothing to be seen. A pale crescent moon rode wanly through the sky, and the stars twinkled thinly through a veil of mist. Nothing moved in the indigo depths beneath the trees, not even the night-prowling creatures of the wood. But Tristan's every hunting sense was fully alive. Except that he was no longer the hunter, he knew. All three of them now had become the prey.

Isolde could hear the thunder of her heart. At last Tristan spoke. "They're out there, I know it."

The low rustle that followed could have been anything. The same was true of the cracking of a twig. But as the clouds parted, there was no mistaking the brief glint of the moonlight on drawn swords under the trees. Tristan turned back into the chamber, a smile of desperate gaiety on his face.

"Mark has surrounded the place with his band of knights. There's no escape for my lady and me. But if you go now, Gawain, perhaps you can save your life."

Gawain gave a cheerful guffaw. "D'you think Mark would let me go? When I'd only make straight for Camelot to tell Arthur what a villain he is? No, no, I'd rather die here with you."

Hefting his sword, he reached for the dagger at his belt. Tristan had to smile. Fighting two-handed like this, Gawain was a foe to be feared and a dear friend to have on their side at such a time.

Tristan raised his sword in the air and listened to Glaeve's joyful call.

"Let them come, then," he said fervently. "We'll sell our lives dearly, the three of us."

"And we'll take Mark with us, or die in the attempt," Gawain vowed. He gave a rumbling laugh. "I shall look forward to that."

Tristan moved toward Isolde. "Oh my lady . . . my love."

*No tears, no fears . . .*

She gave him a flashing smile. "Wait for me, love, on the other side. And before that, sirs, let's give our enemies a battle that will live in memory till the end of the earth. Now, where's my sword?"

# chapter 51

o man is to move from here. Not a single step."

With a sweep of his sword, Mark pointed to the narrow cleft in the hillside ahead. Sweating despite the cold, he cast a baleful eye through the trees toward the hidden grange.

"Guard this entrance with your lives, every one of you. When I go in, I want them caught like rats in a trap. Don't let them get past you alive."

"Sire—"

If Mark had cared to notice, he would have seen Sir Nabon's loyal old face glistening with pain.

"Sire, do not act in haste," the councillor begged. "There may be many reasons why the Queen has taken refuge there."

"And all of them traitorous," Mark hit back.

"And we don't know she's with Sir Tristan."

"Well, Nabon, we soon shall."

Gods above, Nabon thought in dread, where did the King get that venomous smile, that mad, hectic glare? Aloud he returned as boldly as he dared, "We can't be sure, my lord. And even if it's true, every one of your subjects has the right to speak before the law takes its course."

"Nabon, beware who you defend." Mark's tone was dangerous now. He paused for emphasis. "Have a care for your own neck, my friend."

Nabon stared. Goddess, Mother, he cried inwardly, has it come to this? Threatened with death for trying to do right, when I've served the King so loyally all these years? And Mark would do it. He had no doubt of that.

Alas, Isolde . . .

His heart gave way, and he bowed his head. "As you say, sire."

Mark gestured to the knights and men standing round. "You're a good strong fighting force. Now be sure to guard this entrance," he ordered, "on pain of death. You understand, Nabon? No man is to leave this place. I'll take my own knights and flush the traitors out."

Knights, you call them? Nabon looked at the motley crew around Mark and hid his contempt. Among the lower ranks were weasels like Fer de Gambon, men without honor, guaranteed to turn a blind eye to whatever the King did. In the front were a dozen or so fearless and ferocious fighting men like the brutish Taboral. Their task would be to bring Tristan down. Nabon wanted to weep. May your Gods be with you, Isolde. And with you, wherever you are, Tristan, my friend, he prayed.

Mark turned his face up to the glimmering moon. His skin was filmed with an unpleasant sheen and a light of wolfish cruelty gleamed in his eye. He waved his sword round his head.

"Forward," he cried.

NO TEARS, NO FEARS.

How often had her dead mother said that?

*Goddess, Mother . . .*

Isolde's sight thickened and her mother stormed across her mind, raging in full combat as the Battle Raven, riding her chariot in the thick of the fray. Isolde gripped the sword Tristan had given her and wished she had her mother's great weapon of war for the battle that lay ahead. But that was back in Ireland with all the other treasures of Dubh Lein. This would have to do.

*Ireland . . .*

*Erin . . .*

*Home . . .*

She looked at Tristan and Gawain sharing a wild grin of defiance and smiled in her turn. They would all die tonight, she felt sure of that. Tonight her soul would wander Ireland's shores again as she made her voyage to the Great Beyond. Once again she would see the beloved green hills and taste the sweet, silvery rain, and then make the salmon's leap to a better place.

Or perhaps she would visit again the land of her heart, the country of her girlhood, where she had come of age. Now a green hillside swept serenely into her view, its rounded flanks reflected in a lake of sweet shining water as calm as beaten glass, its top crowned with orchards of apple blossom where white doves fluttered and sang in every tree. Isolde's heart swelled with joy.

*Avalon.*

*Sacred Island.*

*Home.*

"My lady?"

Tristan's urgent demand brought her to herself. "Yes?"

The battle glory was upon him now, and he had never looked so fine. He reached out and took her hand, then laid his arm along Gawain's broad back.

"We're all agreed we'll sell our lives as dearly as we can."

Isolde nodded, holding his gaze. *Wait for me, love, in the world between the worlds.*

In a trembling silence, he returned the pledge. *My soul is yours, my lady. You have my undying love.*

Gawain turned to Tristan and hugged him to his chest. Then he knelt to kiss Isolde's hand.

"I am honored to die in company such as this. And the bards will tell stories of this battle as long as stories last."

He reached for his helmet and chuckled ruefully. "The crows that pick over my bones will have to make my farewell to my dear brothers for me. My only regret is not having one more turn with them in the tiltyard at Camelot. I still need to teach Agravain a thing or two."

They armed themselves in silence, hefting their weapons and sharing the armor they had. Together they turned as one to face the door.

"Ready?" Tristan breathed.

Moving as one, they strode out into the night, the two men in the front and Isolde close behind. *I am ready to meet my fate, whatever it is. I have had a good life. Now it only remains for me to make a good death. And to die with Tristan will be the best that can happen if we cannot be together and free to live as we will.*

*Goddess, Mother, take us to your peace.*

"So, traitors!"

A high-pitched cry rang out from the dark. As they stood in the grassy clearing before the door, Mark stepped forward into the light. Behind him came a band of heavily armed men, emerging from the shadow of the trees.

Mark raised a quivering sword and pointed at the three.

"See these traitors, these liars, these adulterous rogues?" he shrilled. "They're your enemies and mine. I want to see them dead!"

"Liars and rogues? Never!" Tristan stepped forward, leveling his gaze at Mark. "I challenge you to single combat here. Make good your accusations with your sword."

"My sword against yours? Great God, you must be mad!" Mark released a snickering bellow of contempt. "D'you think I'd risk my life in combat with you when I can have the pleasure of watching you killed?"

Gawain's great face flushed. "For shame, my lord!" he said. "This is plain murder and treachery, not worthy of a king. How will you look when the tale gets out? All the world will take you for a bloodthirsty killer and a coward, too."

Mark laughed with open glee. "But the world will never find out, because none of you will live to tell the tale. Alas, I regret, Sir Gawain, that you must die, too, but I can't let you carry this story back to Camelot."

"Shame on you then, foul shame," Gawain said quietly.

Mark's eyes bulged. He leaped forward and struck Gawain in the face with his mailed fist. "Shame, yes!" he shouted. "Oh, you and your kind always loved to put me to shame. Well, I'm turning the tables now. None of you will laugh at me anymore!"

Gawain stood openmouthed and speechless, his hand to his bleeding cheek.

Tristan let out a roar and leveled his sword. "Gods and Great Ones—"

"Hold there, Sir Tristan, if you please."

All eyes turned to Sir Nabon as he shouldered up to Mark and swept a deep bow. "And sire, let me say the same to you: hold there. Let me appeal to your knighthood. Do not do this thing. For thirty years I've been the leader of your knights, and I must uphold the code by which we live."

Mark's eyes were very black. "What's this, Nabon? Are you a traitor, too?"

"Never! No man is more loyal to your house than I, except Sir Tristan here." The old knight threw open his arms. "Sire, let me mend this broken love between you all. Sir Tristan is the last kin you have left. He swore his oath of knighthood to you and has risked his life for Cornwall and for your sake. You cared for him dearly once, as the only child of your beloved sister, long since dead. I beg you, take him to your heart again. He will repay you to the last drop of his blood."

Mark laughed hysterically and jabbed his thumb toward Isolde with a disbelieving snarl. "And I suppose I should also forgive this whore, my Queen?"

Nabon winced. "I would not let another man use that word," he said quietly. "You married Queen Isolde in good faith, as she married you. But the love between you did not follow. All you can do now, sire, is to let her go."

"Let her go?" yelped Mark.

"Let her go," repeated Sir Nabon, holding Mark's gaze.

Oh, the good old man! Tears stood in Isolde's eyes. This was the true voice of authority. Mark had to respond.

But Mark was trembling uncontrollably now. He gestured madly toward Tristan and the dark bulk of the hidden grange. "What, turn a blind eye to all this?"

"Yes, indeed, sire," replied Nabon in his strongest tones. "Many people would understand that you had to challenge Sir Tristan when you thought he loved your Queen, and that you had to follow the Queen when she left the leper house. But that is as far as it goes. No one would accept that you were entitled to insult them both in the foulest terms, as you've done here. You've also struck Sir Gawain in the face, which the laws of chivalry say that he may not forgive. And refusing Sir Tristan's challenge will be proof to all the world that you are a recreant knight and an unworthy king."

"Nabon, no more!" threatened Mark. "They are both dead men. Hold your tongue, old fool, unless you want to die, too."

"Sire, I cannot," replied Nabon urgently. "I must speak out. This is the most shameful thing you ever did. You may not disarm and kill two men like this, still less a woman and a ruling queen."

Mark was shaking his head with the same strange smile. "It must be, Nabon."

"Never while I live," cried the old man. "Cold-blooded murder is more than the Gods can bear. The Great Ones themselves will strike you down!"

"Tristan's a traitor!"

Nabon's sorely tried patience snapped. "He's a better man than you will ever be!"

There was a sudden snicker from behind. They're laughing at me! flashed across Mark's mind. His sweating hands hefted his sword.

*Kill! Kill!*

The cry for revenge ran singing through his blood. Blind with fury, Mark turned on the old man and struck him down.

Nabon fell to the ground like a stone. Panting, he raised both hands to the wound on his head and feebly tried to stem the flow of blood. Then his eyelids fluttered and closed and he lay still. For a moment, not a soul stirred. Then a cry of pure anguish ripped through the midnight air.

Tristan leaped across the clearing toward Mark. His sword whirled once against the moon like the flight of a bat and its silver point sank deep into Mark's chest.

Mark's mouth gaped, and his face seemed to fall apart. Rocking back on his heels, he stared at Tristan in wild disbelief. "What—?"

Tristan groaned in horror and threw his sword to the ground.

Mark gave a wheezy laugh through a mouthful of blood. "You swore you were my knight till death."

"And so I was," Tristan said hoarsely.

"I sought your life. Now God has taken mine." Mark's eyes rolled in terror, gripped by a sudden thought. "So I'm bound for the fires of hell. Jesus and Mary, how many thousands of years will it take to pay for my sins? Oh, pray for me, Tristan, intercede for my soul!"

Isolde came forward softly. "Oh Mark, the Old Ones do not punish us for our faults. As we fall asleep, the Mother takes us all into Her arms, then we sleep in peace until we come again."

"You think so, madam? I wish I did, too."

Mark's mouth worked itself into one last spasm, then went slack. He lay on the ground, his mouth still open in his death shout, his eyes bulging as they had done in his life.

"Gods above!" Tristan shouted, hoarse with dread. "What have I done?"

Weeping, he fell to his knees beside Mark's corpse. Nearby lay Sir Nabon, covered in blood from the hideous wound on his head. Hearing his cry, the old man opened his eyes.

"The Gods will forgive you, Tristan, never fear," he said hoarsely. He forced a crooked smile. "You have done the right thing. Come here, sir."

He summoned the leader of Mark's knights with a wave of one hand. The man hurried forward and fell to one knee at his side.

"Hear me, all of you," Nabon rasped. "King Mark is dead. So the throne of Cornwall reverts to his overlord, Queen Igraine. Swear on your knighthood that you and your fellows will follow whoever she appoints as her new vassal here. And in the meantime, take Sir Tristan as your new lord."

"We shall, sir." White-faced, the man obeyed, then retreated to the ranks.

Isolde knelt beside Sir Nabon, drowning in grief. "Don't leave us, old friend."

He favored her with another rueful smile. "Madam, alas I must. I must now take the way of the swallow, the eagle, and the swan. I shall make the great voyage into the unknown and tread the void to the Islands of Delight." He laughed, coughing up blood and painfully turning his eyes to where Mark lay. "And I'll attend my master there as I did here. Bury me at his side, I beg you, for in my lifetime I was never far away."

Isolde bowed her head. "Sir, it shall be. And be assured Cornwall will never forget your name."

Hands clasped, she watched the old man's eyes droop in death as

Tristan and Gawain murmured their farewells. Then Tristan moved across to Mark and closed his eyes. Lovingly, he straightened out his body where it fell, giving him a dignity he had never had in life.

"Oh, my lord," he wept. "You were my mother's brother and my only kin. To you I swore my first knighthood oath, and for you I fought many cruel battles as Cornwall's champion and your own. You wronged me, sir, as a man should never wrong his kin and a lord should not wrong a knight. But your soul will have honor from me as long as I live. I shall bury you like a king and protect your grave. And I shall never forget you while my spirit walks."

Behind him, Isolde closed her eyes and soared soundlessly into Mark's last lament.

*Go, sir, take your soul's flight, wherever it may lead.*

*This day you planned to take three innocent lives, a deed of disgust to all men and women alive.*

*But still we lament your passing and bid you a sad farewell. And we wish you an easeful passage as you go.*

*In your life, you were starved of love. But all your hungers are rewarded now. You are going home. For all of us, a shining star waits on high, where there is no sorrow, no emptiness, no more cold.*

*Look, Mark, your ship stands ready at the quay. Your star beckons. Go with the Mother, then, start your immortal flight.*

*And may your God and mine feed your starving soul and take your lost spirit into Her endless grace.*

# chapter 52

Yet the lament still went on in the depths of her soul.

*Oh, Mark. What you might have been. What you will never be.*

And Gods above, how should she bury him now?

A husband who was no husband, a king who was never a king?

A knight who never lived by his knighthood oath?

An uncle who would have killed his nephew, a monarch who tried to destroy his only heir? And a man about whom the question would always remain: what good did he do in his life? Why did he live?

Enough, no more. After days of hard grieving, Isolde steeled her bruised heart to action. Mark had to be laid to rest, and she would do what had to be done.

But first they buried Sir Nabon, the loyal old lord who had given his life to save theirs. And to save his beloved Cornwall, which was foremost in his thoughts to the very end. Before confronting King Mark, and knowing that this could well cost him his life, he had sent a messenger back to Castle Dore. The man's task had been to rouse all the lords of the Council with a warning to be ready to take command and keep the peace, whatever happened in the wood.

So Isolde and Tristan found that all was calm when they rode back into Castle Dore at dawn the next day. Some had feared that there might be panic and unrest as soon as the word ran round that Mark had been killed. Instead, they found old Sir Wisbeck in the palace firmly at the helm, while Sir Quirian was busy patrolling the streets. There they encountered shock and sorrow at Mark's death, but no loss or grief. Mark would end his life as he had lived it, loved by none.

Or, perhaps, by one. At Sir Nabon's last rites, all the townspeople followed his coffin in tears to its resting place. When Mark was carried up to the chapel on the rock, many lined the streets, dry-eyed, but no one cared to see him to his grave. But a tall, lean woman with midnight black eyes and hair was seen haunting the clifftop before the funeral procession arrived.

Afterward, it was said she was seen there again, cursing and raging at the lowering skies, her long hair streaming in the bitter wind. The Lady Elva for sure, Isolde nodded sadly to herself. Once Mark's mistress, she had almost become his Queen, thrusting herself forward to take Isolde's place. If any woman had loved Mark, Elva had. No one could begrudge her mourning his passing now.

And the meanest soul deserves respect in death. They buried Mark equipped as the King he might have been, had his choices been better and his fates more kindly disposed. They laid him to rest with the battle-sword of his forefathers that no son of his would ever now wield in war, and the carved ivory warhorn that would never sound again. Then they blessed his spirit chariot as it embarked on its great journey, and prayed for its safe landing wherever it came to rest.

"He had no God to anchor his wandering soul," Tristan said heavily. "No woman or child to teach him the secret of love, no soul on earth to love more than himself."

Isolde closed her eyes and brought her clasped hands to her lips. "Take him to yourself, Great One, I beg. Somewhere in your vast realm, find his spirit a home."

"Amen to that, Lord God," muttered Father Dominian, hunched over Mark's grave. The little priest had not yet grasped the reality of his protector's death, Isolde knew. It would be hard for him to accept that from now on, Cornwall would follow the Mother faith again and would no longer be a country where his God would be enforced. But Dominian had taken the sudden change without protest, numbly resigned to what would happen now.

Not so the Pope's messenger, the Cardinal Legate Dom Arraganzo of Seville. No sooner had Mark been laid beside Andred in the chapel on the rock than the lordly Spaniard was knocking at Isolde's door. Admitted to her presence, he wasted little time in pleasantries, but went straight to his concern.

"Who rules this land," he demanded, "now that King Mark is dead?"

Isolde drew a breath. "That is for Queen Igraine to decide. King Mark held his throne as her vassal, and the right to rule Cornwall died with him. Sir Tristan is Mark's kin and his next heir, but the Queen may appoint anyone she likes."

Arraganzo nodded, his worst fears confirmed. "Perhaps even you, madam," he said silkily.

God, God! he cried inwardly, closing his eyes in dread, what is Your plan? You have surrounded us with pagans and sinners here. There's the old Queen Igraine, then Tristan and Isolde, unbelievers all, and the last one the worst. Lord, in Your wisdom, strike Isolde down!

And take the life of the old Queen in Tintagel too, he prayed on. These ruling Queens are against Your will. Why have you placed us at the mercy of these women here?

"So, sir?"

Opening his eyes, Arraganzo saw with a shock that Isolde had clearly overheard his thoughts. The smile on her lips blended pity and amusement in a way he could hardly endure. And was she trying to goad him when she opened her mouth and spoke?

"As you say, Queen Igraine might choose to give power to me, or to any other woman in the land. Would that be such a bad thing in your view?"

Arraganzo curled his long, elegant lip. "God has ordained that only men should rule. Why should we share that rightful power with you? Why should men give power to women at all? Think what you are, my lady, all of you. You're no more than a rib of Adam, the serpent's plaything, the dust of the earth."

Isolde sighed. "Ah, Christian, your ignorance is vaster than oceans, darker than a starless sky. Woman is the circle of the Goddess, through which every man passes at three key moments of his life. The first is in childhood when he is born, the second when a woman takes him into her as her man, and the last when he dies and the Mother takes him home. Every woman is the vessel of the Goddess, bringing new life to the world. And she is the Goddess in her life, in her family, in her home."

"Goddess?" Arraganzo's eyebrows lifted in raging scorn. "There is only one God—"

"And you Christians have stolen from our Goddess to deck him out," Isolde broke in as her faith flooded her veins. "Your holy Trinity is only our Goddess in her threefold incarnation of Mother, Maiden, and Crone. Your holy communion is our Goddess's feast of love, where all are served and none are sent empty away. Even your Grail—why, priest, every woman is a grail! Every man is born to seek the woman of the dream and to find his finest self in that great search. And when he finds her—why then, little man, what you call the Grail is a woman's vessel of her womanhood, forever rich, moist, and full."

The priest was quivering with disgust. When he spoke, he displayed his gathered bile. "Yes, always foul, lustful, and full of sin. How dare you talk of a woman's body to a man of God? Her instrument of generation, her noxious fluids, her rottenness within? These are loathsome things. They're all God's punishment on you for the sin of Eve."

"On the contrary." Isolde threw back her head with a full-blooded laugh. "Our religion encourages us to delight in our bodies and to share with our lovers the joy the Goddess gives. And that sharing, that love, brings forth our offspring, the children we love in the way that the Mother loves us. That's why we stand for birth, while you glorify death. Regeneration, not crucifixion, is our faith."

"But Jesus died for you." He paused, and she could hear his wondering thought. Even for you, madam, pagan and whore.

Isolde shook her head. "Why do I need your man-god from the East, when I have a Mother who was here before us all? All the earth is in the hands of our Great One, who is both land and sea. From her dim cavern underneath the earth she works at two mighty looms. At the first, she weaves life upward through the trembling grass, and at the second, she weaves death downward through the kindly mold. The sound of her weaving is all eternity, and the name we give it here is 'time.' But it is the warp and weft of all that is rich and rare. It is all we know of beauty in this world, though from time to time it comes to us as pain."

Arraganzo spread his fine hands. "Come to us, lady," he said winningly. "The love of our God takes away all pain."

A smile of great wisdom passed over Isolde's face. "Hear me, priest.

There is no life worth living without pain. Even love becomes pain when our loved ones fail and die. But the pain of change is the price we pay for growth. Without love, without life, without growth, we are hollow husks. The Great One gave us this world to enjoy it to the full."

Arraganzo felt his restraint slipping away. "Your Great One, madam," he spat out, "is a Great Whore. When women have the thigh-freedom you preach, it is the end of the world."

Isolde laughed, feeling the joyous mirth surging up uncontrolled. "Our Goddess gives all women the right to choose the man they lie down with, and whose children they will bear. One day even your dark god from the East will accept that women may name their own partners of bed and board."

"That can never be. God has made women weak in body and mind. They must have men to tell them what to do."

Isolde suppressed another wide smile. "Like the two Christian Princesses you brought here to Castle Dore?"

Arraganzo shuddered. God in Heaven, what a witch the fat older girl had turned out to be! And the younger one acting as her familiar spirit, howling and screeching all night like a black cat. Ever since they heard Mark had been killed, they had never let up their cater-wauling refrain, What's to become of us, Father, what about us? And neither he nor Dominian had the slightest idea.

"We won't go back to our father," Theodora had threatened with a red-eyed glare. "Don't try to make us do that."

"When we left, he was glad to see us go," wept the pale Divinia, as full of tears as a month of rainy days. "And we never want to see Castle Dun Haven again."

Never again . . .

Arraganzo came to himself with a shudder. Never again would he tangle with women, however Christian, however young. From now on he would leave it to others to match Christian Kings and virgins as they liked.

Isolde leaned forward. "We can return them to their father's house if they want to go," she said. "Or else they can stay here in Cornwall. You are welcome to leave them with us here in the Queen's House. My ladies in waiting will take care of them."

What, leave them in the home and heartland of a pagan whore? Well, they deserved no better. It took Arraganzo only seconds to make up his mind.

"Madam, I embrace your offer with both hands," he said briskly. "And now I must take my leave."

"Go with our blessing," Isolde returned. "I know I speak for Lord Tristan as well as myself. But when you Christians return, as I know you will, have more respect for the old faith of this magical place. Try to remember that the spirits in the hills and mountains, in the woodlands, in the rushy glens and streams, were here before any human foot trod this soil."

"As you say, madam."

With a flurry of farewells, the Papal Legate bowed himself out of the room. Shortly afterward, Tristan was at her door.

"Lady, I heard the Papal Legate had been with you. What did he want?"

"He wanted to know who ruled the country now that Mark was dead."

"What did you say?"

"I told him Queen Igraine would decide."

Tristan nodded. "Tomorrow we must set out for Tintagel to find out how she plans to dispose of her kingdom here."

Isolde laid a gentle hand on his arm. "Before we go, there's something I can't forget. I want to ask Sir Wisbeck and the Council to get the lepers out of that hovel in the wood and find a better place for them to live. In time, we'll build a new refuge for them with a proper infirmary, and I'd like to put the woman called Madrona in charge. She's the one who fed and succored me, and without her help, I might not have survived."

Tristan leaned forward, somber-faced. "I, too, came across a sick soul in the wood. Like your fellow prisoners in the leper house, she is not responsible for the illness she suffers day by day."

Briefly he outlined the story of Lady Unnowne, alone and unloved in her great castle, struggling to hold on to her wits.

"She may never recover her reason," he finished at last. "And she has only old servants to care for her now."

Isolde shivered and reached out to take his hand. "Alas, poor soul.

Let's send help tomorrow, as soon as we can. It must be the cruelest torment of all, to lose your mind."

Tristan nodded fiercely. "And no cure in sight."

"At least we have good people who'll take care of her and ease her pain." *As I can ease yours, my true love.*

She took him in her arms. In the deep, loving comfort of his embrace, his scent came to meet her, warm and strong. We are safe now, she thought. *Safe at last.*

She turned to Tristan and marveled at the words she never thought she'd be able to say openly, without fear.

"It's late, my love. Shall we go to bed?"

# chapter 53

*I*solde, *Isolde, are you listening, can you hear?*

*Come, I am waiting.*

*Come to me . . .*

Isolde came to herself with a start and did not know where she was. Imprisoned in the cell at Castle Dore? Burning up with fever in the leper house?

Neither of these, no.

Surely not . . . ?

Yes! Tears of relief started to her eyes. *Goddess, Mother, praise and thanks, at peace in my own bed!*

But not with Tristan, as she hoped last night. As they talked sadly in her chamber while the lights burned low, she longed for the comfort of his love with a hunger that had grown greater day by day. But this was no time to feast on his great body or to renew the glory of her delight in him. It was a time of mourning, with Mark not cold in his grave and his fretful soul still hovering over them like a dark shade. The people of Castle Dore were still adjusting to their King's sudden death, and the rest of Cornwall had not yet heard the news.

And Tristan himself would take time to recover from the terrible events of their last night in the wood. She could see he was still grieving over killing Mark, and that grief would be with him for the rest of his life. He knew that the country had to be governed, and he was ready to sit down with her and begin on the task. But it was still too soon, she thought, to take up the reins. Too soon to pretend nothing had happened when so much had changed.

*Too soon, too soon.* Tristan knew it, too, and with the gentlest of kisses, he slipped away to his chamber and left her alone.

"Till tomorrow, lady. Sleep well, my love."

And indeed she had, until now. What had woken her in the dead of night? Half asleep, she rose from her bed and followed the track of the moonlight to the window overlooking the sea. Owls were calling from the forest inland, but the voice that came again was the sound of the deep.

*Isolde, Isolde . . .*

*Come to me, come to me . . .*

In a dream, she left the palace, allowing her feet to take her where they would. Drawn along by the silent call, she found herself tracing the pathway to the sea. Overhead, the moon shone down upon the sleeping world, dusting land and sea alike with silver and gold. But far away in the distance, Isolde could see a vast and misty figure veiled in a pillar of light, scattering its own glow on the midnight air. Her heart convulsed. *Lady—oh, Lady?* Could it be?

She hastened forward. Ahead of her, a tall figure stood alone on the clifftop, muffled in mist and robed in silver spray. Her lofty headdress knocked against the sky, and her gown sighed round her feet like the sea around Tintagel rock.

"Greetings, Isolde," said the mellow and well-loved voice as Isolde drew near. "You have come to tell me your future, have you not?"

And suddenly it seemed to Isolde that the way ahead lay clear and shining through the mists of the years.

"I believe so, Lady," she replied steadily. "At least as far as our earthly lives extend. If Queen Igraine will grant us her consent, I say that Tristan and I should jointly rule Cornwall. He is already the King of Lyonesse. Together we can unite the two kingdoms into one."

The tall figure inclined her head. "Queen Igraine will consent. It is the dream of her heart to find a worthy successor to herself. You and Tristan together will make a mighty force."

Without warning, Isolde's spirit quailed.

"It is a mighty task," she agreed, shivering. A sudden fear gripped her, and the way ahead seemed dark. *Do I have the strength?*

The Lady's warm tones answered her very thought. "Strength is within. You have found it a thousand times in your hour of need."

"But I must not neglect Ireland. To rule three countries—"

The veiled figure held up her hand. "Three candles light every darkness: nature, knowledge, and truth. Fear not, you have them all."

"Yet I failed so badly with Mark..." A wave of remorse overwhelmed her, and she broke off.

"Ah, Isolde..."

The pounding of the surge was louder now. Below the grassy headland where they stood, the incoming tide was slowly gathering speed.

"We all fail," the Lady sighed in a voice heavy with tears, "but we rise and renew the struggle every day. That is our task. At the end of our lives, we hand over to others the work we have done. We are only set here on earth to light the way for those who follow on."

A great warmth suffused Isolde. *Yes, I can do that.*

The deep, musical voice flowed on. "And in that work, we find our dearest delight. There lies our hope of transcendence and healing for the soul, and the same hope inspires the next generation, too. You will find that here in Cornwall. Mark sadly neglected the country, and there is much to do. But for you, there is more."

Isolde fixed her eyes on the tall, diaphanous form. She seemed to have been moving toward this moment all her life.

"Tell me," she breathed.

There was a weighty pause. "Know, then, that you are destined to be my natural successor in time to come. You are the spirit of the sea, just as you are the sovereignty of the land. You were born in the sea, you grew up by the sea, and you will become one with the sea in the end."

Isolde could hardly breathe. "I?"

"You, indeed. You will know the waking sleep of the Druids, the dreaming consciousness in which you see both the future and the past and realize they are one. You will feel every beat of the ocean and the running of the rivers and the standing of the lakes. My two younger sisters, the Lady of Broceliande, the sacred lake in Little Britain, and the Lady of the Lake in Avalon, will hold you as their dearest kin and take you for their own. All this will come once you embrace your fate."

Isolde closed her eyes and clasped her hands. "I do."

Far below, a soft flurry of small creamy waves broke over the rocks, and a deep sigh of contentment echoed over the sea. Isolde felt the mark of the Goddess blazing on her forehead with a calm, painless fire. Her shoulders bore the weight of a shining cloak of feathers, swan or raven, she could not tell, and a bright crown of stars hovered above her head.

"You are crowned now, my dear," the Lady said joyfully. "All the world knows you are the Queen of the Sea."

She stretched out a hand, and Isolde found herself walking the astral plane in a clear and starlit night. From her vantage point above the clouds, she saw heaving, verdigris seas and purple skies, ice-capped mountains and lakes of glass strung out over the surface of the earth like pearls on a chain. High overhead, a radiant moon smiled down. Bathed in its delicate, flower-like silver light, Isolde saw the rounded green flank of a hillside crowned with white blossoms, like a woman lying down. The scent of sweet water rose to greet her, and she heard the drowsy cooing of doves in every tree.

*Avalon.*

*Sacred Island.*

*Home.*

Now the hillside itself opened to her view. In its glittering, cavernous depths she saw King Arthur at the Round Table, surrounded by his knights. Old Merlin stood guard over the starlit forms, all sleeping their final sleep, but all as fine and handsome as they had been in life.

*Oh, oh . . .*

She felt the age-old wisdom of the Old Ones and the innocence and hope of a child new-born. Somewhere her mother was shining down on her, with the blessing of all her mighty foremothers in the land. The life force of the Lady and the power of the sea flowed through her veins, and with it the gift to mediate its fullness, grace, and beauty to the world.

"See, Isolde? You are not alone."

The Lady's voice came from far away. "As you take up your burden with Tristan, remember that there are others who guard and protect these islands, too." One long white arm fluttered back toward Avalon. "What you see there has yet to come about. King Arthur and his knights have not yet fought their final battle and entered their last sleep. But they are the eternal keepers of the land till the land itself is no more."

Now a primeval, oceanic power was approaching with the force of a tidal wave. Isolde saw all the world and all the stars above spinning their way through eternity, and her eyes dazzled with the glory of it all.

The Lady's voice came again. "Watch the wheel, Isolde, always watch the wheel. The wheel is the sea, rolling around our world. The wheel is the world and the lives that flourish there. The wheel is the shape of life and of time itself. Our faith teaches us how to watch that wheel and to follow the wheel of the year every year of our lives."

Isolde cried out in rapture. "I shall follow the wheel!"

The Lady laughed, a rich and joyful sound. "And never fear, Isolde, it will follow you. Wherever you go, you will have that strength within." She opened her arms again in another wide embrace. "See, Isolde, see?"

Far, far below, an emerald-green island floated in a silver sea. Isolde could not speak.

*Ireland.*

*Erin.*

*Home.*

The beloved land, which now she could rule with Tristan at her side. Dimly she heard the Lady's voice again.

"You are the sovereignty, Isolde, and this is your land. It is the home and birthland of the Mother Faith. Once, long ago, a mighty race, the Tuatha Dé Danann, peopled these shores. From the north came the sword of power, which the hero Nuada of the Silver Hand swung against Ireland's foes. He was the chosen one of the first Queen, and she made him her King. The south sent the spear of light from the armory of Macha, battle-queen of great Lug, the God of light. The table of the Goddess-Queen Danu gave us Her loving cup from the west. And from the east came Her ever-flowing cauldron of plenty that the Dagda himself, the ancient father of the Old Ones, had brought to the Western Isle. When the Tuatha Dé Danann left to join the Shining Ones on their thrones, they gave us the Stone of Destiny, *lia fáill*, which still cries out under Ireland's rightful Queen. These are the Hallows of the Goddess, the treasures of Erin."

The Lady paused. "This is your destiny, Isolde, this is your fate. Now you will feel in yourself the force of all things that live and breathe in this world of ours. Every plant, every leaf, every tree will be alive to you, as real to you as you are to yourself. Already the rains of Erin weep in your heart, and her sun shines through your smile. You are the land of Ireland, the blessed land. And it is for you to take forward the message now."

Isolde struggled to find her voice in the glittering void. "I know of only one. Religion should be kindness. Faith is love."

The tall gauzy figure inclined her beautiful head. "We must be saved by that hope. Only faith can save us. Only love."

*Only love . . .*

Shivering, the world around Isolde dissolved, and the tall shape of the Lady began to drift away.

"Farewell, Isolde."

A bubble of fear rose in Isolde's throat. *Don't leave me, Lady! Don't go!*

Then a new calm sprang up in her heart with a deep well of joy. *From now on, I am she, and she will be with me always. Strength is within.*

She raised both her arms and felt her cloak streaming out behind her like great wings. "Farewell, Lady, farewell!"

# chapter 54

*a* mighty peal of thunder rang through the sky. The clouds boiled and rolled and danced round Isolde's head, then without warning she felt grass beneath her feet. As she stumbled against the rough tussocks of the clifftop, a strong hand gripped her elbow and held her up. It was a grip she would have known through all the three worlds and beyond.

"*Tristan!*" She came to herself with a start. "What are you doing here?"

He laughed with joy. "I heard the Lady calling, and I followed you."

"Then you know what she said?"

"I heard it all, my love." A look of unspeakable sweetness passed over his face. "And at last I can truly call you my Queen. Together we'll rule this land and hand it on to the children we shall have."

A pang of fear entered her heart like a knife. "Children? Oh, my love, dare we hope for that? The Lady said nothing about it."

Another clap of thunder drowned her words. Without warning, a great wind drove in from the sea, howling and screaming like a banshee of the Western Isle. The trees on the clifftop groaned aloud and bent cracking to the ground. Above them, the skies were racked with tempest, rain, and fire as a mighty storm took all Cornwall by the throat.

"Here, lady."

Swiftly, Tristan pulled her inside his cloak. Huddled within the shelter of his strong arms, she felt the waves pounding the rocks below. One after another, huge walls of water were rolling in from the sea, hovering for a moment like massive creatures catching their breath, then spending their fury as others behind them pressed in to renew the attack. High over their heads, the heavens were at war with themselves, thunder and lightning raging across the clouds and raining fire and water on the waves below. Isolde shook with fear. *Goddess, Mother, save us when the sea meets the sky!*

The wild waves lashed the coast, and the storm gained in fury with every breath they drew. Hurtling inland, gusts of wind flattened trees and shrubs, rampaging like a madman freed from his chains. The force of the lightning seemed to split Isolde's brain.

"Oh, my love," she howled, her rising fear keeping time with the raging storm. "Remember my mother's curse when we first met?"

He looked at her with eyes wide with fear. "Your mother cursed us? I never knew."

*No, of course you didn't, you were not there.*

Now she was flying on the wings of fear, borne back twenty years and more to a distant past. She saw her dead mother alive and in her prime, maddened by the loss of her lover, killed by Tristan's hand. No matter that the lost knight had invaded Cornwall on the Queen's own command and that Tristan had been forced to defend Cornwall against the unjust attack.

At the time, no punishment was too great for Tristan in the eyes of the Queen. And Isolde, too, had been the unwitting subject of her mother's curse. The memory and the fear of it were with her now.

As was the late Queen herself, her spirit shape stalking the hillside before Isolde's eyes. Shaking from head to foot, the tall, racked body in her favorite black and red clenched her fists like iron and stretched out both her hands.

"*May the man who killed you die a fearful death,*" Isolde heard again. "*May all those he loves, and all who ever love him, suffer until the sea kisses the sky, and the trees bow down their heads at his cursed feet! May the woman who loves him never know peace or joy! May she sorrow for him until her heart turns black, as mine must do now for the loss of my lord!*"

"Goddess, Mother, save us!"

Blasted by the memory, Isolde stood shaking as her mother's shade dwindled away in the mist.

*Mother, yes, your curse has come true. Tristan has indeed died more than one fearful death, by water, fire, and the sword. I have suffered for his love till I knew neither peace nor joy, and my heart has turned black with the death of hope.*

*And just as hope beckons for us, have you come to claim your revenge?* She turned to Tristan in a frenzy. "Oh my love, is this the end?"

"The end, Isolde?"

Soft laughter in the distance brought her to herself. Veiled in the shadows of the darkest hour of night, the Lady shone forth with a last dying ray.

"Oh, Isolde, little one, do you not see that the curse placed upon you both has been lifted at last?" There came another full-hearted chuckle. "Look about you, child. What do you see?"

In a daze, Isolde looked around and saw the seething billows leaping to kiss the sky. Inland, the hawthorn and furze bowed their heads to the ground, while mighty oaks lay prostrate in the earth's embrace. Isolde's soul leaped, too, delirious with relief.

*It is true, then, as the Lady says. The trees are kissing the ground at my beloved's feet, and the sea has met the sky.* She raised a hand in farewell. *All our sufferings are ended, Mawther. Go in peace.*

A sharp bolt of lightning hit the velvet sky. Far off on the headland, the fading image of the Lady gleamed through the last of the night. The tall, fluttering figure leaned forward and unwound her veil.

A radiance filled the night, too bright to bear. As the filmy gauze fell away, Isolde saw the face of her mother alight with its quicksilver delight, its warmth of passion, its unfailing joy in love. But deeper than both was the Lady's thousand-year-old smile. It shone from a face that had suffered in an all-too-human world.

A face with a crown of white hair and an air of majesty.

A face she knew almost as well as her own.

*Why, of course—*

*Igraine.*

She fell to her knees, dimly aware of Tristan kneeling at her side. The storm was dying now, and she could hear the Lady's last words.

"Blessings on you both," came whistling down the wind. "You will rule together in Cornwall wisely and well, and the memory of your love will never die. And blessings on the child that you will bear."

"We shall vow any child of ours to the service of the land," Isolde wept. "But no woman must suffer again what you endured."

"Never, lady!" cried Tristan, his face wet with tears. "Losing Arthur, as you did. Losing your only child."

There was a rustle of dry laughter like leaves in wintertime.

"My child has done well by the land, as well as he might. And so will yours. Any child of a knight like Sir Tristan and a sovereignty-bearing woman of Isolde's acclaim will be a heroine in her own time and beyond. Or a hero of might, for we do not rate men any less."

A last whisper drifted down and around them like a wind from the moon. *Go with your Gods. Make the world a better place.*

Then the Lady was gone. On the headland where she had stood, *lia fáill*, Ireland's ancient stone of destiny, rose up from the mists of ages and shone like a beacon ahead. Around it clustered the ghosts of Cornwall's primeval stones, the vast circles and long barrows built by Old Ones long ago.

Isolde gripped Tristan's hand. "We must renew our vows to the land."

Tristan folded both her hands in his strong, warm grasp. "We shall make it our deepest pledge. We'll do everything Queen Igraine wants us to do. And when she comes again, we'll ask her to bless our rule."

"Queen Igraine!" Isolde marveled, lost in delight. She paused to take it in. "Who would have believed that Queen Igraine is the Lady of the Sea?"

Tristan faced her gravely, still holding her hands in his. "As you will be too, my love."

*Shall I?*

*Can I do this?*

*The Lady of the Sea?*

She gave a decisive nod. *With Tristan, I can do anything.*

Dawn was rising. The tide was turning, and the waves were awakening to the sun, mewling and scratching at the shore like newborn cats. On the wide horizon, a silver-blue sea melted into a rose and lavender sky. Below them lay Castle Dore, Cornwall's stronghold, with Lyonesse beyond. Isolde drew Tristan toward her and pointed to the pathway ahead.

"Come, my love," she breathed.

# chapter 55

The sun rose higher over Cornwall's rolling lands. Most of the country still slept. But from the depths of an ancient greenway rose a strange, high, bee-like drone. An old crooked man on an ambling white mule was raising his anthem to the breaking day.

> "I am the hawk on the cliff,
> The tear in the eye of the sun.
> I am the salmon at the leap,
> And the lake asleep under the gaze of the moon.
> I am life, I am death, I am Merlin!"

"And Merlin has done well," he cackled as he went along. "Arthur and Camelot at peace, the knights all embarked on the Quest..."

A voice in his ear broke into his reverie.

*Ah, but Isolde and Tristan now—*

"Who's there?" Merlin yelped.

There was a mellow laugh. *Oh, I think you know.*

"Igraine?" The flame in his yellow eyes scorched the nearby leaves. There was no one to be seen. But a strong, mellow presence hovered near him in the air.

*Yes, indeed. But I come with no evil intent. All has turned out well for Tristan and his lady, Isolde.*

Merlin thrust his head in the air. "As I knew it would."

*So, old man?* came Igraine's voice again. *Then why did they need Merlin's hand in this? You are fated to be the never-failing guardian of these isles, ever wakeful around our island shores. You were never doing all this for Isolde, were you?*

He flared his eyes again and enjoyed the green spurt and crackle of his fire. A laughing girl rose before him with hair like sunrise and a heart that danced like a wave of the sea. A young woman made of gold but wearing the green, with her love at her side and a soul that would be greater yet.

Isolde.

"Never, no," he said musingly. "She had no need of me. That merry young soul had the leap of the salmon and the spring of a doe in the rut. All that and the hands of a healer and the heart of a warrior queen."

*For her mother, then? You were her lover once.*

Merlin grinned and felt the old heat scratching his loins.

"A wonderful woman, the Queen, one of the best," he purred. "Foolish, yes, and led by her passions, like all women who love men more than themselves. But what a woman she was—what a queen!"

An infinite fondness swept his withered frame. She had made him a man, and he would never forget.

*But would you have done all this for the old Queen alone?* Igraine pressed on. *Braved the wild seas in winter, set Tristan alongside Arthur, your heart's darling, and the work of the House of Pendragon and the future of Britain, too? Why, Merlin, why?*

"Ask me no more," he burst out, wheezing through his teeth.

*I must,* the great voice rolled on. *And you know the reason.*

"You have to protect Isolde." Merlin nodded his aching head. "As I fought for Tristan. Yes, yes, I worked and schemed to save Tristan. I never cared for Isolde, any more than I do for Guenevere. But both of them are happy enough now."

A deep sigh drifted down through the trees. *Tristan was the beating heart of your love and concern.*

"Yes!" Merlin cried and found himself drowning in tears. "Tristan—Arthur—all these sorrowful lost boys. Motherless, fatherless, nameless, and homeless, too, flying boys becoming wounded men."

*And yourself, Merlin. Don't forget yourself.*

"Goddess, Mother, yes," Merlin prayed. "Help the unmothered child—"

He saw through the mists of time the sadness of Tristan's birth, the young mother dying in the depths of the dark wood, the huge eyes full of sorrow, the little body split apart by her travails with her great son.

For Tristan, then, the child of sorrow.

And for the mother who bore the sorrowful child.

"And I did not save her!" he grieved. "Fool! Fool! Triple fool!"

*Well, let her sleep in peace. Cast your mind over the good that is to come.*

Merlin knocked the tears from his eyes. Resolutely, he spun his agate-glinting, golden gaze through all the worlds he knew and the world to come.

Cornwall—safe enough now and for a long time ahead, with Queen Igraine in Tintagel and Tristan and Isolde on the throne.

And the Island of the West—safer still.

Through a mist he saw Isolde and Tristan moving hand in hand into the dawn. As he watched, they paused to look into each other's eyes, and there was no greater beauty on the earth. "Elf-shining," they called that look in ancient days. The future was with them both, he had no fears.

"Joy upon you!" he cried, raising his hand. "May the Shining Ones bring you days of happiness and nights of bliss!"

Now the scene shifted, and his spirit eye looked ahead.

"Ireland, yes," he sang in his high Druid wail.

On the westernmost beach of the sacred Western Isle, a couple rode through the surf as the day broke over the sea. Gilded with the dawn's fierce tints of ice and fire, the woman sat proudly on her horse, great with child. Even prouder, it seemed, was the man riding at her side.

"Tristan!" wept Merlin, weak with joy.

*Tristan indeed, old man, your lost boy no more. The child of sadness is a father now.*

"Joy upon him!" Merlin crowed. "Joy upon all of us."

*Yes indeed.*

He frowned at himself, then laughed. "And where now?"

*Oh, I think you know. Back to the place of your heart, the island the Old Ones loved.*

"The Western Isle!"

Suddenly, Merlin felt the call of the green hills, the land of the ancient trefoil, a land of enchanters and deceivers, of heroes and scoundrels and those who love the *craic*.

He turned the mule's head into the western wind. "Forward!" he cried. "You know the way, my dear."

# epilogue

*C*ome, my love."

"To the ends of the earth and beyond."

*So Isolde followed Tristan into the light of the dawn and above them the love star glowed and pulsed in the sky. That night the moon rose smiling on a love she knew would outlast wind and weather, the coming of winter and the sweet return of spring.*

*For here was a man to love always, a man with love in his eyes, truth on his forehead, and the hero-light shining round his head.*

*Next year she knew, when the celandines woke again like stars in the grass, he would turn to her with the same smile in his eyes. As the primroses peered and the cowslips showed off their spotted throats, she would lie with him in the tender warmth of the sun. Together they would watch the blindworms nuzzling through the grass after their long winter sleep and hear the skylark filling the air with song. And so they would continue through all the springs to come, and the summers and winters, too. And so they would walk with their Gods to the Land of the Living Light to dwell in the Plains of Delight evermore.*

*The moon sailed away in the sky. Here was a love to endure, to reach out, to thrive, to build on and build anew. These two would be part of the fabric of the islands and the future of the world. And thus they wander the star-eyed silence, hand in hand and soul forever in soul, and nothing will part them now in the years to come.*

*In time they will be blessed with a babe born of the sun and the rain, a child of the wave and the woodland to dance with the wind and the sea. The west wind will tenderly bring the infant to life, and the warm wind from the* south will kiss its tears away. Other children will follow, grave-eyed girls and merry-hearted boys, and the joy that they give to their parents will be deeper than tears. But there would be nothing like the joy in the Island of the West over the loving couple about whom this story would be written in times to come.

And in time they will go to join the Old Ones and live forever in dignity and peace. The Tuatha Dé Danaan, as the Old Ones call themselves, will welcome them to their long-ago destined place among the ancient heroic ancestors of all the Celts, living in the enchantment of every new day, in a world of terror and daily miracles. Now they, too, are members of that twilight race, the great ghosts that haunt the Island of the West and the memory of the world yet to be. Not all will understand their story, but those who do will become part of that shining world.

And these lovers will come at last to the place of timelessness, free from the pains of the earthbound mortals who struggle to follow them. Now they will live in the Old Ones' Tir N'an Og, the Land of the Ever-Young, where Avalon's orchards never cease to blow and the blossom and fruit together bloom on the bough. There, with the world's blessed souls, they will remain, forever roaming the Islands of the Mighty, the Happy Isles.

Forever now, Tristan will chase the running deer and Isolde open her arms on his return. For they knew desire beyond joy or tears, and knew no more nor no better than to follow the dream.

For that they live on in the world above kings and princes and queens on their golden thrones. And a new sun will rise for them every day and a new dawn, when lovers rejoice and kiss and fall again in love. And those who have sunlight in their hearts and moonlight in their minds will always be able to follow their love, their dream.

And wherever the children of Erin may roam in the world, She will call them home. Until then, they will send their dreams back to their birthplace, the Land of the Shining, the island the Mother has always called Her own.

IRELAND.

ERIN.

HOME.

# the characters

**Agnomon**  Young warrior of the Picts, nephew of Findra, and cursed with second sight

**Agravain**  Knight of the Round Table, first brother of Sir Gawain, embarked on the Quest for the Holy Grail

**Andred, Sir**  Cousin of Tristan and nephew of King Mark of Cornwall, son of Mark's brother, and mortal enemy of Isolde and Tristan

**Arraganzo, Dom Luis Carlos Felipe da Sevilla y Cadiz y Pinca y Salamanca**  Cardinal Legate, Papal Envoy from Rome to Father Dominian in Cornwall, charged with hastening the downfall of Isolde and the triumph of the Christian Church

**Arthur**  Pendragon, High King of Britain, son of Uther Pendragon and Queen Igraine of Cornwall, husband to Guenevere, father of Amir, and leader of the Round Table Fellowship of knights

**Balan**  Knight of King Arthur, son of Sir Rigord of the Ravine, twin brother of Balin, proud and quarrelsome, who will never refuse a challenge to the death

**Balin**  Knight of King Arthur, son of Sir Rigord of the Ravine, twin brother of Balan, as proud and quarrelsome as his brother, who likewise will never refuse a challenge to the death

**Blanche Mains**  Nickname of Isolde's namesake, daughter of

King Hoel of Little Britain in France, known as "Blanche Mains" for the beauty of her white hands, once in love with Tristan and determined to ensnare him in marriage no matter what the cost

**Brangwain**   Lady in waiting and personal maid to Isolde, formerly maid to Isolde's mother and nursemaid to Isolde when she was a child, born in the Welshlands and thought to be "Merlin's kin"

**Calvaria, Princess**   Fourth daughter of the King of Dun Haven, facing a future in a nunnery

**Cernunnos**   The Horned One, God of dark secrets and ancient, midnight woods, said by some to be Merlin in his incarnation as a stag

**Cormac**   Chief Druid of Ireland, formerly of the Summer Country and once in love with Isolde

**Cunnoch**   Hard and seasoned warrior of the Picts, blood brother of Findra, formerly sword companion to the late King, and doubtful of the new King Darath's ability to rule

**Darath**   King of the Picts, young warrior feared in Ireland as threatening to attack

**Divinia, Princess**   Second daughter of the King of Dun Haven, motherless and unhappy, facing a future in a nunnery

**Doctor**   Healer who has the care of the sick young Lady Unnowne

**Dominian, Father**   Christian priest, head of the Christian community in Cornwall and Father confessor to King Mark, abandoned as a child and cared for by Brother Jerome

**Doneal, Sir**   Veteran knight of Ireland, member of the Queen's Council

**Dun Haven, King of**   Petty king of Cornwall under King Mark, Christian believer and part of Father Dominian's flock, father of a number of motherless girls

**Elizabeth, Queen of Lyonesse**   Late mother of Tristan, wife of King Meliodas and sister of King Mark of Cornwall, lost in the forest when her husband was imprisoned, and died there giving birth to Tristan

**Elva, Lady**   Mistress of King Mark, lover of Sir Andred, wife of a courtier, and enemy of Isolde

**Fer de Gambon**   Knight of Cornwall, companion of Sir Taboral, quick-witted but cowardly, employed by Sir Andred against Tristan

**Findra**   Strong and trusty warrior of the Picts, blood brother of Cunnoch, and uncle of Agnomon, whom he would protect with his life

**Gaheris**   Knight of the Round Table, second brother of Sir Gawain, embarked on the Quest for the Holy Grail

**Galahad**   Knight of the Round Table and destined to triumph in the Quest for the Holy Grail, son of Sir Lancelot and the Grail virgin Elaine, daughter of King Pelles of Terre Foraine

**Gareth**   Knight of the Round Table, third brother of Sir Gawain, embarked on the Quest for the Holy Grail

**Gawain**   Knight of the Round Table, close kinsman of King Arthur, brother of Sir Agravain, Sir Gareth, and Sir Gaheris, famed for his great strength and his prowess with women, which causes him to fall foul of Lady Unnowne

**Gilhan, Sir**   Leader of the Council in Ireland, formerly a knight of the old Queen and loyal to Isolde

**Glaeve**   Sword of power given to Tristan by the Lady of the Sea, inscribed with runic script

**Guenevere**   Queen of the Summer Country, daughter of Queen Maire Macha and King Leogrance, wife of Arthur, lover of Sir Lancelot, mother of Amir, and friend to Isolde from their girlhood days studying with the Lady of the Lake on Avalon

**Hermit**   Holy man, head of a fellowship of hermits and healers living in retreat in the forest, who helps Tristan to give succor to the madman who attacks him there

**Igraine, Queen**   Queen of Cornwall, wife of the late Duke Gorlois, beloved of King Uther Pendragon, mother of Arthur, Morgause, and Morgan le Fay, and supporter of Isolde

**Ireland, Queen of**   See Queen of Ireland, the late

**Isolde, "La Belle Isolde"**   Princess of Ireland, daughter of the Queen and the Irish hero Sir Cullain, lover of Tristan, wife of King Mark, and later Queen of Cornwall and Ireland in her own right

**Jerome, Brother**   Christian hermit and holy man, foster father and spiritual counselor of the abandoned Dominian

**Laboria, Princess**   Fifth daughter of the King of Dun Haven, facing a future in a nunnery

**Lady of the Lake**   Ruler of the Sacred Island of Avalon in the Summer Country, sister of the Lady of the Sea and of the Lady of Broceliande, and priestess of the Great Mother

**Lady of the Sea**   Ruler of the sea, sister of the Lady of the

Lake and of the Lady of Broceliande, and chief priestess of
the Great Mother

**Lancelot of the Lake, Sir**   Knight of the Round Table, lover
of Queen Guenevere, son of King Ban and Queen Elaine of
Benoic, and father of Sir Galahad

**Lazaran**   Leper and leader of the lepers in Cornwall, where
they are outcasts from society and forced to live in the wood,
used by Mark against Isolde to get his revenge

**Lyonesse, Queen of**   See Elizabeth, Queen of Lyonesse

**Madrona**   Former lady of high estate, inhabitant of the leper
house in the wood where she nursed her son to his death
and where she takes care of Isolde and saves her life

**Mark, King**   King of Cornwall, brother of Elizabeth, Queen of
Lyonesse, uncle of Tristan and Andred, lover of Lady Elva,
and husband of Isolde

**Medhebar**   Head woman of the village of Womenswold,
where all the menfolk have been drowned at sea, ready to
accept Isolde's suggestion that they should be courted by
the Picts

**Meliodas, King**   King of Lyonesse, husband of Elizabeth and
father of Tristan, rescued by Merlin from imprisonment
when his wife was lost in the forest and gave birth to
Tristan

**Merlin**   Welsh Druid and bard, illegitimate offspring of the
House of Pendragon, adviser to Uther and Arthur
Pendragon, former lover of the Queen of Ireland, and
protector of Tristan

**Nabon, Sir**   Leader of the Council of King Mark of Cornwall,
supporter of Isolde

**Painted Ones, the**   See Picts, the

**Penn Annwyn**   Lord of the Underworld in Celtic mythology, the Dark Lord who comes to take his children home

**Petrina, Princess**   Third daughter of the King of Dun Haven, facing a future in a nunnery

**Picts, the**   Fiercely war-like tribe of the north of modern Scotland, ancient enemies of Ireland, called Picti, "the Painted Ones," by the Romans for their custom of vigorously tattooing their faces and bodies in many colors

**Queen of Ireland, the late**   Mother of Isolde, ruler of the Western Isle in her own right, descendant of a line of warrior queens, wife of the dead hero Cullain, and lover of many Companions of the Throne

**Queen of Lyonesse**   See Elizabeth, Queen of Lyonesse

**Quirian, Sir**   Knight of Cornwall, member of the Council of King Mark

**Seneschal, the**   Loyal and ancient steward, one of the few remaining retainers at the Castle of Unnowne

**Simeon**   Young monk of the Christian community in Cornwall, pupil of Father Dominian and fiercely loyal to the Church

**Taboral, Sir**   Rogue knight, companion of Fer de Gambon, brutish but big and bold, employed by Sir Andred against Tristan

**Thalassan, Sir**   Knight of Cornwall and member of the Council of King Mark, and a great seafarer in his youth

**Theodora, Princess**   Oldest daughter of the King of Dun Haven, motherless and unhappy, facing a future in a nunnery and determined to change her fate

**Tristan, Sir**　King of Lyonesse, son of the late King Meliodas and Queen Elizabeth, nephew and knight of King Mark of Cornwall, favored by the Lady of the Sea, and lover of Isolde

**Unnowne**　Young mistress of the Castle of Unnowne, alone, orphaned, and sick, afflicted with a number of complaints

**Uther**　Pendragon, King of the Middle Kingdom, High King of Britain, lover of Queen Igraine of Cornwall, kinsman of Merlin, and father of Arthur

**Vaindor, Sir**　Knight of Ireland, former champion and chosen one of the late Queen, and member of the ruling Council

**Wisbeck, Sir**　Veteran knight of the Council of King Mark of Cornwall

**Woodman, the**　One of an ancient line of woodlanders who live in the forest and make their living from what it supplies, but determined to leave the life of his forefathers behind and live in the town

# List of places

**Avalon**   Sacred isle in the Summer Country, center of Goddess worship, home of the Lady of the Lake, modern Glastonbury in Somerset

**Bel Content, Castle**   Name chosen by Tristan to replace the name of Castle Pleure when he became lord of the fortress of Sir Greuze Sans Pitie

**Camelot**   Capital of the Summer Country, home of the Round Table, modern Cadbury in Somerset

**Castle Bel Content**   See Bel Content, Castle

**Castle Dore**   Stronghold of King Mark, on the east coast of Cornwall

**Castle Dun Haven**   See Dun Haven, Castle

**Castle of Unnowne**   See Unnowne, Castle of

**Castle Pleure**   Ancient fortress and grange deep in the heart of the wood, retreat of the cruel Sir Greuze Sans Pitie until his defeat and death at Tristan's hands, renamed Castle Bel Content by Tristan when he became its lord

**Cornwall**   Kingdom of Arthur's mother, Queen Igraine, and of her vassal King Mark, neighboring country to Lyonesse

**Dubh Lein**   Stronghold of the Queens of Ireland, modern Dublin, "the Black Pool"

**Dun Haven, Csatle**   Fortress of the King of Dun Haven in Cornwall, much decayed

**Erin**   Ancient name of Ireland after its Goddess Eriu

**Gaul**   Large country of the continental Celts, incorporating much of modern France and Germany

**Hill of Queens**   Primeval burial ground of the Queens of Ireland since time began

**Island of the West**   Modern Ireland, the sacred island of the Druids and home to Goddess worship and a uniquely Celtic form of Christianity, also known as the Western Isle

**Little Britain**   Territory in France, location of the kingdoms of King Hoel and Sir Lancelot, modern Brittany

**Lyonesse**   Kingdom below Cornwall, home of Tristan, formerly under the rule of Tristan's father, King Meliodas and now Tristan's kingdom

**Middle Kingdom**   Arthur's ancestral kingdom lying between the Summer Country and Wales, modern Gwent, Glamorgan, and Herefordshire

**Orkneys, Islands of**   Cluster of most northerly islands of the British Isles and site of King Lot's kingdom, home of Sir Gawain and his brothers Agravain, Gaheris, and Gareth

**Outre Mer**   Fabled kingdom that lies *outre mer,* "over the sea"

**Pictland**   Kingdom of the Picts in the north of modern Scotland

**Saxon Shore, the**   East coast of mainland Britain, site of the invasions from the tribes of modern Scandinavia and east Germany

**Summer Country**   Guenevere's kingdom, ancient center of Goddess worship, modern Somerset

**Tintagel**   Castle of Queen Igraine on the north coast of Cornwall

**Unnowne, Castle of**   Castle of the Lady Unnowne in the

depths of the forest, home to the sick lady Tristan
encounters on his way through the wood

**Welshlands**   Home to Merlin and Brangwain, modern Wales

**Western Isle**   See Island of the West

**Womenswold**   Fishing village in Ireland that has lost all its
men, now run by the women alone under their leader,
Medhebar

# the celtic wheel of the year

DECEMBER 21
**MIDWINTER SOLSTICE**
THE FEAST OF REBIRTH
*The Yule log is lit*

NOVEMBER 1
**SAMHAIN**
THE FEAST OF
THE UNDEAD
*Bonfires are lit to
keep the living safe*

FEBRUARY 1
**IMBOLC**
THE FEAST OF
THE BLACK MAIDEN,
QUEEN OF DEATH

MARCH 21
**SPRING
EQUINOX**
THE FEAST OF
MOTHER EARTH

SEPTEMBER 21
**AUTUMN
EQUINOX**
*The in-gathering
of crops*

APRIL 1
**LLUD'S DAY**
GOD OF LAUGHTER

AUGUST 1
**LUGHNASAD**
THE FEAST OF
SHEEP SHEARING AND
FIRST FRUITS

JUNE 21
**MIDSUMMER
SOLSTICE**
*Bonfires are lit to
keep the sun hot
and strong*

MAY 1
**BELTAIN**
THE SUN GOD RETURNS
TO MOTHER EARTH
*A three-day feast
celebrating his union with
the Mother Goddess, marked
with fires and flowers*

# the christian wheel of the year

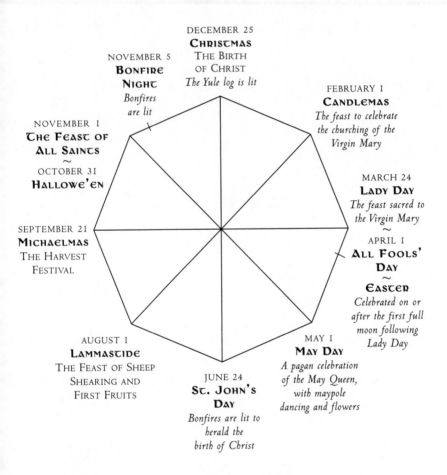

DECEMBER 25
**Christmas**
The Birth
of Christ
*The Yule log is lit*

NOVEMBER 5
**Bonfire
Night**
*Bonfires
are lit*

NOVEMBER I
**The Feast of
All Saints**
~
OCTOBER 31
**Hallowe'en**

SEPTEMBER 21
**Michaelmas**
The Harvest
Festival

AUGUST I
**Lammastide**
The Feast of Sheep
Shearing and
First Fruits

JUNE 24
**St. John's
Day**
*Bonfires are lit to
herald the
birth of Christ*

MAY I
**May Day**
*A pagan celebration
of the May Queen,
with maypole
dancing and flowers*

FEBRUARY I
**Candlemas**
*The feast to celebrate
the churching of the
Virgin Mary*

MARCH 24
**Lady Day**
*The feast sacred to
the Virgin Mary*
~
APRIL I
**All Fools'
Day**
~
**Easter**
*Celebrated on or
after the first full
moon following
Lady Day*

# about the author

ROSALIND MILES is the author of the bestselling Guenevere trilogy, as well as *Isolde, Queen of the Western Isle,* and *The Maid of
the White Hands,* the first two books of the Tristan and Isolde
trilogy. A well-known and critically acclaimed novelist, essay-
ist, and broadcaster, she lives in the country in England.

| DATE | | | |
|---|---|---|---|
| | | | |
| | | | |
| | | | |
| | | | |
| | | | |
| | | | |
| | | | |
| | | | |
| | | | |
| | | | |
| | | | |
| | | | |
| | | | |
| | | | |